LET THE DEAD SLEEP

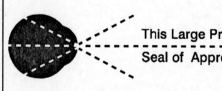

This Large Print Book carries the
Seal of Approval of N.A.V.H.

LET THE DEAD SLEEP

HEATHER GRAHAM

THORNDIKE PRESS

A part of Gale, Cengage Learning

GALE
CENGAGE Learning®

Detroit • New York • San Francisco • New Haven, Conn • Waterville, Maine • London

GALE
CENGAGE Learning®

Thorndike Press® Large Print Core.
The text of this Large Print edition is unabridged.
Other aspects of the book may vary from the original edition.
Set in 16 pt. Plantin.

LIBRARY OF CONGRESS CATALOGING-IN-PUBLICATION DATA

Graham, Heather.
  Let the dead sleep / by Heather Graham. — Large Print edition.
    pages cm. — (Thorndike Press Large Print Core)
    ISBN 978-1-4104-5708-0 (hardcover) — ISBN 1-4104-5708-7 (hardcover)
  1. Antiques business—Fiction. 2. Lost works of art—Fiction. 3. Murder—
Investigation—Fiction. 4. New Orleans (La.)—Fiction. 5. Large type books.
I. Title.
PS3557.R198L48 2013
813'.54—dc23   2013000182

Published in 2013 by arrangement with Harlequin Books S.A.

Printed in Mexico
3 4 5 6 7 17 16 15 14 13

To those who live in and out of the Big Easy and have helped make Writers for New Orleans a true benefit for this beautiful and historic city:

Marvin Andrade; Beti Basile; Molly Bolden; Zach Bolden; Camille Burgin; Tina Callais; Dionne Cherie Charlet; Beth Ciotta; Teresa Davant; Jezabel DeLuna; Rich Devin; Corrine De Winter; Keith Donato; Pam Ebel; Paula Eykelhof; Nick Genovese; Paula and Mike Hardin; Patty Harrison; Jennifer Hughes; Pamela Kopfler; Harley Jane Kozak; Cindy Krempel; Kay Levine; Veronika Levine; Kathy Love; Debra Maas; Lisa Mannetti; Erin McCarthy; Ginger McSween; James, Bonnie and Helen Moore; Stacey, Kaylyn, Scott and Joshua Perry; Kathleen Pickering; Jason, Shayne, Derek, Zhenia, Bryee-Annon and Chynna Pozzessere;

"Suzie Q" Quiroz; Kevin Richard; Debbie Richardson; Helen Rosburg; Bobby Rosello; Dave Simms; Alexandra Sokoloff; Mary Stella; Lance Taubold; Jo Templeton; Greg Varricchio; Sheila Vincent; Leslie Wainger; Pat Walker; Mary Walkley; Adam Wilson; F. Paul Wilson; all the hard workers at the Hotel Monteleone; and everyone at The Vampire Boutique and Fifi Mahoney's . . .

And the amazing Connie Perry!

This story is also dedicated to the memory of Kate Duffy, brilliant editor and friend to so many. She was there at the beginning. She believed that in creating this conference, we could be a nice drop in a massive bucket. I still hear her voice in my mind so often, and smile, knowing exactly what she would have to say in so many situations.

And, finally, I offer it in memory of my one and only sister, Victoria Jane Graham Davant, who loved New Orleans and showed me the magic of the city.

PROLOGUE

"This is it, Ms. Cafferty," Dr. Vincenzo said quietly. He cleared his throat. "We'll, ah, leave you alone to say your goodbyes."

Danielle Cafferty stared at Vincenzo, feeling too bewildered and stunned to cry. Until this morning she'd convinced herself that her father would live forever. He was a big man, hearty and robust, the perfect example of a he-man Highlander, rugged as the Scottish terrain that had bred him. But then the call had come from Billie McDougall that Angus Cafferty was in the hospital. His heart was giving out.

Vincenzo stared back at her awkwardly. Surely, as head of an esteemed cardiac unit, he'd dealt with other situations like this. But he hesitated, then touched her hand gently and left, followed by his sympathetic nurse.

So she understood that it was a matter of time. Her father had fallen into a coma an hour ago and now . . .

She sat in the hospital chair by his bed, holding his hand. She stroked the back of it, fighting tears, feeling as if her head were the size of a melon — dull, aching and hollow. "Hey, I still believe in you," she told him. "I've always believed in you. You've been such an amazing father with your tall tales and stories — I feel like I know my mother, and Mom died when I was four. New Orleans is home, but you've taken me to places around the world. Now, come on, you can survive this! We've been through all these years together and weathered so many storms . . . right, Dad?"

Her father didn't answer.

She glanced at the clock mounted on the wall. The television was on with the volume low; she listened to ads for the year's new cars and the newscaster interviewing a businessman, Brandt Shumaker, about his plans to go into politics. A local blues group came on and she listened to the music for a minute and said, "Good group, Dad. When you're better, we'll go see them."

Her father didn't reply.

She had to keep talking. "I bought a new print last week. A Blue Dog print. I don't know what it is, but I love them. My work's completely different, but of course, that's true for most artists. We all have our individual visions. . . ."

She was speaking inanely. Anything. She refused to accept that his life was slipping away.

And then . . .

Angus Cafferty sat bolt upright, gazing at her. His snow-white hair was mussed and wild; his sky-blue eyes settled on her intently.

"Lass, so late, too late! I should have spoken to you about this so many times, so long ago. I'd thought . . . I'd thought I'd wait until you got to the age of thirty, never thinking this could come so quick upon me. Just a few more years . . . just a few to leave you in a normal life, to know innocence — I was a fool. I have let you down, but you hear me now, Danni, please, hear me now! You mustn't sell the shop. You must never sell the shop. It's our lot in life, that's what it is, and one that matters in a manner most dire. Ah, girl, what have I done? Wanting all to be safe and serene for you. . . ." His Scottish burr, somewhat softened by his many years in the American South, was suddenly strong again. His words were filled with passion. He leaned toward her, gripping her hand so hard that it hurt, but he was alive and touching her and she couldn't cry out.

9

"No, Dad, don't worry, I'll never sell the store. It's *your* store. You'll get better, I can see that now. You'll come home and —"

"No! Ye canna sell the store! And the book, lass, you must read the book. Never doubt what you see or hear, never fear for your sanity or that of the world — turn to the book. The answers are in the book and it will bring you through heaven and hell and all realms in between. Do you hear me, lass, do you hear me? Ah, I love you, Danni, my girl, I love you so much. Cling to my words and live long but, mostly, live well. You're brilliant and beautiful, but the world changes. . . . The book, Danni, read the book, and look to it in all things!"

His grip on her hand eased; he fell back on the bed, his eyes closed and his lips silent.

Danni jumped up and rushed to the door, her tone frantic as she called out. "Dr. Vincenzo, come quickly!"

Vincenzo appeared in another doorway and strode down the hall toward her.

"He spoke to me! He spoke and fell back . . . but he spoke!"

Vincenzo frowned and walked over to the bed. He laid a hand on Angus Cafferty's arm, then turned to face her. "Ms. Cafferty, I know this is a difficult time . . . I was try-

10

ing . . . I . . ." He paused and shook his head. "Ms. Cafferty, he did not speak to you. He had passed when I left this room. I wanted to give you a few minutes alone with him before having him brought down to the morgue."

"What?" Danni gaped at him blankly. "No, no," she said. "My father sat up and spoke to me."

Vincenzo looked at her pityingly. "He's been gone for at least thirty minutes now, Ms. Cafferty. Feel his arm. He's growing colder already. I'm so sorry, I can see how you loved him. But he's what . . . almost ninety. He had a good life. And he was certainly loved."

"No, no, you don't understand. He talked to me. He sat upright and he *spoke* to me," Danni protested.

Vincenzo wasn't going to argue with her. He pursed his lips as if forcing himself to keep silent. "Is there someone you could call to be with you?" he asked. "I can see if we have a chaplain or a priest in the hospital."

She frowned at him, shaking her head. "I haven't lost my mind."

"He's gone, Ms. Cafferty. I'm so sorry, but your father has passed."

Danni winced. She held back the tears

11

that threatened and said with dignity, "I'm fine. I will stay with him a moment longer if that's all right."

He left. She sat at her father's side, and when she took his hand then, she knew the truth — the mighty Scot who had filled her life with love and adventure was dead. Her tears came then in a river.

"Danni?"

She looked up.

Billie McDougall, tall and thin as a reed, a man who had seemed as old as her father but was twenty-odd years younger, stood in the door. He was accompanied by Jane Pearl, her father's office manager, bookkeeper and sometime clerk. They were like family; they *were* her family now.

"Come, lass," Billie said. "Come away now. Your father was old and tired, and he needs to sleep now and rest from the weary rigors of this world. He loved you, lass, and he was loved in return, and that is the true measure of any man's life."

"Danni, we'll take you home. We'll get you a nice cup of tea with a shot of Scotch or whiskey and it will help you through the night," Jane said.

Billie walked in and stood over Angus's body, his cap in hand. "I will continue in your place, my dear friend," he said. And, to Danni's ears, it was like a vow.

As if Billie, too, believed that Angus could still hear him.

Jane set her hands on Danni's shoulders. "Come with us now, Danni. The doctor said you've been with the corp — that you've been with your father for over an hour. It's time to take care of yourself, as he would have wanted."

Jane had strong hands and arms for a woman. She could be forceful.

Danni moved to the door. But then she turned and came back to place a kiss on her father's forehead and laid her head against his chest as she had so many times as a little girl. "I love you," she whispered. "I will always love you. You'll live forever in my heart."

He was growing colder; he was a corpse.

But he was her father.

"Let's go now," Jane urged.

"You will always be with me," Danni told her father passionately as she was led out at last.

Billie remained, looking sadly down at his mentor, his friend and boss.

"Oh, Angus!" he said, anguish in his voice. "She doesn't know yet, does she? I told you that you'd not live forever. Poor lass. Danni has not yet begun to know just *how* you will

stay with her — just what you've left behind!"

CHAPTER 1

It was spring in New Orleans, a beautiful April day, and Angus Cafferty had been dead for three months the afternoon Michael Quinn followed the widow, Gladys Simon, to The Cheshire Cat, an antiques and curio store on Royal Street.

The house itself, now a shop, was one of the few buildings that had survived the Great New Orleans Fire of 1788 that had destroyed 856 buildings — followed by the fire of 1794 that destroyed another 212. It was one of the only structures from the mid-1700s that remained on Royal Street. It had a two-storied facade, with an inner courtyard and balconies surrounding the building streetside. He knew the layout of the old building; the original parlor, study and dining rooms were set up as the shop's display area, while the old pantry was Danielle Cafferty's studio. The basement was not really a basement at all. This was New

Orleans, and even on high ground, the basement was just the lowest level of the house. Six steps led up from the street, and courtyard entries led to the porches and the house. The shop's basement was filled with treasures Angus had collected and kept away from the view of others. Upstairs, above the store, were the office and a small apartment used by the Cafferty family. Billie McDougall slept in the attic, ever watchful, while a second street entry, which had once been a carriage house, was now a two-car garage.

Following Gladys Simon was easy; Quinn was directly behind her and she was oblivious. He felt like a stalker, having to trail her like this, but when he'd discovered that morning that she had the bust, he'd tried to see her. According to her housekeeper, she refused to see anyone. No amount of cajoling had gotten him in.

He'd waited outside her house, but she'd run to her car, turning away when he'd begun to speak to her. All he could do was follow — and pray that she was going to the curio shop.

She approached the shop and so did Quinn, practically on her heels. As they entered, he saw Billie reading a book behind the counter and Jane Pearl, the clerk and bookkeeper, walking up the stairs, presumably going to her office. She paused, however, when she heard the door open.

Gladys Simon was unaware of her surroundings. She headed straight to the old mahogany bar that had been refashioned into a sales counter. Quinn stepped in right after her and feigned great interest in a grandfather clock that was situated just inside the front door.

Billie might have been perfectly cast as Riff Raff in a *Rocky Horror* remake or as an aging Ichabod Crane. He was as skinny as his mentor and employer had been robust. Billie had steel-gray eyes and a shock of neck-length white hair and was dressed in jeans and a Grateful Dead T-shirt. He must have been a startling and imposing figure to a Versace-clad and perfectly manicured matron like Gladys Simon.

But Gladys didn't seem to notice anything about Billie at all. She rushed over to him.

"You buy antiquities, unusual items, don't you? You have to buy the bust from me — you *must* buy it from me. No, no, you don't need to *buy* it. You can have it. Please, come to my house and take the bust away. It belongs in a place like this!"

Billie glanced briefly at Quinn, a frown furrowing his wrinkled brow. "I'd love to help you, ma'am. I'm not the owner, but —"

"Oh, dear! That's right!" she said with a gasp. "But . . . the owner died, didn't he? Oh, please tell me the new owner is available . . . please! I must . . . I can't live with that *thing* anymore. . . ."

"Now, try to calm down, Mrs. . . . ?"

"Simon. Gladys Simon. It was my husband's. He's dead now. He's dead because of that . . . thing!"

"Please calm down, Mrs. Simon," he said again. "The object is a bust?"

"Yes, very old — and exquisite, really."

"You want to *give* me an old and exquisite piece?" Billie's voice was incredulous.

"Are you deaf, sir?" she shrieked. "Yes — I must be rid of it!"

By then, the woman's frantic tone had drawn the new owner from her studio in the back of the store.

Quinn had watched her on the day of Angus Cafferty's funeral. He had chosen not to approach her then; he had kept his distance when Cafferty was laid to rest in the Scottish vault at the old cemetery — the "City of the Dead," where he had long stated he would go when the time came. There'd been a piper at the grave site, but Cafferty was accompanied by the traditional

18

New Orleans jazz band and a crowd of friends to his final resting place. He'd been loved by many in the city. Of course, a tourist or two — or ten or twenty — fascinated by the ritual, had joined in, as well. The vaults in the cemetery didn't allow for the immediate grouping around the grave that was customary at in-ground burials, so he'd been able to hover on the edges of the crowd, paying his own respects from afar.

There was no doubt that the man's daughter had been devastated. And there was no doubt that she *was* old Angus's daughter — she had his startling dark blue eyes and sculpted features, finer and slimmer, but still a face that spoke of her parentage. Her hair was a rich auburn, brushing her shoulders, a color that might well have been Angus's once — when he'd had pigment in his hair. Despite her grief, she hadn't seemed fragile or broken, which gave him hope. Though she was slim, she was a good five-nine and might just possess some of the old man's inner strength.

As she walked to the front of the shop, she was frowning slightly, obviously perplexed by the commotion. She wore jeans and a short-sleeved tailored shirt and somehow appeared casual and yet naturally elegant. She moved with an innate grace.

Gladys heard her coming and turned to her. "You — you're the owner?"

"Yes, I'm Danni Cafferty. May I help you?"

"Oh, yes, you certainly may. I know your father was intrigued by historic objects. I never met him but I read that his shop acquired the most unusual and . . . historic objects," she repeated. "You must come and take the bust."

"Mrs. Simon, we don't just take anything."

"It's priceless! You *must* take it."

"Mrs. Simon, I didn't say we wouldn't *buy* it. It's that we don't *take* things." Danni Cafferty looked at the woman, assessing her with a smile. "I can't believe this is such an emergency that —"

"The bust killed my husband!" Gladys Simon broke in.

Danni raised perfectly arched brows. "Do you mean that . . . that it was used to strike him? If that's the case, the bust might well be evidence —"

"No!" Mrs. Simon cried. "You are not your father!"

Danni seemed to freeze, calling on reserves of hard-fought control and dignity. "No, Mrs. Simon, I am not my father. But if you wish to bring this bust in —"

20

"No! I won't touch it. You must come and get it."

Danni mulled that over for a minute, as if she was still fighting for control. Quinn noted that Gladys Simon's shrill voice had alerted Jane, and the bookkeeper was coming hesitantly down the stairs, one of Angus Cafferty's ebony nineteenth-century gentleman's canes in her hands. A good match for Billie — although the two weren't romantically linked — Jane was slim and straight with iron-gray hair knotted at her nape and gold-rimmed spectacles. She'd been with Angus for the past two years or so, and though she hadn't been a confidant in the way Billie had, she was fiercely loyal to the Cafferty family.

Jane was ready for whatever danger threatened, but seeing Gladys, her slim frame and near-hysteria, she held her place on the stairs, watching Danni to see if she was needed.

"Mrs. Simon, I'm sorry," Danni said. "You're suffering from terrible grief, and I have a lot of empathy for you. But we're not equipped to handle the psychological stages of that pain. We're a curio and collectibles shop and —"

"Yes! You must take the bust."

Danni glanced at Billie, who was following the conversation with unabashed interest.

"Mrs. Simon," she said gently. "Is there someone we can call? A close friend, a relative? Perhaps a minister or a priest?"

"I need you to take the statue!" Mrs. Simon said. Then she raged at Danni. "Oh, you stupid, stupid girl!"

Danni stiffened at the insult but, to her credit, took a deep breath and refused to reply, shaking her head with sorrow instead. "Let us help you. Let us get you someone who can help you."

Gladys whirled around, starting for the door.

"Mrs. Simon, if it's so awful, why didn't you just get rid of it?" Danni demanded.

Gladys stopped abruptly. She slowly turned around and walked toward her. "Don't you think I tried? I threw it in the trash, and it was back in the study the next day. I dropped it in a Dumpster on Bourbon Street, and it was back the next day. I buried it — and it was back!"

She was delusional — or so she obviously appeared to Danielle Cafferty.

"Mrs. Simon, really, you need to calm down," Danni said. "We'll go over and see the statue. Give me an address and we'll come this evening. We close at seven."

A sigh of sheer relief escaped Gladys and she dug into her handbag for a card, which she handed to Danni. "Thank you . . . thank you. You've saved my life!"

"It's just a bust . . . a statue . . . whatever, Mrs. Simon. Please relax. Everything will be fine."

"Thank you, thank you, thank you!" Gladys breathed.

And then she was gone.

Danni picked up the store's old-fashioned phone. She started dialing as Jane came the rest of the way down the stairs.

"You all right, Danni?" Jane didn't hide her concern.

"Of course. But I'm worried about that poor woman."

"Who are you calling?" Billie asked.

"The police," Danni said. "Someone needs to help that woman — perhaps see that she's committed. She's —"

It was time for Quinn to make his move and he did so swiftly, setting his thumb down on the disconnect button before she could dial three digits.

Danni stared at him in total indignation. "What the hell? Who *are* you — what do you think you're doing?"

"Don't call the police just yet. Listen to me. The woman really needs your help. Ask

Billie," Quinn said. "I can try to follow her and get the damned thing, but I've already tried to see her and talk to her. She knows about your father and the shop, so you're the one she needs to trust. You need to go and get the statue. But you don't have to deal with this alone. I'll be there."

Taken aback, she was still angry, but he saw sudden recognition in her smoldering gaze, along with shock and resentment.

Maybe he wasn't handling this well.

"You . . . you were at my father's funeral," she said.

He nodded. "I was his friend. He was a good man. The best. And you're doing him a real disservice if you don't continue his work."

"His work? His work was this shop and I'm keeping it open. Listen, I'm calling the police. That woman needs professional help — and I don't believe you're any more equipped to deal with her than I am," she said.

"Billie?" Quinn turned to Angus's long-time assistant.

Billie cleared his throat, looking at Danni. "Um, yeah, I don't know how to explain it all, but your father would've gone out there and seen the statue."

"Who is he?" she asked Billie, inclining

24

her head toward Quinn.

"*He* is standing right here. I'm Quinn. Michael Quinn, private investigator."

"And you're investigating crazy ladies with statues?" she asked sarcastically.

"You should go see the bust, Danni," Billie said.

"What's the matter with both of you? If I don't call the police, I'll live with a guilty conscience forever. She's deranged! She could be a danger to herself and others."

Quinn stepped back. "By all means, then. Call the police. And maybe they can help her for a few hours — a few days. The danger will continue. I guarantee it."

"Really? And you're so sure of this . . . how?"

"Because I worked with your father on occasion."

Her eyes narrowed. "I don't know you," she told him.

"Um, I do," Billie said. "I know him."

"I've seen him with your father, too," Jane murmured. "But I don't think you should trust him."

"She *should* trust him. Yes, she should!" Billie argued. "No offense, Jane, but you were never part of Angus's real world. You've barely been around two years and you're his bookkeeper, nothing more."

"Well, I never!" Jane said.

"Jane is a wonderful employee and you will not stand here in my store and insult her!" Danni said indignantly.

"Angus trusted me implicitly," Jane declared.

"Perhaps," Quinn said with a shrug. "But that's not important right now."

Danni looked at him warily. "You should state your business, your relationship with my father and then leave the store."

"I helped him. He helped me. I guess Angus wanted to protect you, his little princess," Quinn said. "Well, it's a shame and it's sad and it's probably too late." He felt his anger growing, and he wasn't sure why. It wasn't really her fault if her father had chosen not to share the depths of his life with her.

But she should have figured out that he wasn't just a shopkeeper or a collector! How naive could she have been? On the other hand, maybe she hadn't been that naive. Maybe she'd just been gone too much.

"Like I said, I don't know you, and I was very close to my father!" she began. "Mrs. Simon is suffering and needs help but understand this — I am *not* trained or equipped to deal with mental illness, and I rather think you might have some problems in that area yourself — rather than being a person who's capable of dealing with it!"

"Call the police, then. Like I said, maybe they can at least buy her a few hours." Although Quinn ignored her insult, he felt his fingers knotting into fists. He had to get out of the shop. There was no chance he'd offer unprovoked violence to anyone but he didn't want to break anything there. He studied her for a moment and added, "If you come up with some sense, meet me at the Simon house at five. At five — I don't care if you've closed or not. Billie handles the shop, anyway. He doesn't need you here."

With that, Quinn turned.

As the door closed behind him, he found himself shaking with emotion.

And some of it was anger.

Some of it was fear. Not for himself. He'd long since learned that fear, in itself, wasn't a bad thing. But a man's reaction to fear could be very bad indeed.

He was afraid for the future. He hadn't realized how much he'd depended on Angus Cafferty.

Danni watched the stranger leave, puzzled and trembling inwardly with outrage, indignation, a painful sense of loss. And dread . . .

27

She'd been working until she'd heard Gladys Simon's strident voice. Working idly on the finishing touches to a painting. She assumed she'd been inspired by a face she'd seen on the streets of New Orleans. Dignified, aging, attractive, intriguing. *But her painting was almost an exact image of the woman who'd come into the shop.*

It doesn't mean anything, she assured herself. It was just a resemblance. There were many such women in the South. Old-school, well-groomed and usually ruled by impeccable manners and propriety.

But . . .

She turned her thoughts to the man who'd been in the shop — as if he'd followed Gladys in, as if he'd known why she was coming. Yes, she'd seen him at the funeral. He'd interested her. He hadn't exactly been hiding, but he'd kept his distance from the family and other mourners. It would be difficult, she imagined, for a man like that to really blend into a crowd. He had to be six foot four, and he seemed to be solidly built but not too heavily muscled. He had neatly cropped sandy hair and hazel eyes that seemed to marble to a piercing shade of gold.

"Who is he?" she asked Billie.

And if he knew my father so well, she

wondered silently, feeling a familiar sense of loss and pain, *why did my father never tell me about him?*

I was so blithely unaware! Completely focused on art . . .

Billie looked uncomfortable. "He told you. His name is Michael Quinn. He's a P.I. Used to be a cop with the NOPD, but he left the force to work for himself."

"So what?" she demanded. "He worked with my dad to track down stolen objects or something like that?" she asked.

"Something like that," Billie said, his gaze sliding from hers.

"Hmmph! He's rude," Jane said, resting the cane she'd brought down on the bar counter. "Obnoxious. Like a crazy man. You should stay away from him!"

"No, you should listen to him," Billie insisted.

Jane shook her head. "Report him to the police!"

"Ah, Jane. You'll argue with anything I suggest," Billie said, aggravated.

"Well, rude isn't really the problem at the moment." Danni sighed, looking at the two of them. They could bicker like a married couple; Billie didn't really trust Jane, she thought. But both of them were excellent at their jobs, excellent at helping her run the business. She lowered her head. Most of the time, they were amusing when they were together.

"Billie, sorry. I can't just take the word of some guy who thinks he knew my father better than I did. I *am* going to call the police. I'm worried about that woman."

"Are you going to go and see about the bust?" Billie asked.

"Maybe," she replied. "But . . . I need to report this. If something happened to her — if she was so upset she walked into traffic — I'd never be able to live with myself."

Billie and Jane both stared at her. She called the operator rather than the emergency number and was put through to the right department. Billie and Jane watched as she gave the woman's name and reported her strange behavior in the shop and then answered a zillion questions. Had the woman been armed? No. Had she threatened anyone? No. Had she mentioned suicide? No. But she had talked about a killer statue and sounded as if she needed some serious intervention.

In the end, a public safety officer promised that Mrs. Simon's state of mind would be investigated, and she hung up, feeling frustrated.

Jane and Billie were still staring at her.

30

"What?" she asked.

"Your dad would've found out about the bust. He wouldn't have ignored that poor lady," Billie said.

"You haven't been on any buying trips since he died," Jane added. "No, I wasn't your father's right hand — like Billie — but I knew him well and loved him. Maybe . . ." She looked pained as she spoke again. "Maybe you should listen to Billie."

"Will wonders never cease!" Billie muttered.

Danni lifted her hands in a gesture that said nothing at all. It was still hard; she didn't spend her days crying or moping, but she felt as if there was a huge hole in her life. Angus had expected her to be strong and independent. She'd gone away to school and gotten her own apartment and led a life separate from his.

But he'd always been there. Once she was back in New Orleans, she'd seen him almost every day. She'd traveled with him extensively through the years.

Seeing the sights — at his urging — while he did his buying and collecting. He had spoiled her, yes. But he'd also taught her to be courteous and caring. He'd never walked away from anyone who needed help, whether it was a confused tourist seeking

31

directions or a homeless veteran or down-and-outer needing food and shelter — or a ride to detox.

"I will go see the bust, okay? I'll do what I can for Mrs. Simon."

Billie nodded. "That's what your dad would want."

"I'm trying to keep his legacy alive," she told the pair. "Now, if you'll excuse me . . . I was working. I'll go at five. I'll meet that obnoxious man and buy the stupid bust and hopefully make everyone happy, all right?"

Neither spoke or moved.

With a slight sound of impatience, she passed them by, thinking she'd return to her studio.

But she didn't want to go there. She didn't want to see the painting she'd almost finished, the character study that suddenly looked just like a real person.

Mrs. Simon.

Instead, she headed downstairs to the rooms that had been the most precious to her father. There were glass cases here and there — and boxes everywhere. A full suit of armor stood in one corner while in another an upright Victorian coffin held pride of place. It had never been used for a body but had been a display piece for a funeral home that had once been in business on Canal Street. A mannequin enjoyed eternal sleep behind the small window above the face, a style that was popular at the time. The wall displayed the death mask of an ancient Egyptian queen. One corner of the room held a horrifically screaming gorilla from a movie that was never completed and probably with good cause; the sign on the creature said From The Gorilla That Ate Manhattan.

She paused, glancing around. Other people, she thought, might find the basement creepy. She'd spent so much time working with her father that she'd learned to appreciate the delicate artistry put into so many of the items. The carving on the coffin, for instance, was the result of painstaking craft and labor.

Light filtered in from the old glass panes just above ground level but it wasn't enough for her that afternoon. Danni turned on the low-watt bulbs that helped protect the old pieces of art and artistry and sighed wistfully. Some people might suggest that her father haunted the rooms where his collections were kept.

She wished he did.

"Oh, Dad, if only you were here now!" she said softly.

The book.

He'd been so frantic that she "turn to the book."

It was a very old volume and it sat on a desk, encased in protective glass. Danni could remember it being there forever, she just hadn't thought much about it among the other curios so dear to her father. She walked over to the desk, sat in the swivel chair and looked down at the old tome before opening the glass cover and lifting it out. She'd never held it before, and the book was heavy, the parchment rich and the pages gold-trimmed. It was American, something that always gave her father great pride, and had been printed in 1699.

Carefully she turned pages, wondering what he'd wanted her to read in this book — or why he'd believed it would answer all questions, solve all dilemmas.

She was startled when a piece of folded paper slipped out.

She recognized her father's writing — her name in cursive on the outside.

With trembling fingers, she unfolded the paper.

Danni, dearest daughter, my sorrow is great as I write this. My burden is hard to bear, and yet it will be yours, too. Read with the light on the desk. And remember, the book is only for those who have the heart and the will to understand and to care, and though I have tried to give you the life of a normal young woman, the day will come when you must understand. Of course, I will tell you, talk to you, about all this, but I am writing in case my time comes before I know. Life is fleeting for us all and none can predict the day that we'll be called to a greater reward. My dearest Danni, I believe that love transcends time, and so I am with you, even if I have failed you.

Tears stung her eyes. "You never failed me, Dad. Ever. I loved you so much," she said aloud.

No, he had never failed her. She didn't know that much about his past — only that he had immigrated from Edinburgh when he'd been a young man, that he'd studied ancient history there and spent many years working on archaeological digs. He'd batted around the world until he was in his forties, met her mother — an anthropologist half his age — married her and moved to her home, New Orleans. After her mom died of an aneurysm when Danni was four, he'd done everything for her, acting as both father and mother. Even as an older man, he'd been gorgeous. But he'd never remarried.

A bittersweet smile curved her lips. "I wish you'd make a little more sense, Dad, but . . . no, you never failed me. You were the best ever!"

Danni began to flip through the pages. *The Book of Truth* offered medieval cures for whatever might ail you. One chapter listed herbs and their mixtures for maladies ranging from snakebite to the plague. Another gave instructions for cupping and bleeding.

She went back to the beginning. The print thoughout was large — perhaps to help the elderly and those with poor eyesight. The letters were exquisite, more like calligraphy than print.

She found a publication page. The book had been published in Boston. Maybe accepting herbs as natural medicinal components was something the author had done boldly and angrily, since it was printed only a few years after the calamity of the Salem witch trials.

She quickly discovered that she was right. The author, Millicent Smith, had written an introduction, dedicating the book to the women who had died in innocence, victims of jealousy or greed or even mass hysteria.

"True evil rests deeply and does not enter into the clean souls of those who will not be corrupted by demons." Danni admired the author and printer for their courage, and wondered how many copies of *The Book of Truth* had been created. Were they kept secret during those perilous times, circulating underground? How had her father come across this one?

"Turn to the book," he'd told her.

She shook her head. She didn't believe she'd have to protect anyone from being hanged, pressed or burned to death for being a witch. Maybe he was warning her to guard against prejudice of any kind, because there was nothing so dangerous.

Maybe it was his way of saying that there were people out there who needed to be saved.

"I called the police, Dad," she murmured. "I tried to get help for Mrs. Simon." She sighed. "Okay, I'll meet your bulwark of a private eye and buy the damned statue!"

She set the book back in its case, but as she did, she noticed another piece of paper between the next pages.

The light. Make sure you use the light!

That had been written hastily.

Use the light.

Well, she couldn't read without light, could she? Besides, there were plenty of lights down here.

Determined, feeling guilty although she couldn't understand why, Danni looked at her watch. She'd been down here longer than she'd realized.

If she was going to meet Quinn, she had to get moving.

But she hesitated, drumming her fingers on the glass, frowning. *Michael Quinn.* She vaguely remembered the name and wondered why. She knew she hadn't met him through her father. It was a good old Irish name and there were plenty of those in the city.

And then she remembered. Years ago, the name had been revered. There'd been a Michael Quinn who had hit the sports pages of the *Times Picayune* again and again. He'd lifted his public school from obscurity to stardom playing football. He was offered scholarships to half the colleges in the country. He'd been a local hero, soaring to football glory while maintaining academic achievement and capturing the hearts of adolescent females through the city, the parish and beyond. She was only twelve at the time, so she couldn't really remember the details, but . . .

But nothing. He'd disappeared. There'd been brief articles about him — about his behavior, attending parties known for excessive drug and alcohol use. Then everything had stopped. She hadn't heard anything about him ripping up the college scoreboards or joining the pros. He'd just disappeared.

Might have been a different Michael Quinn.

Gladys heard the voice again as she drove down the street. He was there, beside her, whispering in her ear.

"Do it. Gun it!" he ordered her.

She had ignored him as she'd driven through the French Quarter; you could barely move through the Quarter at times, much less gun a car. People walked into the street heedlessly — especially those who'd gotten an early start on Bourbon Street.

But now, she could see a group of schoolchildren. A crossing guard stood in the street with a large red stop sign, warning drivers that it was a school zone and elementary kids were making their way across the road.

"Gun it. End it for the little bastards — stop the pain for them now. Half of them live in crack houses, you know that. End their pain and yours. Gun it!"

She turned to look at him. He was beautiful. His face was so handsomely structured, with dark hair curling over his brow. His mouth was full and sensual. He moved, and yet he still looked as if he were cast out of marble. It was so strange; the statue in her house was a bust, showing only the head, shoulders and neck of the man, but he seemed to be sitting by her side in full body. He acted natural and at ease. He'd been carved during the time of the Renaissance, but he spoke English and knew modern idioms. He seemed to know modern mores and customs, too.

He was beautiful, yes . . .

And so malicious. Evil to the core. His smile was one of pure cruelty.

"You have to do it, Gladys. Think of the world, always the same. Kill or be killed. You can end their misery and your own. Or if you survive, you'll walk away because of your fragile mental state, the depths of your grief. It's kill or be killed, Gladys. That's the way of the world."

She saw the man in her mind, of course, but he seemed so . . . real. She'd seen him the night her husband had died, seen him standing over the body. And she'd known that Hank Simon was killed by the marble bust he'd been so ecstatic to acquire, the piece that had lain half-buried by the grave of a pirate-turned-entrepreneur in St. Louis Cemetery #1. A former pirate, yes, but a man who'd dedicated himself to good works in the latter part of his life. God knew where the bust had been before that.

He'd stood over Hank where he lay on the floor of their grand Garden District home; he'd stood over him, smiling, while Hank lay broken and bleeding. It looked as if he'd fallen or jumped over the balcony railing, but he hadn't. She'd known it when she saw the man. He had disappeared into thin air and she hadn't seen him again — until he'd appeared at the foot of her bed that morning, telling her she had to do as he instructed, or she'd wind up like Hank.

It was astonishing that her heart hadn't given out then.

No, it was tragic that her heart hadn't given out. Because now he was with her, urging her to kill. . . .

She *wasn't* a killer. She wasn't going to mow down schoolchildren with her Lincoln.

And yet . . .

She felt her foot almost itching to touch the pedal. She felt something inside her suddenly longing to do as he said — hit the gas. Hit it hard. Hit all the children she could. And, definitely, hit the plump crossing guard with her sign and her whistle. . . .

Her foot inched down on the gas with a malevolence that seemed to fill her heart with bloodred fury.

CHAPTER 2

Quinn had thought he'd be able to keep up with Gladys.

Chasing her on foot hadn't been difficult, but following her once he'd gotten back to his car had proven to be a challenge. Parking in the Quarter was a nightmare, so naturally he'd been two blocks down. Still, Gladys Simon wasn't exactly a speed demon, so he should've managed to catch up with her.

But it was the French Quarter. He should have known but never suspected that a parade would close off Bourbon precisely when he needed to cross it.

Gladys had beaten the parade.

He chafed, waiting. There was no turning; there was no backing up.

Assuming that she'd be headed home, he figured he'd start uptown as soon as he could. He tried to assure himself that Danni Cafferty had called the police and that they'd come by — or social services would — to see to her welfare.

But he couldn't be sure.

He knew he had to reach Gladys himself. If Danni wasn't going to take the statue, he had to do it. But he didn't know whether he dared wait long enough to catch up with Gladys since she seemed to be at the end of her rope. If Danni had just agreed immediately to come and get the damn thing, he wouldn't have been so worried.

When he'd tried to call Gladys, she'd refused to talk to him. When he'd tried to see her at home, he'd been put off by a protective housekeeper. He hadn't known that Hank Simon had the statue in time to try and see the man. In fact, he wouldn't even have learned about its existence — other than through vague references in art-history books — if it wasn't for the sniveling Vic Brown, incarcerated now with no bail while he awaited trial.

Vic had sold the bust to Hank Simon. Then, of course, Quinn had found out that Hank had died, which meant his wife now had it.

Vic had shot down three of his associates in the Chartres Street gang before being winged by the police himself. According to Vic, the bust had made him do it.

44

The newspaper had alerted him to the criminal's planned defense. Visiting him in his cell had told Quinn that Vic seriously thought the bust had ordered him to shoot his friends — it was them or his own life. A self-defense plea might actually work for the poor bastard; Vic's attorney, Anthony Everst, was trying to get Vic into a hospital unit. Not a bad call, since the dope dealer and petty crook was ranting in his cell about being damned now that he was no longer possessed.

Despite maneuvering more quickly than the law allowed when he finally cleared the Quarter, Quinn didn't catch up with Gladys on the road. But when he arrived, he saw that her car was in the driveway.

Apparently Gladys had gotten home without incident.

He left his car and hurried up the walkway to the porch of the beautiful old Victorian house where the Simons — pillars of society, philanthropists in the extreme — had lived. The house, he knew, had been in the Simon family since it was built just prior to the War Between the States. It spoke of old money and genteel living, slow breezes and gracious hospitality.

He banged on the door and pressed the buzzer urgently.

It was opened by the battle-ax of a house-keeper.

"You again," she said. Her name was Bertie. He knew that from trying to go through her to speak with Gladys before. He'd begun this quest as soon as he'd learned the bust had wound up at the Simon home.

"Bertie, it's imperative that I talk to Mrs. Simon. I think I can help her. You must know that her mind is unbalanced by grief. I can help her. I swear to you, I can."

"She's in mourning," Bertie said. "And she doesn't need any ambulance chasers trying to get her to sue on her husband's behalf or any such thing." Bertie wagged a finger at him. "I know who you are, Michael Quinn. And I don't care if you were a cop or if you've become a big hero — I heard enough 'bout you and your exploits when you were a boy. No pretty-boy white trash really changes his colors, and that's the truth of it."

"Bertie, this has nothing to do with me and everything to do with your employer," Quinn said, tempted to grab the house-keeper by the shoulders and push her out of his way. "She's nearly unhinged. She needs help."

"Not from the likes of you. You get out of

here, Mr. Quinn," Bertie said.

It really was a matter of life and death; still, he didn't want to force the woman to move if he didn't have to. One thing he'd say for Bertie — she knew his old reputation and could clearly see his size, but her loyalty to Gladys kept her from giving an inch.

"How about you just ask her if she'll see me? Tell her it's about the bust."

Bertie stiffened. She looked at him and either decided that Gladys was in such bad shape that even he might help or that he might be ready to physically set her aside.

"Fine, you can come in," she snapped.

She opened the door, and he entered the foyer with its elegant stained glass. He saw the central stairway leading up to the rooms above and balcony from which Hank Simon had thrown himself to his death. Bertie wouldn't glance in that direction. She stared straight at him and indicated the room to his right. "Go on into the parlor and stay there!" she said firmly.

He nodded and walked in. She followed him, closing the heavy double doors as if that would assure he didn't wander around in the house.

Quinn waited. Handsome portraits of the Civil War–era owners flanked the mantel.

The furniture in the room was an eye-pleasing collection of different decades and styles. The chairs were richly upholstered and the room's central piece — a grand piano — was polished to a magnificent shine.

He sat restlessly in one of the wingback chairs. Bertie was taking way too long.

He stood and walked around the room, feeling a sense of dread, of impending doom. He was ready to break through the doors and burst up the stairs when Bertie reappeared, a look of total consternation on her face.

"You'll have to come back."

"That's what Gladys said?" Quinn demanded.

Bertie hesitated. "I can't find Mrs. Simon," she said.

"What do you mean, you can't find her?"

Bertie crossed her arms over her ample chest. "I mean, she isn't here. I can't find her. So you'll have to come back."

He shook his head. "Her car is in the drive. She was in the Quarter less than an hour ago and now she's here — at least her car is. I was right on her heels. She hasn't gone back out, so she's here *somewhere.*"

"Well, she's not!"

He approached the woman, speaking in a

reasonable voice. "Bertie, listen. You don't know me. All you know about is an old reputation. I'm here to help Gladys — I swear it. We have to search for her. She's not in her right mind."

Bertie's lashes fell over her eyes and she looked downward quickly; she did know that he was speaking the truth.

She looked up at him again. "I have no idea where she is. She'd gone up to her room. Now, she isn't there."

"Which room?" he asked.

"Up the stairs, go down the balcony, first door to your left."

He hurried past her and took the stairs two at a time.

Walking along the balcony, he saw that he was passing the spot where Hank Simon must have hurled himself from the upper level to the floor beneath, breaking his neck. An accident? No . . .

"Gladys! Gladys, where are you?" he called. "I'll get the bust out of here right now! Gladys!"

No reply. He dashed into the woman's room.

Genteel, pleasant, charming. There was a white knit cover on the bed and the pillows were plumped high. An old-fashioned dressing table stood on one side of the room, while a more masculine set of drawers, matching in wood and design, stood against the far wall. White chintz curtains covered the window that overlooked the courtyard. Oils portraying different aspects of Jackson Square and the river graced the walls.

"Gladys?"

The breeze ruffled the curtains. Nothing more.

"Mr. Quinn!"

Bertie hadn't followed him up the stairs. Her voice wasn't panicked, nor did it sound relieved. He walked back out to the balcony that looked over the foyer below and leaned against the rail.

It was solid.

Bertie was standing just inside the entry, but she wasn't alone.

Danni Cafferty had arrived.

"We may be too late," he said.

Bertie let out a gasp.

Danni frowned, gazing up at him with her deep blue eyes. "Too late?"

"Bertie, go through the rooms downstairs. Look in every closet," Quinn said. "You —" he pointed at Danni "— get up here with me and start going through all the rooms on the second floor. Bathrooms, storerooms, closets, you name it."

"Mr. Quinn," Bertie said indignantly.

50

"Mrs. Simon doesn't make a habit of hiding in the closet!"

"Just do it!"

Bertie was worried; that much was obvious. She pursed her lips, not happy taking orders from him but willing at that moment to do anything.

Danni, still frowning, made her way up the stairs. He ignored her and returned to the room Gladys had shared with her husband.

He checked in her bathroom and the huge walk-in closet that had probably been another room or a nursery at one time. He peered under the bed. Then he hesitated, studying the open window. Dreading what he might find, he walked to it, stepped out on the inner courtyard balcony and glanced down.

He sighed in relief. There was no broken body on the patio stones below. He inhaled. Had the woman slipped out the back and gone for a stroll?

Danni came in. "I've been in a study, two guest rooms, a sewing room and an office and there are no more rooms. I opened every closet door — and checked the other two bathrooms. There's no one here."

"It's all wrong," he muttered.

"Why are you so sure of that?" she asked.

"I've seen what the bust can do," he told her. And he had. He'd seen the madness in Vic and he knew what Vic had done.

"The bust is just an object!"

He brushed past her. There was a garage on the other side of the courtyard with an apartment above it. There had to be some kind of entry via the bottom of the U — the traditional design of the house — that surrounded the courtyard. He started down the hall but then paused, noting that the trapdoor to the attic wasn't completely closed.

He cursed, barely aware of Danni standing behind him, watching him as if he should be in a mental ward.

Quinn pulled down the stairs that led to the attic and quickly climbed up them.

At first, he could see nothing. The attic was lit only by a single dormer window and his eyes had to adjust.

Then he heard a scream of horror behind him. Danni had followed him up. She was pointing.

He blinked, and then he saw it. In the shadowed space that fell just to the side of the window, there was a body swinging from the rafters.

He rushed to it, lifting the slim form of Gladys Simon so that the rope around her neck could no longer strangle her. He held her, dug in his pocket for his knife and cut the thick cord, easing Gladys down to the wooden floor. He straddled her, desperate to perform CPR.

But he'd been a cop — and he'd been around.

Gladys was gone.

He kept up his efforts, anyway. He could be wrong. . . .

He vaguely heard Danni calling the police. And he felt her hand on his shoulder.

"She's dead," Danni said softly.

He knew it was true.

He sat back on his haunches, bitterly ruing the time it had taken to reach her. When Danni touched him again, he jerked away.

At that moment, he hated her as much as he hated himself.

Danni felt disjointed.

Horrified and disjointed. The morning had started out like any other — and now she was sitting in the parlor of an uptown home while police and paramedics moved in and out, listening to Bertie cry and Quinn speak with a detective in controlled tones. The way he'd looked at her when he'd given up on resuscitating Gladys had cut her to the core. She felt tremendous guilt, and anger that she should feel that way. She had come when he'd told her to come. She couldn't have known the woman was going to commit suicide! And she *had* called the police, and they'd promised to send social services out to investigate.

She was still sitting here — waiting, as the police had asked — feeling as if the earth had tilted slightly off its axis.

She wanted to leave, to go home, forget the horror of seeing Gladys Simon's body swaying in the shadows, forget she'd seen the woman's face when Quinn had brought her down.

She'd never forget it, though. Something was unalterably changed and she hated it.

"What do you know about this?"

She startled to awareness; the detective — a man named Jake Larue — was standing beside her, looking down at her.

She raised her hands. "I don't know anything. I wish I did. Mrs. Simon came into my shop today, swearing that a bust her husband had bought had killed him. She was extremely agitated. I called the police — not the emergency line, she wasn't walking around with a knife or a gun — and I was assured someone was going to see to her." Her words sounded defensive, like an excuse. They *were* an excuse.

54

Could she have said or done anything that would have saved the woman's life?

Larue turned to Quinn, shaking his head. "She was bereft. Her husband had just died. You're trying to tell me she didn't kill herself?"

"No, I believe she might well have killed herself, but if anyone can answer that question for sure, it'll be the medical examiner. We searched the house before we found her. The police response when Ms. Cafferty called in the death was excellent — I think a cruiser was here in two or three minutes. No one was crawling around the house or the grounds. I didn't, however, get into the garage," Quinn said.

"I have men searching the area now, but if she did kill herself, there's no reason to expect that someone was in the house."

"But someone *was* in here," Quinn said with certainty.

Larue groaned. "You just said she killed herself."

"Yes, I believe she did."

"Then why would anyone have been here?" Larue asked, his eyes narrowed. Danni noted that he wasn't looking at Quinn as if he was crazy; instead, Larue looked as if he wanted to groan again, sink down in a chair and clamp his head between his hands. He held his ground, though, only a long breath escaping him as he stared at Quinn.

"The bust is gone," Quinn told him.

"The bust . . . the bust that supposedly killed Hank Simon?" Larue asked skeptically.

Quinn nodded. "Mrs. Simon was convinced it killed her husband."

"And *you* think a bust killed her, too?" Larue asked.

"It doesn't matter what I think. What matters is what was in her head. If she believed the bust killed him, she might have believed it would kill *her,*" Quinn said. He shrugged. "Or worse — maybe she believed it would have some kind of dangerous effect on her . . . I don't know. I can only say she was acting very erratically and that's why I came here. I'd seen her in the French Quarter, and to my deepest regret, it seems she was in a far worse frame of mind than I'd imagined."

Larue sighed. "Quinn, it's going to get more and more complicated, isn't it? Every time you're involved —"

"Wait!" Quinn protested. "*You're* the one who asked me to check on Vic Brown and his raving about the bust, remember?"

"I'm not publicizing the fact that I brought

you in, you know," Larue reminded him.

Quinn grinned and nodded slightly.

"We were partners once," Larue explained to Danni.

"He's a good cop," Quinn said. "A really good cop."

"And Quinn is a damned good investigator, but I *am* a cop and . . . well, police forces all over sometimes call on P.I.s. With Quinn, I know it's cool because even if he doesn't make big bucks on a case like this, he's going to be okay financially."

Danni sensed that Quinn could feel her looking at him curiously. "I have a trust fund from my grandmother, who managed to buy just the right stocks at the right time," he explained. "So I'm okay when I work on something that doesn't involve a paying client. Something I'm interested in. And I'm always available for Larue when he needs a little help."

"Thank God, since the force isn't rolling in money and I'm going to be stretching the budget to the limit to bring in the overtime on this. I can already see it coming!" Larue turned to Danni. "Thanks to Quinn," he added.

"But you have to admit it's worth it. Because I'm usually a step ahead, and you know I do my damnedest to get answers,"

Quinn finished for him.

Larue was silent for a minute, then sighed again.

Danni was surprised. She'd never imagined that Quinn was actually accepted by the police force — a force he'd left.

"All right," Larue said briskly. "So you figure this bust — which Mrs. Simon believes killed her husband — is missing? That someone broke into the house as she was killing herself and stole it?"

"I don't know if the thief broke in before or after she killed herself, but whoever stole it might have been ready to kill for it, anyway," Quinn told Larue.

Danni spoke up. "No one needed to kill her for the bust. She wanted it out of the house. She would've given it to anyone who asked."

Both of them looked at her — as if they'd forgotten she was there.

"Yes, she wanted it gone," Quinn agreed. "But the person who stole it might not have known she was desperate to get rid of it. That's irrelevant. We were too late, the bust is gone and there'll be more deaths over it."

"You've lost me, Quinn," Larue said. He didn't wait for a response, continuing with, "What about the housekeeper?" He glanced down at the notes on his iPhone. "Roberta

Hyson. She didn't see or hear anyone in the house."

"This is a big house," Quinn reminded him. "And I'm not sure about her eyesight or her hearing."

"Nice . . . I hope people are kind to you when you're old one day."

"I'm not being insulting. The woman is elderly — and she isn't in this room, so she can't be insulted."

It was crazy. *Crazy.* Danni's head was pounding. She stood; the men had forgotten her again, anyway.

"If there's nothing else you need from me, I'm going home," she said. Her voice sounded distant and a little shaky.

Once again, they both gave her their attention.

"Of course, Ms. Cafferty. If we need you, we know where to find you," Larue said.

"You're leaving? Just like that — after this?" Quinn frowned.

"Just like that," she told him, nodding gravely.

She thought she'd made her escape when she walked out the front door, moved down the steps and past the two uniformed officers standing guard at the entry like carved sentinels.

But she'd barely reached the street when

she heard him behind her. And she wasn't surprised when he grabbed her arm.

She spun around, seething. "Let go of me, Mr. Quinn . . . Michael, whatever."

He did, staring at her. She hated the fact that she felt compelled to stare back.

"It's Quinn. Just Quinn." He paused. "I guess Angus didn't talk to you. Either that, or you're an ice-cold functioning psychopath who couldn't care less about the lives of others."

"My father had tremendous patience for people with mental problems. However, I don't. So leave me alone, or I'll shout for that friend of yours who's still in the house."

He shook his head, disgusted. With her. That seemed doubly galling.

And yet she still felt guilty. Gladys Simon was dead.

But what could she have done? She'd never seen the woman before that day!

To her horror, she blurted out, "It wasn't my fault!"

She thought he'd lash out at her and insist that it certainly *had* been her fault.

"No, it was mine," he said, and she realized he was inwardly kicking himself. For some reason, he seemed to believe that if she'd understood the situation, she might have magically saved the day. "It was my

60

fault. I realize now that Angus never really said anything to you and neither did Billie. There are things you need to understand . . . but right now, we have to get that bust back."

"We?" she said horrified. "Look, you don't even know that Gladys didn't stash it in the house somewhere. Maybe it *wasn't* stolen. Like Larue said, you make everything more complicated."

As if Quinn had somehow hired him to play a part, Detective Larue appeared on the front porch.

"Quinn!" he called.

"Yeah?"

"We need some help. You were right. The housekeeper didn't hear a thing — but a window was taken out on the ground level, garage side. The glass was cut out, eased to the ground by some kind of suction device."

Quinn nodded slowly.

"Still doesn't mean the bust is gone. Where did she keep it?" Larue asked.

"I don't know. I've never been here until today. But I'm pretty sure it was kept in the house. When Hank Simon bought it, he was convinced he'd made the buy of the century."

"The den — or the salon," Danni heard herself volunteer. Quinn turned to face her.

"She said something in the store about trying to throw it away, trying to bury it, but it kept showing up back in . . . I'm not sure of the exact word she used, but someplace like an office, den, salon."

"We've checked out Hank Simon's office," Larue said.

"There's a library, but it's not in there," Quinn said. "I looked when we got here and were trying to find Gladys."

Larue motioned to one of the uniformed officers standing by. "As soon as the M.E. retrieves the body and the forensic unit's finished, I want a more extensive search of the house. Go through closets, bathrooms — everywhere."

The officer cleared his throat. "What does the bust look like?" he asked. "The house is filled with antiques and bric-a-brac."

"It's carved marble. Head, neck and shoulders. Curly hair, classic features. It's been described as portraying the face of an angel — or a demon. Some say the eyes are demonic, that they seem to be watching you. It was sculpted with a mantle over the shoulders and at a certain angle the mantle can appear to be angel wings," Quinn told him. "It looks like it belongs in a de'Medici tomb."

"A de'Medici tomb? Would that be a tomb

in one of the St. Louis cemeteries, Lafayette up in the Garden District or out in Metairie?" the officer asked.

"There are no de'Medici tombs around here. No, what I'm saying is that it looks Roman — like something you'd see in a Renaissance church or tomb," Quinn said.

The officer made a slightly derisive sound. He quieted as Quinn scowled at him. "Sorry, Detective Quinn."

"I'm not on the force anymore. I'm just Quinn. I'm simply telling you how it's been described," Quinn added.

"Head, neck and shoulders — it didn't get up and walk out, then," Larue said sardonically.

"No, I don't think it's supposed to be able to walk," Quinn said with equal sarcasm.

Danni wanted to go home. She wanted the day to rewind; she wished she'd never met — and failed — Gladys Simon, and that Michael Quinn had never darkened her door.

"You going to help in the search?" Quinn asked her.

No!

But the way he looked at her . . .

What was she going to do? Go home and wallow in guilt?

Not fair! She really had no idea what was

going on.

She didn't want to agree. She opened her mouth to say *no.*

What came out was, "Sure. You don't think you're going to find it, though, do you?"

"Nope," he said. "But what the hell — we can't be certain it's missing until we do a thorough search."

"What about . . . Gladys? I don't know how to investigate. I'll leave fingerprints all over. The crime scene people won't want us messing things up."

He grinned and reached into his pocket, producing a wad of balled-up plastic. It proved to be several pairs of gloves. "Not to mention the fact that our fingerprints are already all over the place because we were trying to find her."

She snatched gloves from him and put them on. As they returned to the house, Larue said to Quinn, "I'm assuming you have some idea of where to look for this bust or statue or whatever if it's not here?"

"No, not really," Quinn replied. "But I'll try to get a lead on it."

"And if not?"

"If not . . ." He paused for a minute. His eyes slipped over Danni but she wasn't sure he was really seeing her.

"If not?" Larue asked.

"If not, I'm afraid we'll be following a trail of bodies. . . ."

CHAPTER 3

There was really no hurry to search for the statue; Quinn knew it was gone.

Just as he knew Gladys Simon had hanged herself.

So there was no reason to interrupt the work of the crime scene unit and the M.E., Ron Hubert, who came to examine the body of the deceased.

Dr. Hubert arrived as they walked back toward the house, the crime scene unit directly behind him.

Quinn was afraid he'd lose Danni Cafferty while they waited for the forensic team to finish. When Larue called him up to the attic to speak with the M.E., he pulled her along with him. She was reluctant, but she felt the same sense of guilt over Gladys's death as he did, so she followed him.

Hubert was on his knees by the body. Hubert, who was a good man and a good forensic pathologist, had been there through the worst of the city's tragedies, dealing with the aftermath of Hurricane Katrina and the summer of storms and violence that flared in the wake of it. People were bitter, drug lords ignored the police, and the force was at its most vulnerable. Somehow, through the tragedy and carnage he'd seen, Hubert had never lost his empathy for the living or the dead. He'd lived in New Orleans since childhood but his family came from Minnesota, and he had the pale blond hair and pale blue eyes that indicated a Nordic background. He was sixty-plus years of age now, deceptively thin — and still strong. Quinn had seen him easily maneuver bodies that were five times his own size.

"See how the rope is tied?" Hubert asked as Quinn entered the room and knelt beside him. He pointed to the rope. "It's quite awkwardly tied — an inexperienced hand. The way it's situated tells me that she tied the rope herself, hoisted it over the support beam there and used that crate to stand on. There's not a mark on her to say she struggled with anyone. I'll see if there are any hairs, fibers, what have you, on the body, of course, but my preliminary exam suggests she did this to herself." He looked at Quinn. "Don't that beat all? A thief breaks in — but she kills herself. However, unless I can prove that beyond a doubt, he'll probably go up for murder as well as breaking and entering and theft."

"*Can* you prove it beyond a doubt?" Quinn asked him.

"I can certainly testify to the likelihood. Poor woman. The loss of her husband was obviously too much for her. I'm sorry to see her like this. The Simon family contributed to many charities. They doled out help right and left after the storms."

Quinn nodded.

He wished Gladys had talked to him — and he wished he'd reached her in time. He damned well wished Hank Simon had never thought owning the bust would be such a remarkable coup.

But where was the damned thing now?

And how uncanny that a thief had come to steal it — just as Gladys had given in to the darkness. . . .

The Simons had been generous, compassionate people.

He turned to Danni. She was standing exactly where he'd left her, almost as if she'd been frozen there.

"By the way, Dr. Hubert, this is Danni Cafferty. She's Angus's daughter."

Hubert glanced at Danni. "How do you do, young lady? I suppose that question

68

seems inappropriate at the moment. You can't be doing very well." He paused. "I knew your father. He was a fine man."

She smiled fleetingly. "Thank you. Yes, he was."

"Call me if there's anything, please," Quinn said.

"You know I will," Hubert assured him.

Danni had responded to Dr. Hubert in smooth, well-modulated tones, still not moving.

Quinn touched her arm gently, afraid she'd wrench it away from him. Her eyes met his instead, blue and steady and crystalline.

"We'll talk with a friend of mine on the crime scene unit," he said.

She didn't react, but when his touch signaled that she should turn so they could leave the attic, she spun around and preceded him down to the second level.

He found Grace Leon there. She was the head of her unit, a no-nonsense woman with short-cropped graying hair and a slim figure.

"I heard you were on this," she said.

"Sure am. What can you tell me?"

"There was a break-in. As you may have heard, the glass was cut, and then removed with a suction device. We followed a faint trail of dust particles from the lower level to

69

the study — and I do mean faint. I have something that might be a viable footprint from the first stair. I'll let you know what we get, but we'll need some tech to pump it up first."

"Did he — or she — make it to the attic?"

"No, I don't think so. The trail ends in the study. Odd, huh? The old lady hanged herself while she was being robbed. That's how it appears, anyway." Grace looked past him to Danni and then arched a brow at Quinn.

"Danni Cafferty, Grace Leon. Grace, Danni," Quinn said.

"Cafferty?" Grace asked. "As in Angus?"

Quinn nodded.

Grace lifted a gloved hand, then dropped it. "Nice to meet you," she said.

"Thanks. You, too."

"You're free to look around. Just keep the gloves on," Grace advised. "We're packing up now."

"Why don't we do a final check," Quinn said to Danni. He realized he'd been waiting for her to bolt. She wasn't going to.

"All right. I'll take the downstairs," she told him. "And the lower level. You can have the second floor and the attic."

He was surprised again; she seemed all business, as though she knew what she was doing and what she was looking for. She abruptly moved into the parlor.

Quinn found exactly what he'd expected — nothing.

The thief hadn't bothered with the silver or any of Gladys Simon's jewelry. He'd removed the statue and apparently nothing else. While Quinn paused in the study, observing the marvels her husband had collected — a Tiffany lamp, two Fabergé eggs, an Egyptian scepter, a medieval sword and shield, plus walls covered with fine art — he heard someone announcing the arrival of the ambulance that would transport Gladys's body to the morgue.

Dr. Hubert left with the body, saying goodbye to Quinn in the upper hallway with a quick salute.

As Quinn came down the stairs, the crime scene unit moved on out, leaving a few uniforms behind, as well as Larue. Larue was in the foyer with Bertie, who was seated on the love seat that flanked the staircase.

She was sobbing.

"Is there somewhere else you can stay?" Quinn asked her.

"I should be here. I should watch for more wretched thieves," Bertie said between sniffles.

"Bertie, what are you going to do if a thief

shows up?" he asked. "You shouldn't be here tonight. The police will keep an eye on the place and I'm sure there's an alarm."

"The alarm," she said dismissively.

"Was it set today?"

"Well, no, not once Mrs. Simon went out," Bertie said.

"See? We'll set it and the house will be fine. You shouldn't be here."

"I agree," Larue told her. "Ms. Hyson, both your employers are dead. I didn't know them, but I knew of them. You'll be taken care of in their will, I'd bet. But in the meantime, I think that being here could be harmful to your health."

Danni walked into the foyer then, and Bertie studied her for a long moment.

"But the danger is gone, isn't it? The bust is gone." She wagged a finger at Danni. "I *knew* that thing was evil. It was . . . like the eyes watched you all the time, followed you wherever you went. It was creepy. I hated being in the room with it. I didn't dust the study when it was in there, not after that first time. Why, it made the whole room feel . . . dirty. But . . . it's gone now. And Miss Cissy — Cecelia Simon — she'll be coming here now that her mother has . . . passed. I have to keep the place for her. Poor dear, she's just gone back to Baton

Rouge after her dad died. Oh, Lord, I'm going to have to call Miss Cissy and tell her that . . . that her poor mama . . ."

Bertie broke into tears again.

Danni went to sit next to her, putting an arm around her shoulders. "Don't worry, Bertie. Detective Larue will call Cecelia. You just have to be ready to comfort her."

Bertie wiped her eyes and looked at Larue hopefully. "Detective, you must call that poor young woman and tell her. She'll come right back, and I'll be waiting for her. I will not leave when the daughter of the house is coming home."

Larue turned to Quinn, and Quinn shrugged. He was pretty sure Bertie was right; there was no intruder here anymore — and no evil, either.

He didn't say he believed the thief was the one in danger now.

"I'll have someone on duty at the door, Ms. Hyson. We'll watch the house for twenty-four hours, until Cecelia returns, and through the next night, at least," Larue said.

"That's kind of you, Detective," Bertie told him gratefully.

"You through here?" Larue asked Quinn.

"Yes." Quinn knelt down in front of Bertie and pulled a card from his wallet. "The number is my cell. If you're afraid — if anyone bothers you — call me. And if Cecelia wants to talk to me, please have her call."

He was astonished when a big tear slid down the woman's face and she reached out to touch his cheek. "I'm so sorry. I'm so sorry I didn't see that fine spark in you, Mr. Quinn. I just saw the past. Thank you."

"Hey, that's okay . . . you were a good friend to Gladys, a really good friend." He stood, but Danni still sat next to the woman, comforting her. A moment later she rose, too.

"I'm so sorry," she said.

Bertie nodded tearfully.

Danni walked toward the foyer and the door to exit, with Quinn behind her.

He thought she'd leave straightaway, that she would've had her fill of him and the Simon house.

But she waited on the sidewalk. "Who the hell *are* you?" she asked.

There were officers nearby. He hated explaining himself — or trying to explain himself — especially in front of others.

"Michael Quinn," he began, but she cut him off.

"Michael Quinn, yes. Big high school football hero, and then you went on to

74

quarterback for the state and suddenly you disappeared — Oh, yes, after being in the papers time and again for your escapades."

"I was a college kid," he said. "But what you read was true."

"Was?"

"I learned my lesson the hard way."

"Oh?"

"I died."

She leaned back, folding her arms over her chest, staring at him. "You're a dead man?" she asked dryly.

"I was resuscitated," he said, shrugging. She didn't need his whole story just now; she sure as hell wouldn't *believe* his whole story even if he told her.

"It changes your perspective on life," he said.

"How did you know my father?"

"He helped on some of my cases."

"Yes, right — you're a P.I.," she said. Her tone was still cool and skeptical.

He wondered whether to feel sorry for her and try to tell her more about what she apparently didn't know . . . or obey his instinct to walk away.

"Gladys Simon is dead," he said. "Maybe the fates couldn't be stopped — and maybe you're to blame, and maybe I'm to blame.

It doesn't matter. She's past being helped. But that bust is out there. I have to find it."

"The bust is a *thing*," Danni said. "Yes, it was stolen. Yes, it belongs to the estate. But it's a thing. Just a thing."

"You really have no idea what your father did, do you?" Quinn asked her.

"I gather he helped the police at times," she said. "And no, I didn't know. And although I guess it would be to the estate's benefit if the bust was found, it can't be *that* important. It was stolen to begin with, right?"

"It's got quite the history. The bust dates back to the Italian Renaissance. I know some of the background, but not all of it. It graced the tomb of a contemporary of Lorenzo de' Medici's. It remained there, bringing bad luck to the family, or so I've read — until World War II, when it was stolen. According to oral history, it was taken by a supporter of Mussolini who gave it to a German general as a gift. Both men committed suicide. Naturally, it was suggested that they did this because the war crimes they'd carried out were horrendous — and they were afraid that if they were taken in the night by the Russian forces, they'd be tortured before they were killed. From there, the bust supposedly wound up with Hitler himself. After the war, it found its way into the home of a Soviet KGB officer, after which it disappeared until it was unearthed by an American sculptor who smuggled it into the United States. He went on to become a serial killer. His name was Herman Abernathy and he drained the blood of five women in order to make perfect statues of them. The bust went up at an auction house when his estate was sold to pay for his defense and it was bought by a New Orleans entrepreneur and voodoo practitioner. He didn't buy it for his own estate. He had it placed in the cemetery over the tomb of a family known to have practiced white magic. I assume he believed that the dead who were powerful in the ways of good could control the evil in the statue. Then came the summer of storms, the bust disappeared and people started winding up dead."

"Those killer storms are a number of years behind us now," Danni said.

He nodded. "The bust was returned to the cemetery. There was a write-up about its odd history in the *Times Picayune* not long ago."

"I remember the article — but just vaguely," Danni admitted.

"Then it was stolen again. The thief was

killed by a junkie, who in turn massacred a bunch of other junkies. He's awaiting trial now. He sold the bust to Hank Simon right before he was nabbed by the police. And you know what happened after that."

"How did a man like Hank Simon meet up with a junkie?" she asked.

"Hank was a collector. Vic Brown knew that. No killing had been connected to the bust at the time — and Hank was willing to buy a great piece even if he suspected it hadn't been gotten legally. You know how much buying and selling goes on outside the law!"

"That's irrelevant. Anyway, it's a *thing,*" Danni repeated.

"Fine. Well, then, thank you very much, Ms. Cafferty, for taking the time to help out here." Quinn thrust a hand into his pocket and produced another card. "Here, if you feel you really want to understand what your father did, call me sometime. I've got to get on with the search for that . . . thing."

He left her standing on the sidewalk and hurried to his car. He realized she was disturbed by the events of the day and was fighting the possibility that the bust itself could be evil. That was understandable. But . . .

Why hadn't Angus talked to her about the shop?

Maybe, for Angus, separating his life with his daughter — his family — from the shop and his calling had been a method of clinging to something normal.

As he got into the driver's seat, he saw that she was still standing on the sidewalk, watching him.

She stood tall beneath the moonlight, hair curling over her shoulders, and she gave the impression of an Athena — someone who was strong and ready to face the world in defense of the innocent.

He shook his head, emitting a sound of derision.

Yeah. Big help *she* was.

Then he took a deep breath. *Not fair, Quinn.*

He thought about his own past. *You didn't know until . . .*

You knew.

He'd been reprehensible before he'd learned the truth; she was merely ignorant.

But like it or not, he might be moving forward on his own.

With that in mind, he pulled out into the street. Time to hit a few of the shadier spots in the city of New Orleans.

The bastard.

The arrogant, crazy, single-minded bastard.

Danni watched Michael Quinn drive away, her emotions raging. She was furious. It was late — and he'd just left her on the street, going off on his own.

Not that she'd wanted to go anywhere with him. But he'd dragged her into this, and now she felt guilt and sadness that a woman was dead — and total confusion. People could behave brutally, badly, cruelly. But he was obsessed with an object!

As far as she could see, the damage was done. Hank and Gladys Simon were both dead; the bust — the *thing* that had driven Gladys so crazy — was gone. Stolen. But surely the bust itself didn't have any power. Power lay in the minds of people. Somehow Gladys had let herself believe the bust was evil, and therefore, in her particular reality, it was.

"Jerk!" she said aloud.

She headed for her own car in the dark.

As she drove home, she wondered how her father had come to know police officers and forensic experts — without her having a clue. Granted, she and Angus hadn't been joined at the hip. Although she had her room in the shop, where she'd been staying since his death, she'd also had an apartment near Tulane, which, of course, she'd now let go. She'd grown up in the French Quarter, and leaving the sometime-insanity of the area for a place of her own had seemed a logical progression for her. She loved her art, fellow artists and a number of musicians. She went out with her friends; her father went out with his.

She'd just never imagined him delving into police matters. Knowing that Quinn person.

"Jerk," she said again.

She bit her lip as she turned down Royal Street. She was hurt, too. Hurt that so much had gone on that she hadn't known about. She reminded herself that she'd hidden a few things from her father while growing up — not terrible things, but she'd had her share of normal escapades in college. There'd been a few dates she certainly hadn't wanted to share with him, and yet . . .

In all important matters, they'd been close. He'd been friends with Jarett Morrison, the love of her high school life, and although she and Jarett had split up in college, they'd somehow stayed best friends.

Her father had been her rock when word had come that Jarett had been killed on a dusty desert road by a bomb while in the service; he'd held her through the funeral. He'd never met Aaron, the wacky engineer she'd dated for only a few months, or Hardy Wentford, the forlorn guitarist. She'd never brought a man home to meet Angus unless she was serious about him, and she hadn't felt that way about anyone since her mad high school crush on Jarett, a crush that had just faded, as naturally as aging.

Lately, since before her father's death, she hadn't even met anyone she really wanted to have coffee with, much less get serious about.

The point was that *she'd* hidden a few questionable dates; he'd hidden an entire life's project!

Royal Street was quiet but she could hear the distant, competing music from Bourbon Street — like the beating of the French Quarter's heart. The real heart, of course, wasn't in the blaring pop music, the strip clubs or the bars on Bourbon Street. It was in the centuries of history. But tourism kept the city alive, so those entertainers were important.

A few late-night diners were strolling back to their hotels or homes in the Quarter but her block was dead quiet. She hit the remote control button and drove her Acura into the garage. Billie's little Beetle was pulled into its spot, she noted, but she'd expected that it would be. Billie was a homebody. When he wasn't working, he might take a stroll down to Frenchman Street, where more locals played at the pubs and bars, but he was usually home early, up in his attic room, watching *Storage Wars* and gleeful when he convinced himself that no one had ever found treasures to compare with those at The Cheshire Cat.

The garage door opened into what had once been a pantry; now it was a hodge-podge of stored objects. She walked into one of the shop's display rooms. The emergency floor lights were on and she could see the blinking blue lights that indicated the alarm was working. She reset it and moved through the darkened rooms to the stairway, passing the knight in full armor, a life-size voodoo queen doll and a standing display of Anne Rice's *Interview with the Vampire* characters. She paused in the shadows, smiling.

"We were a good team, Dad," she said softly. He'd been the collector, but she'd known how to create displays that made the shop a not-to-be-missed venue in the city. It had gone from a confusion of objects to a showroom worthy of a museum.

She hurried on up the stairs to her own room. It was nearly midnight and she really should get some sleep.

But after showering — she felt she had to; somehow *death* seemed to be clinging to her — she discovered that no matter how hard she tried, she couldn't stop thinking. So she lay awake, hour after hour.

Michael Quinn. He was a celebrity once. But he'd been known for hard living, for dating a different beauty every week and attracting national attention, from sportscasters to pop stars. He'd been escorted out of a few establishments and he'd been escorted into a few jails. Then there was an accident, and he'd disappeared from public view. For a few years, whenever a wicked football game was on, people would say, "If only Michael Quinn was playing!" and then even those sentiments died away.

Danni rose, turning the lights back on. Her iPhone was on her dresser; she walked over, booted up and keyed in "Michael Quinn."

At first, it was all football stories — or stories about Quinn at local establishments. It was true that while he was a phenomenon, he promoted his city and its shopkeepers

84

and tourist venues by being photographed in front of them all the time.

There was a picture of him being arrested. He was still smiling, and it was obvious that he couldn't wave to the crowd because he was cuffed.

His hair had been longer then, falling over one of his eyes.

I died, he had told her.

She searched and searched and finally found an article. At least he hadn't killed anyone else, nor had he had a passenger in the car when his alcohol level had skyrocketed and he had driven himself off I-10 and into Lake Pontchartrain.

Danni kept going from link to link, site to site.

He survived the crash, although his injuries had been extensive.

She came across a poor YouTube version of the news conference he'd held when he left the hospital. He announced he was leaving football, then thanked his family and a priest named Father Ryan and his doctors for his life. He said he didn't know what he'd be doing yet, but probably, if the service would take him, he'd be joining the navy. Something warm stirred inside Danni; he was at a point many people came to. He'd nearly destroyed his life — he could straighten up, or go back to his wild ways. But there was a humility in his speech that touched her. There was sorrow in his eyes when he hugged his mother, a blonde woman who showed her age but, even with the aging he'd no doubt caused, had a gentle beauty. His father was tall and had tears in his eyes when he hugged his son.

The next reference she could find was a small news clip when he was accepted into the service and heading off to boot camp.

She found another brief mention when he joined the NOLA police force. And another, with a thumbnail picture beside it, when he left the force to begin his own business in private investigation.

She sat back, studying the screen, her stomach knotting. Her father was next to him in that picture. They were standing outside the station on Royal Street. Her father had one arm around Michael Quinn's shoulder. She noted an advertising banner behind them for Jazz Fest three years earlier.

Danni sat back, trying to create a time line, trying to figure out how she hadn't grasped a memory of his name when she'd first seen him in the shop. She'd been gone for four years of college, and she'd spent two years in New York City after that, apprenticing at an advertising company and then creating ads for clients. During summer breaks, she'd traveled with her father. She'd left the agency two years ago to come home and start working on her own projects; she'd done well, she could honestly say that. First, she'd sold watercolors on Jackson Square. Then she'd had work accepted by Colors of the World, a gallery down the street.

Her father had insisted they use the shop as a venue for her. She'd fought the idea at first, not wanting to fall back on family. Besides, it was a curio and antiques shop. And she really wanted to make it on her own. But then her dad had asked her to improve the look of the place — and she'd realized some of her oil paintings and watercolors could help in doing just that.

Michael Quinn was five or six years older than she was. So it seemed he'd come back from the service, joined the force and quit while she'd been gone. Not that she'd ever known him; she'd grown up in the Quarter while he'd been an uptown boy.

She clicked back to the picture of the man standing with her father.

And she thought about Gladys Simon.

It was late by then, but she threw on a robe and left her room, following the low-level emergency lights down to the shop and then to the basement level.

She paused for a minute. She'd never been afraid in the shop, her apartment or even the basement in the old house before. She'd always been surrounded by Egyptian artifacts, sarcophagi, coffins, death masks, antique weapons, ghastly movie props and more. She was as accustomed to these strange things as most children were to sofas, family photos on the wall and wide-screen televisions.

But that night, she was hesitant. The corners of the room appeared darker. A mannequin might have moved; a gorilla from a 1920s movie seemed to be staring at her from out of the shadows. A death mask of an Egyptian queen might have blinked.

"Ridiculous!" she said aloud. This was her home, her playground as a girl. She knew to be careful with these artifacts, but they'd never *frightened* her.

She turned on the overhead light, dispersing the shadows and the secrets they held.

She reminded herself again that she'd never been afraid of this room. She'd known and appreciated everything in it all her life.

And then there was the book. *The Book of Truth.*

She started looking through it again.

CHAPTER 4

Never trust anyone.

That was Leroy Jenkins's motto; he'd gone by it all his life, and it had never failed him.

Now was not the time to begin trusting people.

He kept driving, wondering what he should do.

As he drove, he went back by the house in the Garden District. To his amazement, there seemed to be cop cars everywhere.

Sure, it was where big money lived. Sure, the cops cared about big money. But he was stunned. He hadn't figured — in a house with two old ladies — that anyone would even know there'd been a break-in.

He drove quickly by, worried about what was going on.

"You've been betrayed."

Hearing the voice, Leroy nearly went off the road and into the yard of a pretty antebellum house. He straightened the wheel just in time. This was not a good moment to draw the attention of the police.

"They will kill you, Leroy. The cops will kill you. No one is honest. Try to negotiate a deal, and you'll be killed. Leroy, you're not lucky in life. If you come from the gutter, people want to put you back in the gutter!"

Where was the voice coming from?

There was no one in the car with him.

No one . . .

He looked down. The bust he'd taken, the bust he'd planned to get with no muss, no fuss, the bust he could make big bucks on. . . .

It was in a canvas bag, shoved at the foot of the passenger seat.

He dragged it carelessly onto the seat. Hell, the thing had been around for hundreds of years, if what he'd heard was right. It had survived. He wrenched back the canvas so it lay with its cheek on the worn and dirty upholstery. But the eyes were open. It was grinning at him.

"Got your gun, Leroy? Are you ready? They're all out to get you. They want me — because I have the power. You've got to take care, Leroy. You want me to work for you? You want me to get riches for you?"

Leroy sat there in terror. He was ice-cold,

90

paralyzed with fear. A rational part of his brain kicked in.

He'd done too many drugs. Hell, he might just have burned out too many brain cells through alcohol poisoning. He knew the cheap rotgut stuff was giving him headaches these days.

But the damned thing was alive, talking to him.

As he gaped at it, the bust seemed to grow, to become a man. It sat next to him, still grinning.

"It can be yours, Leroy. Money, power, women — everything your heart has ever desired."

Leroy tried to form words. He heard sirens behind him, all around him.

He didn't know if he was more terrified of the bust that had become a man and sat beside him — talking to him! — or the police.

"Everything you ever desired, Leroy," the thing repeated. "And all it will take is a little . . . spilled blood."

Leroy looked straight ahead; he hit the gas and cautiously moved back into traffic.

He'd be damned before he let the police get him.

But he heard a voice, somewhere in the back of his head, trying to shout above the thunder that had sounded in his ears when the bust spoke.

You are falling into damnation this minute. . . .

He couldn't heed the voice.

He kept driving.

Quinn headed to Digger Duffy's bar in Central City.

The area was gradually becoming safer; it had been slowly improving from its lowest point in the thirties — and then Katrina had hit. After that, crime had seemed to rise like a swell from the storm. Now, once again, the respectable citizens of the neighborhood were trying to gain control, but Central City still wasn't filled with streets the casual tourist should wander.

Quinn knew it well enough. He'd been assigned these streets as a cop. He'd had informants in the area and was acquainted with a few junkies who'd happily sell their own mothers for the money to get just one more hit.

Digger Duffy's was a strange establishment. Digger himself was a businessman who had happened to inherit the bar. He didn't do drugs; he didn't even sip on a beer. Two years in prison for knocking over an elderly lady and stealing her watch had given him religion.

He was a good guy. He didn't try to reform folks and he didn't turn them away. If they wanted to talk, he talked. If they wanted redemption, he tried to point them in the right direction. If they wanted a beer or a whiskey, he served it.

Drug dealers kept their business out of the bar, but everyone knew what was going down on the streets. They might be conducting business outside or nearby, but they didn't do it in Digger's.

Digger eyed Quinn as he walked inside, passing tables where men huddled in conversation and where the occasional loner sat gazing morosely into his beer.

Quinn sat at the bar in front of Digger. Digger kept cleaning glasses, raising a brow. "You here for the margarita special?" he asked doubtfully.

"A soda water. Throw in a lime if you want to get fancy," Quinn told him.

Digger nodded, preparing the drink. "Who you looking for, Quinn?"

"A thief."

Digger thought about that for a minute. "Haven't heard 'bout anything major on the market lately," he said.

"This isn't your usual wallet or handbag," Quinn explained. "This is a lethal object —

although not many people would think of it as such."

Digger was skilled at remaining expressionless but his slight frown made Quinn think he might know something — even if he hadn't realized it before Quinn's description.

He leaned close as he set Quinn's soda on the bar. "Some guys figure they can slip through the police cracks and find collectors . . . and some of 'em do. Some 'wind up' with objects they believe they can cash in on. I did hear some talk earlier about a piece of art." He lowered his voice. "There's a collector in the city who likes cemetery art — and is willing to pay a lot for it."

"You wouldn't happen to know anything about the thief or the buyer, would you?"

He shook his head. "Didn't really know the guy who was in here. I'd seen him around before. He's usually into petty stuff — helping himself to a tourist's purse, hanging around the casino to see who leaves a bag hanging on the back of a chair . . . He's never been into violence, hasn't got that reputation, anyway. Heard him on a cell phone, talking about some house in the Ninth Ward and how if the buyer wanted the piece, he could get down there."

The Ninth Ward was the easternmost

downriver portion of the city — the largest ward in New Orleans. It was where the summer of storms had done their worst damage. Celebrities, Habitat for Humanity and other groups had tried hard to pick up the pieces. The destruction and the destitution, even as the years passed, remained prevalent. Crime was high.

"Can you give me a little more on that?" Quinn asked.

He whirled around, aware of movement behind him as he voiced the question. He was licensed to carry his gun, a no-nonsense Magnum, but he'd learned through his military experience and the academy not to draw until he meant to shoot.

The man standing behind him was as old as Digger and his color was gray. He had rheumy green eyes. Quinn sensed integrity as well as sadness in his manner.

"I heard him talking, too," he told Quinn. "And I done hear tales about that 'art piece' that was nabbed. You go get it back, Mr. Quinn. We have enough crime and death going on here. You go get that bust or statue thing or funerary ornament or whatever it is. Bury it deep so it don't come up again. Upper Ninth Ward — I heard someone talking about North Robertson Street."

Quinn thanked him, placed a few bills on

the bar and left. Heading for his car, he put through a call to Larue, asking the detective to meet him on North Robertson.

It was late as he drove through the areas of the city he loved; revelers were still out on the streets but in smaller numbers.

The reconstruction since Hurricane Katrina had been spotty and the demographics had changed drastically. Some decent citizens had returned, but some never would. The face of the Ninth Ward was ever-changing. A hard-working waiter might live next to a hastily reconstructed crack house.

Quinn turned down North Robertson Street. In the darkness and shadows alleviated only by a few blinking streetlights, he slowed to a crawl and looked intently at each building he passed.

He came to a pale blue clapboard house. To one side, a new wooden structure was rising. On the other was a derelict building with a sign that was fading and still proclaimed We Will Be Back.

There was something on the ground in front of the blue house.

Quinn pulled to a stop, braked his car and stepped out. He ran over to the object on the ground, hunkering down quickly when he realized it was a man, a youth of mixed race.

The earth beneath him was soggy with blood; there was no help for him.

He'd been riddled with bullets from some kind of semiautomatic weapon.

Cursing softly, Quinn stood.

He saw a scared child peeping out from behind a curtain at the new house next door. A door started to open.

"Stay in! Stay inside!" Quinn shouted.

More gunfire flared from within the blue house. Quinn drew his weapon and moved toward the entry.

He burst in, but too late.

A woman lay on the floor — young, dressed in shorts that left the curves of her buttocks visible, a halter top and five-inch gold-spangled spike heels. She was dressed like a hooker and — living in an obvious crack house — probably was.

For a split second, he felt torn. The killer might still be in the house.

The bust might still be in the house.

But she lay gasping and trying to breathe.

He hurried to her side and crouched down.

"Help me!" she gurgled, large brown eyes staring into his.

"Lie quiet, don't try to talk," he told her, ripping his shirt for a bandage to staunch the flow of blood pouring from the bullet hole in her chest.

No good. She gripped his arm with bloody fingers as he pressed on the wound.

He watched the light fade from her eyes.

A door to the rear slammed.

Quinn stood; the hooker was dead.

He followed the sound of the slamming door.

The book had chapters on all manner of creatures and things.

One of the first sections Danni read was on witches. It wasn't a bunch of mumbo jumbo about boiling cauldrons and spells; it began with the definition of the word, how *witch* became an evil creature in medieval Europe, and how there was a fierce difference between the pagan religions that had brought forth the medieval fear of witches and the religious practices then common throughout the colonial America.

She felt as if she'd picked up a history book.

But then, as she came to the end of the section, there were instructions on disabling a "practitioner of black magic and those worshipping the evil creations within satanic churches."

Danni sat back, staring at the old tome. It went from being an educated treatise to a magician's manual.

She flipped one beautifully printed and illustrated page after another. There were pages that dealt with ghosts, or "spirits remaining despite the pall of death."

"Where would I find evil statues — or busts?" she murmured aloud. There were all kinds of ghosts, apparently, and a great deal of information on "intelligent or active" hauntings and "residual" hauntings.

There was a section on banshees.

Nothing in these pages on funerary busts.

But then, of course, the book was huge. There were at least a thousand pages in it.

She yawned, blinking, and realized she was exhausted. The words began to swim before her eyes and she decided to give up for the night.

There was nothing she could do for Gladys Simon now. The book wasn't going anywhere; she could continue reading in the morning.

But once again, she lay in bed awake. It suddenly occurred to her that she didn't even know what the bust looked like. She tried to remember how Quinn had described the piece — and as she tried to visualize it, she rose, turned on the lights again and went to her computer.

She keyed in a number of variables,

including funerary busts, New Orleans cemetery bust thefts . . . ancient busts . . . stolen artifacts . . . and assorted combinations. Finally, under a website titled Really Weird Stuff That Really Happened, she found what she was looking for.

The bust was beautiful. It was sculpted out of marble in the likeness of a Roman with handsome, refined features. Even in a picture, however, the eyes were strange. They'd been carved in careful detail. Though the bust had only shoulders and a head, its incredibly realistic appearance was chilling. The shoulders were covered by a mantle, which flowed in a way that seemed to suggest angel wings. But because of the expression in the eyes, the whole of it struck her as far more demonic than angelic.

"It's a thing!" she said once again. "An *object.*"

Still, it was easy to understand how a fragile or damaged mind might see something more ominous in the bust, or even believe that it talked or whispered to them.

The website didn't have much more about the bust — other than that death and mayhem seemed to follow it everywhere. And that, most recently, it had been placed in a cemetery in New Orleans.

Most recently! The site hadn't been updated lately, not with background on the bust.

Now that she had a picture, Danni went through other sites looking for more background information. After an exhaustive search, she was delighted to discover an obscure site dedicated to the bust. The writing was in Italian. She read some Italian, but quickly became frustrated and then remembered that all she had to do was find a translation site on the internet.

That took another few minutes but soon she was reading away — and it was a sad and tragic story. Well, sad for the family of Pietro Giovanni Miro, if not for the brutal man himself.

Tragic for those he'd used and murdered.

He'd been a contemporary of Lorenzo de' Medici, son of the Count of Abacci and heir to his family's fortunes and estates. Ambition had been the driving force in his life — something initially admired by his father and contemporaries. But he hadn't liked to lose, not in battle and not in gaming with his friends and certainly not when it came to his passions.

The first person reputed to die at his hands was a mistress who'd supposedly betrayed him with a member of the de' Medici household; her name had been

Imelda and, perhaps, since her family had a pedigree but no money, she'd been trying to force Pietro to marry her. She died horribly when a fire broke out in the stables at her modest estate and she was trampled by the six massive horses within. An accident, of course. But accidents seemed to occur whenever Pietro was angry. Friends met with bizarre and mysterious deaths. Luigi Bari died when a griffin made of stone toppled from a parapet; he'd won a sum of money from Pietro in a card game. Bartollo Gammino, an actor in a show that spoofed local politicians, including Pietro Miro, died when his costume combusted, burning him to a crisp.

At Pietro's small private palazzo, there were parties every night, but even the noble youths who attended them most often went only once or twice. The depravity practiced at the parties went far beyond their expectations — and their tolerance. Pietro enjoyed provoking an orgy and slaughtering animals over the sexual participants, noting who did and did not seem to wallow in the blood. It was whispered that he was a satanist, killing animals in the name of his evil lord. Many whispered that they'd seen men and women slaughtered there, as well, but none would speak of it to the authorities.

Local girls disappeared after a night with Pietro or at his beautiful palazzo. Most were peasant girls, and at first, little was noted. Pietro always had an alibi or the ability to appear as a victim. Once, when a body was discovered on his grounds, he killed one of his closest servants, blaming the man for the girl's death.

Nobility could get away with a great deal.

Finally, when Lorenzo de' Medici was at the height of his power, one of his cousins, Emiliglio, came afoul of Pietro. It was over a woman again. She was found in the Miro tomb in the la Chiesa di St. Antonio e Maria, outside the city proper — stabbed, disemboweled and decapitated. Just as workers discovered her body while repairing a wall to the crypt, Emiliglio de' Medici was found, strangled in a horse's harness.

Emiliglio, a man with no hope of acquiring the family money or power, was still a beloved figure among the people of Florence at the time.

Lorenzo de' Medici received a petition for Pietro's arrest, but it didn't come to that. Pietro was brought down by a mob in the center of the city, hanged and slashed to ribbons by the furious people whose lives he had touched through his brutality.

His father, bereft, had begged Lorenzo for

the remains of his son's body and Lorenzo had relented — on one condition. The body must be cremated to satisfy the fury of his Catholic subjects who were convinced his evil could only be stopped through the cleansing force of fire. However, his father might have his ashes and the urn might rest in the family vault.

And so, Pietro's father had hired one of the finest sculptors in the city and had the bust carved in his honor. The bust had sat in the family tomb for the next two centuries. Then the family ran into a streak of tragedy and violence until the last male heir died in the nineteenth century. The bust was stolen from the tomb just before the outbreak of World War I and a serial killer was unleashed on the city; it mysteriously reappeared at the tomb when the man was shot down by a local magistrate.

Then came World War II, and the bust was stolen again, never to return to its place at the Miro tombsite.

It had traveled among some of the cruelest dictators in the world . . . and made its way to the United States.

To New Orleans.

And it was still out there now.

Danni leaned back, rubbing her eyes. She glanced at the clock. It was past three in the morning and she hadn't slept. Quinn was out there, too, hunting down the bust. Well, that was his choice. A marble bust was a material object, with no life of its own; it couldn't behave in either an evil or a kindly manner.

But . . .

She drummed her fingers on the desk. The human mind was a powerful force. If Gladys Simon had *believed* the bust was evil, that it could control her, then it might have done so.

Danni had faith and she had her personal set of beliefs and ethics, but she'd never fooled herself about the fact that some of the most heinous acts in history had been carried out in the name of religion. She'd grown up in New Orleans and had dozens of friends who practiced voodoo — without an evil thought or wish in their heads. Nor did she have any evil Catholic friends, although the church had been responsible for events such as the Spanish Inquisition and the burning of thousands of innocents as witches or heretics. And the pious Pilgrims had been responsible for the hanging of nineteen and the pressing to death of one in Salem, Massachusetts. The Pilgrims had *believed* in the devil; they'd believed he could dance in the forests of their bitter cold clime and entice the greedy.

But maybe Quinn was right in being so determined to find the bust. Maybe others had read about the bust and believed in its power, too.

She had to sleep. She knew she had to sleep.

Hating Michael Quinn and wishing he'd never entered her life, she forced herself to lie down and concentrate on sleeping.

In the end, she dozed on and off. But in her thoughts, her restless dreams, she could see her father standing across a vast body of water, reaching out to her. She shouted to him. Despite the distance between them, she saw there were tears in his eyes and she didn't want him to feel any hurt — he had been the best father in the world.

She could hear him shouting to her. She listened so hard and finally she could hear his words coming to her.

Read the book, and look to it in all things.

The water began to churn as if there were a storm coming. She heard the pulse of the waves, heard them pounding.

Look to the book, daughter. Use the light. The light . . .

What light, Dad? This is all so crazy! I never knew. Why didn't I know? You wanted to protect me. . . . Oh, Dad!

*You must never sell the shop. I am with you,
even if I failed you.*

*You never failed me, I swear. I loved you so
much. I'm not weak, Dad, I'm really not weak.
I'm your daughter.*

She woke with a start.

Light was streaming in the bedroom
windows because she'd never closed the
drapes.

And there *was* a pounding. It was at her
door.

"Danni?" Billie called. "Danni — you all
right?"

"Yes, Billie, I'm fine! What's wrong?" she
called back.

"Uh, nothing. I was just checking to make
sure you're okay. It's almost noon."

Noon!

She gritted her teeth. She'd slept away half
the day.

Damn that Michael Quinn.

Could it all be real?

And if it was . . . No, her father had never
failed her.

Would she fail him?

CHAPTER 5

"I'm starting to think I should be more worried about you than the damned bust," Larue said, heaving an exhausted sigh as he sank into the chair behind his desk.

Quinn shrugged. "I'm not saying what's real and what's not — just that death follows that bust."

"Or you — when you're looking for it," Larue muttered. "Another two dead, another precinct involved — and no bust and no explanation," he said. "What happened to bring you out there just in time for that particular murder?"

"I told you. I was in a bar. I asked a couple of guys if they'd heard anything. Larue, listen. There's a buyer somewhere in the city and I need to find out who. Word's out that someone — with money — wants the bust. As long as down-and-outers, as well as habitual criminals, know there's a buyer, people will keep killing others over the bust."

"Why kill the hooker?" Larue asked.

He had crime scene photos in front him on the desk. One photo of the man dead in the yard and the other of the woman Quinn had watched die.

"Because she was there," Quinn replied.

"The first guy —"

"Check out your forensic evidence. I think you'll find that the dead man is the thief who broke into Gladys Simon's house as she was busy committing suicide," Quinn said.

"So, whoever killed the thief and the hooker now has the bust. That's what you're telling me?"

"Yes."

"Do you have any idea of this person's identity?"

"Sure. It's another thief thinking he can buy his way out of the ghetto."

"You don't happen to have a name for him, do you?"

"No."

"Or a way to learn a name?"

"No."

"So, while I'm looking for a killer, without the least conception of who it might be, you're going to be looking for the same man — because you think he has the bust."

Quinn lifted his hands in a vague motion.

"Thing is, when you find your killer, you still won't stop the killing."

"Because of the bust?" Larue sounded tired and skeptical.

"To someone out there, it's a rare commodity and the offer for it is high," Quinn said.

"Why didn't this buyer just contact Hank or Gladys Simon?" Larue asked.

"Maybe they didn't know in time that the Simons had the thing. I didn't know myself until I heard about Vic Brown being in jail, ranting and raving. If a smart thief has a lead on an object, he won't share that information."

"So you have no direction you can give me?"

"All I can give you is what you already have as a good cop, Larue," Quinn told him. "Find out about our dead thief and his girl. Find out who the hell else knew what he was up to. It was taken by someone in his circle. Someone who knew what he was going to do — and where he was planning to make the sale."

Larue picked up a folder and tossed it back down. "Dead man — Leroy Jenkins, arrested three times for possession, out on probation once. His girlfriend? Ivy Hunter, three arrests, all for prostitution. Known associates? Half the dealers in the city, including the new group that poured in to take advantage of the open market after the storms."

"Narrow them down," Quinn suggested, rising. "Although I suspect there'll be more bodies soon enough."

Larue winced at that. "Every time we think we're making headway, there's some other killer who just wipes out the progress we've made. I'm ready to pack it all in."

"No, you're not. You're a good cop — and this is your city. These deaths *will* stop. You just go your way, and let me go mine. I'm going to look for the buyer."

"They'll stop? How? You gonna smash the bust?" Larue asked. "It's marble. It belongs . . . hell, I don't even know where it belongs."

"I do," Quinn assured him.

"Keep me in the loop," Larue said.

"You know I will. That's why you bring me in on these things."

"Yeah, well, let's get this solved — before more bodies pile up!"

Quinn nodded. "I'm doing my best," he said as he left the detective's office. Larue knew him; when others had thought he was quitting the force because he could make a better living on his own, Larue understood

111

what really lay behind his decision — and the event that had caused it.

It was past noon. It had taken all night for the cops to come, to bring Larue in on the murders, wait out the forensic crews and return to the station.

Quinn was bone-tired.

He was more anxious than ever to retrieve the bust, but he knew if he didn't get some sleep, he'd be worthless.

Leaving the station, he headed uptown to his house.

He loved his home, even though a few psychoanalysts had suggested he should live elsewhere. Home, according to the shrinks, could be a "trigger" for bad behavior, for slipping back into drugs and alcohol. They were wrong in his case. It was a beautiful home and he lived in a city he loved.

He'd bought the house from his parents; he kept a garage apartment for them, or for his siblings when they visited the city.

His parents had bought a retirement home near Orlando. His older brother was with the FBI, working in the offices in D.C., his younger brother was in college in North Carolina and his sister was managing a children's theater in Savannah. NOLA remained home to all of them, though. And since he'd purchased the old family house,

it seemed only right to keep it that way —
as the old family house.

It was in the Garden District, within walking distance of the Garden City Book Shop,
plus the house where Jefferson Davis, one
and only president of the Confederacy, had
died, Lafayette Cemetery and at least a
dozen other historic and notable dwellings.
His great-great-grandfather had built the
house, lost it after the Civil War — but lived
to see it bought back by his grandson. There
were pictures on the walls that dated back
to the first days of photography and some
of the furniture was nearly as old. He'd kept
the front parlor as it had always been,
complete with tapestry-covered armchairs,
Duncan Phyfe sofa, a large, nineteenth-
century watery mirror over the fireplace and
occasional tables adorned with various
pieces of antique bric-a-brac.

The kitchen, however, had undergone a
complete redo and what had once been the
"ladies' room" was now his entertainment
center. He watched every sports station, as
well as the History Channel and a few others. His television was state-of-the-art and
wide-screen, and his stereo system had
controls and speakers throughout the house.

Entering, he heard what might have
sounded like a ferocious howl. It wasn't; it

was just Wolf welcoming him home.

The dog didn't jump. He'd been well trained. He'd come from a K-9 unit in Texas and was almost put down when a bullet shattered his hip. Quinn had been in El Paso when the massive drug bust occurred during which Wolf was injured.

He'd been with Angus Cafferty.

They were searching for a Damascus blade that time. It had ended up with one of the most dangerous crime lords ever to smuggle cargo — human and other — into the country.

Wolf had actually saved the day.

The El Paso vet hadn't wanted to put the dog down. He'd explained the intensive surgery and therapy it was going to take for Wolf to have a chance of walking again. Quinn didn't care what it took; they wouldn't have had a successful sting if it hadn't been for the dog. He might have been a fatality himself, since it was the dog that had knocked the knife from the crime lord's hands before he could throw it.

"Hey, boy!"

He bent down. No sense letting Wolf get the notion that he could jump on people just because he was retired.

He didn't have to stoop very far, since Wolf was a large dog. His dam had been a timber wolf-husky mix and his sire a German shepherd. The breeder, out of Wisconsin, sold exclusively to police departments across North America, and carefully bred his animals for their temperaments. That meant Wolf sometimes thought he was a lap dog. He could lick you to death.

He could also hold a suspected criminal with a locked jaw and predatory stare that would rattle nerves of steel.

These days he barely limped and, like an older man, only when the weather was bad. It was always a sure sign that a storm was coming in.

"My boy, my boy," Quinn said, ruffling his ears. "Missed me, huh? Yeah, I was gone for a long time, but it wasn't a day to have you with me. Nothing you could've done for poor Gladys Simon. Sorry affair, Wolf. Three dead — well, four, counting Hank Simon, or hell, eight, if you count from the beginning and include the guys killed by that bastard now in jail."

Quinn regretted the fact that he was too tired to sit in his TV room, with the dog lying next to him, and watch reruns of a few of the games he'd missed.

Wolf whined as if he understood. "Let me check your food and water."

He went back to the kitchen. There

weren't any messes in the house — despite
his size, Wolf had a dog door he could
shimmy through. Quinn also had a
constant-flow water bowl for him and a
feeder that would keep food coming for up
to five days.

It was a big feeder for a big dog, taking
up the space of a small refrigerator.

With the food and water situation fine,
Quinn gave the dog a few bacon treats and
told him, "Sorry, old boy, need some sleep."

He trudged up to his room. Wolf followed,
but curled into his dog bed in the hall, apparently glad that his master was home and
happy just to take up his work as sentinel.

Quinn stripped on his way to the bath,
strewing his clothing, socks and shoes along
the floor. He turned on the water and appreciated its pure, clean feel as he stepped
beneath the shower.

His mind went mercifully blank.

Sleep came quickly when he hit the bed.
He wasn't plagued by dreams of his former
life, the strange occurrence at his "death,"
the stranger who'd reappeared, his time in
the service or on the force. He slept deeply.

He was awakened, he didn't know how
much later, by Wolf's barking. Then he realized he'd been hearing a rhythmic sound
in his sleep. Someone was pounding at his

116

door. Wolf was letting this person know that his or her presence was being noted.

He rose, pulled on his jeans and hurried downstairs. Wolf stood in the doorway in his on-guard position.

Quinn looked out the peephole, a little shocked by the identity of his visitor.

Danni Cafferty had come to him.

The dog was enormous. Wolf, dog, whatever — it was enormous. Quinn was a tall man and his arm was bent as it rested on the dog's head when he opened the door.

Danni was an animal lover, but even so, she took a step back.

"He won't hurt you. He wouldn't hurt a fly," Quinn said. "Unless I told him to."

"How encouraging," she murmured. "May I come in?"

"Um, yeah, sure." Quinn's mind seemed to be moving a little slowly. But then, it was pretty obvious she'd just woken him up. His hair was tousled, his feet were bare — and his chest was, too. She couldn't help noticing that he had a few scars crossing his tanned flesh, his shoulders, chest and abdomen. She also couldn't help noticing that he looked as well muscled and wiry as a triathlon athlete.

"Um, want coffee?"

"Sure, it's almost evening. Coffee sounds fine," she said dryly.

"She's good, Wolf, she's good." Quinn opened the door.

"Wolf?" she asked.

"That's his name."

"Well, of course it is," she said, stepping inside.

The dog — or wolf — whined, nudging her fingers with his massive nose. She stroked his ears. He wagged his tail and followed her as she walked through the house.

She was surprised by the neat and handsome appearance of his parlor. There were all manner of period artifacts about, glass-encased memorabilia in nineteenth-century bookcases and nicely framed portraits and images on the walls. Quinn, however, didn't pay attention to her observation of his living quarters; he was headed straight down a hallway, the dog at his heels. When she hesitated, Wolf came back for her, nudging her hands, leading the way.

"You're not afraid of the dog, are you?" Quinn called back to her.

"No. I love dogs. Except I think this one is actually a horse," she said.

"Are you afraid of horses?"

"No."

"Then you should be okay."

Danni raised her brows but Quinn wasn't waiting for her response. She could tell he was tired and cranky and, since his disposition didn't seem to be the friendliest when he *wasn't* tired and cranky, she simply followed him to the kitchen.

Again, she was surprised. The room had a traditional quality with a display of copper pots and pans over a hardwood island, but the appliances were modern and everything was shining and clean.

"Nice," she said.

He eyed her from beneath a strand of hair that fell over his brow. "You were expecting a hovel with piles of clothing, leftover pizza boxes and roaches?"

"No, I just didn't realize P.I.s lived so well. Oh — that's right. You have a trust fund."

"Yeah, and I got the house for a steal," he told her. "So to speak. And Chessy cleans for me."

"Ah, your girlfriend? Is she sleeping? I'm sorry. I really didn't mean to wake you. Oh, hell, that's not true. I don't care if I woke you. You walked in and turned my world upside down yesterday."

"Chessy is my housekeeper. She's not sleeping, or at least, not here. And I didn't turn your world upside down. It was already upside down — you just didn't know it."

119

He glanced at his watch. "Let's see. It's Wednesday. Chessy comes on Tuesdays and Thursdays. She's worth her weight in gold. In fact, I work so I can afford to pay Chessy. She's the best."

"Apparently."

"What would you like?" he asked. "It's a pod machine — pick a coffee, pop it in, close it and you have coffee."

"I've seen them." She moved toward it to make a selection from the little "coffee tree" next to the machine. She found something marked *bold* and popped it into the machine. He supplied her with milk from the refrigerator.

"Sugar? Or fake stuff?"

"Neither, thanks."

He stood close to her. He smelled clean, as though he was fresh from a shower, which, of course, he wasn't. She'd woken him. They were standing close together in the kitchen and he was half-naked. It reminded her that he was quite a striking physical specimen — even if he was capable of being rude, arrogant . . . and confusing. He chose a coffee pod himself and brewed it, then looked at her.

"Grab your coffee. We'll sit in the playroom," he said.

The term startled her but he ignored her

reaction, moving through a doorway to the room behind the kitchen.

The term he'd used had made her envision a plush, red padded room with sex toys on the walls.

Bad, Danni. The "playroom" was filled with comfortable chairs and couches, a huge television and racks of books, CDs, DVDs, old vinyl records and games. Some video games, but mostly old board games such as Life, Risk, Cranium and Scrabble.

He fell into one of the leather-covered old armchairs, leaving her the matching couch next to him. He sat back, stretching his legs and lifting his feet onto the trunk-turned-coffee-table between them.

"So, what brings you here?" he asked.

"The bust, of course."

"How did you find me?"

"You're in the phone book."

"Oh. Right." He sipped his coffee and seemed to savor the taste. "Good stuff," he murmured. "Bold, but freshly brewed. Not burned."

"Are you interested in what I have to say?" she asked, exasperated. Then she started as Wolf jumped up beside her, and just managed to catch the dollop of coffee that sloshed out of her cup. Tail wagging, the dog set his nose on her lap.

"He likes you," Quinn said. "You're lucky."

"I'm sure he likes lots of people."

"No, he tolerates anyone I ask him to tolerate. He *likes* you. He's a good judge of character, so maybe you're not as bad as I was beginning to think."

She was tempted to get up and leave.

Then she remembered seeing Gladys swinging from the rope up in her attic.

"I'm afraid I don't have a dog, so I can't hope for a creature to improve your manners and position in my mind," she said sweetly. "Do you want my information or not?"

"Yeah."

"The bust has quite a history."

"That's what you came to tell me?"

"You know a lot about it, but do you know the *whole* story?"

"Share it with me, if you'd be so kind."

She took a sip of her coffee, set the cup down and told him everything she'd read. He was silent for so long she thought he'd fallen asleep on her.

"Doesn't make any sense, really," he finally said, opening his eyes. "The way to 'kill' a ghost is usually to burn the bones. If he was cremated . . . there are no bones to burn."

"What about ghosts?" Danni asked. "Have you read that book yet?"

She frowned. "How do you know about the book, anyway? *What* do you know about the book?"

"It's a manual. A manual that your father inherited from his father — and I have no idea where it came from before that. It had obviously crossed the ocean at least once."

"How well did you know my father?" she demanded.

Quinn was silent again. "My dad is an interesting man. He's spiritual but not actually religious — says too many people kill in the name of God. But he managed, years ago, to become best friends with a priest named Father Ryan. Ryan kept my parents sane when I was in the hospital and I flatlined, and then Father Ryan became a friend of mine, too. He's not your average priest. He was also friends with your father. I've done tracking for your dad, and your dad has done tracking for me. Once, he helped me find a child — he saved that child's life." He didn't speak for a minute. "He would call me. I would call him. I loved Angus. Never met a man who was so passionate about the goodness that could be found in people — and so passionate about protecting the innocent. I told him once he was a hero. His response was that if heroes existed, they were quiet men who might be afraid themselves, but *because* they were afraid, they knew they had to act." He shrugged. "Anyway, I asked him once where he got his information, since a lot of it was pretty far-fetched, and he said he had the book. This is an old book, and when it's read correctly, it can give all kinds of information."

"It's very old, of course, but it's like something out of the Dark Ages. . . ."

"No. Uh-uh."

"Oh, please! Come on. Innocent people the world over were persecuted because people believed in demons and witches and dancing with the devil. They were tortured and burned and hanged and . . . It's all a crock!"

He leaned forward, staring into her eyes. Again, he was close — so close she couldn't help being aware of him as a man. But there was nothing teasing or seductive in the way he looked at her. He was deadly serious.

"Yes, the innocent have suffered because of the ignorance, stupidity or superstitions of others. But think about it! If you really had any kind of power, would you just *let* yourself be tortured, burned, hanged? No. Anyone with real power escaped persecution, while the innocent died horrible deaths." He paused, breathing in, agitated. He shook his head. "God, I loved Angus! He was outstanding. But I'm shocked that he didn't tell you *any* of this!"

There was passion in his words — and sincerity when he spoke about her father. There also seemed to be shock and painful regret that Angus hadn't told her about his . . . outside activities.

This was all still impossible to believe.

He studied her. "Why do you think, say, the people in Salem died? They wouldn't claim to be what they weren't. They couldn't come down from a hanging tree because they *weren't* practicing black magic. Half the terror spent on innocents in the world has always come from real fear — and the other half comes from power grabs, pure evil or the greed of others." He paused. "Danni, you believe there's good in the world, right? Goodness in people's hearts? That they're capable of acts of strength and charity in times of trial and desperation?"

"I believe most people are basically good, yes. . . ."

"Where there's good, there's evil," he said. "Yin and yang."

The dog whined and she absently stroked his fur. "You're trying to tell me the statue

125

is evil," she said.

"I'm telling you it carries evil."

"You're really asking me to accept a lot."

"I can't see Russia or China right now — but they're there. Whether or not you believe anything I tell you doesn't matter. Because situations can exist whether you believe in them or not. Whether you even know about them or not." He shook his head again. "You saw Gladys Simon," he pointed out.

"Yes, but isn't it possible that people create things in their minds? Salem, for example. The accused were supposedly dancing with the devil in the woods. The accusers claimed they were being pinched or bitten or whatever. Everyone *believed* them and it turned into mass hysteria. If you've got something in your mind, it can become real."

"You can look at it that way if it makes you happy. Here's the thing — whoever gets this bust *believes* it either makes them kill others . . . or themselves."

"All right, so Gladys believed it killed her husband. And in that belief and in her terrible grief, she killed herself."

"Yes. And the hood sitting in jail awaiting trial — Vic Brown. He had the statue before selling it to Hank Simon. He shot down three rival gang members in cold blood. Not over money — they didn't know he had any. Vic wasn't the nicest guy in the world. But to the best of my knowledge, he has no other murder raps on his record. I went to see him. That's how I found out the bust was out there, causing havoc. The press was everywhere when he was arrested and there are a few seconds of news video in which he's shouting that he's not a killer, the bust made him do it," Quinn said. "You want more coffee? I'm having some. I'm working on —" he checked his watch "— about four hours of sleep."

"I didn't sleep much, either, thank you very much," Danni said.

"Ah, but I didn't wake you up."

"I'd say I'm sorry, but I'm not."

He didn't take offense at that; he grinned. "So, another coffee?"

She nodded and followed him back to the kitchen. This time she noted that the latticed windows could be opened to the "playroom."

She imagined that a century and a half ago, someone had entertained lavishly at this house. She could close her eyes and picture the swirl of antebellum skirts — minus the fifty-two-inch television screen, of course.

They both had a second coffee. Wolf, apparently thinking he should have another wake-me-up, as well, let out a bark and wagged his tail.

"All right, one more of these bacon things, but that's it," Quinn said. "You'll lose that fullback figure of yours with too many treats."

"What does he weigh?"

"Not that much, really. There are heavier dogs. He comes in at about one-thirty."

"Wow, handsome, we weigh about the same!" Danni told the dog.

"He's a good boy," Quinn said, looking at her. He hesitated a minute. "Your father helped me when I first got him."

"Really?"

"We were together in El Paso."

She lowered her eyes, not wanting him to see the mix of emotions she was feeling. Quinn was telling the truth about her father. She remembered his explanation about a buying trip to El Paso a few years back. She hadn't given it much thought at the time; she'd been busy. It wasn't easy, breaking into the art world.

For a moment, she felt guilty again, and angry because she felt guilty. She'd been a good daughter — loving her father all her life. She'd worked hard in school. She'd known that she loved art and she'd assisted her dad at the shop . . . with everything, or so she'd assumed.

She didn't look at Quinn. "How did my dad help you?"

"Wolf was with a K-9 unit. He was shot, and they were going to have to put him down but I wanted to keep him. Your dad came to the vet with me, learned what I had to do to keep him alive after his surgery and got a friend with a private plane to fly us back here." He was silent once again. He couldn't have been studying her this time because her head was down as she petted the dog. "Wolf loved your father. Maybe he senses something of Angus in you."

"Maybe," Danni agreed.

She stood, changing the subject. "So I take it you didn't find the bust last night."

"I found where it had been. A thief stole it from our thief, leaving him and a prostitute dead."

She stared at him. "Two *more* people are dead?"

He nodded gravely. "I was down in the Ninth Ward most of the night, and then at the police station with Larue. Luckily, the bigwigs are seeing all of this as one case and making him lead detective, no matter where the dead show up."

"Larue seems to like you," Danni said.

"Oddly enough, some people do."

She straightened. "So . . . what are your plans?"

"Stay on the hunt until I find the bust."

"Do you know the thief who stole it from the first thief?" she asked.

He looked disgustedly down at his coffee. "No. I have some names. The sad thing is, a great family is living right next to the house where Leroy Jenkins — the drug-dealing thief who took the bust from the Simon house — and Ivy Hunter, his quote unquote girlfriend, were living. Really nice couple of kids in that house, living next door to a crack house. But the father's fighting for his home and hoping to make it a decent neighborhood one day. They weren't acquainted with any of Leroy's junkie friends or buyers. But we did come across a woman down the road — old woman, just trying to keep her head above water — who watched the place. She gave me a list of street names to check out. I was going to start as soon as I got some sleep."

"Did my information about the history of the bust help you?" she asked.

He bent his head, then raised it to smile at her. "Yes, thank you. Anything we know is an improvement. But I can't figure out why the evil, the spirit of evil — or as you would have it, the perception of evil — persists if this young Italian count was cremated. That's what I meant about how it doesn't make sense."

"You wanted something to make sense?" she asked.

Again, he smiled. His voice was soft. "Sorry. I guess nothing makes sense to you. But . . . well, I'm sorry. You're Angus's daughter and the owner of the curio shop. You understand now that very bad things are out there — real or perceived — and this won't be the last time I call on you."

What did that mean? Was this it for the moment? Drive her insane, accuse her of not caring for her fellow man, say thank you — and goodbye?

She stood suddenly. "You need to put on a shirt and shoes."

"I do?"

"Yes, and we should go now. It's getting dark, and Mistress LaBelle makes most of her money at night."

"You're taking me to see . . . a prostitute?"

"You mean you've never met Mistress La-Belle?" Danni teased.

"LaBelle . . . oh! You mean, Natasha, the voodoo priestess?"

She was slightly disappointed, thinking

she might have pointed him toward an unknown source.

"Yes, I mean Natasha. Whenever I have friends in town determined to have some kind of reading, I bring them to Natasha. She reads *people,* I'm pretty sure, and she's dedicated to helping others — and to her voodoo religion. She also seems to know everything that's going on everywhere."

"Very true," Quinn said. "I was going to sleep and then head out to the bars in different sections of town. But I like your idea."

"So . . . get a shirt and shoes."

Wolf barked, as if he agreed. He stood by them, wagging his tail.

Even the tail was like a lethal weapon, Danni thought, feeling it smack against her leg.

She laughed. "Wolf thinks he's going."

"He *is* going. Natasha loves him," Quinn said.

Danni was surprised, but Wolf wasn't. He hurried to the door and waited patiently while Quinn ran upstairs to finish dressing and then ran back down, buttoning his shirt as he came toward them. He grabbed a leash but didn't bother to put it on the dog.

"We'll take my car," he told Danni.

When she might have protested he added quickly, "It's already covered in dog hair."

The car wasn't at all bad; she didn't ask him but assumed he vacuumed often.

Wolf obediently hopped into the backseat. She buckled in next to Quinn and they made the short drive to the French Quarter.

Mistress LaBelle — born Natasha Laroche — kept her home and shop in a building just off Bourbon on St. Anne. By day, tourists flocked to the store. At night, she charged a pretty penny for "consultations" done by candlelight in her courtyard. She would read tarot cards, palms or tea leaves, but mostly she read people, as Danni had said, and she listened. She had, Danni believed, a unique ability to know what they wanted, what they needed to hear. As in, success only came with hard work, a love affair was only worth it if both were committed and involved and, difficult or not, tell children "no!" when it came to something they shouldn't be doing.

"Meet you out back," Quinn said. "Wolf takes up the whole shop."

They split up; Danni went through the main entrance. Quinn walked around to the side. There was a sign on the painted gate: Please Enter Thru Main Shop.

Quinn didn't seem to notice. Or, Danni thought, maybe he'd gone through that way so many times, he knew he was welcome to do as he chose.

The store was filled with the usual objects, but nicely displayed. The walls were rustic hardwood. Domed glass cases held the jewelry Natasha sold, while a round table near the door held gimmicky tourist treasures — spices, the usual voodoo dolls, chicken-feet talismen and other such things. Brilliant and historic masks adorned the entry. The smell of incense was in the air.

Danni walked straight to the counter where Jeziah, Natasha's clerk and assistant, was watching the register.

"Jez, hey, how are you?" she asked him.

He was a beautiful man with mahogany skin, close-cropped dark hair and startling green eyes.

"Danni," he said in greeting. The way he looked at her — as if she was expected and had actually arrived a little late for a party — was unnerving.

"I'm sorry. I realize this is a major business time at the store, or it will be soon, but —"

"No problem," Jez told her. "Natasha's been waiting for you."

"She has? But how —" Danni began.

"She's expected you all day. She knew you'd come before full dark. She's in the courtyard. You know the way. Go on out."

Astonished, although she probably shouldn't be, Danni headed to the back of the shop, through the draperies to the seer's rooms and the ornate door that led to the candle-strewn courtyard beyond.

She stepped outside just as the sun was falling.

Natasha had been sitting in the African throne chair situated behind her covered table. She got up, walking toward Danni to take her hands. "Danni." She kissed both her cheeks.

Quinn, with Wolf lying quietly at his side, was seated by the table.

Natasha was a lovely, exotic woman, about six feet tall. Her hair was wrapped in a turban of orange and yellow that matched her long gown. Her eyes seemed like onyx and her features were slim and elegant.

"It's about time. You really need my help. Word is out on the street already. And if the evil inside the bust knows that you're aware . . . well, then, my dears, you are in grave danger, grave danger indeed."

CHAPTER 6

The sun was setting and myriad shades of pastel fell on the table in the courtyard. Wolf continued to lie placidly at Quinn's feet as he and Danni sat with Natasha. Wind chimes in the trees let out a gentle music that hushed the distant sound of the pop, rock and blues playing on Bourbon Street.

Candles were already alight and the foliage in the small courtyard was rich; there was no sign of the tourist trade here in this private enclosure, and they might have stepped back in time.

Natasha had nodded formally when Quinn walked into the courtyard, as if she'd expected to see him there. Then she'd turned her attention to Wolf until Danni came out.

"Here's the situation," Natasha began. "I don't have anything concrete for you, but you know how it goes — tell a friend a secret, that friend tells another friend, and so on. It's like the whisper game and the facts have all been altered." She stared at them both. "You understand that I honor God and the saints and my religion. We do not have human sacrifices, drink blood or do any of the ridiculous things movies have created out of voodoo." She wagged a finger. "Yes, crazy people who do not respect true religion do the things the movies show, but that is not the way *we* honor our saints and our God."

Danni cleared her throat. "Natasha, you realize that I —" she paused to look at Quinn "— that *we* know you, and we understand that your practice of voodoo is just the same as anyone's practice of more traditional religions. You know me — us — as well, and . . ."

Natasha nodded. "Give me your hand."

Danni seemed loath to do so, but she extended her hand, palm up, to Natasha.

Natasha sighed and laughed softly. "In all these years — and I've known you since you were a little girl — I have never seen your palm. See here?" With a long elegant nail, she traced a line in Danni's palm. "This is your lifeline. It's jagged."

For a moment, Quinn thought Danni would yank her hand back.

"No, no, I'm not telling you anything you

don't want to hear — only what you might expect. It's jagged because these are the times when you must make the right choices. And when, perhaps, you'll find your greatest strength. Quinn — now you."

He raised his eyebrows. She had read his palm in the past. But he extended it to her.

She pointed out the full break in his life-line.

"Here, see? Quinn did die. His life, however, extends here. You see? Not even I can explain it, but most certainly, there was a purpose. I tell you these things because I have wondered, since the death of your dear father, Danni, how long it would be before the two of you met. There are not many who see the haze that drifts between life and death, and because there are so few, it's important that we recognize one another and learn to work together."

"We're here together," Quinn said.

"Your idea?" Natasha asked him.

He felt a flush come to his cheeks. "No. Danni's."

Natasha was pleased with the answer.

"So, the bust is in the hands of the wicked," she said, leaning back.

"Yes. What do you know about it?" Quinn asked.

"There is a cult rising in the area," Natasha said. "Not voodoo. No connection to voodoo. But some of my congregation have told me that they hear people talking about this. It's a group of satanists, or a coven of stupid people who think wiccans could work for evil. There is a high priest or priestess who promises riches and powers to those who will be among the chosen. And death to their enemies. I heard this before I heard about the bust." She hesitated and shrugged, reaching over to scratch Wolf's ears, then looked up and smiled at Danni. "Wolf is my friend, my dearest friend. He saved my life."

"Oh?" Danni said.

"Nothing to do with the occult," Natasha told her. "I was being held up by a no-good lowlife out of Biloxi a year or so back. I'd called Quinn earlier — about something else — and he was on his way but Wolf ran ahead, knocked the bastard down, sent his gun flying and stood over him until Quinn arrived. Wolf, go into the shop. Jeziah has treats for you."

Wolf whined and turned to Quinn.

"Go on," he said.

With a wag of his tail, Wolf obeyed.

"I suspected there was a major buyer for the bust," Quinn said. "What I need to know is whether you've heard anything about who might have it now. Last night, the guy who stole it from the Simon house was killed returning to his own place, where the deal was supposed to be made — according to the information I got on the street."

Natasha nodded. Quinn understood that she wasn't to be rushed.

"Once, it was thought that the world was safe enough. The bust was in the cemetery, guarded by the spirits of those who had done nothing but good for their fellow man. Then it was taken, and the mayhem this caused wasn't part of the death count that followed the summer of storms. Someone managed to return it — until it was stolen again. Word was out that another someone was looking for it."

"The bust was sculpted as the likeness of a man named Pietro Miro," Danni said. "Historically, he was a satanist himself and apparently practiced human sacrifice."

"I knew it was old and Italian," Natasha responded.

"But do you know where we can find it?" Quinn asked her. "Danni did some research last night. Pietro Miro was cremated, so it's not as if we can go to Florence and dig up his body and burn it." He offered Danni a rueful smile. "Not something that's easy to

140

do these days — dig up bodies to burn."

She frowned, obviously wondering how much practice he had in digging up the dead.

Natasha tapped her fingers on the table. "I don't know the name of the person seeking the bust. I've dreamed of darkness, of a group meeting in the bayou. I heard screams while I slept and the beat of a drum. I do know the bust is out there, and I believe its power is growing — and must be stopped. But the men who are jockeying to steal it from one another, thinking they'll be rich when they sell it to the buyer, are not those in the cult. All they want is the money. What they don't realize is that if the bust doesn't kill them or ruin their lives, they will die, anyway. The priest — or priestess! — won't just pay a thief and say thank you. The man who finally sells it to the cult will be their first sacrifice on the altar of whatever their evil belief might be."

Quinn nodded. "Can you give us *anything?*" he asked her hopefully.

"Tell me about last night. I saw the news on the drug war gone bad. You were there."

"I couldn't get much. I did find a woman who gave me street names."

"Let me see the names," Natasha said. "Working here, with people coming and going, I hear a lot about our city's criminal element."

Quinn reached into his wallet and produced a folded piece of paper. There were six names on it. Screech, Potter, Big-Ass Mo Fo, Eyes, Numb Nuts and Butt Kiss.

Natasha studied them for a minute. She pointed at *Big-Ass Mo Fo.* "That's Carl White — odd name for the man, since he's pure ebony. He runs a strip club far down off Frenchman Street. Saddest old strippers you've ever seen. This doesn't seem like his type of deal. The man goes to confession every week, sorry as hell about what he does for a living. You can check him out, though. Screech is Clarence Harvey. He's in the pen right now, doing fifteen on a drug bust. Potter, he's in prison, too. His real name is Bill Flaherty and he's just doing two years, but he won't be out until next summer. Butt Kiss is Bo Ray Tomkins, a sad young white boy who's going to be dead in another year. If he was buying, it was for someone else. Bo Ray doesn't do drugs, he's drinking himself to death. And Bo Ray is the kind who'd kill himself before he killed anyone else. That's what I think the Simons might have done. You'll want to have a talk with him, anyway — he sees things and turns away, keeps his mouth shut. He drinks at a bar on Esplanade off Bourbon, kind of working two worlds, this side of the Quarter and that. Maybe the poor bastard knows he's dying and can't do a damned thing about it. Numb Nuts is Sam Johnson, an old Creole — you can find him drinking at a hole in the wall called Oasis just past the CBD. I doubt he's got the gumption to have stolen this thing." She tapped the paper again. "Eyes. Now, *there* you might have something. Eyes is living like he's legit. His name is Brandt Shumaker. He came down here in 2006, buying up properties people couldn't hold on to anymore — bought them cheap and put a dozen folks out of house and home because they were desperate. He's cold as ice," Natasha said. "He might be your man. He'd shoot you just as soon as look at you."

"Shumaker," Danni said. "He was on an interview I vaguely heard. The day my father died," she added.

Quinn glanced at her. "Politics. Great." He turned back to Natasha. "Thank you. You've helped tremendously. I should've come to you the minute I left Vic Brown's holding cell."

"I didn't have anything but what I could see and hear in my dreams," Natasha said. "I couldn't have helped if you didn't have the names. I can see some things, but that isn't always a blessing. I can see them, but I don't know what they mean or how to stop them. That's your job, right, Quinn?"

He couldn't quite read her expression. Quinn knew that Natasha had always wondered what had changed him so completely. Maybe not *so* completely. He'd never been a crook, never stolen anything and sure as hell never killed anyone. He'd been like Bo Ray Tomkins, on a route to self-destruction, maybe killing his family a little more with each step he took on his way there.

"And you!" Natasha gestured at Danni. "I'm glad you made it to see me at last, young lady. Ever since your daddy died, like it or not, you've got a role to play. Embrace it. You'll only hurt yourself if you don't."

Danni frowned. For a moment, Quinn saw fear and denial in the depths of her blue eyes.

Hell, why not? Until he'd shown up at her shop, she probably thought her life would be filled with art and galleries and vacations, finally-the-right-guy and all manner of good things.

Danni stood. "Thank you, Natasha, for all your help."

"Wait!" Natasha said. She slipped a hand into the pocket of her skirt and brought

144

forth a handful of medallions on chains. She set them on the table and sorted through them. She chose two, untangling the chains. They were cheap metal trinkets, but they bore likenesses of a saint with a halo over his head.

"Saint Michael," Natasha explained. "The patron saint of protection. And your namesake, Quinn. Wear these."

"Of course."

"In voodoo, a lot is taken from the Catholic Church, so you needn't think these are just tourist souvenirs!"

"I would never think that, Natasha," Danni assured her.

Natasha put a medallion around each of their necks. "It's what you believe that's important. But there's one true power, and it doesn't matter what a man calls his power. I believe in goodness. Different roads are traveled by different people, all going to the same destination."

Quinn thanked her for the medal.

He whistled; Wolf came running out to the courtyard.

"You come back whenever you need to. I'm always here for you," Natasha said.

They left by way of the courtyard entry.

"What now?" Danni asked.

"Now I take you back to your car and I

meet up with whoever I can in junkie city."

"What? You drag me into this — and then you want me to go home?"

"It's late, and I'm going off the beaten tourist track."

"I'm not a tourist."

"You're a young woman in designer jeans and a silk shirt. You might as well be wearing a sign that says Mug Me! Or worse. The minute I walk into a place with you, every junkie and whore will clam up."

"The shop and my apartment are close by. I can change."

"Danni —"

"Fine. Take me to my car. We'll split up. I can talk to Bo Ray while you go somewhere seedier."

"You know, I wouldn't want this going to your head, Ms. Cafferty, but in case you haven't noticed, you're young — and you could be described as beautiful. There are bad things that could happen to you."

"Yeah? Then you should watch out for me."

He scowled at her, frustrated and angry. Her eyes weren't in the least timid or frightened at that moment. In fact, the set of her jaw definitely reminded him of Angus.

"Okay, let's go," he said curtly. "It's getting late."

"And it's New Orleans. Late is just the beginning."

Wolf slid up next to Danni, nuzzling her protectively. It seemed even his own dog was against him and for her.

"You'd better have something like coveralls to wear!" he said.

She smiled. "I do."

Danni Cafferty was true to her word. In ten minutes' time, she'd changed into a ragged denim shirt covered in paint stains and an ancient-looking pair of jeans. She didn't carry a bag at all, having stuffed her ID and whatever else in her pockets. Her shoes were Converse sneakers — with holes in them.

He figured there was nothing she could do about her face.

Her face was . . . classic, stunning. He wondered if it would help if he smudged her up a bit. Then again, maybe nothing would work.

"How do I look?" she asked.

Jane was closing down the cash register. "Good grief, Danielle! You're not going out like *that,* are you?"

Danni laughed. "We're slumming tonight, Jane. I'll be fine."

Jane muttered some remark about the

youth of America, shaking her head. Billie, who was setting the alarm on the shop entry door, rolled his eyes. "You need me?" he asked Quinn.

"Not tonight, Billie."

Billie nodded thoughtfully. "Well, you've got Wolf. Good old Wolf." He pointed a finger at the dog, then at them. "You two eat today? Don't forget, got to fuel the machine. I can cook you up something in the attic, you know. I got a little kitchenette up there."

"We'll grab po'boys on the run, Billie," Danni told him.

"Go on out the front, then, before I set this," Billie said.

Walking back to Quinn's car, they stopped at a Lucky Dog stand and bought hot dogs; Quinn gave Wolf one as a treat, just the sausage. With cans of soda in their hands, they continued to his car. "Where are we going first?" Danni asked him.

"I was thinking we might want to see if Bo Ray is at that bar on Esplanade before venturing into the outer regions. If Natasha nails her people right — and I'm sure she does — he may be able to give us more."

He found parking just off Esplanade and lowered the front windows, turning back to Wolf. "Need you to stay in here for a bit, old boy. Guard the car."

Wolf hated being left behind.

"We'll be right back." Danni patted the dog's head. "Couldn't he jump out if he wanted?" she asked.

"That's half the point of rolling down the windows," Quinn said. "If something ever went wrong for me . . . well, the dog wouldn't die here."

When she stared at him, he added, "And he can come to the rescue. Dogs sense trouble."

"He won't just jump out and follow us?"

"Nope."

They made their way over to Esplanade.

Quinn didn't have Natasha's instinct for people but he was pretty sure he knew Bo Ray Tomkins the minute they walked into the bar. He was a wiry young man of maybe twenty-five, already showing the slightly bloated belly of a man well on his way to liver disease. He was hunched over a glass of whiskey, seated in a dingy corner of the dark, undecorated bar.

Quinn indicated that Danni should take the seat opposite him; he pulled up a chair at Bo Ray's table and they both sat. Bo Ray glanced up, panic filling his watery green eyes. He started to rise, and Quinn laid a hand on his. "Easy, Bo Ray. We're not here to hurt you."

Bo Ray looked at Danni and his eyes widened farther with something like awe, and then confusion. He glanced quickly around to see who else might be in the bar. The only other customers seemed to be a bunch of college types who might've been in the city for a bachelor weekend — and had found this particular watering hole for the cheap booze. The bartender was a tired-looking woman of about fifty who was smoking a cigarette while she poured drinks.

"Who are you?" Bo Ray asked. "What do you want?" His accent was Southern, but not local. There was a long drawl to it — Texan, Quinn thought.

"I have a right to be here. I'm over twenty-one and I pay for my drinks," Bo Ray said before Quinn could answer. "And I'm clean. I don't do drugs. You ask the bartender — I keep my tabs paid."

"Yes, you pay for them by scoring drugs for tourists."

Bo Ray flushed. His pasty face became bright red.

"Are you a cop?" he asked Quinn. "Is *she* a cop?" He managed a rueful smile and lifted his glass. "If so, the department's taking a step forward. Hey, I got it — they hired you 'cause they're doing some kind of reality show and reality shows have to have a few pretty people."

"We're not cops," Danni said.

"I'm not doing any scoring — if that's what you're after," Bo Ray mumbled.

"We're not looking for drugs," Danni told him.

"Yeah? Then what?"

"I think you go to a blue house down in the Ninth Ward and buy what you need," Quinn said, "and I think you know about a lot that goes on there."

The red left Bo Ray's face as if a wave had washed over him; he was suddenly white as a sheet. He shook his head vehemently. "No! I don't go there."

"You know where I mean, don't you?"

Bo Ray swallowed so hard his Adam's apple jiggled. He lowered his head. "I don't go there! I'll never go there again."

"You know what happened there, right?"

Bo Ray nodded, wincing, obviously not wanting to look at them.

"Bo Ray, we need your help," Quinn said.

"I can't help you! I wasn't there last night. I swear to God, I wasn't," Bo Ray whispered hoarsely. "Please, go away."

"We can't go away," Quinn told him.

Bo Ray finally looked up. "I don't want to die."

151

"You're going to die because you're killing yourself," Quinn said. "But if we don't find out what went on last night, you're in danger of being killed. Don't you see? It won't matter if you don't say anything to us. If the wrong people believe you know something — whether you do or not — they'll kill you, anyway. We're your only hope, Bo Ray."

Bo Ray didn't speak.

"You think you know who you're dealing with but it's far worse than you can even imagine, Bo Ray."

"Please," Danni said very softly. "If you help us, we can help you."

"How are you going to protect me?" Bo Ray asked, his voice thin.

Quinn reached into his pocket for a paper and pen. "I can't help you myself, but I'll give you the name of a man who can and will. If you think you can get clean, that is."

Bo Ray sat back in protest. "I ain't dirty!"

"Like I said, you're killing yourself. You start with a bottle of whiskey in the morning and when you can't stand your own company anymore, you come out to a place where the well liquor is rotgut and cheap, and you think you're okay because you're functioning enough to come out at all. If you don't want to die — if you want help, if you want to stay alive — this is where you need to go." He finished writing down the information and held out the piece of paper.

"You're probably not a bad guy," Danni said, smiling at him. "I'd take that if I were you. Quinn's right. If you want to live, you need a safe house. You can survive this — and more."

He shook his head, but his protest wasn't what it had been. He kept staring at Danni. Then he said, "You could be all wrong. I just keep my mouth shut about —"

"About what? The bust? You know about the bust, don't you, Bo Ray?" Quinn asked.

Bo Ray winced again, as if he were being beaten by an invisible whip.

Then he let out a sigh. "I don't know that much, honest. I never hurt anyone and that's the truth. I wouldn't put it past some of the guys that scored from Leroy, but I kept out of their way and they ignored me. I was there when Leroy started bragging about a big windfall he was gonna come into. He was acting like a big man that night. Said he was gonna make enough money to get Ivy off the streets — except he might not bother 'cause Ivy enjoyed the work so much. Ivy was real mad and hit him and he backhanded her across the room." He paused. "So, I guess he made his big score. But he made it in time for someone else to come after him before he could get the money. And Ivy paid for it, anyway, from what I saw on the news." He motioned to the television set with its wavy picture that was rigged above the bar. "That's all I know."

"Who else was there when Leroy was talking about his big score?" Quinn asked.

"Three other guys — Numb Nuts, Eyes and Big-Ass Mo Fo," Bo Ray said, looking at Danni apologetically, presumably because of the language. "You ain't gonna be able to touch Eyes — he's got friends in high places. Pretends like he'd never do anything against the law. He has some major offices over in the CBD. Employs a dozen people, supposedly in business. Oh, yeah, he does give to charity, enough to make him look like a real good guy. Old Numb Nuts — he doesn't like guns or knives or anything like that." Again, he glanced uncomfortably at Danni. "Big-Ass Mo Fo . . . well, they don't call him that for nothing. You should see the size of him. He was there that night. He was there, and he was interested. Now, I swear to you, that's *all* I know. Leave me the hell alone."

Quinn rose. "Get up, come on," he told Bo Ray.

Bo Ray sounded panicked. "Hey! You said you weren't the police —"

"And we're not. Come on. I'm going to save your life."

Bo Ray instantly grabbed for the glass in front of him. What the hell, Quinn figured, let him down it. Father Ryan was going to have his hands full. Might as well get the bastard into detox without fighting him any harder.

Quinn threw some money on the table, wanting to make sure there was no trouble with any bills that could bring Bo Ray back. Danni was already up, leading the way out.

"Where are we going? What are we doing?" Bo Ray demanded.

"Darned if I know," Danni said cheerfully.

"What, what —" Bo Ray balked when they arrived at the car and he saw Wolf. "You gonna have that monster eat me?"

Wolf gave a half howl, half bark, then wagged his tail as Quinn opened the door.

"You be good to Wolf, Wolf will be good to you. Get in."

He had to prod Bo Ray to get him moving. Danni took her seat in front and he joined her, quickly revving the car in case Bo Ray decided to jump out.

He looked over and saw that Danni had a curious little smile on her face. "So, where *are* we going?" she asked.

"Church."

He took Esplanade, determined to avoid the crowds that roamed Bourbon Street, and made a few twists and turns. Danni watched their journey with interest.

At last he came to the rectory of Saint Francis at Peace. He parked on the street, got out and opened the rear door for Wolf and Bo Ray. Danni emerged on her side and waited. He took her hand, leading her through the gate to the door.

They were in a poor neighborhood, where some of the homes were historic but so run-down it was difficult to see any architectural value. It wasn't a ghetto; it was an area where the city's hardest workers lived. They could afford to buy or rent here precisely because it *was* run-down and because it was a place where kids who might go bad had a chance to take another path.

And it was where Father John Ryan ruled his parishioners with an iron hand gentled by a silk glove.

The door opened before they reached it.

John Ryan had come from Ireland — via Africa and South America — twenty-odd years ago. Quinn didn't know everything about him, but he did know that the man had studied medicine before becoming a priest. He'd learned about people in his travels around the globe. At sixty, he appeared to be the typical kindly old priest, yet he was anything but. His posture was dead straight and he was imposingly tall, just a hair under Quinn's own height. His eyes were clear gray and he was clean-shaven, bald, well-muscled and ready to dig in and help with manual labor when needed.

"Hey, John!" Quinn called to him.

"It's Father Ryan, my boy, Father Ryan!"

"Yes, sir," Quinn said, amused. He had people with him. John Ryan liked his title used in front of others.

"Wolf! Hello, there, my good lad!" John said, patting the dog who eagerly trotted ahead. "Quinn, to what do I owe this visit? Or should I guess? I've seen the news. Hello, my dear!" he said to Danni, extending a hand. He glanced at Quinn. "Could this be Ms. Cafferty? Forgive me, but you do have something of your father about you. In a far, far more beautiful way, no offense to Angus!"

"How do you do, Father Ryan. I'm Danielle Cafferty. Danni," she said, shaking his hand.

"And this is . . ." John asked, looking at Bo Ray.

"This is a guy who's getting out of here!"

Bo Ray said.

"Bo Ray was at the crack house a couple of days before Leroy Jenkins was killed," Quinn explained. "He knows who else heard about the theft of a bust that was stolen from the cemetery, then sold, stolen — and stolen again, leaving bodies at every turn."

"I really need another drink," Bo Ray insisted.

"He really needs detox," Quinn said.

"Yes, so . . . you're not staying, then, I take it," John remarked to Quinn. "Just making a delivery."

"That's about it, Father."

"Then come in, come in."

The rectory was sparse but homey, filled with books, comfortable chairs and the scent of something cooking that smelled wonderful.

"Soup," John told Bo Ray. "I'll get you some shortly, and then I'm going to make a call." He turned to Quinn and Danni in an aside. "That man will go into seizures if I don't get him situated quickly. I know you have pull with the cops. I'll use your name when I get him into the hospital."

"Hospital?" Bo Ray shrieked.

"You want to live, remember?" Danni said, holding his hands.

"Come on, son. You'll do as I say — in

158

the name of the Lord!" John seemed to tower over Bo Ray, who wasn't short. But Bo Ray was a rail and John Ryan looked as if he could go a few rounds with a heavyweight champ. To Quinn's relief, Bo Ray gawked at John with fear and awe — and disappeared as John led him toward the kitchen.

Quinn was surprised when Danni said, "You know, you're capable of acting like a total jerk — but I guess you're not that bad." She was smiling.

He shrugged. "Trying to keep the body count down, that's all."

John returned to the room alone. Apparently Bo Ray was in the kitchen eating soup.

"I've got him in hand. Now, tell me, what's going on? I've heard rumors about something evil. My flock comes to me for protection. Hard to imagine this object causing so much harm, but . . . I'm a Catholic priest. I know my God is real, and that makes me aware that evil can be just as real. So, what can I do for you?"

"You've already done it," Quinn assured him. "I didn't want to leave Bo Ray on the street."

John nodded. "Well, you two come with me for a minute."

He took them through a door that connected the rectory to the church.

Danni glanced at Quinn skeptically; Quinn shrugged again.

Wolf followed — with no protest from John.

"I have a few of these . . . and you don't have to wear them," John murmured. He'd left them standing before the altar as he went behind it. "You're already wearing Saint Michael's medals. No finer saint with whom to battle evil!"

He came back down to them, his gray eyes serious. "I bless you," he said, "in the name of the Father, the Son and the Holy Ghost." He drew crosses on their foreheads, and then slipped small crosses into their hands.

"These will protect us," Danni said. "Thank you."

"No, not really." John grinned. "Your belief will protect you. These will remind you that there is a higher power, and you are fighting for that power. Frankly — although I do love your medallions — this puts me in mind of that great scene from the mummy movie, when the scroungy little rat pulls out a crescent moon, a cross and a Star of David. No," he said, and he grew serious again. "You'll need your own wits, your strength and your belief to win this battle. I ask God's help to give you everything you require."

Danni stepped forward impulsively and kissed him on the cheek. She reached for the clasp on her chain, undoing it and adding the cross he'd given her to the medallion, then slipped it back around her neck.

"Thank you."

John Ryan flushed.

"Michael?"

"Yes, Father Ryan," Quinn said dutifully. He couldn't quite work the clasp, and Danni came over to do it for him. He felt her fingers on his flesh as he saw the brilliant blue light of humor in her eyes.

He was afraid he'd blush, just like John.

And he was shocked. He was standing in a church, and he suddenly wanted to draw her to him, forget his purpose and feel the warmth of this woman he was just coming to know.

Once upon a time, she would've been the first thing on his mind. But that was long before he'd learned to separate what he did from what he wanted.

"Oh, wait!" Father Ryan said.

Quinn was glad; he felt released from his strange spell.

"We must all go with God's blessing!" He set his hands upon the dog. "God loves all His creatures," he said. "Now go. I will tend to the safety of Bo Ray Tomkins. You, children, must stop what horrors you can."

CHAPTER 7

Soon they were past the Central Business District and Quinn studied the neon lights in the faded section of town. Here, the words *bygone elegance* could definitely be applied. Some of the structures were pre-Civil War; others had been haphazardly constructed through the years. The paint on most of the buildings was chipping, and people — as faded, as hopeless, as the facades of the buildings themselves — sat on doorstops, drinking from paper bags.

"A far cry from your home," Danni said.

"And yours." He sent her a grim smile. "Bourbon Street may be the home of partying, sex and booze to visitors from around the world, but your place on Royal sits on some of the most expensive property in the city."

"I wasn't making a judgment," she said.

"Neither was I."

"You grew up in the Garden District, right?"

"I did." He glanced in her direction. "But I worked some mean streets as a cop and I saw a few places where no one even pretended there was hope for the future. Sorry. I'm still not convinced you should be with me."

She looked straight ahead. "You were appalled that I knew nothing. Now I'm learning," she said. "It's not that I *want* to be learning . . . I'm still . . . well, I'm more openminded. Let me put it that way."

He wasn't sure how to argue with that. He used an age-old response. "You're a girl."

"Yes, that's a fact. And?"

He smiled. "I guess I'll have to take you to a shooting range."

"Actually, I can shoot. At a target, anyway."

"Yeah. It's different, shooting at flesh and blood."

"Look, I don't . . . I don't know if I can embrace all this. I'm afraid. There's a lot I don't like. But I'm stubborn as hell and I've decided I'm going to try to understand. *You* came to *me,* and now I'm not going away."

"You're still . . . a girl."

"Yes, you've proved your powers of observation! I'm involved now, Quinn — and you know I have to be."

They both grew silent. Neon lights were blinking, although most of the businesses there only had a few lighted letters in their names.

They found the bar where they hoped to run into Numb Nuts, also known as Sam Johnson. Quinn hesitated.

"What are we doing?" Danni asked.

"Hoping to park where I'll have a car when we leave," he said. "Oh, screw it."

It wasn't legal but he parked at a broken meter. He noted that Danni nearly stepped on a shattered beer bottle as she exited the car.

"Come on, Wolf," he said to the dog. "Watch Danni."

Her eyes widened as the dog obediently fell into step beside her.

Despite the dog, he set a protective arm around her as they passed a group of down-and-outers guzzling from their paper bags near the doorway. He stood at least six inches over the tallest of the bunch, but they'd fallen silent, watching them. When they passed, someone let out a whistle.

Quinn counted on Wolf to be aware if they were followed.

They were not.

"You're armed, aren't you?" Danni asked in a whisper as they walked through the slatted doors to the bar.

"You have a problem with that?"

She laughed. "No, I'm just glad."

"We're looking for an old Creole named Sam Johnson," Quinn said quietly. "I don't really want to ask for him. I don't want to put him in a spotlight."

"He'll be in a spotlight as soon as he's seen with us, I'll bet."

An ancient air conditioner hummed against one of the windows but Quinn guessed it was more for show — there were ceiling fans blowing and two of the streetside windows were open. The floor was filthy; it was some kind of linoleum that hadn't seen a washing in a decade, and it was littered with cigarette butts and ground-in gum. The woman behind this bar seemed way past retirement age, but she was wiry and strong and busy giving her opinion to a burly man with trousers hung low and BVDs up high.

Two men who looked to be centuries old were playing a game of checkers and three women — old hookers — were lounging, legs spread, on the beaten-up couch that stood against one wall.

Quinn and Danni had barely entered

when Wolf gave a low warning growl.

Then they heard a shout of pain and fear. It came from the group they'd just passed outside.

"I don't know where old Sam is. Ain't seen him tonight," someone cried.

"Where's Sam? You tell me, you low-life bastard, or I'll start shooting at your balls," came the reply.

"Wolf!" Quinn said, drawing his gun from the holster beneath his shirt. He headed for the entry behind the dog, but before even Wolf had a chance to attack, a shot exploded and there were screams and the sound of footsteps running down the alley.

He turned around and shouted to Danni, "Stay here! Stay here!"

When he and Wolf burst back into the street, the group had scattered. Two of the men were racing across the road and one was tearing down the sidewalk in another direction. A fourth had run into the darkness of the alley.

"That way, Wolf!" he ordered the dog, pointing at the corner of the building.

Wolf barked and raced ahead. Quinn tore after him.

Danni had felt brave enough when Quinn was with her, but standing in the center of the tawdry bar — with the hookers and the checkers players and even the bartender and the old BVD guy staring at her — she wished she'd listened to him and gone home.

They seemed unaffected by the sounds from the street; they'd paused to listen, but since no one had come in waving a gun at any of the patrons, they'd apparently decided just to stare at her.

There was nothing to do but stare back. She did so, eyeing them with a frown as she pulled her cell phone from her pocket and hit 9-1-1, reporting her location and explaining that there'd been shots fired. She hung up, trying to look as fierce as possible.

"I guess no one else was going to report the fact that someone might've been shot," she said.

One of the hookers, a skinny woman with frizzy dyed red hair, rose and approached her. "Honey, shots are fired around here all the time. With any luck, the cops will come. But don't hold your breath — takes them a while sometimes. I mean, you know, long enough for a man to bleed out. I guess the cops figure if we're killing one another, there's less for them to worry about."

"I don't think that's true," she said, and yet she had to wonder how she could really think anything about the situation, since she'd never frequented this part of town — and she'd lived in New Orleans all her life. "Human life is sacred."

"Oh, Lordy, Lordy, she might be one of them missionary ladies, Mabel," one of the other old hookers said. Mabel was black. The woman who joined her to study Danni was so pale she must have come from a northern clime.

"I'm not a missionary," she said. "I called the cops because I don't believe they want anyone killing anyone else." They were both studying her now. "Hey, we all need the tourist trade, don't we?"

The pale woman giggled. "Well, I wish the *tourists* I know had a little more in the way of green stuff, but whatever you say, sweetie."

"You come here with Captain America, honey?" the third hooker asked, rising.

Mabel giggled. "After my, er, recent escorts, *I'd* pay that boy, I can tell you! You're a lucky lady, running around with that one."

"He's a good guy. He doesn't want anyone dying," Danni said.

"Quit circling the poor girl!" the bartender called out, walking over to them.

"Oh, Mama Jackson, we didn't mean no

harm!" the blonde said.

"You come on up to the bar, honey," the bartender — Mama Jackson — told her. "Don't pay these girls no mind."

"Um, they weren't offensive, really," Danni said.

The hookers giggled in unison.

"Can I buy a round of drinks?" Danni asked.

They stopped giggling. "Now, that's really sweet. Especially since the cops will eventually get here!" Mabel said. "Seeing that you called 'em. Mama Jackson, this sweet thing is buying drinks. Give us the good stuff — something that has a real label on it!"

"You mean it?" Mama Jackson asked Danni.

"Yes, of course, whatever they'd like."

The checkers players rose and the BVD man turned to look at her.

"Drinks all around," Danni said.

She was suddenly the belle of the bar. The girls cozied up around her and the checkers players smiled at her appreciatively. The BVD man asked, "Hey, that fellow of yours comin' back?" he asked, wiggling an eyebrow.

The blonde laughed. "J.J., you're far too old and ugly for the likes of her!"

"Hey!" J.J. protested. "I ain't too ugly for you."

"You got pretty money sometimes, J.J.," the blonde said.

Mama Jackson started pouring the drinks — shots in dirty glasses. "This will cost you four bucks a pop," she told Danni.

"I'll spring for it," Danni said dryly, hoping she hadn't made a mistake, that she wasn't going to be mugged for the money in her pockets. She didn't think, somehow, that Mama Jackson took credit cards.

But she needn't have worried. They were on the wrong side of righteous, perhaps, but the crowd in the bar wasn't out to hurt her. The blonde introduced herself as Lela, and the third one, a brunette, was Foxie.

"What are you doing in this part of town?" Mama Jackson asked her.

So much for her old painting clothes making her look as if she belonged. She was lucky; she'd never been down and out. She'd been cherished all her life, and her way through school and college had been encouraged and financed. She'd been expected to grow up and have a career.

"We're trying to find a man named Sam Johnson. We're worried about him," Danni said.

"You know old Sam?" Mama Jackson

asked. "Old Numb Nuts?"

Danni shook her head. "But he might have heard about a plan to steal . . . an object and what he heard might have put him in danger."

To her surprise, her newfound friends were willing to help her.

"I thought Sam was acting kind of edgy," Mabel said.

"Yeah, he was talking to me about some fellow and his girl got killed last night," Foxie put in.

"If you're looking for Sam," Lela told her, "you might want to try the old cemetery on Basin Street."

"The cemetery?" Danni repeated. Even if Sam had been killed, he couldn't possibly be in the cemetery yet.

"Yeah, he used to go there on account of his cancer," Mabel said. "You know — he had that man cancer."

"Prostate?" Danni asked.

"Yeah, that's it. That's where he got his name. Numb Nuts. He's a nice old dude. Used to do a lot of talking, only he never had money. After the cancer thing — and the freebie hospital taking care of him — he said that even if he had the money, he couldn't do nothin' 'cause his nuts were numb. But before the operation, he used to go hang out in the cemetery. Said he wanted to get used to being with the dead. Then he told me one night that was where he went when he was scared of some of the bigger bastards around here. Maybe you'll find him there."

"Thank you!" Danni said.

Just as she spoke, they heard sirens; a police car stopped in front of the bar and two officers came in.

Danni turned and quickly explained that she'd called them because a shot had been fired outside. The first officer sighed. Apparently it was true — shots were fired frequently in the area. "Is anyone hurt?"

"Not in here," Mama Jackson said.

Before the cops could exit, Quinn came through the door. Wolf was at his heels, but Danni hardly noticed the dog. He was carrying a man with an ashen face and a bandage, fashioned from Quinn's ripped shirt, on his leg. "I've called an ambulance," he said, bringing the man to one of the chairs. "There's a bullet in his calf. He was lucky. Whoever was chasing him took off when he heard Wolf and me running after him."

"That freak was screaming away about old Sam and I'd a told him where he was if I'd a known!" the injured man said.

173

"Which way?" the cop asked Quinn.

"Down the alley. But I heard a motor revving. You're not going to get him now. I didn't see the car."

He sounded thoroughly disgusted.

Mabel, Lela and Foxie began demanding better police protection, but while the officers tried to impose some kind of order, the ambulance arrived. Paramedics rushed in, asking questions of Quinn and the injured man, Tommy Lee Hutchins. One of the checkers players reached over the bar for the bottle of decent whiskey Mama Jackson had just poured, but Mama Jackson caught him. While the younger officer left with Hutchins in the ambulance, the older officer began to question everyone. Quinn told him about racing down the alley, stumbling upon the injured man and hearing the car rev out on the street when the shooter made his getaway. Naturally, the officer needed to see Quinn's permit, and when he did, he realized that he knew the name, and the two began to talk as if they were old friends.

Then everyone was talking at once, trying to tell the officer what they knew — which really wasn't much — except that Mabel and the girls were able to identify the other men lounging around outside, so at least the cops could track them down and get a better description of the shooter. When Quinn and Danni had finished their reports, it was eleven; he looked tired and worn out, and he told her they needed to go home.

He watched Danni as she paid the bar bill; Mama Jackson and the others raised their glasses to her and told her to come back anytime.

Quinn gave her a curious look. She shrugged and waved goodbye.

"I'm sorry I had to cut out, leaving you in there," he said. "I did tell you not to come with me."

She smiled. "As you see, I can manage."

"I guess." Quinn placed his hand on her back as he steered her out.

"In fact, I managed quite well."

"I just missed him!" Quinn said angrily once they got in the car. "Tommy Lee Hutchins was on the ground screaming, and as soon as I reached him, I heard the car. Wolf gave chase but I called him back. He's a good dog, but he can't stop a car, and I couldn't leave a guy bleeding and screaming in an alley."

"And I don't want to burst your bubble, Quinn, but you couldn't catch a car, either," Danni told him.

"Another near-miss. All this, and nothing," Quinn said, shaking his head.

"Just because *you* got nothing doesn't mean I didn't get something."

He turned to her, startled.

"When Numb Nuts is afraid," she began, "he goes to the cemetery —"

"Which one?"

"Over on Basin."

"At night? The cemeteries are locked at night. . . ."

"Yes, they are. People hop the walls, or so I assume. Unless they pole vault or drop in by parachute."

His brows lowered. "And you know this how?"

"Through my new friends," she said. "Buy a few drinks and . . ."

"You could get mugged. Or worse."

"But I didn't. So let's go to the cemetery."

Tourists did not flock this neighborhood by night — nor did most citizens. Quinn was easily able to park near the cemetery gates.

Wolf made an unhappy little whining sound; he knew he was being left in the car.

"Hey, boy, you're the lookout tonight," Quinn told him.

Exiting on her side, Danni said, "Please don't tell me he's also the getaway driver."

"No, but he's a good lookout," Quinn said. He glanced at Danni, at the cemetery

176

wall and the barbed wire atop it — meant to discourage acts like the one they were about to perform.

"I can go this alone," he insisted.

"No. I'm the one with the information."

"*Can* you make it?"

"I'll need a boost," she said.

They moved along the wall to a place where the top had crumbled, offering a slightly lower purchase.

Quinn lifted Danni by her legs, giving her the boost she needed to reach the top of the high brick wall that surrounded the cemetery. He was glad to see she was agile and had the strength to haul herself the rest of the way.

There was barbed wire on the brick and she had to maneuver around it. This was how the church attempted to keep the drug traders and other reprobates — frat kids pledging and common vandals — out of the historic and sacred burial place of the dead.

It was going to be a little more difficult for him. He called to her softly to meet him around the corner at the gate.

There, beneath a streetlight, he found a place he could climb. Luckily, by then, the honest citizens of the area were in bed, the dishonest were in hiding and the stray street vendor who might prey on tourists by day had long since given up hope of someone needing a can of soda or a questionable wrapped sandwich.

He got a foothold and a few armholds, grateful for the extra strength that had come to him after his near-death experience. He moved quickly — not wanting Danni to see just how good he could be at clambering over heights he shouldn't have been able to maneuver.

He was somewhat surprised that it had been her suggestion to come here. He was still surprised that she'd wanted to go to the seedy bar with him — and that she'd befriended a group of hookers.

But being alone in one of the Cities of the Dead in New Orleans wouldn't appeal to many people, especially at night. Naturally they were all famous for being haunted.

They were also beautiful and new vaults could cost the same as a house for the living.

But there was something more poignant about the old, and this was the oldest of its kind in the city. Along the walls, the "oven" vaults — bodies stacked on bodies in the mausoleum style, but without benefit of the mausoleum structure — were often cracked and broken. Or open and empty.

The walls of many of the small family

vaults were chipped, peeling. Struggling shrubs and flowers grew around stone paths. Only the sliver of a moon joined with the echo of streetlamps, and the cemetery was dark. It was easy to imagine shadowy dangers in the lost mist that rose from the fog as the moisture of day gave way to the cooling temperatures of night.

He looked down the length of the wall by the gate; she appeared out of the mist, walking toward him swiftly and yet with care. In places, the foundations of the vaults stretched out into the paths. Little steps were sometimes hidden by the weeds, and broken cherubs sometimes lay undisturbed wherever they'd fallen.

Despite her attempt at dressing down, she moved toward him like an elegant wraith. She knew the cemetery, he realized, as well as he did.

But even if she wasn't aware of the life her father had led, she was a child of the French Quarter. She had surely brought out-of-town friends to visit the famous funerary grounds — and then, of course, she'd grown up with Angus. That meant a house that had a mummy or two, coffins, urns, not to mention a few movie monsters.

He spoke quietly when she reached him, a slight smile twitching his lips. "You seem to know where you're going."

She was somber, but she didn't seem dismayed by their surroundings. She smiled a little grimly at his question. "I spent a few summers as a tour guide."

The City of the Dead by night did not seem to disturb her. He knew a few hardy cops of whom he couldn't say the same.

"It's a big cemetery, so we should split up," she suggested.

His smile faded. "Don't you watch any horror movies? People always get it with a chain saw or they're attacked by zombies as soon as they split up."

"I haven't heard about zombies terrorizing this cemetery. And I'd hear a chain saw," she told him.

He shook his head. "These are bad guys — with guns," he said.

"Okay."

"And we should move quietly. We don't want to spook Numb Nuts if he *is* here."

She nodded. "Where?" she asked.

"Let's start at one end, follow the rows as much as the jagged streets allow," he answered.

She turned and backtracked the way she'd come. He saw that she had a little penlight that didn't radiate far, but hinted at what lay before her.

They moved in silence, following the perimeter of the wall to the corner, and then taking a left. A bone protruded from a vault. Danni paused; once, such sights might have been common but the church had been trying to keep the graves, mausoleums and vaults better sealed than in previous decades.

Quinn walked past Danni, taking her light. He reached in for the bone.

"Rubber," he told her, pushing the object back into the broken vault. "Someone playing jokes on the unwary."

She grimaced and kept going.

The sliver of moon disappeared behind a cloud.

The pale glow of streetlights touched the City of the Dead. Angels prayed and cherubs looked sadly toward heaven, seeming almost alive in the eerie light.

They didn't find Numb Nuts until the third row. He was sleeping on one of two low vaults that lay side by side, a river of weeds between them.

"Let me," Danni whispered. "You might scare him into a heart attack."

He gave her a sardonic look, but then shrugged.

Danni walked over to the sleeping man and touched his shoulder. He opened his eyes and stared up at her. He didn't seem frightened or alarmed. "Lord Amighty!" he said. "An angel done come for me, right in the old burial ground. Am I dead, then — and not in too much trouble for all the sinning I done?"

"I'm not an angel, Mr. Johnson. My name is Danni Cafferty. I'm here with a man named Michael Quinn, and we're trying to make sure you don't meet any angels before your appointed time."

Numb Nuts struggled to sit up. He frowned as Quinn stepped through the weeds to join Danni.

"Numb Nuts — Sam — we need your help. And I can help you. I can get you into a safe house."

The old man's weathered face seemed sorrowful. "Why, I done thought they'd found me already," he said. "I was kind a glad, thinkin' maybe I'd just gone easy and painless, and that there really are angels."

"If they find you, it isn't going to be easy or painless," Quinn said.

Numb Nuts nodded at that. "All right. I'm not sure as how I can help anyone. I only know what I heard — and that Leroy stole the damned bust, got hisself killed and poor Ivy, too. Why that girl ever stayed with him is beyond me. Well, now, I'm prayin'

182

there's an angel come for her. She weren't really a bad sort. Just an addict, you know? Even so she didn't cotton to hurtin' people."

"Then I imagine Ivy will be fine in the hereafter," Quinn said. "But we need to get you out of here and I need to know who killed Leroy and stole the bust from him."

Numb Nuts nodded again, but didn't move.

"Sam, can I give you a hand?" Quinn asked him.

He agreed, and Quinn set an arm around his shoulders, guiding him into a standing position. "Got no strength left in me, not after all that chemo and radiation," Sam wheezed.

"You're freezing." Danni took his arm to steady him as he stood.

"Nah, this N'Awlins, girl. Maybe, now and then in winter, you get a really cold night. But tonight? It's just the breeze — and the cold of death, I guess. I'm all right."

"How are we going to get him out of here?" Danni asked Quinn. "It was one thing for you and me to get in, but . . ."

Quinn knew he could call Larue; Larue could get the gates opened for him. But he didn't want anyone, not even the cops, knowing where Sam Johnson was. He didn't think they had dirty cops at the department

— he still knew half of them — but even clean cops could accidentally say the wrong thing to the wrong person at the wrong time.

"I can manage," he told Danni.

She frowned, but didn't disagree. "This I've got to see," she murmured.

Yes, she would see, and he was sorry, but there was no help for it.

"Let's go." But then he paused. He heard Wolf barking behind the gates.

"Someone is on to us," he said quietly.

"I don't hear —" Danni began. She stopped as Wolf let out a howl that could wake the dead themselves.

That was followed by the sound of a thud from near the gates. And then another.

"Lordy, Lordy," Sam said. "You two young folk get away from me, you hear? Looks like I am going to meet the angels — or other — this night. Don't want you hurt 'cause of the mess my life has gotten me into."

"Don't be ridiculous," Danni said. "We're not leaving you."

"But we *are* leaving. We're out in the open," Quinn told her. "Come on!"

"Where are we going?"

"The society tomb!"

While they might look like houses, and often had gates that were like entries, most of the tombs were sealed — until there was another death.

Most.

Quinn kept Danni in front of him, pushing her toward the large tomb that housed the remains of at least one hundred members of the Loyal Order of Biblical Brothers. It was a massive domed structure, with a knee-high wrought-iron fence around it. Danni hopped the gate easily; Quinn lifted Sam Johnson off his feet and set him over it, then made the little scissor leap himself.

They crossed the few feet of overgrown rock trail that led to the tomb's gate. The doorway behind the gate seemed to be sealed, but Quinn knew it wasn't. He slipped open the gate, flinching as it squealed in the night. He bent down, pressing the lever at the foot of the seal. The block of concrete that covered the opening slid inward — loudly.

"Get in!" Quinn commanded.

Danni went first; Sam followed her. Quinn closed the seal as soon as he entered.

At first, they could see nothing. Danni trained her little flashlight ahead of her. There was an altar at the rear of the domed tomb. Four concrete tombs stood in the center and, to the sides, were a few rows of chairs. The walls around them were lined with the tombs of long-gone Biblical Brothers.

Dust covered the chairs. Quinn hadn't been in the mausoleum himself in years. He surmised that no Biblical Brothers had recently departed this earth — if there were any left. He brought his fingers to his lips, warning them both to silence as they listened.

"It came from here!" someone shouted in a low, husky voice.

Quinn wished he'd kept the gate oiled.

He could hear footsteps around the tomb. He tried to place the sounds and count the number of men prowling in the cemetery — far too close to the tomb.

"This is tighter than a drum!" he heard, the voice about thirty feet to the other side of the tomb.

There was a third set of footsteps.

"They've got to be in one of the big ones," another hoarse voice said. The three were trying to whisper — difficult when they needed to be heard by one another.

He thought quickly.

If he'd been alone . . .

If he'd been alone, he could have waited, ready to ambush the trio from the tomb.

But he wasn't alone. Although he was big and even "blessed," he wasn't sure he could

186

outfire three paid assassins on his own.

In the pinprick light he saw Danni's eyes — they were wide, somber, and her expression assured him that she was awaiting his lead.

He hurried across the tomb, seeking the drawer with its spiderweb-covered brass plaque that read Angel Morrero.

"Quinn?" Danni asked.

He ran his hands along the tomb, trying to find the lever. To his relief, the marble slab that covered the tomb rotated, sliding to an angle and revealing a black void.

"Get in," he said. Both Danni and Sam stared at him.

"Now!" he urged.

Danni plunged into the darkness.

Sam followed.

He listened; he heard footsteps as their pursuers hopped the low gate.

He went in after the other two, entering the cold darkness of the tomb.

CHAPTER 8

Somehow Danni kept from screaming.

Her hands seemed to sink into a pile of ash. Was it a decayed body — or the naturally cremated remains of a man?

She could see nothing before her, but could tell she was on a slant. Numb Nuts, Sam, was close behind her — nearly on top of her — in the stygian darkness. She could hear his heartbeat and smell his fear.

And his unwashed body.

He crashed into her as Quinn came into the tomb, pushing them forward so he could slide the marble covering the "drawer" back in place. She wondered where they would go.

And then, as she squeezed farther to allow Quinn room, she began to slip, pitching downward.

She managed not to scream as she fell — into a fetid pool.

Sam fell against her. He almost let out a

yelp, but she knew Quinn was with them and that he'd clamped a hand over the other man's mouth.

"Walk forward," Quinn said. "Stay low or you'll crack your head."

Moving forward, Danni realized she was in a bit of awe and a bit of shock. She'd lived here all her life and had never imagined that such a tunnel existed. The French had built the Vieux Carré on high ground, but even the high ground in New Orleans was below sea level.

So it made sense that the tunnel was filled with water. Icky, smelly, horrible water.

She was bent over as she moved because the tunnel was narrow. The water came nearly to her ankles, and she could only guess what might be in it. She didn't know where she was going but it was so tight there was no way Quinn could get in front of her.

It felt as if they walked for an eternity.

She remembered she had her penlight — actually clenched in her fingers. She pressed the little button seconds before she would have banged her head on a rock wall.

"Dead end!" she whispered.

"Push on it until you feel it give," Quinn said.

She could hear Sam Johnson breathing hard. He was trembling behind her. She groped the cold earth and stone before deciding that, no matter what she'd seen so far, Quinn was crazy. There was no way out of here. Then, just as her frustration was reaching the panic stage, she pressed harder and heard stone scrape against stone.

They had to back up as the slab swung around.

There was another dark gaping hole ahead of her. She crawled into it. It was even tighter, scattered with some kind of soot or remains, as well.

"Push until you find the right pressure to make the outer slab revolve!" Quinn whispered from behind her.

She took a breath, holding her nose, fighting the waves of claustrophobic panic that were washing over her. She pressed and pressed . . . and something gave.

A minute later, she landed on a floor. Her little light fell from her hand and rolled away from her. Crawling on the tomb's floor, she groped for it blindly.

She nearly screamed when she touched some small furry creature.

A squeal sounded; she gulped back another cry as she realized it was a rat.

Her fingers finally curled around the light. She turned it on. They were in another tomb, another "house" in the City of the

Dead. This one barely had room for the three of them to stand between the shelves holding the dead.

"I gotta get outta here, man," Sam muttered. "Can't move, can't breathe —"

"They get you with a couple of bullets, you sure won't be breathing," Quinn told him

They were jostled and shoved as he reached into his pocket for his cell phone. Though it was dark other than for Danni's little light, she was certain he'd hit speed dial because a minute later he was speaking softly into his phone, asking that patrol cars get to the cemetery as fast as possible — sirens blaring.

She felt Sam shaking and placed her hands on his shoulders. "Breathe. Just breathe slowly and you'll be fine."

She sensed that his eyes were on hers. "You're going to be okay. You're going to be okay."

He spasmed for a second, trembling rapidly. Then she heard him take a deep breath. They were going to make it.

Whoever Quinn had called — she assumed it was Larue — had power.

Although sixty seconds seemed like an hour in the tomb, it couldn't have been more than a few minutes before she heard sirens, the sound coming closer and closer. She felt Quinn move and the pressure of his fingers against her lips.

"Listen," he whispered.

She heard what he was waiting for — the sound of footsteps as three people ran past the tomb.

"Hold on — just a few more minutes," he said.

Then, finally, he pressed the right point on the slab that was really a false front for the tomb they were in. The iron gate opened.

And they could feel the rush of cool night air. Sweet, clean, fresh, *delicious.*

Officers surged toward them, warning them to halt, to raise their arms. Quinn called out, "It's Quinn. Whoever was in here ran over to the rear wall."

For a moment, Danni was blinded by the high-beam flashlights trained her way. Then she saw a man walking through the uniformed officers.

It was indeed Larue.

"Hell, Quinn, what are you doing in here?"

"Trying to keep this man alive." He dropped his hands and approached Larue, indicating Numb Nuts, explaining that they'd heard a rumor he hung out in the cemetery. Larue looked at the old man and then at Danni. Sheepishly, she lifted her hand in greeting.

"We'll try to get it all untangled at the station," Larue said with a sigh.

Quinn had no idea just how repulsive they were until they were seated in Larue's office. He glanced over at Danni. She was obviously uncomfortable — and she resembled a ghost. She was covered in dust. Bone dust, dirt . . . some of it turned to mud from the flooding in the tunnels.

Wolf sat by Quinn's side, the cleanest among them.

He was loved at the station house. Quinn knew the men there were usually far happier to see the dog than him.

Stroking Wolf's head, Quinn watched the man they'd saved and decided that he liked old Numb Nuts — Sam Johnson. Sam sat there humbly, trying to tell them what he knew.

"I guess I was expectin' to die," he said, lean elbows on his knees, chin sunk into his hands. Quinn thought that at one time Sam had probably been an intriguing man. His skin was a light café au lait and his eyes were large and expressive, very dark. He spoke with both humility and dignity. Since he'd learned that life could beat a man down —

or make him soar so high he didn't know he'd ever crash — he wondered about the Sam Johnson who might have been, before he'd succumbed to scratching out a living in any manner he could find.

At the moment, of course, he looked like a sewer rat. But he had a fine bone structure and he sat as if he wasn't covered in slime.

"I mean, I'd heard about the shooting out in the Ninth Ward," Sam said quietly. "I figured there was something going wrong." He shrugged. "I like the old cemeteries. I like 'em a lot. I figured if I was hanging out there, only my friends would know where I was and, if I was found, I wouldn't bring others down with me." He offered Larue a weak smile. "Yeah, it's illegal to be there at night. But, hey, I *am* a Catholic."

"I'm not holding you for being in the cemetery," Larue said. "We need your help."

Quinn realized, yet again, why he liked Larue. Larue wasn't making Sam feel like trash; he was treating him with the respect due a human being.

"Well, as you surely know," Sam began, "I was out there — out at Leroy's — for illegal purposes. But there was a group of us that day, and Leroy was saying he was going to be flying high. He was going to manage the easiest break-in ever and come away with

one stupid object that would make him rich
the rest of his life. It was strange because
Ivy didn't seem happy about it. He was telling her to shut up every time she told him
she didn't like it and that he really needed
to quit his bragging. And now . . . well,
other folks are turning up dead and . . . I
guess the person who wanted the *object* got
his hands on it and killed Leroy instead of
paying him. And poor Ivy," he added.

"What do you know about Eyes, Sam?
Brandt Shumaker?" Quinn asked.

"Eyes himself doesn't come around a
whole lot. He doesn't dirty his hands."

"Okay, but I got word that he went to Leroy's to acquire his illegal substances,"
Quinn said.

Sam raised one shoulder. "Might've been
his big black limo drivin' around that night.
Yeah, hell, there aren't that many big black
limos in that area. Eyes . . . supposedly, he
has *eyes* everywhere and that's how he got
his nickname. That car of his . . . filled with
his goons . . . it's like this black monster
that moves in the night all on its own.
Everyone steers clear of him."

"But you didn't see him? You didn't hear
that he'd threatened Leroy or anyone?"
Larue asked.

Sam shook his head. "All I heard is that

this *object* is more valuable than all the money in the world — if you know how to use it. Supposedly it's something that can give the owner incredible power over others. Sounded kind of religious or satanic to me," Sam said. "Sounded like something you want to keep away from. Besides, I thought they were all talking rubbish. And if some idiot thought he could get the devil to do his will through it . . . well, then, as long as Leroy didn't go 'round hurtin' nobody, it didn't matter a damn to me." He looked troubled. "Some say Eyes has fooled around with strange groups. That he's not into voodoo like those who see it as a real religion, but into voodoo kinda Hollywood-style, you know — all the hocus-pocus, raising the dead, sticking needles in voodoo dolls and all that crap. Blood sacrifice."

Larue turned to Quinn.

"You can question Shumaker, at least. Intimidate him a little," Quinn said. He knew that Larue had been hoping for more.

Larue nodded. "We can question him, but I don't have anything on him other than that he's driven around in a black car and he may or may not have been in Leroy's neighborhood. But thank you, Mr. Johnson," he said to Sam. "Thank you for telling us what you know."

Sam's expression was troubled. "I guess someone is out to kill me now. If it's Eyes, I'm good as dead."

"We'll see that you're kept in a safe house while the search goes on," Larue said, getting to his feet. "It's not much, but you'll have an officer with you, watching over you."

Sam's eyes became huge, and he trembled slightly. "You'll . . . put me somewhere, and have someone watch me?"

"Yup."

"You mean a jail cell?"

Larue smiled. "No, more like a cheap room, but it'll have a shower and we'll keep you fed while we're sorting this out. It's obvious that your life is at risk — and we really are here to serve and protect," he said dryly.

Sam looked over at Danni and she clasped his hand. "You're going to be okay," she promised him, not for the first time.

"It *was* an angel I saw when I opened my eyes this evening," Sam said.

"Well, Sam, it's the police, not the angels, who are going to work hard to save you," Quinn told him. "And, in return, if you think of anything, you make sure you tell us right away."

Sam appeared pensive. "There's something bad, I can tell you that. Something real bad. And it's not like you can just arrest Eyes, even if you find a reason. This is more than one man. There's a bad element here. People who are looking for something they don't have — and they think this . . . thing can get it for them."

"We'll be careful." Larue tapped his intercom. "Officer Boyle, will you come in here, please? We need to take Mr. Johnson to the safe house. Can you get him some clean clothes for after he's showered and a meal?"

Boyle, a big, well-muscled man, must have been waiting right by the door; he was there in seconds. He nodded at Sam and said, "Come along, sir. We'll have you squared away in a few minutes."

Sam paused, looking at Quinn. "How you know about those tunnels in a place where there should be no tunnels? Are you one of them Biblical Brothers?" he asked.

Quinn sensed Danni studying him, waiting for an answer.

"No, I'm not a Biblical Brother," he said. "I just have a lot of . . . friends."

Sam didn't push it. He turned back to Larue. "I look like scum — and smell like it, too. But I swear I never sold nothing to kids and I never sold nothing harder than marijuana. Ain't legal, I know that, but

198

didn't seem so bad to me. Never saw no pothead split open someone's skull like I seen in bars."

Larue shrugged. "You may be right, Sam. But, right now, it's not legal."

"If it was, half of us wouldn't have had nontaxable work. Anyway, you're helping me. I want you to know I never willfully hurt another human being in my life."

"That's good to hear, Mr. Johnson," Larue said.

Sam smiled and looked at Quinn, touching his shoulder. "Thank you."

"My pleasure."

Sam turned to Danni. "Angel, you take care."

"You, too, Sam."

When Sam had left the office, Larue coughed loudly. "Sweet Jesu, but you all smell like hell!"

"Yeah, a shower would be in order," Quinn agreed.

Larue pointed a finger at him. "When you knew what you were doing, you should've told me. We could've been there earlier — and we might have a lead on the men who were in the cemetery."

"If a dozen cop cars had shown up, Sam would've disappeared," Quinn told him. "Hey, come on! You don't think I wasn't hoping we'd get our hands on one of those goons! Especially since it looks like the one we're trying to get is Eyes."

Larue waved a hand in the air. "Out of my office. You really stink. Even Sam smelled better." He shook his head. "Wait! Who else knows about that tunnel?"

"The Biblical Brothers, of course," Quinn said.

"I thought they all died years ago."

Quinn couldn't help grinning. "It's a secret society these days. So, if you are a Biblical Brother, I guess you don't tell anyone."

"I can find out about the last entombment," Larue said.

"I'm sure you can. Me, I don't know who it was. I had an old friend named Ben Wheedon — he told me about the tunnel. When he died, he was buried at Lafayette Cemetery with his family. We through here for now?"

"God, yes!" Larue said with disgust, holding his nose. "But, Quinn, remember. You've got to keep me informed on this. The dead are piling up."

"Yeah." Quinn stood. "Thanks for getting the troops there so quickly tonight."

"Sure." Larue nodded. "It's what I do," he said sarcastically. "Now, for the love of

God — go bathe. Even poor Wolf is wrinkling his nose at you."

As if in agreement, Wolf whined and thumped his tail on the floor. Quinn and Danni rose, and the three of them left the station.

It was very late.

They might have found a trail, but they hadn't managed to follow it very far.

Danni was thoughtful as they drove home. They were both tired — no, exhausted — and with the mud created by bone and tunnel dust combined with the water they'd crawled and sloshed through, she couldn't have felt more physically gross.

She wondered if she was too tired to think rationally.

But she felt somewhat numbed . . . and shocked, once more, at the situation in which she found herself.

"Did my father know about the tunnel?" she asked Quinn, turning in her seat to face him. "Did he know everything you know? How *do* you know what you know?"

He glanced at her, then looked ahead again and shrugged. "I'm a friendly guy. I can't be sure whether your dad knew about that tunnel. We never had occasion to need it when we were together. It's a long story and I'm not trying to hide anything from you, but it's late and we have to get started again in the morning. I'm pulling up in front of your place, so . . . Lord, Larue was right! We *are* rank."

The car stopped. They were at her shop and home. She felt a cold nose and warm muzzle brush her neck — Wolf, saying good-bye from the backseat.

Quinn opened her door and she got out. His good-night smile seemed a little grim. "I'll see you in," he told her.

"You think someone might be after me?"

"I think it's the French Quarter, and stray drunks and muggers and pickpockets might grab a woman on the street."

"Well, then, thanks." She dug out her key and walked to the shop. He watched her as she went.

"Hey!" he called.

"Yeah?"

"Take Wolf."

"What?"

"Take Wolf for the night. He's perfectly behaved. Give him a minute outside, and he'll be great until morning."

"Quinn, that's good of you — I appreciate your concern. And I love Wolf. But I'm not set up for a dog right now."

"Take him, anyway."

"Quinn —"

"Please."

She hesitated, thinking that perhaps it wasn't a bad idea. The world had changed so much. She didn't even know if she felt safe in her own home — the home she'd loved all her life — anymore.

"These guys have big guns! If someone's shooting at a dog . . . well, a dog can't dodge a bullet," she reminded him.

He countered that with, "Wolf has a big bark, which is a nice warning sound, and a bigger bite."

The dog hopped out of the car, tail wagging.

"I don't have any dog food," she said.

"He's fine with a full English breakfast."

She nodded slowly and smiled down at the massive dog. "Wolf, want to stay for a slumber party?"

He wagged his tail more vigorously and looked at Quinn.

"Watch out for her, boy," he said. "Now, if you don't mind, let yourself in so I can leave with a restful mind and get to a shower!"

She studied him a moment longer. Even stinking of fetid water and muck and whatever else had adhered to them in the tunnel and tombs, he was somehow attractive.

Maybe it was his courteous concern for her. More probably it was his size and physique — eyes, facial structure and his rueful smile.

She cringed inwardly. *I'm starting to like him!* she thought.

"I'm going in. And you text me when you're home safe, all right?"

He gave her a brief salute, leaning on the car door until she'd unlocked the shop and stepped inside. Then he went around to the driver's seat, gunned the motor and headed down Royal.

"Well, here we are," Danni told Wolf. "What do you think? Or have you been here before — and I just don't know it?" The dog wagged his massive tail again. No answers there. "Let's go out to the courtyard . . . and you can do what dogs do."

It occurred to her that she'd have to clean the courtyard in the morning; with Wolf's size, she might as well be keeping a horse overnight.

Wolf quickly went about his business and returned. She locked up, then checked the alarms and hurried upstairs to her bedroom, exhaustion really setting in. Wolf lay down inside her room, right in front of her door.

She realized she liked the idea of having the dog. There was something so . . . reassuring about Wolf. He made her feel safe, secure.

Like his master.

The shower beckoned like a long-lost lover. Danni stripped and threw her clothing straight into the bathroom trash can, then stood under the spray of water, relishing the heat and steam, before seizing the soap and energetically removing all the slime — real and imaginary. She zealously scrubbed her hair, and when she emerged at last, she thought she might have scrubbed some of her flesh raw. But it felt wonderful.

She slipped into a T-shirt and boxers, patted Wolf and climbed into bed. She was afraid her mind would race, that tired though she was, she'd never drift off.

But in seconds, she was deeply asleep.

She had no concept of time passing but she awoke to the thunderous sound of the dog's barking. It was loud, jarring, and she shot out of bed, confused, as she fought off the remnants of sleep.

Wolf was standing at the door, barking — and howling. He looked back at her, then jumped up, scratching the door.

"What is it, boy, what is it?" she asked.

He barked again. He wanted out of the room.

In all her years in the French Quarter,

she'd never had a problem. No one had ever tried to break into the store. And now, of course, if there'd been an attempt, the alarm would have gone off.

The alarm hadn't, but Wolf was definitely sure that danger threatened from somewhere.

"Wait!" she commanded the dog.

She glanced around her room. She'd never worried about a weapon for self-defense before. She hadn't played Little League baseball, so she had no leftover bat to grab.

The best she could find was a high-heeled shoe. It was one of the only pair of spikes she owned. It could make a hell of a weapon, she decided — in a movie, anyway.

But she wasn't too sure about her ability to wield a shoe. . . .

She gripped it hard and opened the door to her room. Wolf raced out and down the stairs as she trailed more slowly behind him.

Arriving downstairs, she realized she had a wealth of weapons as she seized a mace from the mannequin clad in the suit of armor and hurried through the shop, following Wolf to the courtyard doors. He stood there, barking, begging to be let out.

"Hey, I'm not getting you shot, Wolf," she said, trying to peer out the windows.

She heard something and swung around.

For a moment, she tensed, her fingers tight around the mace.

"What is it?" came a whisper.

Billie had come down from his attic room.

"I don't know," she said. "The alarm didn't go off, but the dog's going crazy."

If Billie was surprised or dismayed to find a horse-size dog in the shop, barking and jumping at the door, he didn't show it.

He walked to the door. "What is it, Wolf?"

He keyed in the code on the alarm pad, then cautiously opened the doors. Wolf bounded out, barking, and dashed to the side-street wall, where he stood and continued to bark.

As Billie moved past Danni and into the light, she saw that he was carrying something — a small pistol.

She'd never been aware that he owned one.

He followed the dog out into the courtyard, where Danni watched from the doorway.

Billie patted Wolf on the head, then turned from the wall and came back to Danni.

"They're gone now."

"*They're* gone?" she asked. "They — who?"

"Whoever was trying to break in. I don't know if they would've gotten past the alarm, but it's a good thing Wolf scared them off. I mean, if these guys are running around with guns, they might've figured they had time to shoot the place up before the police arrived. Wolf informed them they couldn't get away with it."

She frowned at Billie. "How long have you had that?" she asked.

"Pardon? Oh, this," Billie said, gesturing with the gun. "Maybe fifteen years? Small, but it's rifled, and my aim is still darned good." He looked at her. "They won't be coming back tonight. They found out you have the dog and they must realize you have a direct line to the cops."

"Billie! What do you know about this?" she demanded.

"I know I'm here to protect you," he said. He stood tall — skinny as hell with his wild, thin white hair — but still as dignified as a knight of old.

"That's fine, Billie, thank you," she said. "But —"

"Same service I performed for your father, Danni. I wish he'd told you more. He just didn't see the end coming so soon. I do know this — whatever is out there, you have to bring it in or destroy it. I also know that your father trusted Michael Quinn, and between them, they did what they needed to do. You have to take on his role in the world. I can't explain it, but that's the way it is. Let's get some sleep."

"Oh, no, no!" Danni protested. "Let's have some tea instead. Let's talk."

Billie groaned softly. His face twitched, but he didn't argue with her.

She led him to the kitchen in the shop, switching on lights as she went. Once there, she put on the kettle and brought out tea bags, milk and sugar. She set them on the table while she waited for the water to boil and indicated to Billie that he should sit. He did, clicking the safety on his little pistol as he placed it next to him.

Wolf lay beside them, half underneath the table, head on his paws, ears alert.

"Cookies?" she asked. "I have shortbread cookies."

He raised one thin shoulder, his expression uncomfortable.

"Cookies, it is," she said. She brought the canister. The kettle began to whistle, and she poured the water into a teapot, along with a couple of the bags. Arranging everything on the table, she joined him.

"Now talk, Billie," she said sternly.

He lifted his hands. "I have been your father's assistant for years and years," he began.

"Since before I was born," she agreed. "You even knew my mother."

"Lovely lady, truly sweet and good and beautiful," he said reverently.

"Which is all very nice," she responded. "But you're here for more than that."

Billie sighed, leaning back. "Your grandfather collected in Scotland," he said.

"Collected what?" she asked.

"What needed to be collected."

"Billie!" she said with exasperation. "We sell things here. We've had the shop open forever. I sold a Tiffany lamp the other day. I've sold all kinds of paintings, sculptures, costumes, clothing, toys — you name it and we've sold it. So what does this really *mean?*"

"It means there are things out in the world that shouldn't be there. It means that every now and then, there's something that causes heartache and . . ." He paused. "And death and mayhem and grief."

"Like the bust," she said.

"Like the bust."

"But there are lots of things in the basement. Many things my father added to his private collection. If they're somehow evil, how could my father keep them here?"

Now Billie looked really uncomfortable. "Billie!"

"If he kept them, he cleansed them," Billie said.

"With Michael Quinn?"

"In the past several years, yes."

She drummed her fingers on the table, realizing he wasn't going to volunteer anything; she'd have to keep asking.

"Why Michael Quinn? Did he meet him through a special group or secret society?"

Billie shook his head.

"Then how?"

"He came to see your father."

"Because?"

"He'd been hired to find a child."

"And so my father . . . helped him find the child? Wait — was the child found? Alive?"

Billie smiled at that, nodding his head fervently. "Quinn came to your father to ask if he'd heard about any wacko group that was maybe planning a child sacrifice. Your father had recently purchased the contents of a long-deserted warehouse. A man and a woman had come in, trying to buy things from that warehouse, but nothing had been cataloged as yet. They went away, said they were coming back. They'd left a number where they could be reached when the contents were cataloged. Your father had begun looking into the contents of the warehouse, trying to find out who'd died and left everything there to rot with no family to make a claim. Anyway, he eventually discovered that the man who'd owned the storage place — under an alias, of course — had been none other than Gruesome Gus."

Danni blinked at him. Gruesome Gus was a serial killer in west Texas. He'd been apprehended and sentenced to death — and he hadn't fought it. He'd actually died of lethal injection a few years back.

"Did my dad know the stuff had belonged to Gus before he bought it?"

"No, but he would've taken it if he had — just to make sure."

"To make sure of what?"

"That it was safe," Billie told her.

"All right. So Michael Quinn came here. Because he thought Dad could help him."

"Yes."

"Why? How did the two of them connect in the first place?"

"I don't know. You'll have to ask Quinn."

As if recognizing the fact that they were discussing his master, Wolf whined softly.

Danni gave him a shortbread cookie. It probably wasn't good for him, but she didn't have dog biscuits. If Wolf was going to be hanging around, she needed to invest in dog food and treats.

"Trust me, I will ask Quinn," she murmured. "Go on."

"With what?"

"What happened then?"

"Oh, well, that couple? They'd asked for a scepter. Your dad found it. He didn't feel there was anything special about it — it was the type of thing they sell in wiccan shops or costume shops."

"So?"

"He told Quinn. And Quinn used his contacts to backtrack the cell number your father had been given. It was pay-ahead, the kind you supposedly can't trace — but they were able to discover where the phone had been sold, ask some questions — and get an address for the people. They'd taken over a fishing shack on the bayou. They'd gotten hold of some old Greek or Etruscan or some such book that promised eternity if they provided the sacrifice of a child and did all the right incantations, used all the right props. Anyway, Quinn went out there and got the kid back."

"What gave Quinn the idea? That this child might have been stolen for something so . . . obscene?"

"You'll have to ask him," Billie said again.

Danni nodded thoughtfully. "What's your part in all this?"

"I assist. That's what I do. Whatever your father asked of me. I guarded the place, I made calls, I read, I did whatever he needed done." He smiled, petting the dog. "I watched over Wolf with them, when they were afraid poor Wolf might not make it." He looked her in the eyes, his face solemn. "And I'm here for you. For what you need. I don't have the touch myself, you see. So, I assist."

"What do you mean, the touch?"

"Some people are just . . . special."

"Oh, Quinn is special, all right," she said.

Billie grinned, leaning toward her. "Some people know what they have to do in life. Some become priests or rabbis or whatever. Some look after the innocent — they somehow know they're supposed to and they find the way, even if there are a lot of detours. Your father . . . he came from a long line of men who knew they'd been touched by the hand of an ultimate power. Quinn . . . now, he had a few detours. But he doesn't give up. With you, I remember asking your dad once or twice if he was worried that he didn't have a son. He'd tell me that girls were brighter than boys and then he'd wink at me in that way he had. 'Smarter, Billie. They tend to be smarter. And they know how to think with their hearts. My girl will be just fine.' But then he died. And he hadn't said anything to you. You are his child, so I will be there for you no matter what you do, if it means looking after the shop and babysitting when the time comes — or marching into strange battles. You lead, Danielle Cafferty, and I will follow. But as to Quinn . . . I can tell you only that he is a good man. Almost reminds me of a medieval warrior. Someone as unique as the things in your father's private collection. But you — you have to find your own path. Make your decisions. Learn the ways of your father — if you choose." He took a long swallow, finishing his tea. "Thank you. Now we really need to sleep. Or I need to sleep." He smiled weakly. "I'm not as young as I once was. In fact, I may not be the squire anymore who should be running behind you, carrying your lance and shield."

Impulsively, Danni rose and kissed his cheek. "I'd have no other squire, Billie. No other."

That obviously pleased him, although he lowered his head so she wouldn't see.

They left the tea service in the sink for morning. Arm in arm, they climbed slowly up the stairs. Danni went back to bed, encouraging Wolf to jump up beside her. The dog was doubtful at first, but then curled at her side.

She couldn't help wondering what had turned an alcoholic womanizer into a medieval knight.

Curiosity kept her awake for a while.

But again, when she slept, she slept deeply.

The sun had risen high when she opened her eyes.

CHAPTER 9

Quinn's first stop in the morning was the rectory; he wanted to talk to Father Ryan and find out how Bo Ray — Butt Kiss — was doing.

Ryan opened the door, apparently expecting him.

"No Wolf?" he asked.

"I left Wolf with Danni last night," Quinn told him.

"I have coffee on. Come in," Ryan said.

Quinn followed him into the rectory's homey kitchen. Father Ryan poured a cup and handed it to him. "You hungry?"

Quinn shook his head. "I ate a few of those power bar things — they taste like cardboard but they fill you up. So, how is Bo Ray? And for that matter, how are you — since I dumped the junkie on you."

Ryan smiled. "I've got him in the hospital — under an assumed name and under guard. He's cleaned up, by the way. He's a worn-out, skinny young man, but he looks better. Good-looking kid, actually. Pretty smart, well-read and all that. If he got it together, he could shake up the world. Or at least contribute to his own community."

"Well, let's hope."

"You came out all right," Ryan pointed out.

Quinn shrugged uncomfortably. "Dying kind of makes you want to watch it, you know?"

Ryan nodded without saying anything else on the matter. "How'd the night go?" he asked.

Quinn told him what had happened.

"I can see how Eyes might be in on this," Ryan said. "He plays the generous, charitable businessman — but he's out there campaigning for anything that might line his pockets. He has a lot of workers who . . . well, they stick it out because they have to. He's cruel and rude, and treats maids and anyone doing a menial task as if they're no better than slaves. He's talked about running for public office."

"How could he be elected if he's an ass — and everyone knows it?" Quinn asked.

"Politics, I guess. Make the voters think he's the lesser of two evils?"

"I don't doubt that Eyes is in on this.

But . . . I'm trying to figure out how he'd even know about the bust or where he'd get the idea that this object would help him create a political campaign. Besides, he's really dirty. Wouldn't the cops be able to come up with *something* against him?"

"As far as I know, that's been the problem for years. The cops don't have anything on him. He pays his bodyguards, security goons, really well. They protect him. Whenever anything around him smacks of the illegal, one of his employees has taken the rap. Not a single one has ever turned on him."

"But now people are dying," Quinn said.

"The dead don't talk, do they? Not on the witness stand, anyway."

Quinn had to agree with that.

He left the rectory and drove to the police station to check in on Sam.

Larue assured him that the man was doing well, happily playing cards, checkers and chess with the various officers watching over him.

"They tell me he's a heck of a chess player," Larue said. "So, where are you going from here?"

"I'm just planning to observe humanity."

Larue looked down with a shudder. "Try

not to make your . . . observing illegal, will you?"

"I'll try not to," Quinn said, grinning. "But you do know that's why I quit the force."

"Quinn —"

"I'll stay on the right side of the law!" Quinn told him. "Did you get anything from the guy who was shot in the leg the other night?"

"Sure. He's still in the hospital, howling. His description of the shooter is 'Big guy. I think he was white. Might've been mixed. Probably around thirty. Maybe forty. He had hair. No, he was balding a little. He was wearing a hoodie. Maybe it was a long-sleeved tee.' "

"And no one saw anyone racing away from the cemetery, either, right?"

Larue shook his head. "Thing is, if you're part of the criminal element in certain areas, there are all kinds of holes you can crawl into. We find them eventually — and more holes pop up. You can't go knocking on every door in the city. Well, you could, but we don't have the manpower. I do have detectives crawling the streets. Watching. Listening."

Quinn thanked him and left.

Outside, he looked at his watch. He hadn't

wanted to call or waken Danni yet; it had been a late night. He smiled, wondering how she was doing with Wolf — and how Wolf was doing with her.

He hoped she hadn't fed him too much junk.

He headed over to the Central Business District. He could eat, and if he found the right restaurant, he might run into a few of those who worked — in one way or another — for Eyes.

When Danni woke, she showered quickly and hurried down to take the dog out to the courtyard. She made herself coffee and was in the kitchen when Jane came to join her.

She knew Jane often seemed strange to people who came into the shop. They sold some of the weirdest things in the world, along with antiques, art and more typical collectibles, but Jane was the preppiest-looking person in the world. An aging preppie . . . Today she wore a blue dress with a Peter Pan collar, little black pumps, and her hair was pulled back in a neat bun. She sent Danni a troubled frown. "You bought a dog?" she asked. "I know you miss your father, but buying a dog that size . . . you might have given it a bit more thought."

"Oh, he's not mine — and don't be afraid of him. He belongs to that man. Michael Quinn. He was in the other day." She gave Jane a rueful smile. "He's my guard dog, I guess, for the moment."

Jane nodded. "I'm not that much of an animal person. But he's sitting very nicely by your feet. Hello, boy," she said.

The dog stared at Jane with his wolfish eyes. Jane didn't try to pet him.

"Well, it *is* your shop," Jane murmured. She looked at Danni worriedly. "I read about all the bad things that've been happening and I haven't seen much of you, lately. Are you okay?"

"I'm fine, Jane."

"But you need a monster dog to protect you?"

"I really like the dog!"

"Okay," Jane said. She shivered, making Danni think of a nervous terrier, but managed to speak bravely. "If you need me, need my help, you know I'm here."

"Of course, Jane. Thank you!"

"I believe Mrs. Simon's daughter is in town. There was a little piece about her in the paper. Anyway, I was checking up on the place before locking the doors last night and I peeked in your studio. That painting you did of Gladys is wonderful. So beautiful and elegant. I was thinking . . . maybe you'd like to give it to her daughter."

Danni started; she'd forgotten all about the painting she'd been working on when the woman — whom she was sure she'd never seen before, unless it was in the society pages — had walked into the store. She forced a smile. "What a nice idea," she said.

Jane smiled in return and went back out to the shop.

Danni drained her coffee, then walked through to her studio to look at the painting again. The resemblance to Gladys was uncanny. "I did see her picture somewhere," she said aloud. "I *must* have. And she was a beautiful character to paint. So much kindness in her eyes and such strength in her cheekbones!"

At her side, Wolf stirred. She absently set a hand on his head.

She was more disturbed by the fact that she'd been painting Gladys when the woman walked into the store than by her night in the cemetery.

Jane had made a really nice suggestion, though. Danni had something of a name in the local art world, so the painting might be appreciated by someone who'd just lost her mother.

After losing her father.

Yes, she would give it to Cecelia Simon. That would also get the painting far away from her.

As she studied it, she felt her cell phone ringing in her pocket. She answered and heard Natasha's voice.

"It's Natasha. If you have a chance, take a walk down here."

"Okay. What's up?"

"A friend came in, reminding me that I promised to officiate as priestess at a ceremony for my parish this evening. There were some people who followed — I can't talk now. Come on by and I'll try to explain why I believe you two should come now . . . *and* tonight."

"I'll be right there," Danni promised.

She decided that Wolf would like a walk and a little socializing. Natasha had said *you two,* and she probably wasn't referring to Wolf. Natasha assumed that she was working with Quinn. Well, she was. She was somewhat surprised that she hadn't heard from Quinn; she had his dog, after all.

She slipped out through the courtyard, Wolf at her heels.

Tourists abounded on the streets. Spring in New Orleans seemed to bring people in droves, although, to Danni's mind, there was nothing wrong with winter in her city. It could get cold, but not like it did in the north. The weather was pleasant and the shops were decked out for the festive season — a beautiful time in the Crescent City.

She moved down Royal, pausing here and there as someone exclaimed over Wolf and she stopped to allow him the attention he deserved. Restaurants and bars seemed to be booming, which was a relief, since they depended on tourism to survive.

Jimmy Joe Justin was on the street and she found herself stopping again. Jimmy Joe was an incredibly talented man. He played several instruments — sometimes, a couple at once, such as the harmonica and guitar. He had a voice like honeyed silk and could sing jazz, pop, rock and show tunes. She'd told him once that he should have been appearing at the biggest venues in the country; he told her he loved the French Quarter and the people there, and did just fine with the money that piled up in his guitar case.

She threw in five dollars, then hurried on to Natasha's shop.

When she arrived, Natasha was in the courtyard surrounded by a tour group. "Voodoo really has many names," she was telling them. "Vodun, vaudin, vudu . . . and more. It's a religion that brought roots from

Africa to the New World when the slave trade came here and then it drew upon the Catholicism of the French and Spaniards who were often the masters at the time. In voodoo, there is a supreme being — God as so many know Him. But in voodoo, He is far away — or perhaps He's really busy. We can all imagine that, with the state of the world today, yes?"

Laughter followed her words. Natasha went on to explain. "Like many Christians, we seek intervention through saints — many of the same saints. On our altars you see images of angels and saints. We are a flourishing religion. There are about eighty million worshippers worldwide. Men may be priests and women may be priestesses. Members join a parish, just as many Christians do. Those who are true believers do not practice *petro* — or the black form of voodoo that would do harm to others. We also believe the soul or spirit has two parts — *ti-bon-ange* and *gros-bon-ange*. We also believe the spirit lives on, but that there must be a ceremony a year and a day after a loved one has departed to see that both halves of the spirit are united. We do believe in possession by spirits, and we dance and sing to let them possess us so we may hear their messages. Most religions are very good

— a positive voice. It's what men do with them that can be bad. Don't assume that what you see about voodoo in movies is true! If you were curious about Islam or Judaism or Christianity or any other religion, you'd ask someone who's involved, who knows. So feel free to ask questions. We love to share our beliefs!"

Natasha had seen Danni and Wolf at the back of the courtyard. She invited the tour group to enjoy her shop and then started to make her way over to Danni. She was frequently stopped by the curious — just as Danni was stopped by a number of dog lovers.

At last the courtyard began to clear out, and Natasha finally reached her. "Thank you for coming so fast. I'm afraid you didn't come quite fast enough, though. I thought he'd stay, but I'm sure he'll be at the ceremony tonight."

"He?" Danni asked in confusion.

"Carl White. His street name was among the ones Quinn gave me — Big-Ass Mo Fo."

"What's the ceremony?"

"Gerome Vasquez is a parishioner of mine. His brother, Andrei, died a year and a day ago. As you know, the *ti-bon-ange,* or little angel of the soul, does not rest unless the *gros-bon-ange* is brought back, so that the soul might find peace and rest as one. I couldn't tell if Carl was with Gerome when he came in or if he knew him and knew what was going on . . . or if he just happened to be here. But I suspect he'll show up for the ceremony tonight. It'll be out on the old bayou road heading west toward Houma. That's where the peristyle we use for our worship is located. You've been there, although you might not remember."

"Yes, I've been there. I came with my father," Danni murmured.

"You must come tonight. And you'll see if others come . . . searching for something they won't get from us, but searching there nonetheless." She rolled her eyes and grinned. "Our city is filled with *everything* — vampires, spiritual vampires, frat boys and girls, a 'Cult of the Werewolf' and so on. But for some reason, tourists all believe that they'll see the dead burst out of graves or a human sacrifice if they come to a voodoo ritual. Or they think they'll find black voodoo, and although it exists, it's never among the true followers. But when people hear through the grapevine that there's a ceremony, they show up."

"We'll both go, Natasha," Danni assured her. "When is it?"

"We'll begin at eleven. It's as much for

the survivors as the deceased. Our belief is that if we don't join the soul, there may be sickness and evil and other bad things around the loved ones left behind by the dead."

"Thank you, Natasha," Danni said. "I'll get hold of Quinn and we'll be there. I remember where it is."

She realized, as she walked Wolf from Natasha's shop, that she was glad of the excuse to call.

Ridiculous. She had the man's dog. She could call him anytime!

She started to punch in his number but before she could finish, she bumped into someone and heard her name exclaimed with pleasure.

"Danni!"

It was Jenny LaFleur, one of her close friends from high school, with whom she'd reconnected when she returned to New Orleans to live. Jenny's eyes were bright with laughter and excitement. "Hey, I was going to call you and make sure you hadn't forgotten! You *have* forgotten, haven't you? I can tell. It's tonight!"

Danni looked at her blankly. "Danni!" Jenny blurted, hurt in her voice. "Brad and I have that gig tonight on Decatur Street. We're using the backdrops you painted for us and we're going to promote the shop and your art. Remember? You promised to come." She giggled. "We're counting on our friends, you know?"

Friends.

Yes, she actually had them. She'd forgotten with everything that had happened since Gladys Simon walked through her door.

"Oh, Jenny —"

"Don't you *dare* tell me you're not coming!" Jenny said. "We're finally being recognized as a talent in our own hometown. Please come," Jenny begged.

Jenny came to every one of her gallery showings. Brad had been the musician of their class, a clown when he was young. He was now in love with Jenny, but had always been a friend to Danni, as well.

"I'm so sorry. Things have been a bit crazy lately."

"Your dad wouldn't want you sitting at home, pining for him, Danni. He was a great guy — and so proud of you. He wanted you to live your life. Tonight will be great. And if it's not great . . . we'll *really* need you!"

"I . . . just forgot. What time are you on?"

"Nine o'clock."

Danni nodded. "I may have to cut out a bit early, but I'll be there," she promised.

"What a great dog," Jenny said, bending down to pet Wolf. "When did you get him? He's huge!" She giggled again. "He must be a menace in the shop, with that tail. He's beautiful, though."

"He's not mine. Belongs to a friend."

"Who?"

Danni waved a hand in the air. "Oh, I don't think you know him. I'm sure you'll meet him at some point. Anyway, I've got to get going. I'll be there, clapping and cheering my fool head off, okay?"

"Better be!" Jenny told her. "Okay, see you soon!"

As she walked down Royal to her home and shop, Danni lost her enthusiasm for calling Quinn. Yes, she'd been given a lead.

And now she'd be saying, "Hey, I might have learned something about all the horror going on. But we have to stop by a bar first and listen to some music. . . ."

She kept walking. Well, he hadn't called her, either. Maybe he was on to something himself. Maybe he didn't intend to call her.

Maybe she was supposed to head out to the voodoo ceremony by herself. Alone.

She wouldn't be alone, she reminded herself.

She had Wolf.

■ ■ ■ ■

Quinn made his first stop in Brandt Shumaker's offices.

They were modern offices, all glass and chrome, the walls lined with posters of properties the firm was handling and pictures of oil investments, along with propaganda on why the oil digs and platforms were so important to the survival of Louisiana. He went through a secretary and then an assistant, and when he'd convinced both of them that he had a small fortune to invest, he was led to Shumaker's office.

He wasn't surprised by the office; while it was glass and chrome like the rest of the place, the walls held custom cabinets with a variety of antique and intriguing objects — including shrunken skulls from New Guinea, South American tribal spears and Etruscan sacrificial bowls.

Shumaker rose when Quinn entered. He wasn't a tall man, maybe five-ten, broad and stocky with graying hair and a square face. He wasn't particularly handsome but he was dressed to the nines in an Armani suit and exuded an air of power and authority that gave him a certain appeal. He extended his hand to Quinn. "Mr. Quinn! I've heard of you. Way back when, I thought we'd be seeing you pick up a Super Bowl ring!"

Quinn took the indicated seat before Shumaker's desk. "Ah, well, I tried living a bit too hard when I was a bit too young," he told Shumaker.

"A regular bad boy," Shumaker agreed, friendly as he took his own chair again, folded his hands on top of the desk and studied Quinn. "I heard you ran off to the military and then became a cop."

"Yes, but I went out on my own a few years ago," Quinn said.

Shumaker lifted a brow.

"I'm a private investigator."

Shumaker appeared to digest that information, still smiling. Then his dark eyes grew hard, and Quinn felt a change in the man that was palpable. "So, you're looking for a major property investment?"

"Yes, land seems to be the only thing worth buying these days. Even when the market drops, if you can hold on, you have something more than a piece of paper. The stock market is just wicked."

"That's bull, Quinn, and you know it. You're investigating me. My employees aren't exactly idiots, but apparently I haven't found the sharpest knives in the drawer for my office. Private investigators don't make the kind of money those dunces think you're about to spend. So, what the hell is it, Quinn? I'm going to have you thrown out — but I'm curious. Who sent you here?"

Quinn smiled. "You better hire tougher dunces in the office, Shumaker, if you plan to throw me out. I'll go of my own volition. But you're curious? No one sent me. I'm here because there's a trail of dead, Shumaker, and your name comes up in connection with this trail. The cops can't touch you — yet — because you hire thugs to get the blood on their hands. But you deal drugs as well as land, and you're involved in something you can't begin to understand, something that will eat you alive. Let me say that I'm here with fair warning." He pointed to the shrunken skulls. "It's obvious that you're into collectibles, Shumaker. Be careful. The collectible you're after intends to collect you."

Shumaker rose, his face a mottled shade of purple. He set his hands on the desk and leaned toward Quinn. "You want to warn me? Let me warn *you,* Mr. Quinn. I'm a legitimate businessman. You won't ever find anything on me. In fact, I'm going to run for office and I'll probably wind up running this state. People love me. I give them what they want and what they need. I'll have followers up the wazoo and, I promise you, I'll be untouchable. So I suggest you stay out of my way. I also intend to report that you threatened me. Which you have. I'm going to get my legal team on this, and they'll see to it that you're not allowed within two hundred yards of me. I don't know what you think you'll get from me, but there's nothing for you here. Now, Mr. Quinn, I do believe you should leave my office."

Quinn stood, too. "Shumaker, I believe I just got exactly what I wanted. Thanks for your time," he said.

He left the office, thanking the staff pleasantly as he did.

He felt that he did have exactly what he needed, but he figured he'd keep at it. He was in the area, so he decided to try a few of the restaurants and bars frequented by the employees at Shumaker Properties.

He was nearly coffee-ed out, but he headed into a place that was known for its excellent and, most importantly, cheap po'boys. The restaurant was not at all fancy and situated in the far corner of a not-very-attractive 1930s building. As the aroma suggested, the food was the appeal. He realized the power bars he'd eaten that morning had worn off. He certainly didn't need more coffee, so he opted for a shrimp po'boy and a soda.

A group of five men and women in cheap business suits were situated in a vinyl-seated booth in the corner. Beneath his jacket one was wearing a tailored white shirt with Shumaker Properties embroidered on the collar.

Payday at last. Well, maybe. If they said anything.

Quinn found a vacant seat within hearing distance. He took his chair just in time to hear one of the two women in the quintet say, ". . . weirder than ever. And meaner."

"Hush!" the young woman next to her said, glancing around. "I think the bastard has spies everywhere."

"Yeah? Well, I don't see any of his 'security' force around now," an older man said.

"He told me he's had a few late nights — working, of course," another said. He shook his head. "He *is* meaner than ever. One of guys at the shop who works on that limo of his came in and talked about the underbelly of the car being scratched up by going over a construction site or something — told him to watch where he was driving if he wants the car to work all the time at a moment's notice. Shumaker went into a fury at the guy and said it wasn't his place to tell him where he could and couldn't drive." He looked around and lowered his voice. "Then one of those big-ass goons he keeps on as 'security' came into his office. Sandy — you know, his secretary — told me later that she heard the guy from the garage got driven off the road. And Shumaker's been seeing some strange woman. Every time she comes in, Sandy says, he goes on and on about how he's going to be mayor, and then governor, and then what the hell, he'll rule the world!"

"I wish I could afford to quit," one of the women muttered.

"I just might quit whether I can afford it or not. Hell, I'm ready to tap dance on the street and see if I can collect some money in a hat," the older man said.

The second woman spoke softly. "Don't quit. Franco Quinero in accounting quit two weeks ago. Odd — he had a car accident, too. I'll bet he'd tell us he got driven off the road if he could. But he can't, since he's in a coma."

Quinn sat and listened to them; the rest of their conversation consisted of worries about their health and the economy.

He was startled when his phone rang.

He was annoyed at first, and then dismayed at the sense of pleasure that filled him when he heard Danni's voice.

"Quinn? Where are you?"

"Eating a po'boy," he said. He was sure that the members of the group didn't have hearing as acute as his but he wanted to act natural.

"Eating a po'boy?" She sounded confused. "Well, *I've* been working."

"Really. Good. With Wolf."

There was silence for a minute. "Yes, with Wolf. Finish your po'boy," she told him. "Then get your sorry ass over here."

She hung up before he could respond. As he closed his phone, he felt a smile slip onto his face. She was, after all, proving to be Angus's daughter.

"You're mad at me for eating a po'boy?" Quinn asked Danni. She was evidently in a huff. Strange thing was, he still felt like smiling. She was in a *regal* huff, and she was beautiful when she seemed cool and controlled — and steaming with emotion beneath. Her eyes were blue rockets, her posture was rigid, and yet she paced her studio with long strides that betrayed her agitation.

"Silly me. I had it in my head that if you hadn't called, you were pursuing the truth, stamping out terror — saving the universe."

He nodded. "I was."

"By eating a po'boy?"

"It was a shrimp po'boy, really good," he said. "Danni, I was in the Central Business District, hanging around a place where I figured Shumaker employees had to eat."

"Did you learn anything?"

He shrugged. "I think there's a woman involved. Isn't there always?" he teased.

The glance she shot his way suggested that she was not amused.

He grew serious. "It seems a woman's been coming to his office of late. Every time she comes, he runs around saying he's going to rule the world. And . . . the undercarriage of his car was roughed up. I'd say he was definitely prowling around in the construction areas of the Ninth Ward. His temper has flared more than once and it seems that anyone on his bad side ends up in the hospital. Or dead."

"They told you all this?"

"I'm a talented eavesdropper. Your turn."

"We're going to a ceremony tonight. A voodoo ceremony."

"Oh?"

"Natasha called me. She's officiating at a ceremony for a member of her parish. His brother died a year and a day ago. And before that —"

He cut her off. "She thinks someone in her parish might be involved in this?"

"We're fixated on Eyes. But she told me that Big-Ass Mo Fo was at her place today — and she's pretty sure he'll show up at the ceremony."

"Eyes could be in on it. As far as he goes, I'm thinking in another direction."

"Oh?"

"I stopped at Shumaker Properties today."

"And?"

"He was defensive. He wants to get a restraining order out on me for threatening him."

"Did you threaten him?"

"I warned him."

"Quinn —"

"I'm not lying! I just said I thought he was looking for something dangerous. And he instantly became very angry. So . . ." He paused. "They could be in on it together — Shumaker and another of our suspects or even someone else," he said. "Who knows? But we'll definitely go to the voodoo ceremony."

She watched him oddly, then took a breath.

"And before that, right before, we have to go see a group playing down on Decatur."

"We think it has something to do with musicians?" he asked.

She shook her head, flushing slightly. "I have to be there. They're good friends, they've been to all my art openings and . . . I have to go."

"Can we make both?"

"They're playing at nine. The ceremony doesn't begin until eleven."

He was thoughtful for a moment. Bo Ray was in rehab, Sam Johnson was in protective custody. Two of the other names he'd gotten were of men who were in prison. That left Eyes and Big-Ass Mo Fo.

Danni was still watching him, stiff, straight, regal — beautiful. She was, beneath the pride of her stance, hoping he'd agree with her.

"I love a good musical group," he told her.

He started suddenly. He could have sworn he'd heard a sound just outside her studio door.

But Wolf was with them. Wolf was sleeping; he hadn't moved. If there'd been any danger, the dog would have gone into a frenzy.

Still, he stepped over to the door and looked out. Nothing there. His hypersenses were on heightened alert and not really working, he thought. They were overworking, if anything. Of course, he was never completely sure if he actually had hypersenses. After he'd flatlined at the hospital and begun his long journey back to health, he'd seemed to have more strength, to see more clearly — to hear with greater clarity.

Maybe it had been so long since he'd been clearheaded, in those years before his death, that it just *seemed* he had hypersenses.

"What is it?" Danni asked.

"Nothing."

"Are you sure?"

He nodded, eyeing the dog. "So, we'll go down to Decatur this evening," he said.

"I really just need to show up and stay for a bit — and clap a lot."

As they started to leave the room, he hesitated and looked back at the painting of Gladys Simon.

"I'm going to give it to Cecelia Simon. Jane suggested I do that. I thought it sounded like a nice idea," Danni said.

"Yes, nice," Quinn agreed.

They left the room, but before he closed the door, he looked at the painting again.

She was definitely Angus Cafferty's daughter.

CHAPTER 10

The bar on Decatur was old. The building had housed apartments since the mid-1800s and still did.

The bar was next to a souvenir shop. Just as it had housed apartments from the time it was built, it had housed shops — and restaurants and bars.

Danni had always liked the bar. It combined the best of the old with the new in a way that created living history and a comfortable environment. The bar itself had been there since the establishment was opened as a tavern. Booths were old, but covered with new upholstery. The stage was about a foot and half off the ground and, when they arrived, Jenny and Brad were just finishing the setup, along with their drummer and bassist. The group stopped their sound check long enough to say hello. Of course, Jenny had shouted her name with a whoop from the stage as soon as she'd seen her enter.

Danni swung around in Jenny's exuberant hug and then she did the same with Brad, and — what the heck — she knew Steve, the drummer, and Luis, the bassist, so she greeted them with warm hugs, too. When she was back on the ground, she turned to introduce Quinn, except that Jenny was already talking to him. "I know you — I mean, I know about you. Wow, that's not coming out right. You're Michael Quinn, one of the most brilliant quarterbacks to go through our high school and then you were a college darling and then —" She broke off, blinking.

"Hey, man," Brad said, stepping in and shaking Quinn's hand. "I heard you died on the table, but they said you made a miraculous comeback and would make a full recovery. But you never went back to the game."

Quinn was pleasant to Brad and Jenny, giving Jenny that smile that had surely collected hearts all his life and grimacing as he replied to Brad. "No more football. I went into the military, got out, joined the P.D. and finished up my degree."

"So you're a cop now?" Jenny asked.

"Worse," Quinn said solemnly. "A private investigator."

They laughed at that. "We've got to open at nine on the dot," Brad said.

"Go, go, finish your setup," Jenny told him. She stood back, looking at Danni with happiness. "I was so afraid you were going to ditch me!"

"We can't stay long, but . . ."

"Long enough to give us an audience until the drunks and tourists come in!" Jenny said. "Thank you, thank you."

"It's just that if we disappear in the middle of one of your sets, please don't be upset."

"Grab a table. Looks like we're actually getting people," Brad said.

"It's a bar. Of course, we're going to get people!" Jenny scoffed as they returned to the stage.

Quinn pointed out a table where they'd have a good view and not be directly under the speakers. He asked Danni what she'd like to drink and she asked for a zinfandel. She slid into the booth they'd chosen, then casually turned to watch the door. There were obviously tourists walking in, but she noted that a few of her other friends from days gone by were arriving, as well.

When Quinn joined her again with her glass of wine, he had a dark beverage for himself.

"What is that?" she asked him.

"Coke," he told her.

"I guess I shouldn't have gotten this since we're heading out to a ceremony. I'm glad you're the designated driver."

He shrugged. "Not to worry. I just don't do much these days," he said.

"Much of what?"

He'd slid into the booth next to her and was watching the stage. "Don't do much of anything, really. Don't do drugs, seldom drink." He turned to look at her. "Let's see, I went from being a decent kid with great grades lucky enough to have size and physical coordination — to an idiot who took every pill and bottle offered to him and fooled around with all kinds of girls, careless of anyone who actually cared about me. And then I died. I had alcohol poisoning *and* I was hit by a car. My folks nearly had heart attacks themselves that night. Hey, guess what else I figured out the night I died?"

"What?"

"I like the world when I see it through an unaltered mind. Okay, sometimes the world sucks. But music is great when you really hear it."

She smiled at that. "Do you play anything?"

"Guitar — but not like your friend, I'm

sure. You?"

"Piano. I had a lot of lessons. My dad wanted me to learn the bagpipes, but he tried to start me so young, I couldn't hold the damned thing, so . . . I went to the piano."

She fell silent as Jenny welcomed the crowd, announced the band and then looked at her and thanked special friends for coming.

Jenny and Brad and their group — the Night Walkers — were good. They did a number of covers that were loved in the city, but they did some original songs, too. They played for forty-five minutes, then took a break.

Brad and Jenny came over to join them. Jenny, flushed with pleasure, said, "It's going well, isn't it?"

"Great," Quinn told them. He asked Brad something about his guitar; Brad got up enthusiastically and encouraged Quinn to follow him.

Jenny leaned toward Danni. "Oh, my God! Where did you *meet* him? I've seen his old pictures in the hall at the school, you know, in uniform. And I saw him in dozens of news stories years ago, but . . . wow. He's better in real life. He's so tall. He's so . . . built. He's so mysterious — I mean, he was

247

a candidate for either rehab or prison . . . and here he is. With you!"

"He was a friend of my dad's. I didn't know it until recently," Danni explained.

"I guess you got him at a good point. Strange, he was such a local superstar in the sports arena — and I think, in his heyday, he even did some commercials. For some brand of sneakers. He was given just about everything in the world, and I guess he took it all as his due. He went through women like toilet paper, but they still flocked around him. Hey! Has he told you about his near-death experience? Wait, how can it be *near*-death? He flatlined on the table, but then he came back. So, what would you call that?"

Danni lifted her shoulders in a shrug. "He doesn't like to talk about it. But he got a second chance. Maybe a second chance makes you clean up?"

Jenny grimaced. "I don't know. We had a few friends who had miraculous second chances — but they couldn't do it. They're dead now. But, hey! Are you two an item? That is so neat!"

"No, no, we're not an item. We're . . . friends," Danni said. They *were* friends; they'd gotten that far.

"A P.I.! How cool," Jenny said. She leaned

even closer, a mischievous look on her face. "You should be an item. But then again, you threw Elliott Carver away as if he were . . . toilet paper."

He was! she thought.

Her last half-serious relationship had been with a local filmmaker. He'd let his successes go to his head. He became rude in restaurants and pretty much heedless of anyone but himself.

"Elliott and I saw life differently," she said.

Jenny laughed. "I haven't seen him in a while. He used to hang out on Frenchman for a while, but I guess he's above us locals now. So, what about this guy?"

Danni raised her eyebrows. Quinn could come across like a bulldozer, but that was only when he was in hot pursuit of someone — or something.

"So far," she said, "he seems to be very polite in restaurants."

Brad and Quinn came back to the table then. Quinn looked at his watch and gave Danni a questioning glance.

Danni saw that the place was filling up; people were three-deep at the bar.

"We're going to get out of here. Looks like you're doing just fine."

Jenny sent her a happy smile. They went through the ritual of saying goodbye, with hugs and handshakes all around. Brad and Jenny returned to the stage, and Quinn and Danni slipped out the door.

"Thanks for that," Danni said.

He looked at her with a smile. "I like music. No problem. Your friends seem nice."

"They are."

"And curious."

She looked back at him. "Well, people *are* going to be curious, you know."

He nodded. "We don't ever really live down the past."

"But you've redeemed the present — and future."

"Said like a true schoolmarm," he told her. "Very uplifting."

"Hey!"

A few minutes later, they were driving out on I-10. "Wolf is all right at your place?" Quinn asked.

"Billie loves him."

"I get the impression he makes Jane nervous."

"She's never had a dog . . . I don't think. And besides, she leaves the shop by eight every night. If we're open late, Billie closes up." She turned to face him. "You never left Wolf with my father."

He kept his eyes on the road.

"Oh, I see. You didn't feel my father

needed protection. He could take care of himself."

He seemed about to speak but she could tell he wasn't sure what to say.

"Never mind — I get it. My father *could* take care of himself. We need to go back to a shooting range. And maybe I should get a weapon."

"Not until you know how and when to use one," he said.

"That's reasonable."

They exchanged another smile.

They really had become friends. And quickly. Maybe running around in a cemetery, beneath a cemetery, in fetid water and in dusty tombs helped form a lasting bond.

Quinn seemed to know where he was going; she assumed he'd been out to a ceremony or two.

The road that led to Natasha's peristyle was nothing but dirt and rock — and flooded in bad weather. She owned the property, though, and Danni knew that over the years, no matter what the weather or circumstances, Natasha had been available to her parishioners.

The peristyle was a hut with a thatched roof that had been repaired and rebuilt dozens of times. The sides were open and the platform flooring was about five feet above the ground. It could accommodate a number of crates and dozens of people. There were steps and a ramp for the aged or handicapped.

When they arrived, there were already many people in attendance. The majority were African-American or of mixed race, but there were at least ten who would be labeled white. A few of the parishioners viewed them as outsiders, but they were immediately greeted by Jeziah, Natasha's assistant, and it seemed that once he'd okayed them, they were all right.

They hadn't been there long, conversing with others — accepting some kind of drink that tasted like pure rotgut alcohol — before Jez began the setup. The crowd naturally made way for him, and he announced their intentions for the night: to put to rest the full spirit of the departed. He spoke about the voodoo belief in, respect for and love of their ancestors, and he spoke about Natasha. At a very young age, she'd been bitten by a snake — a snake that would kill most people but she had survived. And she was alive with the powerful spirit of the snake; the snake was her *loa.*

Then Natasha appeared. She spoke in Creole, addressing the crowd, and Danni tried to follow her words. She talked about the deceased, about his goodness as a human being. She said he must be given the rest he deserved. It was the fault of his surviving family if his spirit became sick as it wandered, if it created sickness among his family and friends, and brought them harm. Thankfully, the deceased had a loving family. They would ask that the departed man's *gros-bon-ange* join them that night and meld with the *ti-bon-ange,* so that eternal peace might be found beneath the all-powerful spirit through the gentle guidance of *Mawu,* the moon, and *Lisa,* the sun, both parts of the great Nana Buluku, male and female aspects of the supreme being.

And then she was offered a massive snake — a constrictor rather than a viper — and she began to dance. Other snakes were taken from crates by several people, following Natasha's movements. As she moved, drumbeats sounded, and soon, everyone was joining her in the exotic pulse of the dance.

Danni didn't understand all the words being spoken, but she was carried away with the others, moving on the platform. Quinn, doing the same, towered over almost everyone.

Jez danced near Danni to warn her, "Do not touch Natasha, because she is the priestess here. It is bad luck. Some believe it can cause injury or death."

She nodded; he moved on. The dancing continued. She was surprised by the power of the chanting and the beat as they rose up. And she was astounded to feel as if energy did rip through her, as if she were part of the whole. There was definitely a carnal feel to the movements — sensual, fluid, erotic — although no one had disrobed. No one even touched another.

The drumbeats rose to crescendo. Then they halted.

Many of the dancers fell to the floor.

Natasha cried out and bent over.

All on the platform were silent.

But then Danni heard sobbing from the rear of the platform. She looked in that direction.

She didn't know how she hadn't seen the man before. He was enormous, about Quinn's height, and broad with heavy shoulders, enormous legs and a massive presence.

He had to be Big-Ass Mo Fo.

She realized that Quinn had seen him, too, that he'd slipped through the crowd to get closer to the big man.

She'd been distracted; she heard Natasha speaking again. She was using some kind of feathered talisman to wave over the crowd as she spoke.

Then she heard people speaking the way they'd speak on the street, greeting one another, saying goodbye, making plans to meet for lunch. . . .

Conversations that might be heard anywhere.

People said respectful goodbyes to Natasha. The crowd thinned.

Danni heard sobbing again from the rear corner of the platform.

The giant known as Big-Ass Mo Fo — Carl White — was on his knees. Quinn knelt beside him, speaking gently.

Natasha, too, heard the sound, and sent away the last of her parishioners with a somber nod that assured them she cared for them, but that she was needed.

Danni felt an urge to join the small group in the most quiet and nonintrusive way possible. When she reached them, she felt as if the world had gone away. It was quiet in the bayou, other than the man's sobbing and the sounds of insects and the occasional splash as a fish jumped or a gator thrashed by.

She went down on her knees by Natasha, facing the man. Natasha was speaking to him in Creole; her words were so quickly spoken Danni became lost. She saw that Quinn was looking at her.

Natasha suddenly spoke in English. "Come, we'll go to the house. This may take some time."

Danni didn't know what house she meant but taking her cue from Quinn she rose. Natasha led the way. She paused to speak with Jez, who was collecting the talismans they'd used that night and securing the snakes in their crates to go in the back of his truck. He nodded gravely and kept up his task.

"Come," Natasha said again.

It was a good thing that Quinn was tall and fit. The big man leaned on him heavily, still muttering in Creole as they moved through the growth by the swamp. Natasha led them along an overgrown trail to a wooden shack that sat on pilings just over the bayou. She went up the steps, pausing to get matches and a lantern from the porch. She struck a match and lit the lantern, then let them into the little shack.

It was one room. There were old upholstered chairs across from a fireplace, a cot covered with an antique quilt to the side, and in the far back corner of the room, Danni could see a water pump, a few cabinets and a counter.

"It's chilly. Perhaps a fire?" Natasha said to Quinn.

He nodded and began to build up kindling to light the logs. Natasha brought Carl to a chair, urging him down with a soothing singsong voice as she spoke to him in Creole. Danni struggled to follow her speech. Natasha was telling him that Quinn and Danni could help him.

Natasha went to the water pump, filled a kettle and returned to set it over the fire that was beginning to burn.

"Tea. Tea is always good," she said, reverting to English. "I had a great-great-great-grandfather who was Irish. His ways have come down to us," she said cheerfully.

Quinn stepped away from the fire. He took a seat opposite the big man and nodded to Danni, who sat on Carl's other side.

Natasha checked the tea water and joined them.

"Now, Carl, tell Danni and Quinn what happened. Tell them about Leroy — and the night he was killed."

Carl inhaled, looked at Danni and Quinn, lifted his massive hands and released a long sigh. "I do business, yes. I buy and sell some drugs — nothing dangerous, I swear it. No heroin, no fancy street drugs cut with who-knows-what . . . and I own clubs where women sell their bodies, but only those who choose. They are treated well by me. I have been a bad man, perhaps, in the eyes of many. But I have never been an evil man."

He sounded so sincere, his voice full of emotion.

"We're not judging you, Carl," Quinn told him.

"I have never taken another man's life. I have never ruined a man or a woman. I throw men out if they act with cruelty, you understand? My girls work for me because they know I will protect them and that I am fair and honest."

"Carl, honestly, we're not here to judge or punish you," Quinn said. "But you know something."

"I know that I *don't* know something and that I don't want to — and it's scared the hell out of me!"

"What is it that you don't know?" Quinn asked.

"Start at the beginning," Danni suggested. "You were at Leroy Jenkins's house to buy some drugs when Leroy was talking about breaking into the Simon house, right?"

Carl stared at her a moment and then looked down, his shaved head low. He took a breath. "Leroy, he was talking about something big going on, something that would make Mistress LaBelle and all the other priests and priestesses — and vampire groups, covens and all else — look like child's play. He was going to be richer than Midas. He was going to have all kinds of power, just through breaking in, hurting no one and getting some antique bust. He was bragging like crazy. So I took my stuff, put my order in . . . and left." He inhaled again, and exhaled. "I came back a few days later. When I was almost there, I saw that big black limo Eyes drives around in. He never gets out of the car — I seen the inside of it once. It's all plush and nice, has a refrigerator between the seats in the back and a work tray. He always just sits in there and lets his bodyguards do his dirty work. Anyway, I seen it driving *away* from Leroy's place — after I heard gunfire. So, I didn't go there. No sirree, I was smart and I got myself away as fast as I could."

"But you know the car belonged to Eyes?" Quinn said.

Danni thought he seemed a little disappointed. That he was wondering if they'd gone through all this to discover what they already knew.

Carl nodded solemnly. "I figured I hadn't been seen. That I could just get out — and the police would take things from there.

And the police did come. I heard the sirens while I was heading out. I figured the whole mess wouldn't have anything to do with me."

"But you were wrong?" Danni asked.

He nodded again. "First, I get this message that I didn't think anything about."

"What was the message?" Quinn glanced at Danni. She knew the two men — Carl and Shumaker — hadn't been in collusion, but Shumaker must have recognized the potential in Carl.

Carl spoke at last. "It was a text. It was on my phone." He grinned sheepishly. "I read it a bunch of times after that. It said, 'You could be among the chosen. Give over to the power. Answer to the nature of the beast, and you will survive. You can't handle the power. It will kill you. I know how to wield the power.' "

"Do you still have this message?" Quinn asked him.

Carl reached into his pocket. He produced his cell phone and handed it to Quinn.

"There's probably no service out here," Natasha said, rising to attend to the now-boiling water.

"I can bring up old messages," Quinn murmured, touching various icons on the phone.

Danni watched as he brought up the message. Like Quinn, she looked for an ID. The phone announced that it was Unidentified.

"Then what happened?" Quinn asked.

Carl shrugged. He almost smiled. "Check out my answer."

Quinn's thumb stroked over the phone, bringing up the reply.

She read, " 'Hey, you sorry asshole, I'm all the power I need and I want no beasts in my life. Go fuck yourself.' "

They both looked at Carl, containing grins.

"And then?"

"Then I get a call at work. I have a legitimate business, you know — an office, staff. My secretary put it through. There's some guy on the other end telling me I'm a sinner and that God has already damned me to hell. I have one more chance. Come into the fold with all the fold desires."

"And what did you say?" Quinn asked.

"I said —" he hesitated, looking at Natasha and Danni "— I said again what he should do with himself. So then he tells me I better prepare my soul for an unwelcoming hell — that I know about the bust, and the bust knows about me."

"What did you do?" Danni asked him.

"I hung up."

"And then what?"

"Then one of my girls, Shirley, comes in to see me. She shows me a text message she got from Unidentified Caller. The message said, 'You're going to die because your boss is a Big-Ass Mo Fo.' "

Danni felt a chill seep into her bones. "And?"

Carl White shuddered, and it seemed that the whole shack trembled.

"I told her that she worked for me, that I'd protect her. But . . ." He paused, gazing up at them, his brown eyes damp as if tears threatened again. "But," he said in a whisper. "She died. She died this morning."

"How?" Quinn asked.

Carl swallowed visibly. "Her family called around ten. They don't know exactly what happened. She worked at the club last night until about 3:00 a.m. and then went home. Her cousin went over there early — they were supposed to go to a studio together. He was having her do some backup for a recording. She had a voice like a lark, Shirley."

Quinn leaned forward. "Carl, how did she die?"

"They're doing an autopsy on her. She was dead in her bathtub, eyes open in the water. She drowned, they guess, but how does a girl just get into a bathtub and drown? I guess they're suspecting that she overdosed on drugs, but Shirley was one of those smart girls who didn't do drugs. She wanted to sing, you know? So there's Shirley — a good girl — dead. And I heard about the shoot-ups with Butt Kiss and something going down around Numb Nuts and I figured that this beast, this bust, whatever it is, has my number. But if I'm going to die, I'm going to do it with my high priestess knowing what's been happening and doing the right things for my soul."

Quinn sat back, turning to Danni. "Eyes doesn't have the bust. He thinks one of the others has it."

"He thinks Carl has it."

"Holy Mother!" Carl breathed. "I don't have that *thing*. I'd never have that thing! But if the bastard thinks I've got it, I'm dead. I have faith. I have my faith — this is my faith. Natasha is all goodness and I come to her. But now, I — I'm afraid."

"We're not going to let you die."

Carl shook his head sadly. "Do I look like I'd go easy, man? But there's something out there, and it don't matter how big or tough you are — it can get to you."

Quinn spoke with strength in his voice. "Carl, I don't care how big and bad this thing is — we can fight it. But you've got to trust me."

Natasha had poured mugs of tea and went about serving them as if they were having a social chat.

Carl looked at her beseechingly as she handed him his. "You listen to Quinn, Carl. You listen to him, and you help him and Danni, just like I said."

"First, I need to keep this phone," Quinn said. "I'm pretty sure the caller is using pay-as-you-go phones that can't be traced, but who knows. They have digital teams that can do amazing things."

"Okay." Carl seemed uncertain. "Cops. You gonna call the cops on me? You want me to tell 'em I was buying drugs?"

"This isn't a drug bust, Carl. It's a murder investigation — and much more."

"I'd rather go to hell than Angola State Prison."

"You're not going to prison. Your clubs are legal and no one's going to bust you for pot and cocaine they can't produce. I need —"

He broke off as a phone rang. Danni jumped up and slid a hand into her pocket, but it wasn't her phone that was ringing; it was Natasha's.

She answered it, listened then frowned

and hung up. When she spoke to them, her voice was obviously controlled through force.

"That was Jez. He said there's a car coming down the dirt road." She looked at Quinn. "He made it out to the highway but . . . someone shot at him from the car. They let him go. He's on I-10 heading back to the city. He says he'll call police, but they'll never make it out here in time."

Quinn rose in a flash, putting out the lantern. "Carl . . ." He paused, as if searching for someplace a man of Carl's size might hide. "Let's get outside, under the pilings. Now!"

Although the fire still burned in the hearth, the little place seemed very dark. Danni felt Quinn's hands on her shoulders as he urged her up and out the back door that led to a porch directly over the water. Natasha's place sat partly on land and partly on pilings over the bayou.

A three-quarter moon was up.

Quinn prodded her. She half jumped — and was half pushed — into the bayou.

As the water, cool by night, swept around her, Danni could make out trees, dripping with moss and bowing low as if the weight of the world lay upon them. She sucked in her breath, fighting a wave of panic. She'd grown up in the city, not in the bayou, although she'd been out here now and then — often enough to know that snakes and gators did prowl the area. It was their home, after all.

Her feet sank in muck.

But they'd all plunged into the water in the nick of time.

She heard the rumble of tires over the grass and bracken on the overgrown path.

The high beams of a car nearly blinded her and she sank lower into the water.

She clearly heard car doors opening.

And then the unmistakable snapping of foliage as men exited the car and made their way toward the little shack in the bayou.

CHAPTER 11

Quinn listened as footsteps approached the house. The headlights went off, giving him an advantage in the darkness. He heard the men as they entered the little shack and drew his finger to his lips, hoping that Danni — or any of the others, for that matter — wouldn't cry out if something slithered by in the water.

They were all dead silent.

He waited until he heard the men enter the shack. When they'd done so, he gripped the flooring and heaved himself up. Dripping, he crouched low and moved over to peer through the window.

Two men were in the shack. They both carried guns — Smith & Wesson pistols with silencers, although there was no reason for silencers out here.

They held their guns easily and he had a feeling that they were fairly competent with the weapons.

He debated his next movement, not wanting to shoot men in cold blood. But then again, if he let them, he knew they'd shoot down their little group in the bayou.

"There's no one in here," said the first, the taller of the pair.

"Check under the cot and under that pump," said the smaller, broader man. "They're here somewhere. There are still three cars parked out on the road to that hut thing the voodoo priestess uses. If you see Big-Ass Mo Fo, remember, just wound him. They want him alive. The others — get rid of them any way you can."

As he listened, Quinn realized that he could hear someone moving stealthily around the side, toward the rear of the shack and the porch that stretched out over the bayou.

"Shh!" said the taller guy. "Artie's out there. Something must've caught his attention."

"The back," the shorter one said.

As he spoke, Quinn heard a startled scream from below.

Danni.

He took aim and fired into the house, double, and fast. He had no real shot but was rewarded by a scream as the short guy gripped his calf and the second screeched

— shrieking as he surged forward, hands on his buttocks. Quinn turned and saw that someone else was in the water now. Carl White was slumped over and Danni was struggling with a man on her back while Natasha pulled at his hair.

Leaping into the water, Quinn had no choice but to thrust Natasha aside and grapple with the man throttling Danni. He hauled him off, but the guy was a brute. They went down in the water together. The man had a knife and tried to slice him with it as they fought, but Quinn refused to release his grasp on the man's throat — a grasp that kept his combatant beneath the water.

The thug went down hard; even with the strength he fought to maintain, Quinn found it difficult to render him unconscious. But when he heard muffled screams coming from above the water again, he managed to jackknife his knee into his opponent's jaw, and the guy finally went down. When Quinn came up, he saw that Danni was struggling with the tall man from the shack, while Natasha was being drowned by the shorter one.

He thanked God that his piece worked wet or dry — he had a clear shot at the short man who had nearly killed Natasha.

He fired, hitting him in the brain. He

didn't dare assure himself that Natasha was alive. Instead, he dove down, his hands snaking around the other man's ankle. He jerked him off his feet, forcing him to release Danni. She surged for the surface.

He turned. There was a gun in his face.

The man took the time to smile. He fired.

It was a misfire.

Quinn lunged at him, throwing him to the muck below and slamming him down with his own weight.

He had to rise for air. When he did, he saw Danni, drenched and grim, staring back at him. She screamed and threw herself forward; his opponent had risen but before he could take aim to fire again, Danni pushed him off.

Quinn felt a savage fury that these men sought to dispense death as if human life meant nothing. This time, his force sent the man deep into the muck, and he smashed his fist into the killer's face, holding him there.

When he ceased to move, ceased to struggle, Quinn fully rose. Chest heaving, he looked around. Danni was watching for him anxiously, sodden hair plastered to her face. Natasha had rolled Carl over and was trying to drag him to the rise of the shack's porch. She could never handle such a weight.

"You okay?" he asked Danni.

She gave him a white-faced nod and he hurried to Natasha. She had a gash on her forehead and was gasping for breath. Quinn took Carl White's water-borne weight and told her, "Get out. I have him. Get me . . . blankets."

With a tremendous effort, he lifted Carl's weight, prodding him up onto the porch platform. Danni had clambered to her feet and caught Carl, rolling the big man so he wouldn't plunge back into the water. Quinn leaped up himself, crawled on his knees to Carl's side and immediately began CPR. Danni was versed in the procedure, and started to count and press on Carl's chest while Quinn breathed into the man's mouth. A moment later, as he rose and Danni pressed, Carl suddenly coughed and a stream of water spewed from his lips. He coughed again.

Natasha had rushed out with a blanket. "Thank the Lord by any name you call Him!" she whispered, falling down to wrap the cold man in the warm blanket.

As Quinn stood, stretching his back to shake the pains he'd just noticed, he heard sirens.

"The cops are coming," he said.

"Yes, Jez would have called them." Natasha looked down. Two of the dead men were bobbing to the surface. "We'll be in a station giving statements all night — but thank the Lord again, we're alive to do it."

He glanced over at Danni. She was pale and quiet and once again sodden. She had the unique ability to somehow look beautiful in such a state. Maybe it was more than beautiful; she had an air about her that was almost beyond anything carnal. Then again, he hadn't felt that way when he'd watched her while they were dancing to the voodoo drums.

He'd felt entirely carnal then.

He gave himself a mental shake. Yes, indeed, she was proving herself to be Angus's daughter at every turn.

It had just been a hell of a lot easier and more straightforward to work with Angus.

"I'll get him into the shack," he said.

He hunched down and lifted Carl White — who had to weigh a good three hundred and fifty pounds. He felt his muscles straining, but he got the man inside and placed him on the sofa between the chairs. The fire was dying down; he got it going again. They should probably get Carl to a hospital, and he wondered how they could manage that.

They needed to keep him hidden — as well as the fact that men had come to the bayou and died there.

"How are we going to explain this?" Danni asked, warming herself before the fire.

Quinn shrugged. "I hope we won't have to, since Larue will be with them."

"How do you know that?" she asked him. "Born-again ESP?"

He smiled at her. "Nope. I know Larue. When Jez called it in, Larue was alerted, and he'll be with the squad cars headed out. This is tearing up his city. He'll be here. Mark my words."

He was grateful to discover that he was right.

Larue's car was in the lead, followed by two others. There were six officers all together, but Larue waved the others aside and approached Quinn, where he awaited him on the path.

"How many dead?" Larue asked, stopping in his tracks.

"Three. They wanted to take Carl White with them and kill us. I didn't have a choice. Carl's inside. He was struck by something — to keep him quiet, I imagine — but he nearly drowned."

"Danni Cafferty?"

"She's fine. Drenched, but fine."

"And Ms. Laroche?"

"Natasha is fine, too."

"Okay, so what the hell happened?"

He indicated the bayou behind him. "I haven't fished out the dead men. Carl White is in the shack, along with Natasha and Danni. We went there to talk after the ceremony. Next thing I knew, Jez called to warn us someone was coming — with guns. We hid in the water. I thought there were only two, but there was a third. I injured the first two, but the third guy was attacking the women. When I fought with him, the others limped bleeding into the water and kept trying to kill us. They didn't mean to kill Carl, but in their struggle to kill us and our struggle to survive, he inhaled a lot of the bayou. He's breathing now, but still unconscious. He needs an ambulance. And I think the others are dead — at least they quit trying to shoot, strangle and drown us."

Larue lowered his head, shaking it.

"No, I don't know who the hell they were," Quinn continued. "Goons who worked for Shumaker — Eyes — is my bet. Maybe we'll be able to prove it. We have something this time — bodies."

"There always seem to be bodies around you, Quinn," Larue said.

"Nice way to look at it, Larue. What about, 'Hey, Quinn, glad to see that you and the women survived'?"

Larue raised his head and grinned. "You know, I wasn't really worried about you. Sorry. I was hoping to get here before you had to kill the goons."

"You've got more faith in me than I do," Quinn told him.

"God, you stink again."

"Sorry."

"Hell," Larue said. "Let's start cleaning this up."

"Larue."

"Yeah?"

"We may have something. Carl White received threats on his cell phone. And one of his girls was threatened. She's dead — died in her bathtub this morning."

Larue swore softly. "Where does this end?"

"When we find the bust. It's still out there somewhere. And apparently someone's still looking for it. That someone thought Carl had it. We have to find the bust and stop his dreams of riches and power. That's where it will end."

That night, Billie was waiting up when they returned to the shop. He opened the door to the courtyard, letting Wolf out to greet

275

them as they arrived.

"You look like bloody shite!" Billie said, his brogue strong with his emotion.

"Yeah, I guess." Danni was hugging Wolf. She loved that the dog seemed as happy to greet her as Quinn. Well, maybe not *quite* as happy. He let her stroke his head for a few minutes, but then seemed to need Quinn to make a fuss over him.

"I have tea," Billie said gruffly.

"Tea," Danni said, smiling.

"Hot tea with milk and sugar and a good dollop of Jameson whiskey, if you feel the need," he said firmly. He pointed at Danni. "Up to your room, change into something dry. And you, sir — up to my attic chamber. I haven't a thing that could pretend to fit you, but I pulled out a few old pieces that belonged to Angus, and you can make do with them. Then you'll come down and catch me up on what's going on."

"It *is* three in the morning," Quinn reminded him.

"So it is. You should get moving."

Quinn looked at Danni and grinned crookedly. She looked back at him and felt as if her heart had stopped beating. She could well imagine his old days, when all he had to do was give out that smile and people fell over themselves to be near him. He was physically imposing, and that grin was sheer seduction.

Yes, she was really liking him, really caring about him — and almost pathetically attracted to him. But he was different. He heard things before anyone else did; the strength he'd betrayed tonight had been astonishing. He'd hefted Carl White around as though he'd been no more than a baby, and there was no questioning why that man had gotten his moniker.

"Clock's ticking," Billie told her.

"Yessir!" She turned and raced up the stairs.

It was hard not to stay in the shower for a long time. The spring days were getting warm, but the water in the bayou at night had been chilling — not to mention everything that had gone on in it. She tried to weigh her feelings. She'd been numb, in a way. Men had tried to *kill* her. She could still remember the terror of grappling with them, of not being able to breathe . . . of being certain she was about to see her father again.

Drying off, she studied herself in the mirror. Marks from the hands that had tried to strangle her remained on her throat. She tried to conjure up the man's face. All she could remember was his look of brutal determination. She realized that she'd never seen any of the men clearly.

She brushed out her wet hair and pulled on sweatpants and a T-shirt. When she got downstairs, Quinn was dressed in one of her father's old flannel shirts and a pair of his jeans.

They came to his ankles, but Quinn seemed warm and dry. She was surprised that he looked at her with accusing eyes. "You didn't tell me there was almost a break-in here," he said.

She was startled and glanced at Billie. "Um, we don't know if it was an attempted break-in. Wolf barked. And Billie came down. With a *gun,*" she added, raising her eyebrows.

"Honesty is a good thing here, between us," Billie said.

"Yes — we honestly don't know if it was going to be some kind of break-in," Danni said. "And you! You talk about honesty!"

"I haven't been dishonest," Billie protested. "I hold down the fort — and do whatever I'm asked. But I need to know where you are and whether you're all right, young woman. I'm too old to pace around like a mother hen waiting for a teenage daughter to get back from a date. Now, drink your tea."

She laughed out loud. The terror she'd felt that evening was slowly leaving her. When she looked up, she saw that Quinn was studying her.

"You could have died tonight," he said quietly.

"I could have. And you could, too. Again."

"I'm living on a second chance as it is," he said.

"Which makes it that much more precious," she returned.

"It's no good fretting about each other. It is what it is," Billie told them. "But from now on, you keep me up on what's going on. Thank God for Jez tonight and the fact that he called me *and* the police. You could've been killed by those thugs." He turned to Quinn. "You would have heard the car, but Jez bought you a few minutes that might have been all-important. So — the bust is out there. Somewhere. Eyes, or his men, killed Leroy and Ivy. Maybe Leroy was holding out, trying to get more money . . . who knows? Shumaker's goons might have been getting ready to torture it out of Leroy when they realized you were coming, Quinn. But if he's still killing people —"

"It's not because of what he thinks they know. It's because of what he thinks they have — or know where to find," Quinn finished.

Billie nodded, his face grim. "Tonight goes to show that *you two* are in danger, real danger. More so than those poor fools who just get in the way."

"We'll be careful, Billie," Quinn promised him. "Wolf will be with you until this is over."

"And then who is with *you*?" Billie asked. "Angus, he had me. You had Wolf."

"I want Wolf with Danni," Quinn insisted.

"Hey, I'm in on this, too, remember?" Danni said. "And I have a solution."

They both looked at her.

"Until we find the bust, Wolf and Quinn both stay here. My father's room is empty. So Quinn can stay there."

"I have a house," Quinn said.

"A great house," she agreed. "But here's the deal. We keep you *and* Wolf."

"How is that a deal?" He laughed. "A deal usually means some kind of give-and-take."

"Yes, usually."

He nodded slowly.

"You must be wearing her down, Quinn. Danni didn't want anyone else even going through Angus's things."

"I happen to like living," Danni said. She saw that she hadn't touched her tea. She swallowed down the contents of her cup and rose. "And sleeping. We don't seem to be getting much of that around here lately. Good night. Oh, by the way, I let Wolf in my room," she told Quinn.

She left them in the little kitchen and started through the shop. In the darkness, it should have been eerie with the sarcophagus and other funerary items, medieval pieces and tribal fetishes.

But she wasn't afraid of the shop, and she realized that was because nothing in it was *evil.*

Somehow, her father had seen to that.

And now . . .

She turned back, thinking that, first thing, they should find out exactly how Carl White's girl, Shirley, had died.

But Quinn was still speaking to Billie, and although she shouldn't have eavesdropped, she found herself listening in.

"So, how is she working out? Is it like being with Angus?" Billie asked.

"She's his daughter," Quinn said. Danni smiled. It was probably the greatest compliment she could receive. But then he added, "It's harder. Much harder than working with Angus."

"How's that?" Billie asked.

"Well, Angus wasn't built like a *Sports II-*

lustrated swimsuit model, for one," he said, and went silent for a minute. "And I wasn't falling halfway in love with Angus all the time," Quinn continued. There was something in his tone that touched her soul. After a few seconds of silence, he lightened the mood. "Angus wasn't my type at all, you know. Too big — and hairy."

Both men laughed. But there was warmth in the laughter. These men had loved her father in very different ways.

Falling halfway in love . . .

Was that what she was doing, too?

Not a good thing, she thought.

He was too strong, too aware, too —

I died, he had told her. And it was true; he had flatlined on the table.

His life was a second chance. . . .

But if she was following in her father's footsteps, what was hers?

282

CHAPTER 12

Quinn wondered if he would actually sleep that night; he was overloaded with the remaining adrenaline.

And tea.

To his surprise, exhaustion from the past few days kicked in, and soon he was out like a light.

He woke up hearing Wolf's nails clattering on the wooden floor outside the bedroom door. He sat up quickly, pulling the covers to his chest as the door opened and Danni and Wolf entered the room.

Danni looked great — bright-eyed, fresh and beautiful. She was wearing jeans and a tailored shirt, and it all seemed to hug her body perfectly. He was glad of the covers.

"Ten o'clock, rise and shrine. The hell with that not going to bed till 4:00 a.m. thing," she said, sitting on the foot of his bed. "Larue called on the shop phone — since you weren't answering your cell. He wants you down at the station right away. I think he's getting worried about keeping Carl White safe."

"Why do you think that?" Quinn asked her, struggling to really awaken.

"Because he said, 'I'm worried about our ability to keep Carl White safe.' Well, he didn't say that, but I'm assuming he figures that Shumaker knows you're on this case and maybe he knows about your affiliation with John Ryan. If so, he may go after Father Ryan, and then he could go after nuns and nurses and doctors. . . ."

"Yeah, I get it," Quinn said. "All right, I'm getting up."

She stayed on the foot of his bed, staring at him.

"Once you're out of the room," he said. He grimaced. "Your dad didn't have any pj's that fit me."

"How did you do it?" she asked him.

"Pardon?"

"No human being without superpowers could have lifted Carl White the way you did last night. And you hear things before other people do. I'm not sure what else. I'm going to have to be more observant." She kept staring at him, obviously determined.

Wolf gave a little whimper. He stood by the bedside and nuzzled Quinn's hand.

"The strength . . . the hearing — they're gifts, I guess," he said huskily.

"From whom?" she asked carefully.

He smiled and said, "I don't really know."

She folded her arms over her chest. "The story, please?"

He pulled a pillow from the other side of the bed, placed it on his lap, then sat up and looked at her. He'd never seen eyes bluer than hers at that moment, or more intense.

"You know most of the story, don't you? I had everything. Loving parents, a great family. I did well in school with no effort, sailed through, became known as the high school player to watch. I graduated, went to college, got a reputation as the college player to watch. Everyone loved me — or loved being in the sunshine that seemed to surround me. And I was an ass, a total prick. I couldn't count the girls I had in a night and I discarded the decent ones as easily as the — forgive me — sluts. I just took everything offered to me. Including tons of alcohol, pills, cocaine . . . you name it. Then I overdosed. I was hit by a car. They were trying to pump my stomach and do surgery to sew up the gashes at the same time, and I died." He paused, saw that she was waiting for more. And there *was* more.

He inhaled on a deep breath. "I know you've probably heard this story before, too — maybe not in connection with me. *I saw it happen.* I was there, but floating over my body. I saw the doctors and the nurses . . . and in the waiting room, I could see my parents and my family, crying their eyes out. I thought about what an ass I'd been and I wanted to comfort my mother so badly. . . ."

He grimaced, took another breath and met her eyes again. "Then . . . I saw a doctor walk in. A man with scrubs on over jeans and a leather jacket. He was about forty, I'd say — dark, wavy hair . . . good face. I saw him down there, giving instructions . . . and when I turned — up where I was floating — I saw him again. He looked at me with pure disgust and said, 'What a waste. What a pathetic waste. You had the stuff to make a difference.' I looked down at my bedside and he was still there, telling them to rev up the heart blaster one more time. They did. I remember feeling as if I'd been struck by lightning. I think my body jumped off the bed. During the next few days in the hospital, I couldn't shake what I'd seen — or imagined I'd seen. And I knew it had all happened because my sister had never entered the room that night, but I'd known exactly what she was wearing. As I began to heal, I realized I was stronger than ever and that I could hear every word the nurses were saying when they whispered at their stations. I asked about the doctor I'd seen, but no one knew what I was talking about. I dropped it.

"When I was finally in shape to get out, I spent some time telling my family how grateful I was for them and begged them to forgive me. I was going to sign up for the navy. I did my two-year stint, then went through the police academy and started with NOPD. I worked for the department several years, and got a degree — I studied criminology. I thought that being a cop was what I was supposed to do." He stopped speaking again. Danni hadn't said a word. She was watching him with steady eyes. She didn't seem frightened or even entertained. Her look was dead serious, as if she was glad of what she was hearing.

"Did you want to say anything?" he asked her. "Maybe tell me that the neurons flapping around the brain at time of death probably cause such visions?"

"I'm sure physicians do have an explanation for it — whether they're right or you're right, I don't know. But there's more."

He nodded. "One night, I was off-duty. I was at a bar on Frenchman Street and a fight broke out. I ignored it at first — there were other cops on duty. The fight went outside, and I followed. The one guy was ripped to shreds. I realized that the on-duty cops hadn't intervened. They felt those two should bash the hell out of each other, since they were both junkies. I stepped in and they remembered they were supposed to enforce the law — not make judgments. Anyway, I left the bar to head home and ran smack into the man I'd seen at the hospital."

"The doctor who was telling them to hit you with the paddles again — and who was with you, floating above the scene?"

"Yep. He was angry. He told me I wasn't supposed to wait for others to step in. I wasn't getting it. I needed to do more — and take help where I could get it. I felt him brush by me. I thought about that meeting for a few days and then I resigned and got my P.I.'s license. For a while, I wondered if I'd made a mistake. All I got at first were cases where someone wanted me to spy on someone else . . . until the little girl disappeared. I took the case right away. The father was an old friend I'd gone to school with — a real friend, one who hadn't enabled me, but who'd been there for me when I needed to talk. He told me the police were trying but he wasn't sure they were trying everything. I agreed. I'd picked up vague hints of some Satanic activity but didn't know how to investigate it, how to pursue it. Later that same day, I gathered up a pile of clothing I hadn't worn in ages. I was going to have it cleaned to give to Goodwill. I emptied the pockets . . . and I found your father's card. Once I met him . . . well, everything clicked. I had a few cases that were mundane, that I managed on my own. But I found that little girl because of your father, because of what he knew — because of what he did.

"So . . . do I really have any answers about myself? No. I've seen the man a few times since — in a crowd, sometimes, giving me a push in the right direction at other times. Literally and figuratively. But who he is — what he is — I don't know. I have no idea what name he goes by, if any. I don't even know if he lives in my mind, if I got that card the night he brushed by me . . . or if I picked it up somewhere. I do know that I'm finally doing what I'm supposed to do."

She was thoughtful as she studied him, chewing her lower lip. "So that means I should know what I'm supposed to do," she said softly.

"You seem to be doing it — and very

well," he told her.

"And I made you go see a band," she said regretfully.

He shook his head strenuously, reaching out to clasp her by the shoulders. "You were right to see the band. You're right to live your life as normally as possible. Life is nothing if we don't enjoy every second that we can."

"So . . . you live normally?"

"Danni, I still have friends. And I'm lucky — a great family, too. They're not in NOLA anymore, but they come back and visit, and they stay at the house. We always have a great time together. You have to *live* life. Not to do so is a sin, just as much as enjoying it at the expense of others."

She nodded. She was so beautiful. And they were so close. He could sense her, smell her, feel her; he knew her breath and her heartbeat.

And he was naked beneath the covers.

He let his hands fall and he sat back. "You have my story now — all of it, I swear. I'd better get down to the station and see Larue."

"I'm going to take the painting to Cecelia Simon. She should be at the house by now."

"I'll call you when I leave the station. If the bust is still out there, and as far as we know, it is, that means Shumaker is still searching for it. We have to figure out what Leroy Jenkins did with it — before he was killed. That might mean tearing apart his house and yard, except I can't imagine Shumaker hasn't done that. And the cops and crime scene people were all over it that night. Still, being on the police force taught me to be methodical, so it's something we need to do — no matter who's already done it."

"Is Wolf with me or you?" she asked.

"You — and if they don't want him in that house, you don't go in, either."

"Yes, sir." She spun around with a mock salute and exited. Wolf looked at her and then at Quinn. "Go, boy. Go with her," Quinn told the dog.

Danni arrived at the Simon house just after one in the afternoon.

Bertie smiled as she opened the door. And then she saw Wolf.

"Hi, Bertie. I hope you're doing all right," Danni said.

"Yes . . ." Bertie seemed like a sentinel, standing dead center in the doorway. "What are you doing here with that . . . dog?" she asked.

"Wolf is an angel, honestly," Danni said.

Bertie gazed at her stonily.

Danni cleared her throat. "Um, I'm an artist by trade, Bertie. I'd done a likeness of Mrs. Simon and it came out quite well. I thought Cecelia might like it."

Before Bertie could say any more, Cecelia Simon came sweeping down the stairs. "Who is it, Bertie? What's going on?"

Danni realized she'd probably seen Cecelia in the society pages, the same as she'd seen Gladys.

To say the young woman was elegant would be an understatement. Cecelia had light blond hair cut in fashionable layers, a slash of long bangs falling over one eye, highlights enhancing the style. She was dressed in a form-hugging military-style bodysuit and platform heels. Her makeup was perfect.

Danni would've expected someone whose eyes were swollen with tears. A bereaved daughter heedless of her appearance at the moment.

"She's with the cops," Bertie explained, gesturing at Danni. "Or was with the cops. Or that Quinn fellow."

"I'm Danielle Cafferty, Ms. Simon," Danni said. She'd thought that after her earlier visit, the then-sobbing housekeeper had decided she liked her. Now, she wasn't sure. "Your mother came to my store right before she died. I thought you might want this painting I've done of her."

"That's very nice of you, Ms. Cafferty," Cecelia said. "Please, bring it in."

"There's the dog, Miss Simon," Bertie said.

Cecelia waved a hand in the air. "He's a beautiful monster. Part wolf, is he?"

"He belongs to a friend but, yes, if I remember correctly, he's a mix of a few breeds, including maybe a quarter wolf. He's kind of a rescue — extremely well trained and a *very* good dog," Danni said.

"Bertie, he won't do anything *dirty* in the house." Cecelia looked at Danni. "Will he?"

"No, he will not."

"Then please do come in," Cecelia said.

Danni entered, carrying her brown-paper-wrapped, framed rendering of Gladys Simon, Wolf at her heels. They came in as far as the entry. Danni remembered the last time she'd been at the house — when they'd found Gladys swinging.

Wolf sat obediently at her heels as she unwrapped the picture. Cecelia's eyebrows shot up. "You've depicted her wonderfully. It's lovely. What can I give you for it?"

"No, I don't want anything. It's a gift," Danni said. "Your mother seemed to be an incredibly nice woman."

Cecelia nodded but showed no emotion. "Seriously. You're a real artist." She smiled. "Artists are always struggling, aren't they?"

"It's a gift, Ms. Simon, if you'd like it. My father has passed away, too. He left me with a shop that does very well."

Bertie sniffed. "Not well enough to buy the stupid bust!"

"I was coming to the house to see about the bust when . . . when we found Mrs. Simon," Danni said.

"Well, apparently the bust is gone," Cecelia said briskly. "And so is my mother. I feared for her after my father died. I like to imagine the two of them are happy together now. They lived for each other, you see, Ms. Cafferty. Well, then, thank you — I accept this gratefully. Is there anything else?"

Danni realized she was being dismissed. "Nothing at all. My sympathies to you," she said.

"Thank you." Cecelia glanced at her watch. "I believe I'm due at the mortuary. Mother's body hasn't been released yet, but I do want to plan for a beautiful funeral."

"Of course."

Danni turned with Wolf and left, feeling very odd about the encounter. She supposed she'd expected . . . tears, grief, a display of emotion?

She'd done what she could, giving the woman a portrait of her mother.

She had nothing else to do. Until she heard from Quinn.

She patted Wolf as they left the house and the door closed behind her.

"Home, boy," she said. "We didn't get a terrific welcome, did we? Not that I thought she'd offer tea and crumpets, but . . . whatever!"

She strolled to her car. Wolf jumped in beside her and they began the drive back to her shop in the French Quarter.

Jake Larue pushed a file across his desk toward Quinn. "Autopsy report on Gladys Simon. Looks like she did kill herself. I'm not a scientist. I don't know how the M.E. and the crime scene people figure it all out, but apparently the way the rope was tied . . . They're sure she killed herself. They're going to release her body this afternoon."

That wasn't much of a surprise to Quinn.

"Carl White doing okay?" he asked.

Larue nodded. "This is going to get expensive for the city, Quinn. We've got Carl in one safe house, and your second friend, Sam, in another."

And Bo Ray Jenkins was being watched

over by Father Ryan.

"We need some answers. I have men working all over the city, trying to trace that damn bust, trying to find out what's going on. The price tag on this is escalating. I have officers working off-duty hours, which is adding up on the time clock, to keep these men safe. Men some people think should be allowed to wallow in the violence they create."

"Carl and Sam are not violent men," Quinn said.

"But they run in violent and illegal circles," Larue reminded him.

"What about the men who were killed last night? Do we have IDs on them? Any way to tie them to Brandt Shumaker?" Quinn asked.

Larue picked up another file. "Derby Halloran, Beau Headley and Grant Finaker. All three were from Detroit and had rap sheets for armed robbery. Derby had only been out a few weeks. All three checked into different hotels — as if they were ordinary tourists."

"Okay, so where were they staying in New Orleans? What about the car they came in?"

"Rental car. Finaker rented it when he landed at the airport two days ago. There's no tie we can find to Shumaker."

"Great. So these three men just came to town on a whim and then drove out to Natasha's place on the bayou to kidnap Carl White and kill anyone with him," Quinn said.

Larue looked pained. "Come on, Quinn, you know *I* have to work within the confines of the law. Hell, I went in first thing myself to speak with Brandt Shumaker this morning. He was polite, all business. He was appalled to hear about the violence and, of course, he wanted to know why I'd think that he — an upstanding citizen — would have anything to do with this. He was, to all appearances, totally cooperative, and he didn't even try to bribe me with a massive contribution to a police benevolence society."

"Did you *really* think he was just going to confess to murder because you walked in?"

"I felt he should know we were suspicious of him."

"He's probably smiling with amusement and lighting up a Cuban cigar to enjoy with a glass of Patron right now," Quinn said, shaking his head.

"May I point out again — *I* have to work within the law," Larue said.

"And you're suggesting I don't?"

"I'd never suggest such a thing."

"Okay, then. I don't think Shumaker has the bust yet. I believe that's why he's trying to kill people, why he's threatening them and trying to prove he means business. I think it's why he wanted me, Natasha and Danni dead — but Carl alive."

"What the hell can this bust do?" Larue asked, sounding exasperated.

"Power can be in a man's mind. It can mess with the chemicals in the brain. I've seen people hyped up on drugs perform insane feats. Hell, I performed a few myself. But look at it this way. If this trail of dead is what we're getting when he *doesn't* have the bust, can you imagine the terror he'll unleash when he does? When he believes he's all-powerful?"

Larue looked at him with dull eyes. "You know we're not just sitting on our hands. I have officers in the street and — although some would grumble if they knew — following up every lead I get from you."

"Yeah, I'm grateful for that," Quinn said. "What about the death of Carl White's stripper, Shirley? Did you get anything from his phone?"

"You soaked the damn phone," Larue complained. He raised a hand. "Yes, yes, you were trying to save lives and you did that quite nicely. I told you we weren't just sitting on our hands. Our techs were able to get some information off it. They clearly read the threats to Carl and they traced the number those threats came from. But the phone was purchased at a massive electronics store in Baton Rouge. Pay as you go — as we all expected. Dead end. Bought with cash, and no one remembers who bought that particular phone, since they sell hundreds. It wouldn't matter, anyway. I doubt Shumaker bought the phone himself. Shirley is Shirley DuPree and she's due for autopsy this afternoon."

"I'll go over for that," Quinn said, and rose. "But, Larue, what I'd like to do — with your permission — is get into Leroy Jenkins's house. He has to have stashed the bust *somewhere* after he stole it — if no one else has it and Shumaker is looking for it."

"You have my permission and my blessing. The place is still surrounded by crime scene tape and I have officers on duty in the area, patrolling the neighborhood. I'll give them a call and tell them you're coming."

"You know what?" Danni told Wolf as they returned to her house and she drove her car into the garage. "My feelings are hurt! That was a damned good likeness of Gladys. You'd have thought her daughter would've been more appreciative!"

Wolf gave a sharp bark, as if he were in total agreement.

Her first step, she decided, was to go back into the shop, see how things were going. There were a number of tourists and shoppers there, oohing and aahing about the oddities and knickknacks to be found.

People gushed over Wolf as they were prone to do, and she assured everyone that he was a friendly dog and that they were welcome to pet him.

Wolf received the attention with his usual dignity.

Jane was at the cash register. "How are we doing?" Danni asked her.

"Very well," Jane said. "Spring always brings out the tourist trade in NOLA. Did you take the picture to Cecelia Simon?"

"I did."

"She must have been incredibly grateful."

Danni shrugged. "She wanted to pay me. She's kind of a cold fish."

"She should've been thanking you with tears in her eyes!" Jane said. "Maybe she doesn't know that you're an up-and-coming, well-respected artist!" she added indignantly.

A woman was politely trying to look around Danni into the display case at the cash register. Danni smiled and moved aside.

Billie was showing another customer some of the reproduction medieval mail they carried. He looked over at her and she shrugged again.

They had the shop well in order, so Danni decided to go back to the "basement" to study her father's book while she waited to hear from Quinn. She pulled her phone from her pocket to make sure she hadn't missed a call. She hadn't.

She turned on the lights and went over to the book, which she'd put back in its glass encasement on the desk. She didn't sit in the desk chair but reverently picked up the tome and curled into one of the old plush chairs near the life-size model of *The Gorilla That Ate Manhattan*.

Wolf was unimpressed with the items in the basement. He curled up at her feet.

What else is there to find? she wondered.

She'd read about Pietro Miro, and it made sense that anything related to him might be unpleasant or upset people. But how could it make people do evil things?

And if it was possible, how did they stop it?

She flipped the pages carefully.

"Okay, Dad, where do I go from here? I know the history. But how do I stop what's going on and get the bust — and then what should I do with it?"

She looked through the table of contents, impressed at the number of subjects covered. The sections on ghosts and poltergeists were long. She thought that if the bust was haunted, maybe she should read about ghosts.

She did.

But despite the beauty of the language, she wasn't sure she'd discovered anything that wasn't already urban legend, or well-known paranormal lore. As she'd already learned, there were two kinds of hauntings — active and residual. "Residual" hauntings were the saddest. They included cases of soldiers fighting the same battle over and over again, the moments that led up to a murder, the despair of a person about to commit suicide. "Active" or "intelligent" hauntings occurred when the soul knew that it was caught in the veil or the mist between this world and a different dimension, torn between solving something in life and walking into the light.

The best help for a ghost, of course, was to discover why he or she remained behind and solve all past issues. . . .

The way to stop a ghost from tormenting the living — when it would not accept its own demise, when it chose to create havoc, pain and even death — was to see that the body was rendered to ash, including the bones.

But Pietro Miro had been cremated hundreds of years ago. How could he, in any mist or veil on the way to the afterlife, be causing trouble?

She groaned inwardly. A week ago, she'd have laughed at such a question. She did laugh aloud as she read another of the suggestions. *Know thy ghost.*

"I read all about our ghost!" she said, skimming down the page.

She was so involved in her reading that she nearly jumped sky-high when her phone buzzed in her pocket. She answered it quickly.

As she expected, it was Quinn. She was surprised by the pleasure she felt when she heard his voice. But then, she was constantly surprised by Quinn.

That morning, he'd been honest and sincere. And she hadn't wanted to leave the room, to remember that they were together because . . .

People were dying.

"What are you doing?" he asked.

"Reading."

"Want to go on a treasure hunt?"

"Sure. Are we bringing Wolf?"

"You bet. He loves a treasure hunt. I'll swing by for you in ten."

"We'll be ready."

Danni returned the book to its glass enclosure, then glanced over at it. "I've read the book, Dad. With lots of light. What am I not seeing?"

The gorilla seemed to stare at her, as did the eyes of the mannequin in the Victorian coffin. Nothing in the room seemed to have an answer for her.

Danni was waiting with Wolf at her side when Quinn drove down Royal to collect them. The street was thronged with tourists. As he pulled to the curb, she hurried toward him and he found himself astonished again at the way she'd come around to the idea of taking her father's place. He smiled, remembering how he'd thought on that first day that he'd have no more help from the shop in his future quests. She saw his smile as she slid into the car, allowing Wolf to jump in the back.

"Was it a good morning? Why are you grinning?"

"It wasn't a bad morning. It wasn't a good

morning. But I did get permission from Larue to go and search Leroy Jenkins's house."

"And that's making you smile."

"No, *you* made me smile."

"Oh?" She seemed skeptical.

"Yeah. I thought you were an absolute disaster that first day. Now you've been shot at, you've gone swimming in the bayou . . . you've danced at a voodoo funeral rite —"

"Hey, I know and respect voodoo. I grew up here, remember?"

"But not being attacked, nearly drowned and all that."

"No, not all that," she agreed.

They were silent as he looped around to head west toward Esplanade by way of Bourbon. Then she said, "You're smirking at me."

"I wasn't smirking."

"You were. But that's all right. I thought *you* were the biggest jerk in the world."

"And now?"

"Now you're a jerk with a mission."

He shrugged, still smiling. He knew damned well that he was attracted to her, that the scent of her subtle perfume — a scent he was coming to know well — instantly stirred something inside him. He gave his attention to the road, waiting for a few happy tourists sipping New Orleans's famous Hurricane drinks from plastic traveler glasses. Music from half a dozen venues blared loudly enough to become a cacophony on the street as he drove. He shook his head.

"Anyone would think you're not a music lover," Danni teased.

"I am. That's why this is overkill to me. I enjoyed seeing your friends — before the gunfire, the voodoo dancing and nearly getting killed in the bayou. If they keep playing regularly, your friend Brad said I can sit in with them sometime and play guitar."

She looked at him with wide eyes. "You'd do that?"

"Uh, yes. Why does that surprise you?"

She laughed. "I guess I never imagined you doing anything besides . . . well, hunting down a Renaissance funerary bust."

"Great. But remember I told you — I have family and friends. And life is precious."

"Yes, very much so," she responded soberly.

A few minutes later, the scenery seemed to underline that ideal as they passed areas that were still, after all the years gone by, a pile of wreckage from Katrina with signs of *precious* life few and far between.

Then they reached Jenkins's house. There

was a patrol car in front, but the officer waved as Quinn drove up.

Larue had kept his word.

"So . . . you think the bust is still here?" Danni asked.

"No, I don't. But if we don't look, we can't really be sure that it isn't."

She nodded. She hadn't seen the house before. She stared at it as they approached, Wolf close on their heels.

A chalk outline in the shape of a body remained where Leroy had lain dying the night he'd gone there. Inside, they saw another to indicate the position in which Ivy had been found. There were little plastic numbers indicating blood spatters and other places where the forensic team had noticed possible evidence or clues.

"We're allowed to just . . . search?" Danni asked.

"We are." He paused as they walked inside. "It's a life-size bust, so I doubt it could be stuffed in a small cranny. I also believe Shumaker's had men in here — slipping past the patrols that have gone by. But we'll look. We'll see what we can see."

He began by surveying the living room, opening drawers, closing them, opening a closet, closing it.

Leroy had been less than tidy.

There was black powder on windowsills and doors, a leftover from the forensic crews' attempt to lift prints. He avoided the powder. Danni went into one bedroom and he heard her going through closets and doors.

They'd been there a few minutes, earnest in their endeavors, when Wolf started to scratch at the back door. Quinn hurried toward it, aware of Danni behind him.

Out back, it looked as if a giant plow had gone over the ground.

"I guess Brandt Shumaker's men *have* been here," Danni murmured.

"Yep. Not a big surprise."

"So, if he'd buried the statue, they would've found it."

"I would think," Quinn said.

"Should we give up?"

"Let's look around awhile longer."

"Okay."

They turned and went back in. Quinn wasn't even sure what he was looking for, but he couldn't help feeling that something in the house would give them a clue as to what Leroy Jenkins would've done with his prize until he got his money — or negotiated for a higher amount.

Danni disappeared into a bedroom. "This

is pretty yucky, you know!" she called to him.

"Yeah, old Leroy wasn't much of a house-keeper. Neither was Ivy, I guess," he called back.

He looked through canisters in the kitchen. One held coffee; one held some pretty aromatic pot.

"Quinn?"

"Yeah?"

He went into the back bedroom to join her. The bed was unmade with the sheets not even stretched over the mattress. Dirty towels lay in a corner. A dresser was laden with makeup and perfumes.

"What did you find?"

"Maybe nothing. The police searched here, so they must have figured it was just doodling or a piece of trash. What do you think this is?"

She handed him a crumpled sheet of paper. It had a bunch of squiggly lines and a sketch that appeared to be an airplane drawn above a pile of squares. Between the airplane and the squares was an X.

"I'm assuming the plane means the air-port," she said.

"The squares might indicate the cemeter-ies," Quinn added. "I-10 goes by this area, and Airline Drive, which goes to the airport.

But there's a line from the X toward the bayou. Hmm. You've got Greenwood Cemetery, Cypress Grove Cemetery — thousands of vaults and mausoleums. But after the cemeteries . . ."

She pointed at the paper, tracing a line with her finger. "Heading toward the water, you have a few old house and mill ruins, some in better shape than others, but most of them abandoned."

"Let's go," he said decisively.

"We're going to search, vault by vault?" Her voice was incredulous. "Quinn, that could take days!"

"Yeah. May as well get started."

"Haven't you ever heard about letting the dead rest in peace?" she asked.

"Not when we need the dead to give us a hand."

CHAPTER 13

Even he had to admit that it was like looking for a needle in a haystack, Quinn admitted hours later.

Either that, or there were just too many dead in New Orleans.

They couldn't simply walk the rows and streets of the Cities of the Dead; he had to tap on tombs, watch for recent entombments and try to determine what a man like Leroy Jenkins would have done with a funerary bust.

At least it was daytime. There were tourists thronging the cemeteries. There were also licensed guides all about, plus those who were visiting the tombs of their loved ones, and those who were curious and a bit morbid.

That was good; he doubted they'd have trouble with crowds of visitors all around.

But it was bad, too.

He tried not to check iron gates and seals

in front of people. Every once in a while, someone turned a corner when he wasn't prepared, and he had to smile and make up something about a superstition.

As he examined one vault where the seal was chipping, a couple turned onto their row or "street."

They scowled at Quinn with obvious disapproval.

"Oh, this is the tomb of . . ." he said, quickly looking at the vault for a name.

Danni was faster. "This is the DeMarie family tombs and chapel. It's good luck to knock on it three times and say 'Let the dead sleep, peaceful and deep,' " she invented on the spot.

"Yo, wow, nice!" the man said with a heavy New York accent. "Honey, there's nothing wrong with a little luck!" he announced to the woman at his side.

Quinn and Danni left them at the vault, tapping and chanting.

"We're not getting anywhere, you realize," Danni said.

"Okay, Vic Brown stole the bust from a cemetery. He started shooting up his own gang members, and he wound up in jail. But he'd sold the bust to Hank Simon before that happened. Hank killed himself, and Gladys believed it was because of the bust. Gladys killed herself, and the bust was stolen again. By Leroy Jenkins. Then he was shot — and we now think that he hid the bust before he sold it. If it was stolen from a cemetery, kind of makes sense it would be hidden in a cemetery."

"We don't have enough manpower to do this — just the two of us," Danni said.

"We can bring Billie in," he suggested.

"You know a lot of cops," she reminded him.

"Yes, but . . ."

"But?"

"Everyone who touches that thing becomes tainted somehow. Everyone we know who actually *had* it is dead — except for Vic Brown, and this is Louisiana. Death penalty state. If Vic's attorney doesn't convince a jury that he was mentally impaired, he'll get a death sentence."

"And you think *we'll* be safe from the bust?" Danni asked.

"Let's hope so," he said. "But that means *we* have to find it."

"We can't keep looking right now," Danni told him. "You have a dog in the car, Quinn. We can't keep him there for hours and hours. And, somehow, we have to narrow this down."

"I know," he said with a frustrated sigh.

"How?" he asked her. "Any ideas?"

"Maybe some research on these cemeteries. Originally, the goodness of the family whose vault it 'decorated' here in New Orleans was supposed to help contain the bust's evil," Danni said.

"That didn't stop Vic Brown from stealing it."

"But it was dormant for a long time. Besides, what matters now is what Leroy believed, or what he thought would be safe. If we do some research, we may discover another such vault — or a mausoleum full of some kind of holy men or women. If we can get back to my computer —"

And then his phone rang. He frowned, seeing the caller ID, and answered it immediately.

"Quinn, I need to see you." It was Father Ryan.

"Okay," Quinn said. Danni was looking at him with arched brows, waiting. "What is it?"

"I can't tell you."

"John —"

"I'm a priest. I can't break the sanctity of the confessional."

Quinn groaned. "John, you're calling to ask me to come over — but you don't plan to tell me anything?"

"Just come. I'll . . . I'll figure out a way to give you the pertinent information without betraying a vow." He was silent for a second. "Somehow," he said.

Danni was still watching him expectantly.

"Wolf can get out of the car at our next destination," Quinn said. "Come on."

"Where are we going?"

"Church."

Danni wasn't sure whether to laugh or cry. Father Ryan was, beyond a doubt, a good man.

He'd invited them for lunch; he wasn't saying much of anything. But after lunch had been served, he began to talk about shrimp boats and places out on the bayou.

"We have incredible plantations along Plantation Row," he said conversationally.

"Yes, we do," Quinn agreed. He was studying Ryan intently.

"But, of course, the great houses that remain — especially cleaned up, with re-enactors, tours, all that — are merely the tip of a once huge iceberg," Father Ryan continued.

Quinn leaned forward. "We could just play charades, you know," he said.

Father Ryan grinned at that. "People always think that *plantation* means Tara,

315

right out of *Gone with the Wind*. As if a plantation had to have a massive and expensive mansion. Really, *plantation* meant *farm*. Back before the majority of the populace started moving into the cities, there were small plantations or farms all over the place. Naturally, they were on the river or a bayou that connected to the river, because you had to get your goods to market. There were all kinds of plantations. Big grand plantations owned by the rich — and smaller plantations that belonged to those who were just getting by. They could be really individual in style, too. You've both been to Oak Alley, right?"

Danni smiled. "I think it's illegal to claim you're from this area if you haven't been on a school bus out to Oak Alley."

"Gorgeous house, beautiful property, so much history." Ryan nodded. "And the Creole plantation, Laura, is open now, too. Goes to show that, although they had similarities, these places were different. I mean, you can keep seeing more and more. San Francisco plantation is exquisite, but . . . I like the smaller plantations, not so grand, where you get to see how hard and heavy the work was — still is! — out on the cotton and produce farms."

Quinn murmured to Danni, "What the

hell is he going on about?"

Father Ryan poured them all more coffee. "Our rich history and diversity," Father Ryan said. "And the fact that time can be brutal to houses and property. Time — and poverty, of course. Before the Civil War, there were rich houses, poor houses, great plantations, just plain old working plantations everywhere. Along the bayou, along the river. Some of the smaller of the old plantations are in ruins along the rivers and bayous now. And abandoned sugar mills, too. Why, they're down dark trails, overgrown with foliage. Kind of like Natasha Laroche's old shack out on the bayou, but on dry land."

Danni looked at Quinn. "He wants us to go back to the bayou area."

He nodded. "I think one of his parishioners confessed to something that happened in bayou country."

"I would never divulge words spoken in the confessional," Father Ryan said.

"No, because then he'd sound like a crackpot on speed," Quinn muttered. "Not to cast aspersions on his flock or anything."

"Hey!" Danni protested. "He's discussing history with us. He's telling us there's an old plantation house with an abandoned sugar mill. And something's going on there."

Quinn rolled his eyes. "I presume this has to do with preventing a murder."

Father Ryan sighed with impatience. "If I *knew* there was going to be a murder, I'd call the police. All I learned is that one of my flock was tempted by something he heard while smoking dope at a crack house. I encouraged *him* to call the police. Because of my faith and my need to honor those who trust in my silence when they talk to me in the confessional, I can say no more. I'm counting on you not to be stupid, Quinn! Lord, what has happened to this boy?" he asked, gazing heavenward.

"He's talking about a lot of ground to cover," Quinn said, "without being very specific."

"You have national preserves and wilderness," Father Ryan said. "These wild zones give you an idea of what the Europeans first saw when they came to New Orleans to start building the French Quarter. Why, right near Bayou Sauvage there's land that is still privately held, although no development has gone on in decades. You have ruins in that area. Ruins of old homes — on sugar plantations destroyed by floods and storms through the years, in different stages of neglect. Developers buy up a lot of this property, hoping the levees will hold, that the water will be diverted and one day they'll be worth building up again."

Quinn took the paper they'd found in Leroy Jenkins's house out of his pocket. He traced the X mark from the cemetery with one finger and turned to Danni. "This could be the Bayou Sauvage area."

"And it wouldn't be really big because so much of it is part of the national wildlife refuge. That means nothing else is too close. It's far out in the swamp area where people aren't wandering around at night," Danni said.

He brought the paper to Father Ryan.

"Father, do —"

Father Ryan lifted his hand, looking away. "It's easy for people to become disenfranchised with the church — to see the bad in the world, feel the everywhere pain and lose faith. When you lose faith, you begin to look for something to believe in. So you start listening to the newest faith healer out on the market. Doesn't matter what brand they're offering, as long as there's some reward. Sometimes it doesn't even matter what the price is to join. I think you two should go exploring tomorrow and see what you can find. *Tomorrow!*" he stressed, turning to Danni. "You should always have a good dog with you. Dogs can often see and hear what we don't. And God knows what kind of reptiles you could run into, so you really want to be armed. Danni, you can shoot?"

"I have held and shot a gun," she said.

He shook his head. "That doesn't mean you can shoot. Quinn, get her to a shooting range and get her something she can manage without shooting her own feet."

"All right," Quinn said carefully.

"Do it *now*," Father Ryan told him. "She should know how to handle a gun by Saturday night."

Two nights away, Danni thought. Something was going to happen — or Father Ryan believed something was going to happen — out on private land near the Bayou Sauvage National Wildlife Refuge.

"Now," Father Ryan repeated. "Go, shoo . . . get on it."

"Thanks for the hospitality," Quinn said.

"Sure."

With Wolf trotting obediently behind them, they left. As they did, Quinn looked up at the sky. "Night is coming on soon. Not a great time for cemeteries or the bayou."

"But there are lights at shooting ranges," Danni said.

They went by Quinn's house first, leaving

the dog for a few hours. He produced a gun for her and explained how it worked. She'd gone skeet shooting a time or two with friends, but couldn't have identified the make or model of the gun she'd used.

"This is a Glock 22. The bullets are hollow point — they don't rust. It carries fifteen shots and it's used by law enforcement agencies around the globe. Handle it, get to know it, become familiar with the safety. Never point that gun at anyone unless you're ready to pull the trigger."

The only two guns she could recognize were the British Brown Bess and an ancient flintlock in her father's collection that had last been fired in 1715.

Quinn chose a range on Lafayette Street in nearby Gretna. He taught her how to draw and how to aim. He warned her that most times speed was of the essence. He impressed her with his accuracy and his steadiness — and with his dead-straight aim.

She couldn't begin to compare with his accuracy, and she was surprised when he seemed satisfied with her progress.

"You'll hit him somewhere in the head or chest. That's what you need," he said.

They'd been working closely together. She realized she'd been so intent on her lesson that she hadn't thought about the way they'd been touching each other through most of the late afternoon and early evening. But as the lesson came to an end, she was aware of his hand on hers, showing her how to hold the gun, and she appreciated the length of his fingers, his clipped, clean nails and the strength in his grasp.

Just his size made her feel secure.

He quickly squashed any confidence that idea had brought her.

"Remember, the biggest, meanest bully goes down when he's got a bullet in his head or his heart," he told her. "I don't care how tough. A knife in the gut will kill. But a bullet in the right place — that's your best bet. Knives can be ripped out of someone's hand. A gun can be shot from a distance. I should have started you on this from day one."

"There really haven't been *that* many days," she said.

"Yeah." He smiled. "Seems like I've known you forever, though."

She wasn't sure if that was a good thing . . . or not.

"We should do some research on the computer," she said. "Let's see what land is still privately owned — and where there might be some ruins. What do you think Father Ryan heard from a parishioner in *confession* that he was trying to tell us without telling us?"

Quinn was thoughtful as he led her out. "One of his parishioners must have confessed to joining some kind of group that holds secret ceremonies out in the bayou country."

"That could be voodoo —"

"It's not voodoo," he broke in. "Father Ryan determined that much. He has many friends who are deeply religious and practice voodoo. He has friends who are rabbis, ministers . . . you name it. He has his own faith — and he respects the beliefs of others. He studied theology and he loves culture and religion. As long as a religious practice doesn't hurt anyone."

"Where was *he* throughout history?" Danni murmured.

"Sadly, not around. What I'm saying is, I know him so well. He's trying to give us what he's learned without breaking any of his vows. So, that means one of his parishioners has come to him in terror because of a ceremony he witnessed or took part in. I don't even want to know the name of the poor dumb slob who got involved. He — or she — is going to need all Father Ryan's prayers. I think if we find out where this group is meeting, we'll find a way to get to

Brandt Shumaker. I'm convinced he's behind this. All the evidence points to it."

"This is America, remember? Even if he's a satanist spouting the most noxious views in the world, he won't be doing anything illegal."

"He will be if he's inciting a crowd to riot or if he's practicing any kind of sacrifice."

"Voodoo practitioners sometimes kill a chicken."

"If Brandt Shumaker *is* a satanist, he's sacrificing a lot more than chickens," Quinn said. "Besides, I intend to find this place where I suspect he's holding his ceremonies before he conducts his Black Mass or whatever he'll be doing in two nights. If we can pin down a general area —"

"In a huge bayou."

"There'll only be certain places with ruins — on land that isn't owned by the government. If we can narrow it down that far . . ."

"It'll still be a huge area of bayou."

"Ah, but we have a secret weapon."

"We do?"

"Wolf!"

They stopped at a po'boy shop for a quick supper and then headed back to Quinn's place to get the dog, arriving at the shop just after nine. When they entered via the courtyard, Billie was at the counter.

"I thought you closed at seven," Quinn said to Danni.

"We do, but if people are in here, we let them browse until they're done. Sometimes, if you don't close the door fast enough, more people wander in." She smiled. "We *are* a working business, you know. Sales pay the bills."

Quinn noticed a slight sound. He turned to see that Jane, frowning, was coming up from the lower level.

Jane gasped when she almost ran into Danni. "Child, you just scared me half to death! You and that . . . dog."

"I'm sorry, Jane," Danni apologized. Then she asked, "What were you doing down there?"

"I should have sent Billie," Jane said. "That basement . . . it gives me the shivers. Of course, why wouldn't it, when these rooms are filled with such creepy stuff."

Danni laughed politely. "So why *did* you go down?"

"I thought I heard something moving — maybe someone who didn't realize it's off-limits to shoppers."

"If you hear things, Jane, don't go down there. It could have been a thief," Danni said.

"She's right," Quinn told Jane firmly. "Let Billie check out any noises you hear."

"What was it?" Danni asked her.

"Nothing. I didn't see anything or anyone." Jane's eyes widened. "Rats! Could we have rats?" Her voice rose with alarm.

Rats had been an enormous problem in the city after the summer of storms. They were still prevalent in certain areas, although Danni hadn't had any in the shop in a long time.

"I'll take a look," Quinn offered.

"I hate rats. I really hate rats!" Jane said shakily.

"I'll bring Wolf down, too." Quinn gestured to the dog, who edged closer. "He'll find them if they're there."

Jane ran her hands down her skirt, as if afraid they might be dirty. "I hate to kill anything, but . . . they spread disease, they get into food. So, yes, please, if you can do something, go ahead. Let me help Billie get the last of these people out of here. Thank you!" she said earnestly to Quinn as she walked toward the counter.

"Do you think someone's bringing the hunt for the bust here? To the shop?" Danni whispered.

"I don't know. I mean, if you believe in the power of the bust, then you'd probably believe in the power of this shop. But like I said, I don't know. Wolf and I will go and check it out now."

Danni nodded. "I'm going to run up to my room and get started on the computer."

Quinn hurried down to the lower level while Danni went through the shop to reach the stairs.

It was dark when he got to the basement; Jane had turned off the lights. He stood in the darkness for a moment, letting his eyes adjust, listening. He didn't hear a thing.

He turned on the lights.

The basement hadn't changed since he'd been in it months ago — with Angus. The book sat in its glass-enclosed case, the mannequin in the coffin slept in death and the giant gorilla stared at him balefully. Crates and boxes and ancient statuary remained where they'd been stored.

He moved through the area, checking behind boxes and along the walls. He didn't see a single dug-out hole or anything that would indicate that a creature — human or non — had been there.

Had Jane really heard something down here? Or had she been *searching* for something?

Jane had been with Angus for almost two years before he died, Quinn reminded himself. Angus had evidently trusted the woman.

Wolf was at his side. "Find anything, boy?"

The dog looked at him and wagged his tail. Nothing.

"Let's go on up."

He glanced around the room one last time, then he hesitated by the light switch. "Angus," he said softly. "We miss you. We really need you on this."

If he expected a voice to whisper in his ear or a cold draft of air to pass him by, he was disappointed. But he sensed that the spirit of the man was still there — strong and good. He turned off the light and walked up the short flight of stairs to the main level.

He heard Jane telling Billie she was leaving and heard him wish her a nice evening. Quinn walked over to join Billie as he escorted Jane to the door. He assured her that he hadn't come across any rats.

When she'd gone and the door was locked, Billie frowned. "Do you think —"

"I think Jane just imagined that she heard something. Nothing was disturbed. And I'm sure you don't have rats."

"Nevertheless, don't you worry, Quinn. I'll be sleeping with my gun at my side."

Wolf barked.

And Quinn smiled. "He's telling you that you don't need to worry, Billie. He'll alert us if anything is wrong."

"All right, then," Billie said with a nod. "I'm off to bed. And I'm glad the two — I mean, three — of you are in. These late hours are hard on an old heart that beats a little faster when the time goes by and Danni isn't home."

"It's a research night, Billie. We're here."

Danni's door was ajar when he got to the second level. He tapped it and she told him to come in.

He would never have imagined that she'd appear so seductive wearing flannel pajama pants and an old T-shirt. She was seated at her desk chair, one foot on it, arms resting on her knee, chin on her arms. She seemed to glow; a scent of soap hovered around her and her hair flowed down her back in smooth dark waves.

"I hopped into the shower," she said. "I love cemeteries. I feel reverent toward them. But," she added, a slight smile curving her lips, "even when I haven't been crawling through sewage or bone dust, they make me feel as if I should shower quickly."

"How are you doing?" he asked. "*What* are you doing?"

"Reading and going from site to site."

329

"I'll grab a quick shower, too. Be back in ten."

Wolf didn't follow him into Angus's old room. He found a place between the two rooms in the hallway and curled up, one ear tilted slightly as if he were already listening and on guard.

Quinn showered but returned to jeans and a T-shirt. He left his holster and gun on the table by his bed; Wolf would warn them in plenty of time if he needed the weapon.

Danni was still in the chair, still reading. Only now both her feet were on the floor and she leaned over the desk, intent on the computer.

"You found something?" he asked her.

Without looking away from the screen, she nodded and lifted a finger. "A few on possible vaults in the cemetery. And one —" she swung around, an excited expression on her face "— one site where things might be going on! Listen to this! 'Hunter Martin was rumored to be exceptionally cruel to his slaves. While nothing was ever proven, it was feared that a few of his "punishments" became beatings in which men and women died. Neighbors would ask after one slave or another and be told to mind their own business, that he could use his "property" as he chose. In the end, it was never known just what happened to him. Some suspected that in the confusion of the Civil War — perhaps in 1862 as the Union took hold of New Orleans — he was murdered by the slaves he'd treated so cruelly. He was not seen after the Union takeover. The slaves he'd owned either wandered off, found the Underground Railroad or joined with Union forces. By the end of the war, his plantation home, known as Martin's Hold, was in a sad state of disrepair. His sugar mill, long abandoned, was overgrown and deserted. The location of the property contributed to its continued downfall. Bayou flooding was frequent and it was neither taken over by the local population following the war nor coveted by the carpetbaggers who made their way south. Flooding due to its proximity to the bayou and marsh made any attempt to redeem the house or mill an unprofitable venture. Today, it remains unattended in the wilds of swamp, bayou and marsh. The land was sold at auction in 1898 and changed hands several times over the years. It is still private property and the grounds are considered dangerous as well as illegal to visit. However, the Bayou Sauvage National Wildlife Refuge offers opportunities to see some of the beautiful foliage, trees, birds and other wildlife that thrive in this kind of landscape.' "

"Martin's Hold," Quinn said slowly, lying back on her bed and lacing his fingers behind his neck.

"You've heard of it?"

"I think so and you may have heard of it, too. It became part of an urban legend. We'd tell campfire stories about it — although that wasn't the name we used. He was supposed to be an evil old tyrant, and there are lots of tall tales about the way he was killed. In the stories I heard as a kid, he was just known as Hunter, and we made up any number of ghost stories about him. Legends grow, and some people thought the plantation was closer to Houma than it was to New Orleans. I'm sure there are other stories about other people who were cruel or behaved badly and that these various stories merged into one. Some people say his slaves hung him, and others say they drowned him in the black cane molasses at the sugar mill. Some have it that they beheaded him and that he runs around the bayou at night, just a body, screaming for his head. I have no idea how he screams, now that I'm old enough to realize you can't scream if you don't have a head. But urban legends are usually based on *something,* so

I'm assuming the stories I heard were based on Hunter Martin."

He dug his phone from his pocket and glanced at the time. It was after ten, but he went directly to his speed dial. At least he wouldn't be asking Larue to come and get him out of another fray that involved gunfire and bodies.

"What are you doing?" Danni asked.

"Calling Larue. I want him to find the info on who owns the plantation."

"This says it's owned by the Detona Group."

"That could mean anything. But thanks. I'll get him searching."

Larue answered almost immediately. His voice was level — but wary.

"All is fine," Quinn assured him. "With the two of us, anyway. No guns, no bodies."

"That's a relief," Larue said.

Quinn explained that he needed to know about a piece of property. He gave Larue the particulars and then received his lecture on private property and constitutional rights. That was followed by a warning about trespassing.

"We can't just burst into that place. And neither can you. Legally, I'm saying. The key words here are *private property,*" Larue said.

"If you have to arrest us, we'll make bail."
Quinn could almost see him rolling his eyes.

"If you call for help, of course, we'll have to come in."

Quinn smiled at that. "See what you can find out through all your *legal* sources, okay?"

Larue told him he'd call back in the morning.

He hung up. Danni was watching him.

"He'll call us tomorrow," he said.

"Larue is a good guy, huh? You two seem to get along."

"We do. I worked with him. We were partners once. After I left the force, he got a raise and now handles major crime throughout the city."

"You're lucky he doesn't think you're some kind of weirdo."

"Oh, he probably does. But we're friends — and I'm a weirdo who gets results, so . . . yeah, I guess I'm lucky. What else have you got?" he asked, rising up on an elbow to watch her.

"Comfy?" she asked him.

"Yes, thanks. What else did you find?"

"Well, the way I see it, we have three possibles. In one cemetery, you have a large mausoleum that was built for the Sisters of Mary's Virtue. The sisters were cloistered

334

nuns who lived in a now-demolished convent before the Civil War. They spent their days in silence, tending to people stricken with contagious diseases. Then, next door, so to speak, you have a mausoleum built for the priests of the Little French Chapel. It's also gone, but their mausoleum still exists. And there's one more place someone might notice and expect to be sacred. It was built by the Society of Angels. They were a mixed group — doctors, priests, nurses — who set to work *following* the war to support and heal wounded soldiers from both sides of the Mason-Dixon Line. They raised money to help amputees and others who were disabled, and they, too, cared for patients most people didn't want to touch, such as malaria victims."

"We'll bring Wolf and Billie and check out all three," Quinn promised.

She got up from her chair, stretched and yawned.

He started to rise but she came over and sat on the foot of the bed, studying him.

"You didn't . . . become an *angel,* did you?" she asked him. There was a teasing note in her voice. Was she serious?

"What? No! Far from an angel, I'm afraid."

"Hmm."

"Why?"

"Just curious."

"In what way?"

"Well . . ." To his surprise, she stretched out beside him. He was instantly aware of her, although she wasn't touching him at all. Her expression was somewhat perplexed, as if he were a great mystery. And she hadn't made any effort to seduce him — although, in her flannel pants and a T-shirt, she had far more appeal than a half-naked beauty queen. She had those enormous dark-framed blue eyes, and that flow of mahogany-red hair. And he loved the way the soft cotton of her T-shirt clung to her breasts. . . .

He felt his breath catch. He forced himself not to move, raising an eyebrow instead.

She grinned suddenly. "Did you take a vow of chastity?"

He smiled in return; he couldn't help it. "No."

"That's it? No?"

Good God, *was* she seducing him? "Um, no . . . I didn't take a vow of chastity."

"Oh. Oh, well, okay." With a shrug, she began to get up.

He reached out, drawing her back to him. "Oh, well, no — not okay. What was *that* all about?"

His hand lay on her arm. They were actually curled toward each other now. Close. He felt feverish, his skin heated.

She glanced at his arm, and then her eyes, so very blue, met his. He thought he could as easily be lost within them as in any sea or sky. There was a dazzling sparkle of amusement, too. She wasn't looking at him as though he *shouldn't* be touching her.

"I guess I was wondering if there's something wrong with me," she said.

"Wrong with you?"

"Yes. I was thinking that you're a healthy free heterosexual male, and I'm a healthy free heterosexual female and . . . well, you're lying in my bed and you don't seem interested in coming on to me."

Quinn blinked. He laughed.

"Don't go adding insult to injury!" she warned.

He shook his head. He wanted to pull her straight into his arms. He felt as if he were soaring on a high that no drug could ever create.

But he held still a few seconds longer. "Yes, at the beginning I thought you were a spoiled debutante —"

"Better than an obnoxious hulk!"

"But . . ."

"But?"

He did pull her to him then. He drew her close and adjusted his weight, bracing himself on his elbows, staring down at her.

"But now — and I'm pretty sure you know — I all but worship the ground you walk on," he told her huskily.

"Wow. Worship the ground I walk on!"

"It's an expression."

"I like it," she said.

"But . . ."

"Another *but!*"

"You're who you are, and I'm who I am. We are . . . what we are."

"You're the one who told me we're supposed to live normal lives."

"Yes," he said.

He leaned in. Her lips were damp and full, inviting. He felt their heat as he kissed her, the brush of his lips gentle. He rose just inches above her, determined to see her eyes again. "At this moment, not much else seems to matter — if you're sure I'm what you really want. And I'm not prepared . . . I mean, I don't walk around with condoms, whatever my past might have been."

She grinned. "I'm on the pill. I *have* had relationships before. Not many, but once upon a time I did have a life."

"Oh."

She smiled. "Would you ever have made a move?"

"I . . ."

"Answer yes!" she whispered.

"Yes, God, yes!" he said.

He kissed her again, molding his mouth to hers. He felt passion embrace him, kissed her long and deeply and with trembling force. She kissed him wickedly in return. He felt her tongue as it slipped into his mouth, arousing every carnal desire within him.

She rose against him as their lips remained locked. They broke away, breathless, looking at each other again for the eternity of seconds, and then began reaching for each other — he to tug her T-shirt over her head, she to pluck at the buttons on his shirt. Her fingers were unfastening his belt buckle as his lips touched the naked flesh of her shoulder and he'd never felt more alive, hungrier, more in need of a woman's touch. . . . He shimmied out of his jeans and briefs, traced his fingers down the length of her torso and rid her of the flannel pajama pants. They moved together again, and he relished the feel of their bare bodies touching, both eager to feel, to surrender to their base and yet beautiful desires.

She made love as elegantly, as passionately, as uniquely, as she did everything else. Her fingers were like feathers as they teased his body; her kisses were light and taunting and giving. He drew away at one point just to look at her, to savor the way her long hair curled around her breasts, to gaze at the smoothness of her flesh. Then he dropped reverent kisses onto her breasts, tantalized her with his tongue, brushed her torso with his fingers and edged down the length of her body. She moved erotically against him, a rhythm beginning between them. He felt as though he were drowning in the scent and taste of her, wanting more and more. He rose above her, finding her lips again, and they shared another fiery kiss as he thrust within her. They held each other in an eternity of savoring what they had, before frantically plunging into a hip-locked dance that became everything in the world.

He fought against his climax and yet the need was savage, desperate. And then he could hold back no longer, crying out in the night as she shuddered and trembled in his arms, melting into him as the frenzy slowly eased from them both.

She was still in his arms, legs entwined with his, when his eyes met hers once more.

She reached out and touched his cheek.

"I'm not sure I've ever felt so alive," she murmured.

He caught her fingers and kissed them. It seemed a miracle that she'd come into his life, a miracle that he'd found someone like her.

"Well, you might say something, you know," she whispered. "Like, was it as good for you as it was for me? Or . . . thank you?"

And she could make him laugh . . . she could make the world worth fighting for.

"Thank you," he told her solemnly.

That brought a tap to his cheek. "Hey!"

He turned to her. "I'm just afraid . . ." He couldn't find the right words. He worried that he'd insulted her, but to his astonishment, she understood what he was saying.

"I know," she said. "We are what we are. I'm just learning that, but it seems we have odd roles in life. Don't worry, Quinn. I know we have to do what we have to do, that lives — souls, perhaps — depend on it. You've shown me the legacy my father left behind. I'll never forget that. I'll be very serious when we're . . . when we're looking for the bust, when we're trying to solve this puzzle." A smile raised the corners of her lips. "And I promise I'll be extremely focused when I'm being shot at and the bad guys are trying to knife or strangle me."

He pulled her back into his arms. "We're going to try damned hard *not* to let that happen again."

She freed herself, leaning over him, her hair teasing his flesh and the feel of her breasts seductive again although with no intent. "But that's the point, isn't it, Quinn? If I become who I must, we *will* be in danger."

She was right, of course.

But he wasn't an angel. He was just a man who'd been given a little help and shown a different path.

He would always try to protect her.

His life had changed so much since his wild and wicked days, since he'd died. He hadn't become celibate, but his affairs were few and far apart.

And she was touching him. . . .

He didn't reply. He didn't argue or agree with her words. He kissed her again. Slowly. And he made love to her again, as she made love to him. Hours seemed to pass before they both lay together, spent and silent.

He started to leave the bed. She stopped him. "Where are you going?"

"Back to your dad's room. Billie and Jane will be around in the morning and —"

"And it's my house, and I don't care what

they know. Jane disapproves of any premarital sex whatsoever, but realizes it exists. And Billie . . . well, I believe Billie will think it's just great or par for the course or . . . or he won't think about it one way or the other. Stay here. I want to sleep beside you. Please."

"There will never be a sleep so sweet!" he told her. He grinned, remembering her made-up quote in the cemetery. "Ah, to be asleep at your side, peaceful and deep!"

She smiled. "Now that, Mr. Quinn, is a very good line."

He lay down beside her again.

And he did sleep sweetly. And deeply.

CHAPTER 14

Danni woke late, feeling as if she were still cocooned in the warmth of the night. She stretched out a hand, but she was alone now. Quinn had already risen.

She showered, then dressed and went downstairs.

There were several people in the shop. She slipped through to the little kitchen and poured herself a coffee before investigating what everyone was doing.

Jane was showing jewelry at the counter.

She heard Quinn speaking with Billie in her studio, and she made her way there.

She found Billie pointing out a few of her paintings on the walls. "Shouldn't we get moving today?" she asked as she walked in.

"Yes, but we were talking about the portrait you did of Gladys."

"I gave it to her daughter, who wasn't very appreciative. I told you that," she reminded Quinn.

"I know, but I was thinking about the painting itself," Quinn said.

"We were talking about the fact that you'd never met her before she came into the store," Billie added, "but you were doing a painting of her right when she did."

"It was weird, eerie. Uncomfortable," Danni said.

"Do you feel the desire to draw or paint a tomb — or the bayou?" Quinn asked.

"What?"

"I was wondering," Billie said, "if maybe you can draw . . . *things.*"

"Things," she repeated.

"Not to get too creepy about it, I'll put it like this," Quinn began. "We know that as human beings we only ever make use of a small part of the incredible computer we all have — the brain. Maybe that's why some people have ESP. It's a function they've managed to cultivate that others haven't. Danni, you might have a way of processing thoughts — thoughts you don't actually know you have — into some kind of fore-warning."

"I looked at pictures online for a good hour last night. Maybe I'd just be imitating a picture I'd seen and we'd end up wasting a lot of time."

"What made you do a portrait of Gladys

Simon?" Quinn asked.

"I didn't *know* I was doing a portrait of her. I sat down and got to work. That's all."

Billie, Quinn and even Wolf stared at her.

"I wish it was something I *could* just do," she said. "But I'm not feeling the urge to sketch or work with oils or watercolors at the moment. Sorry."

Billie shrugged. "Figured I'd ask," he said. "I made some egg sandwiches. Want to grab one before we get started?"

They ate, had more coffee and prepared to leave. Danni ran back to check on Jane first, asking her if she'd be all right on her own for a few hours.

"Well, of course, Danni, I'll be fine," Jane assured her. "Where are the three of you off to? Somewhere fun, I hope."

"It'll be loads of fun, I'm sure," Danni said. "See you tonight."

She left quickly, telling herself to ask Billie whether Jane knew about . . . what her father had done. And now, what she was trying to do.

Not that she could explain it herself . . .

"Where to first?" she asked.

"The cemeteries. We need to try and get our hands on that bust. Then we'll visit the property you found online," Quinn said.

"Do we know anything about that property yet?"

He nodded grimly. "Detona Group is a 'doing-business-as.' The parent company is something called 'Properties.' "

"So what does that tell us?" Danni asked.

"It's a real estate firm — and the biggest shareholder is Brandt Shumaker."

"Oh," Danni said. "Not really a surprise."

"No," Quinn agreed.

All three religious society mausoleums were in different cemeteries, but at least the cemeteries were close together. They decided to start farthest from the city and work their way back. Then, if the bust was found, they'd get it down to Angus Cafferty's private collection as soon as possible.

Wolf clearly wasn't happy about staying in the car, but he waited obediently as they entered the first of the cemeteries. The Little French Chapel was larger than the customary family vault, but not immense. The seal hadn't been touched in a hundred years, and there was little decoration on the brick structure, just a large cross erected above it.

When they returned to the car, Wolf was anxious. Danni saw Quinn frown and look around, but there was no one parked near them and the few sightseers seemed to be nothing more than that.

The next cemetery contained the great memorial built in honor of the Society of Angels. The structure was beautiful and well-tended, but it was plain, and while it had been there for over a century, as well, it was designed with the sleek modernism of the time, a style that left little room for gothic angels, cherubs or busts. Billie walked around and called out excitedly. Over the rear window, there were several little guardian statuettes — but they were two cherubs and a weeping angel, nothing that resembled the bust they were seeking.

Returning to the car again, they noticed that Wolf was even more agitated. Danni saw that it worried Quinn; he stood still, carefully surveying the area.

"What is it?" Billie asked.

"I don't know, but Wolf senses something. We're going to take a roundabout route to the last cemetery — and I'm going to call Larue."

He did, then drove them to the third cemetery. When they left the car, Quinn lowered the windows completely. "Keep an eye out, boy," he told the dog.

He paused at the gates. There were a few people ahead of them with cemetery guide maps, but no one else about.

Danni led the way, heading for the tomb

of the Sisters of Mary's Virtue. It was certainly the oldest of the tombs they'd come across and the most ornate.

And it was large, built in a T-shape with the entry on the vertical side.

A three-foot wrought-iron fence surrounded the structure. The grassy area inside was overgrown. The tomb had been built in the style of a gothic church, with two gargoyles guarding the main entry. There were stained-glass windows in the front and Quinn thought there might be more around the back.

They climbed over the little fence and Danni followed as Quinn hurried toward the entry. A gate protected it, and beyond that, a door, rather than a seal, allowed access.

"I'm checking the back," Billie said. "This is a big one. There could be another entrance." He began to walk around.

Quinn pulled at a rung of the wrought-iron gate; it opened without a squeak. He glanced at Danni, shrugged and set his hand on the heavy wooden inner door. It, too, gave without protest. They went in.

For a minute, the sudden darkness in the tomb after the bright daylight cast Danni into momentary blindness. She blinked a few times and then she could see. The tomb was set up as a chapel. There was an altar toward the rear and two hallways going to the right and left behind it. She realized that almost every inch of wall space was a ledge for entombment.

A large gold cross sat on the altar and on either side were statuettes of the Virgin Mary, hands folded in prayer, her eyes raised to heaven.

"I'll go left, you go right?" Danni suggested.

Quinn nodded. "This place is enormous, but I'll be able to hear you if you shout. Call if you need me."

Danni strode ahead to look past the altar. From the rear, stained glass let in a strange and eerie light.

To the left, a hallway passed rows and rows of deceased sisters. She started down it. As she walked, she saw plaques on the walls, most in French, that gave simple names and dates of the sisters' births and deaths. There were breaks along the way with little altars. Icons of saints sat on the ledges, along with other pieces of funerary art such as paintings of children cradling little lambs, images of a dying Christ in the arms of his mother, cherubs and angels. She tried to move quickly and yet make sure she saw them all.

Empty sconces would have held torches at one time; now their brackets were skeletal and rusted. At the far end of the tomb, she saw a single ledge — with a bust on it.

She began to walk toward the ledge and then paused.

There it was.

After reading about it, the bust was exactly what she'd expected. It was life-size, depicting a man with generous lips that should have made him appealing. Instead, the curl of the lips seemed to indicate a careless cruelty. Rich hair waved over the forehead. The entire face was classic and striking.

The eyes . . .

They were open.

Watching.

As she was about to call out for Quinn she heard a loud thump that seemed to come from the rear of the tomb.

She started back but heard him shout, "I'm on it!"

She felt an impulse to stop him, but Billie had been around back. Something might have happened to him; she wanted Quinn to make sure he was unhurt.

She whirled around, hearing a sound like stone sliding along stone. Then, nothing. The tomb was silent.

She hurried back along the hallway and

paused abruptly. Someone was behind her. It wasn't Quinn. She knew that before she turned.

She screamed even as arms reached out for her. . . .

And a hand clamped down on her mouth.

Billie had guessed correctly — there was more than one entry to the vast mausoleum. Quinn had assumed it might have been at the rear of the tomb, in one of the wings, but it wasn't. It was located to the far right of the main chapel area and it wasn't actually a door. The opening was low to the ground and he realized it was how a coffin would be slid into the tomb — or out of it.

He crawled through it and walked around to the back.

At first, he didn't see Billie.

Then he did.

The elderly man was on the ground, half-covered by the grass growing long and thick in the little fenced yard around the mausoleum.

Quinn's heart thudded with fear as he rushed to Billie, hunkering down to check for injuries and a pulse. No pulse, but no blood, either; he hadn't been knifed or shot.

A moment later, Quinn found a weak beat at the side of Billie's throat. He looked around, swearing. The police had yet to arrive.

Quinn pulled out his phone and called for an ambulance. As he did, Billie groaned and tried to sit up.

"Lie still," Quinn told him. "Lie still. Help is coming."

But Billie grasped his arm. His gray eyes were filled with misery, his bone-thin face contorted.

"Three of them. I saw them just as they got me . . . hit my head, butt of a gun . . . Leave me . . . they're in the tomb!"

Quinn stood, drawing his gun.

And heard a scream.

"Don't move. Don't whisper. Don't fight me!" the man said.

He was tall and wiry-strong; Danni felt she was held in a death grip.

She saw, from the corner of her eye, that he was wielding a knife.

A butcher knife. Large. Even in the shadows, its razor-sharp edge seemed to glisten with just a hint of what it could do to human flesh.

"Which one is it?" he demanded.

She shook her head, pretending she didn't know.

He dragged her down the hall to the ledge,

her feet scraping on the stone floor of the mausoleum.

"Damn you," he growled. "I will slice you from ear to ear, and don't think your boyfriend is going to save you. I'm not alone."

They got to the end of the tomb — and the ledge. To Danni's surprise, he stopped. He didn't need her help anymore. He seemed to be listening to someone who wasn't there.

"Yes, yes, I'm here. I'm here for you!" the man holding Danni said.

She thought there must be someone near . . . but there wasn't! Quinn had to be close by, though — if he hadn't been ambushed. This man had just said he hadn't come alone, but . . .

He shoved Danni away from him and tossed a burlap bag at her. "He says you're to pick him up, cover him, get him in the bag."

He was referring to the bust.

She got her first good look at the man. He was wearing a shoulder holster, and she could see the sheen of his gun. He was carrying the knife tightly in his left hand. She wondered if he was ambidextrous.

Just her luck.

"Do it!"

She turned. The bust was heavy, but then it was marble. The eyes seemed to stare at her as she lifted it and got it into the burlap bag.

The lips seemed to curl in complete enjoyment.

As she turned back, the man took the bag and slung it over his shoulder with an audible grunt. At the same moment, he pulled her to him using his knife hand, the blade nicking her flesh.

"Let's go. He said not to kill you until I'm in the clear," the man said.

Danni was numb with dread, but she had no choice. She felt the steel of the knife against her throat as he propelled her to the front entrance of the tomb.

Quinn raced around to the main entrance. He didn't dare take the coffin slide — he'd be trapped with no vision and no aim. He sidled around the main door, looking in. He heard nothing for a moment. And then a voice called out.

"I can see you," it said. "Move outside or she dies."

His eyes adjusted. A bulky man he'd never seen before held a knife to Danni's throat, a heavy burlap bag thrown over his shoulder and a gun tucked in his holster. Quinn was furious with himself. He'd taken Danni to learn how to shoot. Why hadn't he insisted she carry the gun today? He'd assumed they'd have another chance at the range, so she could become more proficient. And it hadn't occurred to him this morning that she might need a weapon. . . .

He heard the grass rustle behind him. He turned in time to see a second man stealthily coming his way. The man saw him and raised a gun.

Quinn shot first, hitting his target in the chest. He whirled around but the man with Danni was charging him, blocking any chance he had of shooting because Danni was his shield.

The stranger approached in a whirlwind, thrusting Danni toward Quinn so hard and fast that they were both thrown backward. As Quinn scrambled to right himself, the man took off. When Quinn got to his feet, he heard a shot and he saw that the man with the burlap bag was racing among the myriad tombs of this City of the Dead.

He started to take aim but a shot rang out in his direction and he ducked low.

He stayed down as another shot came from a tomb to his left. The bullet ricocheted off the stone beside him and plowed into the ground just inches from where

Danni was scrambling to rise.

He saw that the shooter had partially emerged from the tomb, the muzzle of his gun trained on Quinn.

But before the man could fire, something came leaping out at him.

Wolf!

The dog seemed to appear from nowhere, bared teeth sinking into the man's gun wrist. He screamed. His gun went flying, and Wolf bore him to the ground, standing over him, fangs at his throat.

"You all right?" Quinn asked Danni.

She nodded wildly. "Go! Chase the man with the bust!"

He ran, weaving through the vaults. Tourists were rushing out of the cemetery; they'd heard the sound of gunfire — and now sirens. The police and an ambulance were arriving at the gates.

He jogged around more vaults, looked down "boulevards" and "streets," but the man had vanished.

He ran back to the tomb for the Sisters of Mary's Virtue. Danni was still on the ground, catching her breath, watching Wolf keep his prisoner pinned down.

"The bust — the bust is gone," Danni told him. "It was my fault. I didn't see or hear them."

Quinn pulled her to her feet. "It's not your fault, it's mine. They've obviously been stalking us, and I led them right to it. Thank God you're alive. I'm alive."

"Billie . . ." she began anxiously.

"Billie's going to have a headache, but he'll be fine."

He saw that a trickle of blood dripped onto Danni's throat. She'd nearly died. He tried not to shake; he did slip an arm around her, drawing her close. "How badly are you hurt?" he demanded.

"What? Oh, just a scratch," she said. Gesturing at the man on the ground with the dog over him, she asked, "Should we . . . go help?"

"Let him stare at Wolf's fangs a little longer," Quinn said bitterly. He touched Danni's throat, assuring himself that she was telling the truth.

Then he walked back to the man who'd tried to jump him — the man he'd shot and killed. He'd never seen him before. He was a stranger, about thirty-five or forty, with a number of gang tattoos. But it wouldn't matter who he was. He'd been hired from somewhere else by someone with no name. He'd been given a hefty payment and promised a great reward.

They did have one man, though. One

who'd survived. Who could perhaps give them a lead.

But it was true, Quinn thought angrily. This was his own fault. He'd led them right to the bust.

And the bust was gone.

"Quinn, we got him! Call off your dog!"

He turned. Larue was in the cemetery. The place was now swarming with police. Danni ran to the emergency medical techs who'd come, leading them around to the back of the tomb and the place where Billie lay.

Quinn whistled for Wolf and walked over to Larue. "They have it. They have the bust," he said.

"They who?"

"There were three of them. One dead, one that Wolf ran down — and one who got away with the bust."

"I'll get men searching immediately. You have a description?"

"Big guy, carrying a burlap bag. Fortyish. Tattoos. Brown hair, ravaged-looking face. A few pockmarks on him."

"But we've got one of them. And the other —"

"Yeah, the other's dead. When someone attacks me with a gun, I shoot to kill."

Larue nodded. "Well, you know the drill.

Let's get started on the paperwork — and questioning the man who's alive."

Danni went to the hospital with Billie. He had a mild concussion and they were going to keep him overnight. She had the cut on her neck treated, but luckily — especially considering its location — it was a superficial wound.

In the hospital, Billie was a bit of a problem. He didn't want to stay. He was disgusted with himself for having been jumped so easily, but Danni convinced him they'd all been taken by surprise.

When she left him, getting dropped off at the police station by one of the med techs who was ending his shift, she began to wonder just how they'd been found. Who the hell had known where they'd be heading? Or had the shop been spied on all this time? Had they been followed whenever they'd come and gone?

At the police station, she was led into an observation area where Quinn watched Detective Jake Larue in another room, grilling the man Wolf had taken down. Wolf was next to Quinn; someone at the station had rewarded him with a nice bone. He was happily chewing away, but did pause to look at her, giving a happy thump of his tail before returning to his bone.

"Is he getting any information?" she asked anxiously, nodding at the one-way glass.

"Sure," Quinn said. "The guy's name is Peter Huxby, and he's from Detroit, like those other guys who showed up at Natasha's. Whoever's pulling the strings on this must have some connection with the underground in that city. The man heard there was big money to be made in New Orleans. The only person he ever saw once he got here — until today — was the guy who escaped. The man who has the bust. His name is 'Bigsy.' And that's all Peter knows. Bigsy was the one who met him when he came down, and he's the one who paid him. Cash. Worn bills, nothing bigger than hundreds. Oh, and naturally, he was given a pay-as-you-go phone, and naturally, Bigsy got hold of him using a pay-as-you-go phone."

As Quinn told her what they'd heard so far, Larue rose, left the interrogation room and joined them in the observation area.

"What's up?" Quinn asked.

"He just requested a lawyer," Larue said.

Quinn shrugged. "Par for the course."

Larue's phone buzzed. He answered it, listened a moment and said, "Thank you," before hanging up and turning to Quinn again.

"The man you shot was named Alex Renault. He's got a rap sheet a mile long. He was born in this area, but he's been hopping around from state to state — when he hasn't been in the pen. What are your plans now, Quinn? I suggest you think out your next moves very carefully. I know a statue doesn't kill people, but people are killing over that statue. You may want to leave it alone. We'll nail Shumaker eventually." He paused, narrowing his eyes. "You might notice you've been in a few dangerous positions while tracking this thing down."

"I can handle it, I was a cop, remember."

"Ms. Cafferty was not," Larue argued.

"I'm okay, really," Danni insisted.

"But we'll think about all the complications," Quinn said. "Wolf, come on, bring that bone if you want, but it's time for us to go."

"Quinn, keep me informed," Larue said wearily. "I'm glad that, so far, the bodies I keep picking up in your wake haven't been yours or Ms. Cafferty's."

"Me, too," Danni whispered. "Me, too."

A few minutes later they were in Quinn's car, heading toward Royal Street.

"Why are we going to my place?" Danni asked.

"Because Larue is right. I don't want to get you killed."

"Well, then, you should've thought of that before you walked into my shop," Danni told him flatly.

"You could have died," he said. "That's not the first time, either."

"And *you* could have died today, too."

"Danni, I was a cop, I was in the military. I know more about self-defense."

"Something, again, that you should've thought of before," she said stubbornly.

"I have to protect you."

"Because we slept together?"

"Maybe. Maybe not." He turned to her with a mischievous smile. "Something *you* should have thought about before."

She shook her head and said, "Quinn, we also had a discussion about being who and what we are. You're going out to Martin's Hold and you think you're dropping me off at the shop? Well, guess what — you're not. So just keep driving."

"If you're going to go running around like this, we really need to get you back onto a shooting range, buy you a holster —"

"And nothing's happening until tomorrow night," she reminded him. "Let's go there now and see if we can find any sign of the activity that's supposed to take place — or the bust."

Once again, Quinn wished with all his heart that Angus Cafferty was with them.

Or that Danni Cafferty had proven to be a miserable shrew or a spoiled princess.

"You *are* going to keep driving, right?"

He sighed. "Yes. I'll keep driving. After we make a stop."

"Oh?"

"We're going to pick up the little pistol I had you working with. Just make sure you don't shoot me with it, huh?"

"Hey!" Danni yelped. "That's insulting!"

"No insult intended. I think you'll be a real expert one day. But you don't have any experience yet."

"I'll try very hard not to shoot you."

They made a quick visit to the shop so Danni could run upstairs and change her clothes. She considered telling Jane what had happened to Billie in the cemetery, but she couldn't do that without more of an explanation than she had time for or wanted to give. She'd say something tomorrow if necessary, keeping the details as vague as possible.

Jane was busy at the cash register, so Danni decided they'd just slip out. Hopefully, Billie would be home soon.

They headed out of town and toward the bayou country.

"What do you think we'll find?" Danni asked.

"A trail of dead, I'm afraid."

CHAPTER 15

Bigsy Taylor looked at the burlap bundle next to him and laughed with delight. He had it, he alone. He possessed the bust and *he'd* be the one to make the fortune, shared with no one. He wasn't a double-crossing SOB — *he* hadn't made his fellow conspirators go down in a rain of bullets and a dog attack. It had just happened. So the bust was his.

As he drove, doubling through the city a few times as he'd been ordered, he began to feel an eerie sensation sneaking along his spine.

That usually meant cops.

He checked around; they couldn't have found him yet. He'd parked his car around the block from the cemetery and he'd seen the cops who were chasing him running in all the wrong directions. The dog had already been occupied. His escape had succeeded. There was no reason for the cops to be after him.

"Get this off me," someone said.

The voice was so close that he jumped. He nearly ran off the road.

"Drive as if you know how to!"

He looked to his right. *The voice was coming from the burlap bag.*

It was a trick. It had to be some kind of trick. He reached out and ripped the burlap from the bust. To his amazement, the bust seemed to grow . . . like one of those trick pictures in a booth at an arcade.

There was a man sitting next to him. Thirty or so, dark-haired, wearing a ridiculous toga thing around his shoulders. But Bigsy didn't laugh. He stared — and nearly drove off the road again.

He felt the man touch him. Something raced through him, like an electric pulse.

"Go. Go straight to where you're supposed to be. Now."

Terrified, Bigsy drove. He was afraid to look to his right.

"You've got your gun?"

Bigsy nodded.

"When we get there, you shoot anything that moves, you understand?"

Bigsy nodded again.

He pulled off the highway and found the old road. It had never been paved and the car jolted as he drove. Tree roots made for more bumps, and foliage slapped the windows. Finally, he neared the ruins of the old mansion and mill.

"There . . . there are people here!" the man said. "Start shooting!"

Bigsy got out of the car, holding his gun. He saw vaguely that there were people in front of him, people expecting him — it was an ambush! He raised his gun and began shooting wildly, missing his mark.

A volley of bullets came his way. The first caught him in the stomach and he was aware of blinding pain.

The next caught him dead center in the forehead, and he went down like an ox.

Brandt Shumaker walked to the car, followed by his priestess. He kicked Bigsy, making sure he was dead, even though the giant hole in his head assured him the big man was gone.

"What the hell caused that?" he asked. "No matter. I was going to have to get rid of him, anyway."

"The bust. We don't know if he has the bust," the woman said.

Shumaker opened the door. The bust lay on the seat. Just seeing it, he felt power surge through him.

"Are you going to set it up for the ceremony?" the woman asked.

"Hell, no. That thing stays with me wherever I go," Shumaker said. "But we've got to dispose of the body and the car."

Shumaker wasn't concerned about hurrying. He walked around to the passenger seat and looked at the bust for a minute before cradling it in his arms. The second he touched it, he felt fulfilled. "My friend — the things we can do!" he said.

He saw the eyes open; saw the smile that curved the marble lips.

"Yes, my friend. We will rule the world."

Quinn glanced at Danni and then back at the road as he drove. "There's going to be a dead man somewhere. Bigsy, whoever he is, doesn't have much of a chance now. He's had the bust in his possession."

"You think it kills that . . . quickly?"

"I think the bust has been seeking a certain personality type — with a certain level of intelligence."

"The bust can call out to who it wants?" she asked skeptically.

"It's possible. I also think the bust demands the utmost loyalty. When people won't commit an act of brutality, they end up taking their own lives."

"Like Gladys Simon."

"Like Gladys," he agreed. "Count them up. Hank apparently plunged from a balcony. Gladys hanged herself. Vic Brown killed a bunch of people before he went down. Everyone involved with the bust winds up dead. And we know Shumaker is as evil as a man can be. He'd kill his own mother to further his ends. But what I think the bust wants is the kind of power Pietro Miro wielded in life — political power."

"But . . ." Danni began, then fell silent. They'd pulled off the highway and were driving onto a lonely road near Martin's Hold. "That car!" she said, pointing out a black sedan. It had veered off the road, tires bogged down in the marsh.

Quinn stopped behind it. "Stay," he told Wolf. "You, too," he said to Danni.

"Quinn —"

"Cover me from the car, will you?"

She nodded, removing the pistol from her bag. He walked over to the car and opened the front door and then the back. She saw him take out his phone and make a call.

Then he returned to his own car.

"What did you find?" Danni asked as she replaced the gun in her purse.

"Nothing. It might just be an abandoned car. I called it in to Larue. He'll send a couple of men to check it out."

Danni studied the terrain as they drove. She couldn't see anything that remotely resembled a road. Quinn circled a few times, and then seemed satisfied that an area with broken foliage was indeed a road.

He parked the car nearby and they climbed out. "I don't want to warn anyone that we're coming," he told her.

They hadn't gone more than a hundred yards down the dirt path before she was attacked by a swarm of mosquitoes. She could've kicked herself for not remembering to bring repellent.

Danni loved New Orleans, the city's surroundings and, in fact, the entire state of Louisiana. She didn't love the bugs in the bayou area.

She swatted at them. Quinn looked over with a shrug. "I offered to leave you at home," he said.

She sent him a warning glare. He smiled — and shut up.

Wolf moved ahead of them, barging into the brush. "Where's he going?" she asked.

"He must have found a shortcut."

They followed the dog and in a few minutes, they broke through the bracken and brush to see the facade of the old Martin's Hold estate, set in a field of long grass. It was crumbling, decaying. The sugar works — what remained of them — were to the right of the main house.

"I don't think it has much of a roof," Danni said.

"I don't think it has a roof at all. Maybe just an overhang," Quinn said.

For a moment, they stared at the house.

"There's been a car here recently, so there has to be another path in." Quinn pointed out the flattened grass.

Danni looked around and then gestured behind her. "It came from that way, north of where we came in," she said.

"Double tracks. It pulled out that way, too."

Wolf let out an excited bark. He was eager to go up to the house.

Quinn and Danni went after the dog. She saw that he was watchful, but unless someone was hiding quietly in the brush, they were alone.

Besides, Wolf would have known if anyone *was* hiding there.

Because the door of the house had long since fallen off, they walked in unimpeded. A staircase led up to nothing but the open air. Although remnants of the first floor ceiling remained, the outer walls of the second story had crumbled.

"We stay together," Quinn said.

Danni nodded.

The house had a hallway. There was broken furniture in one of the rooms, including a desk, a faded seascape on the wall and chairs missing a leg or two.

Danni told Quinn, "The architecture seems to be on par with a lot of old Victorian houses. The first room on the right was a plantation office, and beyond that was a ladies' room and a music room. Over on this side, we'll find a grand ballroom. . . ." She was correct. A still-standing pocket door was open, creating a room that stretched almost the length of the house.

"And there'll be a pantry behind that and a kitchen and —"

Quinn shook his head. "And nothing. It doesn't look like anyone's been here in eons."

Wolf barked.

Quinn's hand instantly dropped to his holster, but Wolf hadn't sensed danger. He wanted them to follow. They did, passing through the large ballroom area; as Danni had predicted, there was a pantry behind it.

"When the pocket doors aren't open, the front room on this side is a parlor and the second is a dining room."

A canted, decaying table seemed to prove

her right.

"There'll be another pantry behind the dining room," she said.

She walked ahead and, again, she was proven right. Bits of broken pottery were scattered about, but there were no signs that anyone had been in the vicinity in a long time.

"There's no basement — it's barely sea level here," Quinn murmured.

"Satanic rituals usually take place in a basement?" Danni asked him.

He raised one shoulder. "Basements are good places to hide many a sin," he told her. "Unless, of course, you're underwater. Which should mean we don't have all that much sin in New Orleans. But our whole conception of heaven and hell depends on heaven being up, while hell is down. So if you're going to sin —"

"Sin in the basement," Danni finished.

There was nothing in the house. They walked toward the remnants of the sugar mill.

Through a rotting roof, the sun cast half shadows over the massive mill. Huge vats where the syrup had been boiled lined what was left of the structure. A brick chimney remained, along with implements for stirring, long-rotted cane and a sickly sweet smell. To the sides were the ghostly relics of wagons used to haul the cane and what appeared to be rusted manual cranes. They were silent as they walked through the ruins of the mill. The very air seemed to carry a miasma.

"There's nothing here," Danni said.

"*Too* nothing."

"What does that mean?"

"Well, think about the years that have passed. Kids daring one another or out to be spooked on Halloween must've come here. There should be gum wrappers or cigarette butts or beer cans — at least *some* trash somewhere," Quinn said.

"Ah." Danni nodded.

Suddenly Quinn bent down. She did the same, not at all sure what he saw.

"Footprints," he explained. "Lots of them."

She blinked. She could more or less recognize what he was talking about. He pointed to the ground. She could make out the lines left by the bottom of a sneaker.

"So you think Shumaker is coming here and officiating over some kind of cult?" she asked.

"I know he has something going on. Whether he's twisting voodoo, Christianity, Santeria or anything else — I don't know.

But he's got *something* going on." Quinn straightened. "The bust isn't here," he said.

"No."

He looked at her. "You're not going to argue?"

Danni hesitated. "I saw it, you know. In the tomb."

"And?"

"It's just . . . odd. I think I'd sense if it was near us. But I don't understand . . ."

"Understand what?"

"Well, supposedly, if a ghost is haunting someone, making that person's life miserable or whatever — *killing people* — it's stopped by being burned to ash. Pietro Miro was cremated, so I don't get how this can be happening. We're looking for a bust. So I'm assuming the spirit has to materialize somehow, at least in the minds of those holding it. But, by all accounts, the evil spirit of this man shouldn't be able to wield such power. And then, why is he tied to the bust? If he's an evil spirit because he *wasn't* really cremated, wouldn't he just be able to walk or drift around as he pleased?"

"Danni, I don't have those answers. I do know we have to find the thing."

She straightened. "Let's walk the property one more time. We'll split up so we can cover ground more quickly."

"We'll move quickly. But, Danni, I've told you before — we *don't* split up," Quinn said firmly, rolling his eyes. "I'm going to have to introduce you to some of the cheesier horror films. When it's a monster, people are always caught when they're alone. Now, if we were after a giant reptile or humongous killer crocodile, it would be different."

"Scared?" she teased him.

"You bet. Come on, Wolf, we'll do this with speed and organization. We'll walk on each side and between the vats."

Wolf wagged his tail. They walked, finding nothing but the telltale scuffles they'd already seen on the dusty floor.

It was when they neared the remnants of the old brick chimney that Wolf barked and raced ahead. He seated himself in front of the fallen bricks by the chimney, waiting for them.

Quinn ducked down first. "Someone's been here," he said.

"What is it?"

"Not good." He pointed. There'd been fires lit in the gaping hole that went up the chimney. In the ash, but not burned, were two dolls — one male, one female. The male had light yarn for hair, the female a crimson color. There were needles through the eyes

377

of both dolls and through the hearts. They lay beside the kindling that was set for another fire.

"Us?" Danni whispered.

"Let's get them to Natasha."

"Natasha isn't into voodoo dolls," Danni said angrily.

"She'll know what to do with them," Quinn told her. As he spoke, his phone rang. The buzz startled them both.

When he answered it, they could hear Larue's voice.

"Where are you?" he demanded.

"The sugar mill ruins."

"Okay," Larue said. "I'm a mile down the bayou from you. Get out on the main road and then take a road that says Bayou Grigsby South. You'll miss it if you don't look hard — it's not much of a road."

Quinn glanced at Danni. "You've found a body?" he asked.

"What's left of one."

There was nothing at the end of the road except for a small, weather-beaten fishing dock. Danni thought it was probably only used by a few locals. The dock stretched out over marshy ground that offered little in the way of an embankment; as she tried to reach it, her feet sank into water.

Wolf didn't like it, either. Walking at her side, he whined softly.

Larue was at the end of the dock with a few members of his forensic team, along with the medical examiner.

"You can wait, if you'd like," Quinn said.

"Wait where? I'm not staying alone anywhere around here!" Danni could see two fair-size gators sunning themselves on the opposite bank. They were regulars in the bayous of Louisiana and she had a healthy respect for them.

"Fisherman dragged him up," Larue said, indicating the mass at his feet. "I'm surprised the guy got as much of him as he did."

The sight on the dock hit every gag reflex in her system but Danni swallowed hard.

This was the man she'd last seen in the cemetery or — as Larue had said — what was left of him.

He was missing his right arm from the elbow down and his right leg from knee. Gashes tore across the body and the face was torn.

"Do you know him?" Larue asked.

"It's Bigsy. The man from the cemetery," Danni said.

There was a loud splash in the water. She glanced over at it. Water droplets spun and dazzled, and she saw that in the bayou, two large male alligators were apparently becoming territorial with each other. Wolf barked; Quinn calmed him.

"Coming through, coming through!"

Danni turned around. It was Ron Hubert, the medical examiner she'd met at the Simon house, followed by an assistant. His pale hair glowed in the afternoon light and he looked like a mad scientist as he made his way along the dock. He nodded at Danni and Quinn, then hunkered down by the body.

"Is this where he was found?" Hubert asked Larue.

"A fisherman snagged him. He caught the shoulders first and pulled him up, thinking he'd just fallen in and might be saved. He dropped him on the dock, as you see him now, and called 9-1-1. He was pretty shaken up. I let him go home."

"So," Danni murmured. She squinted at the gators, feeling acutely uncomfortable. "He came here — and walked into the bayou and was . . . eaten?"

Hubert, kneeling by the body, looked up at her. "I won't know cause of death for sure until we get him into an official autopsy, but I'd say he was most likely dead before he hit the water. Slugs in the head and chest have a tendency to render a man dead."

"Then he was shot and discarded in the swamp," Larue said.

"That would be my guess," Hubert told him. "At least he was dead before he was half-eaten. That was one small mercy. I'm surprised the gators didn't finish the job."

Danni turned away, walking back toward the road. Wolf, after a brief hesitation, accompanied her, as if he knew his role was to protect her at all times. Quinn joined them a minute later. "You were right," she said.

"Being right doesn't make me particularly happy at this moment. It means Shumaker does have the bust."

"That means there'll be a ceremony tomorrow night. And Shumaker will use dolls that represent us. And —"

"No." Quinn shook his head. "I think there was already a ceremony with us. He's going to want something more for tomorrow night."

"If there was some hex put on us, it didn't work" she said.

He smiled. "No. It didn't work, and it won't work, but let's get the dolls to Natasha, anyway."

"Okay. Still, hexed or not, I have to shower first."

"Okay. What matters is that we know he has the bust and we know when he's going to use it."

He set an arm around her shoulders as they returned to the car. As he started the drive back into the French Quarter, Danni asked, "Won't he have people all over, guarding the grounds?"

"Probably."

"Then if we go, we're dead meat. We have to get Larue to do a raid."

"Larue has to work within the law. He'll be ready, but we'll have to be there to give him a reason to come in."

"Except we're not allowed to be there! It's private property and we're not invited."

"We wandered in and found ourselves at risk for our lives. That'll work."

"What if we *are* at risk?"

"Like I said, Larue will be ready. But you should be at the shop — with Billie."

Danni groaned aloud. "We've been through this. You wouldn't have said that to my father."

"I might have," he told her. "Once we have the bust, we'll need to figure out what to do with it. Usually an object can be cleansed of a spirit or there is no spirit. It's just people who believe an object has power and can make them behave in a certain way."

"But I've seen this bust," Danni said. "Quinn, the eyes on it are creepy. I didn't feel as if it was taking hold of me or anything, but it watches. It . . . thinks. It speaks to people."

"We need to destroy it."

"It's marble. That won't be easy."

"Well, my point is, that's why you need to be at the shop. You need to be reading. Doing research."

"You feel there has to be something in the book. If so, Quinn, I didn't find it."

"And you read it from cover to cover?"

"Quinn — it's a tome! I read the pertinent parts."

"There's a pertinent part we're missing," Quinn said. "When we reach the city, I'll park, you shower — and I'll run over to see Natasha with the dolls. When you're done, start going through the book again."

Annoyed, she nevertheless agreed.

At the shop, Quinn parked but didn't come in. Danni ran up to rid herself of her swamp-soaked clothing and took a few minutes to revel in the heat of the water and the clean scent of soap. She got dressed, ready to head down to resume her reading. But voices from the shop attracted her curiosity and she peered around a Venetian statue to see what was going on.

Her heart leaped to her throat and seemed to lodge there.

Brandt Shumaker was in her store. He was wearing a polo shirt and jeans. She was his height, but he had brawny arms and a barrel chest. His hair was neatly clipped and he was clean-shaven and looked strong and reassuring — the perfect politician. She'd seen the man on the news often enough; she was immediately certain it was him. And he was chatting with Jane at the counter. They sounded like old friends.

She felt anger surge through her. A man who was responsible for at least half a dozen deaths was standing on her floor.

Danni walked up to the counter, tension radiating through her. She fought to keep her expression neutral, but didn't think she'd succeeded.

"Oh, Danni! Mr. Shumaker, this is the shop's owner, Angus's daughter, Danielle. She'll know if we have any such objects secreted away! Danni, this is Mr. Brandt Shumaker," Jane said, turning to her. Danni's expression must have startled her because she mumbled, "Oh. Oh, my."

"We have nothing for you in this shop, Mr. Shumaker," Danni said coldly. "You're not selling by any chance, are you?"

Shumaker studied her with amusement.

384

"Me? Selling? No, I'm a collector of the fine and the unusual. You must come to my office sometime. You'd love my collection. That's why I'm here. I'm trying to organize everything in my collection into different displays. I'm working on several now — one on Santeria, one on voodoo, one on witchcraft. I was looking for an antique wand. I hate the replicas they're making these days. I prefer something from the 1600s, but up to the 1800s would do. I was also interested in any fetish pieces you might have. Not art or contemporary collectibles, but the real deal."

"I have nothing for you, Mr. Shumaker," she repeated. She wished then that she'd called Quinn back. But what could he do? Her shop was public. Quinn might have started a fight that would've gotten them nowhere.

Shumaker continued to study her. Finally he smiled. "Well, thank you, Danielle. A pleasure to meet you. Perhaps we'll do business in the future."

"I sincerely doubt that, Mr. Shumaker."

"Oh, don't be so dubious, Ms. Cafferty! I do believe we'll meet again."

He offered her his hand; she ignored it.

"Danni!" Jane chastised softly.

She ignored that, too.

"Thank you, Jane," Shumaker said. "It was a delight meeting you."

"Likewise," Jane said.

Shumaker turned to leave the shop.

"Danni! What is the matter with you? How could you be so rude to a customer? Not just any customer, but Brandt Shumaker. Danni, he's probably going to be our next mayor!" Jane said, obviously distressed.

"He's not a customer, he's a monster," Danni exploded, still feeling the tension. "I don't want him in here — and if he comes back, you can make that clear to him."

"Oh, I'm sure he'll never come back," Jane said. "You couldn't possibly have been ruder — unless you'd used foul language! Thank heavens you didn't do that."

"Jane, I mean it. The man is a monster. I don't want him in the store." Danni tried to control her voice and her emotions. "He uses other people to get down in the dirt, but he's a drug dealer and God alone knows what else."

"Danni, that's just rumor by people who are jealous of his success," Jane said, apparently mystified.

Danni leaned on the counter. "Please, Jane, I don't want him in here, okay?"

"Well, okay, but it seems you've managed to tell him that yourself!"

Danni didn't want to argue. She walked quickly away, heading downstairs to the book.

Natasha was in her store explaining certain herbs and their powers to a customer when Quinn arrived. She glanced up at him when he entered — and then looked him up and down. He realized he'd clumped in a pile of mud and flushed in embarrassment. Danni had been right; with no imminent danger, a shower would have been in order first.

He indicated that he'd be in the back. He and Wolf walked around to the courtyard entrance and waited for her. He sat at her wrought-iron table, setting the dolls on it. Wolf lay down, his nose on his paws.

Natasha came out a minute later. "Something's happened?" she asked anxiously.

Quinn gave her a brief rundown of their day. "And these were at what I assume is Shumaker's ceremonial site — the sugar mill. Beside a fire."

Natasha picked up the dolls and studied them. She shook her head. "These are not part of any legitimate voodoo, but the attempt to mimic a form of black magic is evident. According to these, you should be blinded. You need to be careful." She paused for a moment, adjusted her turban and picked up the dolls. He caught only a few words of her Creole as she began to murmur a prayer. *Cleanse* and *bless* were words she used, along with *protect* and *strengthen.* As she spoke, she removed the pins from the dolls. When she was done, he placed his hand on hers, met her eyes and smiled.

"Thank you," he said.

"These are just dolls, you know. Belief is what we have faith in, and what we're willing to give in to. Your belief, Quinn, is in creating good in the world around you. These dolls could not have any effect on you, whether I blessed them or not."

"Ah, but I believe in *your* goodness, Natasha!" he told her. "So it feels better."

"We're both more concerned with what it means that they were there — not with the dolls themselves," Natasha said.

"Yeah. He knows Danni and I are together."

"I'm sure Brandt Shumaker did his research on you," Natasha said. "And he would also have found out that there was something unusual about the shop. Maybe he knew about Danielle's father."

"In any event, we took the dolls. He'll know we were out there. It stands to reason that we should stay on the offensive." Quinn

388

said as he started to rise, "Thank you, Natasha."

She set a hand on his arm. "Be careful."

"Natasha, I'll be extremely careful. The police are backing me. We'll go in, and the minute we see anything out of the ordinary — which we will, since he does have the statue — I'll call Larue and he'll have a brigade of patrol cars and troopers ready to go in."

Natasha nodded, troubled. "Jez overheard customers talking in the store. People he didn't know, maybe tourists. They were talking about a ceremony someone had told them about. They seemed to think it would be fun and adventurous to go out and dabble in satanism."

"So that's what he's practicing — satanism?"

"I don't know if it could even be given a name."

"Natasha, we'll take care. I promise you."

"I will be praying for you," she said.

"Come, boy," he ordered Wolf. As he walked the short distance to Danni's, he noted that Royal Street was crowded with happy tourists, shopping, laughing, enjoying the music in the Quarter. The world seemed far too normal for something as evil as the bust to exist.

He went in through the side entry. There were people in the shop, but he didn't see Danni so he hurried down to the first level.

She was seated behind her father's desk; she'd taken the book from its glass case and brought it there. She looked up at him, white-faced.

"What is it?" he asked urgently. "What did you find?"

"He was here, Quinn. Shumaker was here — trying to buy wands and fetish items. For his collection."

He turned away, his temper, and his fear, soaring.

Danni leaped up and came around to face him, setting her hands on his shoulders. "He's gone, Quinn. I told him to leave."

"You should have called me."

"Why? You would've started a fight, you would've won — and he'd have gotten you locked up. Maybe that's what he was hoping to do."

Maybe.

He pulled her close to him, holding her tight.

Shumaker was trying to tell him in his own less than subtle way that he knew exactly how and where to find Danni.

Somehow, he had to keep her away from

that sugar mill. Shumaker had the bust. And he might be planning a grand sacrifice. . . .

CHAPTER 16

Jane locked up for the day soon after Quinn arrived. Billie would be in the hospital until the following morning, and Danni decided they should cook their own dinner that night. "Honey, we've been out so often lately. Let's stay home," she teased. "I have some steaks in the fridge and we can toss a salad. If that sounds okay to you."

Quinn said it sounded great and went up — finally — to take his shower while she puttered in the kitchen. He returned to help her, setting the table, watching the oven grill while she tossed the salad.

It felt good to be here, together, at her house. Except for the tension she was feeling.

Quinn must have been feeling it, too.

He watched Wolf now and then, but Wolf seemed content and tired, sleeping on the kitchen floor.

"You set the alarm, right?" he asked.

"Yes, it's set."

When they were almost ready to eat, she said, "I'm sorry if I've unnerved you. I hated that he was in here, that he was chatting up Jane as a potential voter!"

Danni took the steaks out, turned the oven off and discovered that he was behind her, gently drawing her into his arms. "Don't worry. He's never going to come up for a vote."

"I just feel —"

"That he somehow sullied your shop."

"Yeah, I guess," she said quietly. "And I guess I'm lucky he didn't come in here and start shooting."

Quinn put the steaks on plates and the plates on the table. He didn't sit until Danni came around to take her chair. When she did, he took his own and said, "Whoever, whatever, resides in that bust isn't stupid. If Brandt Shumaker came in here shooting, he'd never make it to his grand ceremony tomorrow. There'd be witnesses and he'd find himself taken down to the station. As far as we know, he's never actually pulled a trigger himself. He's always gotten someone else to do it. But I suspect he came in here today to taunt us. He wants to tell us that we may know about him, but he knows about us, too."

"He's going to assume we found those dolls."

"Natasha did her voodoo thing over them, by the way."

"That's good. Although . . . Quinn, are we immune?"

"I think so."

"Great. You *think*."

He reached across the table to take her hand. "It's like hypnotism. The bust can't make us do what we would never, in our heart of hearts, do."

"Gladys killed herself."

"Gladys didn't understand what she was up against. Pietro Miro wanted her to commit an evil act. She *couldn't* do it, and suicide was her way out. Neither of us is going to kill ourselves. But — now hear me out on this! I want you to stay here tomorrow night. I will get the bust, and when I have it, we need to know what to do with it. Your father's private room — that's where things like this go. Down there, with the book, is where it may lose its power. I need you to be here, ready when I do get the bust thing in my hands."

She shook her head. "You're suggesting I let you go alone."

"I won't be alone. I've talked to Larue. He'll have a small army ready to come in the minute I give him the call."

"You're the one who came into my shop like a crazy man, demanding I get the statue — and learn who and what I am, although I haven't quite figured that out yet."

He smiled at her. She liked the look in his eyes and the slight curve of his lips. "I can't help it that the stakes have changed," he said. "I'm not a chauvinist. I'm an equal-opportunity guy. But your father was a crack shot, something else you might not have known. He could wield many a weapon. He was big and tough and . . . you're not. You could actually put me in danger tomorrow night because I'll be too worried about you to pay attention."

Danni felt the truth of his words. She was afraid herself — but she wanted to go. She wanted to be what she was supposed to be, learn to face the demons and difficulties of the role she'd somehow been cast to play. She didn't want him going alone.

But she knew that he would die for her. Not because of who she was, but because he was who *he* was.

She sat back in her chair and nodded slowly. "All right. I guess it's like the don't-split-up rule in a horror movie, huh? Don't let the bad guys force you to show yourself. Then they'll just kill both of us."

"Something like that."

"All right," she said again.

"Billie will be back tomorrow. And . . ." He hesitated. "And I've asked Larue to see that he keeps a man stationed in the street. That way . . ."

"Half the police force will already be involved, if you're telling me the truth and —"

"I'm not lying to you, Danni. I don't lie. Larue's worried that he'll go through a song and dance with the courts if he just bursts in and Shumaker can prove he's simply having a religious ceremony on private property. There's nothing illegal about that — even if he's practicing satanism. The separation of church and state allows him to do that. Larue wants something he can use to really put Shumaker away."

"Did you tell him about the dolls?" Danni asked.

"Nothing illegal about having dolls, Danni."

"Fine. I'll stay here — because I don't want to endanger your life," she told him. "But," she added, rising, bringing her plate to the sink, "I don't like it."

Quinn rose, too. She didn't look at him as he came up behind her but he slipped his arms around her, his face buried in her hair.

His hands slid over hers in the soapy water, stroking along the length of her arms and she turned into him, into his embrace, lifting her face to his, eager for the feel of his lips on hers.

"Dishes can wait?" he asked huskily.

Dishes could wait.

She wound her arms around him, feeling the sweet pressure of his mouth on hers, the hot, wet hunger in his kiss. They stumbled away from the sink, still in each other's arms. His hands glided beneath her shirt, caressing the bare skin of her torso and her breasts. She lost her balance and he backed away, catching her, and they half landed on the table, laughing.

"We're all alone tonight," he whispered. "Well, except for Wolf."

"He's such a well-mannered dog. He'll look the other way."

"But we could be romantic," Quinn teased.

"Really. How?"

"Well, you know, I can sweep you off your feet and carry you up the stairs."

"You do have wonderfully strong arms."

"Yeah, and when you're my height and size, a bed is more comfortable than the kitchen table."

She laughed again as he swept her up.

They moved through the darkened shop to the stairs, heedless of the paintings on the walls, the statues, medieval swords, eighteenth-century vampire-killing kits and the other curiosities they passed. The staircase was narrow but Quinn swore that he could maneuver it and he did, and in a few minutes they were in the bedroom, tearing at each other's clothes.

Her drapes on the courtyard-facing window remained open. The moon was nearly full and cast a soft light into the room, as if highlighting the bed in the midst of the shadows. Danni was glad; she loved seeing his eyes, the bronzed color of his shoulders, the grace of his hands as he touched her. They fell, entwined at first, shoving stray pieces of clothing off the bed. Then he was above her, looking at her, and their lips met with the fire of arousal. She found herself bathed in the heat of his mouth as his lips trailed over her flesh, eliciting desire wherever he touched. Hunger filled her and she touched him in turn, relishing the tremor and tension in his muscled form. Her lips caressed his shoulders, her fingers skimmed the length of his back. Then she felt his touch going lower and she clutched at his hair. She was aware of the color of the room, the coolness of the sheets, the beauty of the moon beyond, but soon she became aware of nothing but him, his touch, the fire burning deep inside and radiating through her until it seemed to leap into an inferno that was all-consuming. She tugged at his hair, his shoulders, writhing and drawing him back to her and then deep within her. Soon they were rolling and twisting on the bed, seeking each other again and again, desperately needing release while never wanting this to end. She felt the climax coming and clung to him and felt the power in him as he climaxed, too, and then the shuddering of his body against hers. Their lips touched, and the world seemed to explode between them, and they shuddered together, still entwined.

He smoothed back her hair and said softly, "I'm definitely *not* going to die tomorrow. Not when I can return to you."

She curled more tightly into his arms. "You can't die. I have no idea what I'm doing."

"If you have no idea what you're doing, we should keep it that way," he said with a laugh.

"You know what I mean," she said, nipping his shoulder.

"I do," he told her. "Danni, all I have to do is get in there — and call Larue."

"What if Shumaker isn't doing anything but holding a ridiculous ceremony?"

"Then I'll have to get out."

"What makes you think you'll manage that so easily?"

He rolled onto his back, gazing up at the ceiling. "Because I'm a Louisiana boy, born and bred. I've been out in that bayou country a million times since I was a kid. Shumaker hires his goons from afar."

"He has the bust."

"And I have . . . I don't know what I have, but I have it."

"What do you mean?"

"I came back from the dead, Danni. I came back for a reason — and because I had some kind of protector who wanted me to."

She propped herself up on one elbow to look down at him. "Was he real? The man you saw when you died? Maybe he was created by neurons or whatever the scientists suggest. Maybe we should both get out of this now and let the police do their job."

He gently pushed her down, his face serious. "Danni, I've never wished so fervently that I could just forget the world — which I actually did a few minutes ago," he said. "But we can't go back to what we were. *I* can't go back. Even if we wanted to, we're already branded by Shumaker. But that doesn't matter. Don't go to the sugar mill tomorrow night."

She stroked his hair, studying his eyes. "Yeah, I thought you'd say that. How annoying and yet . . ."

"And yet?"

"And yet it's the mystique that makes you so . . ."

"So?"

"Palatable!"

"Palatable! I'll show you palatable!"

She laughed, and then she was shrieking, and they made love again until they were both spent and exhausted.

She lay with her face on his cheek, thinking she'd be awake all night, tormented by worry about what was to come the next day.

But they really had exhausted each other. The extent of their physical exertion took its toll; lying in his arms and thinking she would never sleep, she slept.

Quinn woke with a start because something wet and cold was touching his hand. He jumped up. It was Wolf, of course. But the dog had been shut out of the room.

"Danni?"

He stretched out his hand across the bed. She wasn't in it. Glancing at the radio on the bedside table, he saw that it was just after 3:00 a.m.

He scooped his jeans off the floor, then fumbled on the bedside table for his gun. Wolf ran to the door, waiting for him and Quinn followed quickly. He wanted to shriek her name; but at the same time, he didn't want to alert anyone to his presence.

But if someone had been in the house, the dog would be barking furiously. Wolf would never have left Danni if she'd encountered trouble.

Still, he moved down the stairs silently and carefully. The alarm hadn't sounded. The drapes had been open upstairs but the doors to the balcony were locked. He would have heard anyone entering by the bedroom. But then, when Danni got out of bed, he should have woken. It had taken Wolf to come and get him.

At the bottom of the stairs he looked around. Silent eyes in the various statues and paintings stared out at him from the shadows. The jewelry display at the counter gleamed in the streetlights. He could see that Danni wasn't in the shop. He tried the kitchen, the pantry — and went down to the first level. He looked into Angus's private collection, at his desk, through the rows of artifacts and boxes. The book lay in its enclosure. There was no sign of Danni.

Wolf licked his hand, and he realized —
the dog knew where Danni was.

"Bring me to her, boy."

He followed the dog down the hall to the
rear of the shop and Danni's studio.

She was there. She was seated at a chair
before a canvas, a table bearing watercolors
beside her. She was still naked, exceptionally beautiful as she sat there, hair curled
over her shoulders and falling in disarray
about her face. Her eyes were open, but she
didn't seem to be aware of what she was
doing.

She was painting.

"Danni?"

She didn't respond to the sound of his
voice. He went on bare feet to stand behind
her and see what she was painting.

A full moon rose in the night sky. There
was rich foliage in the picture; the bayou
could be seen in the background. He saw a
building with a broken roof that allowed the
moonlight to enter, but there seemed to be
a dozen fires burning, as well, fires that
came from torches set in the ground. He
saw vats — sugar cane vats — and the
chimney they'd seen earlier. Now, in front
of it, stood an altar and, chalked on the
ground, a pentagram with various symbols.

Displayed on the altar was the bust. The face was marble and cold, the eyes unseeing. Behind the altar was a man in a robe, holding something that looked like an ancient Sumerian knife, curved, with a wicked niche in the blade. It was silver and glittered in the light as the man held it aloft.

A form lingered behind the man, a form that didn't seem quite solid; it was the ghostly image of a man dressed in a short tunic, a red mantle over his shoulder. He moved as the living man in the robe moved, as if he were a puppeteer.

There were dozens of people in similar robes scattered throughout the ruins of the mill. But the worst image in the painting was that of a woman chained to the remnants of the chimney. Her head was down, and she was covered by a gray-and-red mist that emanated from the fire.

The human sacrifice?

Danni reached toward the painting with her brush, about to add something to the canvas. He didn't know why, but he had to stop her.

"Danni!"

He rushed forward and grabbed her, dashing her hand away. She started violently. Her eyes flew to his in complete confusion.

"What . . . Quinn — what . . . Oh!"

She was still confused — and she seemed horrified.

"Hey, it's all right. You were sleepwalking. You didn't tell me that you sleepwalk!" he said.

"I don't!" she protested.

"But —" Her eyes fell on the canvas. She jerked back violently and he caught her in his arms.

"I — *I* — painted that!" she said. *"In my sleep?"*

He nodded, stroking her hair.

"It's horrible!"

"No, it isn't, Danni. It's a little scary, but it isn't horrible."

"I painted what we're expecting," she said. "Except . . . do you think he'd really kill a human being right in the middle of his ceremony — *in front of witnesses?"*

"Oh, I think with the bust he'd do exactly that. Maybe Pietro Miro's spirit can only take complete hold if there's some kind of sacrifice."

"Well, that's that," Danni said. "You can't go there alone."

"I won't go alone," he told her.

"So I'm coming with you?"

He shook his head. He didn't want to say aloud that the woman in the painting frightened him — *that he was very afraid Danni was the intended sacrifice.*

"No, you're going to be here with a cop outside the door, Wolf at your side and Billie sitting tight with his gun."

"Then?"

"I'm going to go see a friend in the morning — see if he wants to accompany me."

"Who?"

"Father Ryan," he said. "Come on. I know it's hard, but we have to try and get some sleep before tomorrow." He tried to lighten the mood. "And you're not exactly dressed for chitchat in the shop."

"Oh. Oh!" she said, realizing her situation.

"Lots of people walk around naked in their own homes. Of course, they don't all have display windows facing the street."

She spun around and left him, tearing up the stairs. Quinn started to follow her but paused to study the painting carefully.

A week ago, she'd done a rendering of Gladys Simon. Gladys Simon had died soon after walking into the shop.

He gritted his teeth, feeling both dread and determination filled him. He'd keep Danni far, far away from the ruins of the abandoned sugar mill in the bayou.

Business as usual. Billie called from the

hospital, grumpy and eager to get home. Quinn made the short drive to pick him up as Wolf watched over Danni while she whipped up omelets for a welcome-home breakfast.

Disturbed by what had happened during the night, Danni steered clear of the studio.

Quinn returned with Billie, who'd been apprised of events since he was hospitalized. He clasped Danni in his arms when he saw her — so tightly that it hurt — but she made no protest, looking at Quinn past Billie's head. He winked at her discreetly.

"So, we run the shop, and you go for the bust — with Larue and half the city's finest at your beck and call," Billie said, accepting his plate and sitting down.

Quinn nodded. "That's the plan."

"When are you going?"

"This afternoon. I want to find my hiding place before Shumaker and his followers start to arrive," Quinn said.

"I'll be with Danni, come what may," Billie swore.

"No one can sneak up on you. You'll have Wolf," Quinn said.

"And you won't," Danni reminded him.

He smiled at her. "I won't be alone. I've already called Father Ryan."

"And you're not worried that *he* might

put you in a situation where you'll have to show your position before you can get the cops?" Danni asked.

"Father Ryan got around before joining the priesthood," Quinn said. "I'm not worried about him. Pass the butter, please," he said, and calmly began to butter his toast. "When we've finished breakfast, Danni, you get back to the book. Billie —"

"I'm going to check my gun and ammo."

"And keep an eye on the store. Brandt Shumaker was in here yesterday. If he shows his face, stay in the shadows but see that he doesn't cause trouble. However, I don't think he'll come today. He has his own plans to complete for the evening."

"So, why did he show up yesterday?" Billie asked.

"He came in person as a threat," Quinn said. "He's on to us. I accosted him at his office. As for Danni . . ."

"Maybe, via the underbelly residents of the city," Billie said. "He knew about Angus — knew that he was dead — but that the shop's still here. Or maybe one of his people followed Gladys before he got that fool to break into her house to steal the statue. And it's not as if you and Danni haven't been seen together."

"True." Quinn finished his breakfast and

brought his plate to the sink. "I'm going to drop in on Larue, make sure he's ready for tonight. And then I'm going to stop by and see Father Ryan, make sure he's ready, too."

"Will you be back before you head out?" Danni asked him.

"I'll come back briefly," he promised her. "You may yet find something in that book." He glanced at Billie, then turned Danni to him and gave her a quick but impassioned kiss on the lips. Billie cleared his throat and focussed his attention on his eggs.

Quinn left. Billie went upstairs. Danni decided to rinse all the dishes and place them in the dishwasher, then get to the book.

She heard a key twist in the lock, but Wolf barked happily and ran out to the shop with Danni behind him. Jane had arrived for the day.

"Good morning!" Danni greeted her.

"Morning!" Jane said. "There were half a dozen people peering in the window when I walked up. Got to hurry and open — I can feel it! It's going to be a good day for business."

"I'll be around if you need me," Danni told her. "And Billie is here, too."

"Thank goodness he's back. I've missed him! How he fell down and hurt himself is

409

beyond me. Well, maybe not. We're not spring chickens anymore — Billie *or* me!" Jane said. Smiling, she went to turn on the computer and check the cash.

Danni hurried back to the kitchen and dealt with the dishes. Then, as she'd planned, she took the stairs down to the first level. The book awaited her, and she picked it up reverently. Wolf was constantly by her side, curling up next to her feet as she sat at her father's desk.

Where to look now?

She studied the cover page again and the author's name.

"Millicent Smith!" she said aloud. "What were you thinking when you wrote this book? And what did people think of you for writing it? And where would you have information on destroying the already-cremated Pietro Miro?"

She was deep in a chapter on satanism and deals with the devil when Wolf let out a little woof and she heard a tap at the door.

The door was open but Jane stood in the doorway, waiting politely.

"Hey," Danni said, petting Wolf. "It's just Jane."

Wolf settled down. "He's fine, Jane. Come on in."

"I think he's starting to like me. I bought

him dog treats, you know."

"Treats — the way to a dog's heart," Danni said, smiling. Then she frowned. "That man isn't back, is he?"

"No, no, Danni, that man won't come back. I'm still surprised you were so rude."

"You know my opinion of him."

"But . . . never mind. Danni, are you okay?"

"Of course. Do you need me?"

Jane shook her head and entered the room slowly. "I was dusting and I walked by your studio. I didn't mean to pry but I saw your painting."

Danni realized she should have made sure the studio door was closed.

Jane swallowed. "It's a pretty sick painting," she said. "I'm worried about you," she added in a rush. "I know a good psychologist. This may be fear and grief you're feeling since you lost your father so suddenly."

"Oh, Jane, I'm fine, really." Danni tried to think of words that would reassure her. "I watched a ridiculous horror movie last night. It was one of those slasher movies and it took place in an abandoned sugar mill. Don't worry, I'll rip it up and paint a pastel of Jackson Square next. I'm all right, I swear it."

"Okay, Danni. But you're a sweetheart,

and you know I care about you. If I can help you in any way . . ."

"Thank you, Jane. I appreciate that," Danni said.

Jane nodded and turned to leave. Danni went back to the book.

" 'Time has little meaning in other dimensions,' " she read aloud. " 'Evil may lie in hibernation until it finds the opportune moment to strike. Those who have made covenant with Satan exist in that realm where hours and minutes are of no consequence. Pacts with Satan allow for souls to await the corporeal bodies that will give them the reward they craved when they signed in blood.' "

It seemed a bit like fairy tales — Grimm's version, but definitely something out of fantasy and the more primitive folk tales. Did this mean that even Brandt Shumaker was to be a sacrifice, giving over his body to the spirit of Pietro Miro? If so, she was certain Shumaker didn't know it. But in his careless orders to cut off all life that stood in his way, hadn't Shumaker made his own deal with the devil? And if so, how did two souls inhabit the same body?

"Quinn, I can't just park a dozen cars in front of the property. First, you'd hardly have an element of surprise, and second, Shumaker will be calling the mayor, the governor and God knows who else claiming police harassment. And we still don't have proof that the man is doing anything illegal," Larue said. He had a map spread out in front of him. "But I'll be here — on the road closest to the entry. And my backup will be through here. The land next to his is government, so I'll have some officers — out of uniform — close enough to run in if the roads are barred for any reason." He looked at Quinn. "You seem even more convinced today that something's going to happen. I hope so. I hope it's tonight. I can only drag out half the squad so many times, you know?"

"I do know," Quinn replied. "And I am positive." He hesitated. "What do you have on missing-persons reports at the moment?"

Larue arched a brow. "Why?"

"I believe Shumaker plans a human sacrifice."

Larue turned to his computer. "Last seen in NOLA?" he asked. Studying the screen, he shook his head. "We have a few. A grandmother from Uptown — no, she was found wandering in a grocery store. A Loyola student but they're not sure he's missing. He took off on a nature walk and we have officers and rangers looking for him. A young woman from Savannah who was supposed to meet up with friends for a bachelorette party, a middle-aged man from Detroit —"

"Just the women. Young ones."

"Three," Larue said.

"Well, we may find one tonight."

"You see a girl, you get on the phone immediately, you hear?"

"I'll be checking in with you often."

"Except, of course, I don't know you're in there," Larue reminded him.

"I'll use your cell. Don't worry."

"And what if something happens to *you*?"

"Father Ryan will be with me," Quinn said. "I'll see that he's in a position to call in, regardless of what's happening," he added grimly.

Quinn left Larue's office and headed out to see John Ryan, who was waiting for him at the rectory door. When Quinn walked in, he saw that the priest had an arsenal that included far more than holy water.

"You *are* ready," he remarked.

"I heard someone sneaking around last night," Ryan said.

"Don't parishioners come to you?"

"My parishioners knock at the door. They don't crawl around in my bushes."

"I've put you in danger," Quinn said regretfully.

Ryan grinned. "Quinn, I'm God's warrior, whether I'm listening to confessions — or pointing a Colt .45 at some bastard trying to murder innocent babes. I saw enough of that in Liberia. I know what I'm doing and what we're up against. I've got the weapons I need — holy water, a good Bowie knife and my trusty Colt."

"I'm not sure the Vatican would approve."

"In some things, most churchmen have realized that it's better to beg forgiveness than ask permission."

"Okay, then we're on," Quinn said.

"When do we leave?"

"In an hour."

"I'll drive. I borrowed a parishioner's car. No one will recognize it."

"Good plan," Quinn said.

"See? I'm already useful!"

Quinn drove back to the shop. As he walked in, Wolf rushed up to greet him, so he knew everyone was safe. He saw Jane helping customers at the counter and sprinted down the steps to the first level. Billie sat in a corner of the room, his gun in his hands. Danni was behind her father's desk, reading.

"Anything?" he asked her.

She shrugged. "Well, according to Millicent Smith, the author, Pietro Miro might intend a real comeback — taking over Brandt Shumaker's body."

"I doubt if Shumaker knows," Quinn said.

"My thought exactly. I'm trying to find out what happens if a spirit like that chooses a person who might have made his own pact with the devil. So far . . . I'm still reading. I'll call you the minute — No, no, I won't call you. Someone could hear. I'll text you. Can you feel a buzz when you get a text?"

He felt ridiculously like teasing her. He leaned over the desk and said softly, "I always get a buzz when you text," he said. "Oh, that was bad, wasn't it?"

"Don't ever use it as a pickup line," she advised.

"I'm in here, you know!" Billie said.

"Yeah, and I'm leaving," Quinn straightened and looked at Billie. "Close your eyes for a minute, huh?"

He drew Danni up, into his arms. He kissed her and experienced a sensation that wasn't so much desire as a feeling that he had finally found something, someone, so right. It gave him strength, promising all the things that made life worth living.

She kissed him back, then met his eyes.

"Gotta go," he told her.
"I'll be here," she whispered.

CHAPTER 17

It was nerve-racking, waiting.

She found it difficult to read and pay attention, yet Danni knew it was important. She read through the chapters on satanism again. First, the author severely chastised the Pilgrim perpetrators of the Salem witchcraft trials; Satan had little use for old women and for those who were truly pious, she said. The people condemned at Salem had obviously loved and been in awe of their God. Even with the threat of death, they had not admitted to any pact with the devil. But evil existed as surely as goodness, and the devil had no use for anyone not capable of exercising cruelty and brutality. The devil sought out those who already had a penchant for hurting their fellow man. He relished souls who would gleefully rape, rob, murder or commit torture for their own ends. He had a supply of such souls to choose from.

"How's it going?" Billie asked.

"Hmm? Oh, fine." She stretched. "I just don't have anything else I can work with."

"Hey, don't feel bad. Angus only had the book, too."

That made her think of her father. She missed him deeply. If there was going to be a ghost inhabiting her world, why couldn't it be her father?

She leaned back in her chair, remembering him. He'd been ever-cheerful in her presence. She thought about the countless buying expeditions she'd been on with him and how she'd been a fool, always believing he had a "business meeting, lass — you'd be bored!" when he'd approached a dangerous situation.

Had he ever planned to tell her the truth about his life? Had he hoped, maybe, that hers could be different?

She remembered his voice on the day he died. She recalled that day as if it were a film she could replay before her eyes.

The book, Danni, read the book and look to it in all things. . . .

"I'm reading the book, Dad!" she told him softly.

"When your father was reading it," Billie said, "he didn't just use the overhead light. Maybe his eyesight was failing and we didn't know. He used that little lamp there — the old stained-glass lamp on the corner of the desk. It was a gas lamp once. He had so many unusual things, but he sure did love that lamp!"

Danni frowned, looking at the lamp on her father's desk. How old *was* the damn thing?

She suddenly remembered the little piece of paper she'd found when she'd first started reading the book. *Use the light. . . .*

Her father hadn't meant that she should use just any light!

This was the light!

"Thanks, Billie," she said, and switched on the lamp.

Wolf stirred, raising his head to look at the door. Jane stood there. "A lull in the shop," she informed them. "I'm going to make myself a sandwich. I'll bring you some tea and sandwiches, too."

Wolf barked, wagging his tail.

"Oh, yes, and I won't forget you, Wolf! I have dog treats. They look like real meatballs. Might taste better, too, depending on who made the meatballs," Jane said.

"That's great, Jane. Thank you." Danni smiled, grateful for Jane's kindness.

"Oh, there's the bell on the door," Jane muttered. "Might take me a few minutes but I'll bring you some food down here. You seem busy," she said, glancing at Danni. Turning to Billie, she frowned. "You don't!" she said pointedly.

"We've been talking about my dad," Danni explained.

"Of course, dear, of course."

Jane hurried off, and Danni looked at the page and nearly jumped.

There were lines between the lines. They hadn't been visible — until she'd turned on the light directly over the book.

She studied the lamp; she didn't recognize the type of bulb.

"Billie, there's a strange bulb in here," she said.

"Oh, it's not strange. I bought those for Angus at the hardware store. They're special black-light bulbs."

She nodded at Billie and returned her attention to the page. " 'There wouldst be those so committed in soul and spirit as they that find a way to cling to the earth, though they be not of it.' "

"Thanks a lot. Big help!" she murmured.

She started to go back through the entire book, but then realized she'd been in the right place. She turned to the beginning of the chapters on satanism.

Jane came bustling into the room again,

bearing a tray of sandwiches and hot tea. "Here are the meatballs for Wolf," she said.

"You give them to him," Danni suggested. "That way, you two will become better friends."

Jane bent down, feeding Wolf the treats, and the dog gobbled them up.

"I guess I like him," Jane said after a minute.

"And he likes you, too," Danni assured her.

Jane smiled and went back upstairs.

Danni quickly texted Quinn. Everything okay?

She waited anxiously but he texted her a few seconds later. Just finding positions.

She sent him a smiley face. Setting down her phone, she picked up a sandwich and took a bite. Jane had made tuna on rye.

"Not enough mayo," Billie said.

"But you're eating it."

Billie grinned. "I'm hungry. Not the best, though. I should've made lunch myself."

She took another bite or two of her sandwich. It wasn't that good, and she put it back on the plate. Unlike Billie, she wasn't very hungry. In a while, she'd get up and prepare something herself.

They'd parked the car out on the far road,

alongside those that belonged to others visiting the park. Ryan was still wearing his Roman collar and black shirt, but besides that, he might have been any average Joe. His knife was in a holster at his ankle and his gun was covered by the khaki jacket he wore, one that matched his khaki pants.

Quinn had chosen similar clothing — tan fishing pants and a dust-colored shirt, and although he didn't have a knife strapped to his ankle, he did have one folded in his pocket. His gun was in his holster, also concealed by a windbreaker.

Standing on the highway for a minute, he listened. From a distance, he could hear the chatter of visitors exploring the wonders of the Louisiana bayou. He could hear the grunt of gators in the swamp water and the movement of birds in the wetlands. A different kind of grunt warned him that wild boars were in the area, but the last thing he was worried about was a boar.

"Let's go. It may be later than we think." John flipped the gold crucifix he wore so it hung over his shirt. "You got yours?"

Quinn reached for the chain at his neck. "One holy medal from Natasha — and one from you," he said. "Thanks. Haven't taken them off."

Father Ryan nodded. There seemed to be

no one around so they chose the dirt road. As they neared the ruins of the house and the mill, they ducked into the brush, moving as quietly as they could, trying not to let twigs snap. Ryan was better at it than he was, but not even he knew all the places Ryan had been during his early years in the military and the peace corps.

He paused as they were about to emerge from the brush. A car had just pulled up in front of the house, coming from the dirt road. Quinn held his breath, Ryan motionless behind him. As they watched, a woman got of the car, surrounded by three men who looked like the goons Shumaker had a tendency to hire; despite the humidity they were all clad in suits, wearing sunglasses — and obviously packing weapons. That was clear when two of them took handkerchiefs to wipe their brows at the same time.

One of the men stopped to look around. Seemingly satisfied, he led the way to the broken-down mill.

"Didn't have a clue we were here," Ryan whispered.

"What Shumaker never realized is that he needs a good dog," Quinn said. "We can get across now — head straight to the back. There are a bunch of old wagons there. Piles of rotted cane. Plenty of old barriers."

He was unhappy about their sprint across the open but the woman and the three men had gone into the mill and there was no one to see them. They entered through the rear, where the massive wagons hauling the cranes had come.

Quinn felt his pocket buzz. As soon as they were in, hidden behind a broken wagon, with a good view of the crumbling chimney, he pulled his phone from his pocket. He smiled. The text read, New light on an old subject. May find answers. All well here.

He texted a reply. In position. The party is beginning. All is well.

A smiley face answered him. He pocketed his phone again, glad that she'd seen reason and stayed behind.

At his side, Ryan was watching the movements of the four people, who'd now reappeared. He didn't speak. He looked at Quinn and drew an inverted pentagram in the dirt.

Quinn strained to see through the vats.

They were drawing a chalk pentagram, just like in Danni's painting.

" 'Though one may be ash, if ash and bone remain as one, if they are given a place of honor — as if to make whole — then the

425

spirit might inhabit the world, confined to the receptacle in which it rests,' " Danni read aloud. "That would be in a mortuary or tomb somewhere in Italy, I think."

She yawned. Sitting here was getting to her. Or her lack of sleep last night was getting to her. She was *so* tired.

"Billie?"

Billie didn't answer. She glanced over at him. He was in the chair, snoring, his gun in his hand, both laid on his chest.

"At least it's not just me." She got up to stretch and nearly fell back in the chair.

"Whoa," she murmured, sitting again, her foot sliding out. She accidentally kicked the dog, but Wolf didn't move or howl or do anything. Uneasy, she stooped down to look at the dog. His eyes were closed; he was completely still.

Dead?

It hit her all at once.

The sandwiches! The dog treats!

Jane?

She fumbled, trying to open the desk drawer where she'd shoved the gun Quinn had gotten for her. Her fingers wouldn't obey. As she tried, she heard Jane talking to someone, coming toward the stairs.

". . . out like lights, I assure you. The wretched dog, too. I put his into some of

426

those ridiculous meatballs. He won't hurt you. Don't know how much I put in them. He may never hurt anyone again!"

Danni was astonished that in her own state of danger, she wanted to rip Jane's throat out for what she'd done to Wolf.

Now what? She couldn't make her muscles work and her mind was fuzzy.

They were almost upon her.

She leaned over and turned off the light.

And slumped back in her chair. She closed her eyes.

She couldn't fight. Best to make it look as if she had no idea what was happening. If they'd meant to kill her through Jane, they'd have done so already. No, she had to hope they'd take her, and leave Wolf and Billie, and that Wolf was still breathing, just sleeping deeply, and that wherever they took her . . .

Quinn would find her.

As the afternoon waned and night began to fall, people arrived. They looked like any group attending a religious meeting — except that this group was mostly dressed in black. They weren't exactly Goths; they came in all sizes, ages and types.

A van drove up filled with boxes. They could see it through the rotted slats on the side of the mill. The woman who'd come in the first car was now wearing a black robe, and a large silver inverted pentagram hung around her neck. She greeted them all the way a preacher's wife would, welcoming them formally to the gathering.

Still no sign of Brandt Shumaker and no sign of a sacrifice. Ryan nudged him and pointed. Two of the men were bringing in an altar, which they set in front of the ruined chimney.

Quinn felt his muscles tighten. Still nothing Larue could use to shut them down.

Ryan mimed a drinking motion. Another two men had arrived bearing boxes, which they placed on a makeshift table composed of wagon pieces and opened. The boxes contained bottles of wine and plastic party glasses.

So, not everyone got to drink the sacrificial blood.

Yeah, a nice Bordeaux was good on any occasion, he thought dryly.

Preparations were in full swing. More and more people began to show up. There were certainly down-and-outers among them, grateful when they were handed capes that were better quality than the clothes on their backs. Some didn't seem to be destitute at all; he recognized a man who owned a catering company on Magazine Street and a woman who ran a dress shop on Conti in the Quarter.

Father Ryan leaned in close. "Some of these people — they're just disfranchised, looking for a fix, looking to belong, looking for something better than what they have. But her . . . she was born with a silver spoon!"

"Her who?" Quinn asked.

"The priestess or whatever she calls herself." Ryan glanced at him quizzically. "You don't recognize her?"

"You mean the woman who got here first? The one who seems to be in charge? Who is she?"

Ryan grinned. "That's Cecelia Simon. Daughter of Hank and Gladys Simon."

Shocked, he stared at the woman. She was fairly young. She was attractive. She'd inherited a small fortune.

She'd nearly had the bust in her grasp. Her father had possessed it. Then her mother did.

And now . . .

Now she was in league with Shumaker. How had he gotten to her? Or how had the bust gotten to her?

Had she assumed she'd get it from her mother's house, once her mother was dead?

Cecelia Simon. Brandt Shumaker. It

didn't add up.

Or maybe it did. Maybe Shumaker had put out a call on the grapevine, searching for the bust, and when it disappeared, Cecelia had joined with him to get her piece of the action. She didn't act in the least like a grieving daughter. Perhaps, somehow or other, she'd learned about the bust, perhaps she'd encouraged her father to buy it, thinking she'd get it that way. She would've known Shumaker, since he belonged to the same business circles her father had.

As he watched, another woman followed a man, bearing more boxes. These, too, were opened on the makeshift table. He squinted to see what was being unloaded. It appeared to be French bread.

"Black Mass!" Father Ryan whispered. "Body and blood. Most will drink wine. Some will drink blood, and some will dip their bread into the blood of whatever sacrificial creatures they bring."

"I believe the creature will be human," Quinn whispered back.

"God help us! Larue is ready to burst in, right? I've counted five men with weapons — so far. And forty or fifty of these *followers.*"

The odds weren't great.

But he said, "Larue is ready." Hoping it

was true . . .

"The lord high priest will be here soon!" Cecelia Simon announced. "You will remember that you are about to join a sublime covenant, a covenant that will bring you great riches and incredible wonders. Give yourselves to him, our dark lord — for he knows all. He will see that you are playing games if you do not really give yourselves unto him. Anyone not willing to entrust him with their hearts and very souls, leave now, for his displeasure is full of wrath — while his pleasure gives you all that you could ever desire!"

"Dark lord!" Ryan muttered. "Dark lord, my ass!"

But at Quinn's side, he closed his eyes. His lips moved.

Quinn realized that he was praying and his words were in Latin.

The priest was preparing to engage in battle, be it with his fists, his gun — or his faith.

⬯

"I told you," Jane said, pride in her voice. "I told you I'd take care of it all. You had me get this job to watch what old Angus was up to, and when he died, you said I could leave. But I know this girl! I knew she'd be in it up to her elbows because she could never let anything go. You hired all those fool men who blew it every time — and *I've* taken care of what you needed!"

Danni dared to open her eyes a slit, certain that with the way she'd slumped, her hair gave her cover.

Brandt Shumaker was back in her shop. He seemed to be alone with just Jane, but then she noticed that another man was with him.

"Kick the old coot over there. Make sure he's in nighty-night land."

The man did as bidden. He kicked Billie hard. Billie fell out of the chair but didn't move a muscle in protest. He fell in a heap on the floor.

Shumaker himself shoved a booted foot against Wolf's flank. But Wolf didn't even whimper. "He'd make a nice rug," Shumaker said.

Danni was afraid that tears would sting her eyes; she wanted to jump up and bite the bastard, heedless of giving herself away. It didn't matter, since she lacked the muscle power to do it.

But Billie *was* alive. She had heard him snoring. Maybe Wolf was, too. She had to pray he was.

"Get rid of her," Shumaker said quietly.

She assumed at first that he meant her.

But then she knew he didn't.

"What?" Jane cried out in disbelief. "Brandt — make him stop. He's pointing that gun at me!"

"Jane, Jane, Jane!" Shumaker said. "So proud of yourself. You get above yourself, woman. You're an idiot."

"I did this for you — for me! *You!* How can you be doing this? I've worked in this wretched shop for almost two years, just watching and reporting, once you suspected Angus Cafferty of being more than he seemed. I stayed on after the old bastard died and I came to you the minute Michael Quinn walked into the shop because he'd worked with Angus. I've done everything you asked."

"And I paid you well all the while — on top of your salary here," Shumaker said, shrugging carelessly. "You've collected a hefty sum through the years. You had it easy, Jane."

"You promised me a fortune when I came to work for you. You promised me money and everything else I wanted, Brandt. You said I'd be closest to you, that we'd —"

"Jane, seriously, do I look like a man who'd settle for an old hag like you?" Shumaker sounded amused, but he walked over to Jane, grabbing her chin in his hands. "So, you drugged their food. Idiot. The cops will find the drugs in them. They'll know you poisoned them. So obvious, Jane — the leftovers from the lunch *you* made them are right in the room. No, I'm sorry, but you're no longer an asset to my company. You made yourself a burden, Jane. And you know I don't carry burdens. Get rid of her," he said again, pushing her away from him and walking toward Danni.

"No!" Jane cried, trying to throw herself after him.

"Make it look like she did it herself. Leave the gun there."

"No!" Jane let out another anguished cry. "You can't —"

Her words were cleanly cut off. Danni heard a popping sound and a whiz in the air. Shumaker's man had used a silencer. Jane went down at Danni's feet. Her eyes were open.

Blood streamed from the back of her head.

"And now," Shumaker said, "for this one!"

She braced, waiting for that sound, waiting for a bullet to crash through her flesh.

The man with Shumaker reached down and took her into his arms, threw her over his shoulder and went up the steps. He was wearing gloves; there would be no prints in the house. Shumaker must be wearing them, as well.

No one would be left in the house. She would just have disappeared. . . .

But Billie wasn't dead. And Wolf . . .

She had barely touched the tuna sandwich.

And she was awake and aware, and she assured herself that when the time came, she would fight. She might not win. . . .

But if she went down, she was taking this bastard with her!

They'd been so busy observing, Quinn hadn't noticed just how stiff he'd become. Now there were so many people in the ruins of the old sugar mill that he didn't have to worry about moving. He adjusted his position, stretching his muscles as he did.

The arrangements for the ceremony were being completed. He realized they needed to be closer to the altar and the chimney area; when the night's event started, he might not have much time to stop it. He motioned to Father Ryan, who nodded his bald head. Ryan shot out first, sliding along what remained of the walls, and dived beneath the next wagon. There were enough piles of earth and broken crates to cover their movements.

They made it to the last of the wagons.

From here, their view was no longer obstructed by the giant vats that sat in the mill, creating aisles on each side, almost as if it were a church.

Ryan nudged him. Whatever the major event of the ceremony — *the blood rite?* — it was about to begin.

Danni had known everything that was happening to her.

She'd known where they were going as they set out, but she was shoved down in the back of the sedan with Shumaker. She'd longed to move; being near him was so repugnant that she had to steel herself not to retch. She'd known she had to wait, wait until she could gain a weapon of some kind.

The drive to the sugar mill seemed to take forever.

Eventually, she'd known, they had to get out of the car.

They did. But the second they arrived, there were men outside waiting to welcome their high priest; they were like pop-star fans given backstage passes, greeting Shumaker as if he were a god himself. They were all around him. And they were all armed.

"Your faithful has gathered," someone said.

"They're ready. All is ready for you,"

another said. "And for *her.*"

"Everything is exactly as you asked," the third said effacingly.

Before she could budge, hands were grabbing for her. She decided to continue playing possum for a while, even though her fear was overwhelming. She'd made a mistake; she should have fought at the house. If she had, they would've shot her but at least she would have denied them a sacrifice.

The men dragged her out of the car. One of them picked her up. She hung there, limp, listening.

"Where's my cape and cowl?" Shumaker demanded.

He was quickly dressed, with the assistance of his acolytes. Then he lifted a hand, telling the man to hold her as he entered the broken-down sugar mill.

Danni cracked open one eye. The man shifted to adjust his hold and she had a fleeting glimpse of a knife inside a slot in his gun holster. As he juggled her, she flopped around — and slipped the knife into her own hand.

Hiding it was more difficult but she managed to slide it down her shirt.

A moment later, he carried her in.

Quinn watched tensely as the high priest —

the puppeteer responsible for all that happened — made his entrance.

Brandt Shumaker!

Cecelia Simon stepped forward, arms held high. "All kneel!" she commanded.

Quinn shook his head, his jaw locked. He was astounded that people could be so easily deceived, so ready to follow someone they knew next to nothing about.

So willing to kneel when they owed no humility to a con man.

The high priest looked like a Ku Klux Klan member wearing a black headpiece and black robes. He raised his hands as he strode toward the altar. His voice boomed out and it was a voice Quinn had come to know all too well.

A man in the audience started to rise, but one of Shumaker's henchmen nudged him. "He didn't say to get up. Stay there."

That was when Quinn felt an odd sensation; he turned and nearly fell over, almost grabbed for his gun, almost gave away their position.

There was someone at his side. He'd had his eyes on the room the whole time. No one could have come near him without being seen. But someone had.

Before he could draw his gun, the man lifted his head.

Quinn froze.

He'd seen the man before. Seen him when he'd drifted over his own body the night he died. Seen him again when he'd been told he needed to do more.

And there he was, his fingers to his lips. He pointed. Quinn saw that one of the boxes by the wagon wasn't an old crate; it was new. It was from a costume shop. The robes were in the box, he realized.

He nodded. Tapping Father Ryan's shoulder, he reached carefully into the box and pulled out two of the robes. He turned back, but the man was gone.

"Did you see him?" Quinn asked Ryan.

"Him? I see the bastard at the altar, all right. Is that who you mean?"

"Uh, yeah," Quinn said quietly.

He kept still while Ryan scrambled into one of the robes. Then he struggled to work his own arms into the sleeves of the other, all the while hiding behind the broken-down wagon. Successful, he touched Ryan's arm again. "Wait," he said.

Ryan nodded grimly. "You got that phone of yours on speed dial?" he asked.

"Yes."

Shumaker walked behind the altar. He continued to hold his hands above his head, as if acknowledging the acclaim that was rightfully his.

Quinn saw him place an object on the altar.

The bust. The bust of Pietro Miro.

It was just an object, marble and artistically carved. But the eyes of the bust seemed alive, almost as though it added something palpable to the air, a tension and an excitement. The fire in the sconces set around the silo seemed to burn brighter; sparks flew and the shadows seemed to move and breathe.

"Welcome to the Cult of Miro, my friends. Tonight, you will see magnificent things. You will see the power that shall come to you if you keep your covenant. There will be nothing you dare not ask — the health and welfare of a child or . . . the death of an enemy. The great lord you worship knows human needs and desires. He seeks to fill them all, but he demands your utmost obedience. And he demands your blood!"

There was a murmur in the crowd. Father Ryan looked angry enough to explode. Afraid he'd move, Quinn set a hand on his arm.

"Not yet," he whispered.

"Fear not, my friends! You need only give a drop of your blood, symbolic of your faith in him. He demands sacrifice, yes, but not

440

from those who love and worship him. You will come forward in this communion. You will give blood before you drink the blood of power and riches. You will bind your soul to our great dark father, and learn the promise that he makes."

He raised his hands again and began to chant in Latin.

"We have to stop this," Ryan said.

"Father, it's against everything you know and love, but it's not illegal — yet," Quinn reminded him.

"He mocks God and worships Satan," Ryan fumed.

"Patience, Father," Quinn warned.

Ryan hunched tautly, ready to spring.

Shumaker's men urged the participants along. As Shumaker chanted, each was led forward to scratch his or her finger with the ceremonial knife — exactly like the one Danni had painted — and then led back to take a place in the crowd.

When this was done, Shumaker began to speak again. "We eschew the humiliating denial of the so-called godly!" he cried in English. "We will seek the carnal pleasures we so desire without fear of reprisal. We will lie with whomever we please, whenever we please, and revel in the free sensuality of the beasts that we are!"

Shumaker's words brought a roar, but Quinn realized that Shumaker's men were beginning these responses, goading the crowd.

"We will be one, one there for all. As a group, defending one another's freedoms, we will be free. We will smite our enemies and rise to the top of the world, the job world, the money world — the have-what-you-will, do-as-you-will world!

"Is someone hurting you, bullying your children? Has someone moved up the career ladder and pushed you down? No more! With the power of the beast you will not be subjugated as lesser men!"

Another roar sounded. Three cloaked women stepped forward like an out-of-sync Greek chorus. They began a chantlike singing. They sang in Latin; Quinn didn't know what he was hearing. He did know that the middle woman in the group was Roberta — Bertie — Hyson, the Simons' housekeeper.

Had she been in on it all along? Had she been the one to report the presence of the bust to her employer's daughter? If so, how had she and Cecelia come to recognize each other's evil nature?

Between Shumaker's words and the rising chorus, the beat of a drum that joined in and the swaying of the crowd, the ceremony was well underway. The followers appeared to be hypnotized by the man who was speaking.

Quinn blinked, wondering if he was seeing an optical illusion. The bust seemed to burst into flame — and yet it was still there. But there appeared to be someone behind Shumaker, a little to his left.

The man the bust portrayed. He stood tall, and although he wasn't solid, his arms, bared beneath the mantle, shone with sleek muscle and strength. A sound of awe rippled through the crowd; if this was an optical illusion, others were seeing it, too.

The man's face was chilling. The structure was as strong and cleanly handsome as any image of a Greek or Roman god. The eyes were deep and large and seemed to shimmer with amusement — and cruelty.

At his side, Quinn heard Father Ryan fervently whispering his own prayers in Latin. Ryan's jaw was taut even as he whispered the words, and Quinn felt that the priest's anger — and his belief — would see him through. They both had to be in control.

In his pocket, his phone buzzed. It wasn't a great time to answer Danni, but she might have found something valuable in the book. He pulled out his phone.

The message wasn't from Danni.

It was from Larue.

"Cop in front of the curio shop not in his car. Officer going in."

His heart seemed to stop.

"And so, tonight, you will see the beauty and the strength and the power!" Shumaker roared. "We are sworn by our blood to silence about what we see and hear tonight. Death to those who defy the cult. This will be sealed when we give the devil his due!"

That was when he saw her. She was carried out, apparently unconscious, and she was bound to hooks that were imbedded deep in the brick of the fireplace.

The woman from Danni's painting.

And the woman was Danni.

CHAPTER 18

Danni kept her hair over her face, her eyes ever so slightly open so she could see. The place seemed suffused with a hazy light. There were people chanting, people swaying. Drums were beating and everyone seemed drunk or drugged, crying out for blood — for a blood sacrifice. The man, her captor, held his bulk against her for balance as he slid ropes attached to the brick chimney around her wrists. Letting her head fall to the side, she saw the altar. She saw Shumaker there, the bust — and the knife. And at Shumaker's side, she saw him. Pietro Miro. He wasn't quite in the flesh.

The man, the image — the damned soul of Pietro Miro — turned to stare at her. He knew she could see; he didn't care. She felt his eyes as they raked over her. His lips moved and she could hear him as if he spoke. "How sweet your blood, my dear. How sweet that all your shimmering goodness should fail!"

"The blood of our enemies shall feed our savior and our dark lord!" Shumaker cried, raising his head and the knife.

It was now or never. They'd assumed she was unconscious and therefore a powerless victim. She hadn't been properly tied.

She lifted her head, tossing back her hair, surveying the crowd.

Quinn was out there somewhere. He had to be ready to help. And Larue . . .

His men were coming.

Could they come fast enough?

"Let the dark lord feed his dark lord!" she cried. "For all that Pietro Miro seeks is the body of one who holds power — and then he will cast you out, Shumaker, and you will rot and burn in his hell for eternity!" She freed herself from the loosely tied ropes.

"Bitch!" Shumaker bellowed, apparently forgetting his Latin. He turned, the knife aimed at her, but she dived as he plunged his blade into the brick. She rolled on the floor while Shumaker tried to extricate the knife.

"Stop her!" he shouted. His men had evidently not been prepared for their sacrificial victim to fight back.

Someone lunged toward her, someone in a black cape. She was ready to fight, fumbling in her shirt for the knife, when she heard a voice. "It's me, Danni, stay down!"

Quinn rose, drawing her up with him. "It's true! Stop what you're doing. The so-called dark lord will take you, Shumaker, and take them all!"

"It's that bastard, Quinn! Shoot the son of a bitch!" Shumaker roared.

Quinn dived down with Danni. Shots did ring out — but they weren't aimed at Danni and Quinn. They were fired over the crowd; they were being fired into the air.

"I am the voice of God!" someone thundered. "Get thee from this place lest you feel true wrath!"

People were screaming and running, shedding their black cloaks as quickly as they could. Shumaker's men tried for order, but they couldn't tell where the voice was coming from and began firing wildly. Another man in a black cloak came walking toward the altar. A blast from something seemed to throw him back, but he rose again.

Danni heard a shrill cry of pain. She saw a woman go down in the crossfire. It was Bertie.

"Go back to hell!" the man commanded. Latin streamed from his lips.

One of Shumaker's men rushed out, taking aim. Quinn rolled to his knees and shot first, and the man fell. Shumaker leaped from the altar onto Quinn, clutching his sacrificial knife. Danni tackled his back and she rolled with him.

"Quinn!" she yelled. "Get the bust! Break the bust! Break it wide open!"

"Ryan! The bust," Quinn shouted, wrenching Shumaker from her before he could wield the knife in a second attempt to kill her.

Ryan pushed forward, as if against a great hot wind. He reached out and got his hands around the bust of Pietro Miro, smashing it with all his strength upon the ground.

Bone and ash from within were caught in the wind. They blew and scattered while Quinn dragged Shumaker to his feet. One of Shumaker's black-suited men came forward, ready to shoot Quinn. Danni screamed in warning.

Quinn whirled Shumaker around.

The bullet tore into Shumaker.

For a moment, Danni saw the man's face. It seemed that she saw the would-be politician's face, then that of Pietro Miro and then Shumaker's again. His eyes were wide with shock and denial.

Quinn released his hold and the man slipped slowly to the ground.

They heard the sounds of sirens and cars jerking to a halt — Larue and the police were there. Quinn gathered Danni in his arms.

Father Ryan stood over the remains of the bust and the bones and ash that were Pietro Miro. He pulled a vial from his jacket and poured holy water over the remains, saying prayers as he did. He was, after all, a man of God.

Larue came running in, followed by a number of patrol officers; they knew what they were doing. They rounded up all those who weren't running through the brush trying to get to their cars.

Larue stopped in front of the two of them, exhaling a sigh of relief. He quickly hid his emotion and asked, "What's he doing?" indicating Father Ryan.

"Ending it," Quinn said.

"You really all right?" Larue asked Danni. "We found our man from your patrol car dumped behind a bar on Bourbon Street. He's okay, thank God. The uniforms burst in and found Jane dead and Billie —"

"He's okay?" Danni interrupted.

"Raging mad, but he's fine," Larue said. "Your shop woman wasn't much of a poisoner."

She didn't even want to glance at Quinn.

"What about Wolf?" she asked anxiously.

"None the worse for wear."

She was so relieved, she felt her knees wobble. Quinn steadied her. "We're going to get out of here, okay, Larue?"

"I'll meet you at the station," Larue said. "You know the drill. . . ."

"Yeah, yeah — paperwork," Quinn finished. "We're just getting out of here, but I don't have my car. I came with Father Ryan."

Ryan came up to them then. "My work is done. That is, Detective Larue, if you'll be so good as to see that all this ash and bone is truly scattered. Thrown-in-the-swamp scattered!"

There was an officer standing nearby. "Sir?"

"Do what Father says," Larue told him.

"Father?" the officer said in confusion.

"Father Ryan, son. Come by and see me at the church anytime." Ryan shook his hand, saying, "Get others to help with this. See that it's done properly, please."

"Yes, sir, yes, sir."

"God bless you," Ryan said pleasantly.

The tension had left him; he seemed on top of the world. He set one arm around Danni's shoulder and the other around Quinn's. "Let's get out of here, indeed.

450

These gentlemen can handle it from here. Once again, goodness has prevailed!"

He led them out. There were patrol cars all over the property now. Officers had people clustered around the cars, and all the former participants were talking fast. Danni noticed that two of the black-suited men were in the backseats of patrol cars; a few others lay dead.

They started down the road, away from the frenzy that was still going on. "Now, that was close!" Ryan said. "Too close. But there you go. You do everything you think you should to stay out of danger, and it comes from a source you never expect. Danni, you must be far more careful when you hire your next clerk, you know."

She was surprised that she was able to laugh. It was over, really over. She didn't have to collect the bust; it was gone. Father Ryan was a powerful man.

"How did you know to just break the damned bust?" Quinn asked.

"I found it in the book right before . . . before they showed up. Oh, Quinn, I was so scared for poor Wolf. I mean, don't get me wrong — I love Billie, and human life is more precious than anything . . . but I'd heard Billie snoring and Wolf wasn't moving and —"

"Shh," Quinn said. "I know. I understand. What I *don't* understand is how we never saw the evil in Jane Pearl. Not even your father! He hired her, and she was working for Shumaker all along, spying on Angus, on you, on everything that happened at your place!"

"Well, she paid the price," Danni said.

"As will you!"

They were stunned by the voice that suddenly rang out.

A cloak-and-cowl-wearing figure stood before them, blocking the path. Danni felt Quinn moving for his gun but the figure stepped forward. "Draw, and I shoot her faster than you can draw in a breath, you bastard, Michael Quinn. You two ruined everything! My fool mother couldn't stand the bust. I told her I was coming to take it, and she went and killed herself!"

It was Cecelia Simon.

"You know, Ms. Simon, your parents would be so disappointed in you," Quinn said calmly. Danni kept very still; she knew that he and Ryan were planning something, but she was afraid that whatever they could do, whatever they could silently plan, it would be impossible to save all three lives.

"My parents were namby-pamby assholes willing to give my inheritance away," she spat. "They never approved of me, but they did hold the pursestrings. Even Bertie knew they were nothing but a pair of Goody Two-shoes who'd contribute to every charity in the whole world — but wanted *me* working my ass off. Thank God that woman was really *my* bitch."

"Your bitch is dead," Danni said.

"Oh. Too bad." She gave the slightest of shrugs. "When I first learned about the bust, I had to get Bertie to extol its virtues to my father over and over again, talk him into believing he needed this 'object of beauty' as he liked to call it. But the old fool offed himself before I could get there — and then my idiot mother did the same. They were so *weak*. Always threatening me! If I didn't shape up, my father would leave everything to charity! To the church and — get this — animal shelters! My inheritance to a bunch of dogs! Well, I almost got it all. You ruined everything. And save your speeches. The cops will arrest me, and I don't need any sermons about not getting away with this. But if I'm going down, I'm taking one of you with me. Which one? A priest? That would be rich. Or you — Quinn. No, I think it should be the great artist here who created such a lovely image of my dear mother. That way, Quinn, you'll live to suffer for what you caused — and you, Father, you can pray for her lost soul the rest of your days!"

Danni knew what they planned. Quinn would shove her behind him and take the bullet and Ryan would pull a gun. She had to stop it, but a bullet could fly in a split second and she didn't have the strength to intercept Quinn.

Her thoughts were rapid.

But as Cecelia raised her gun with a demonic smile, they heard a shot.

She fell flat in front of them.

The next thing Danni knew, Wolf came running through the trees that bordered the wetlands; he nearly knocked them over, jumping up in his frenzied greeting.

Then, as they stumbled, trying to remain standing and greeting the dog, Billie came walking up to them.

"Bloody hell, but thank the Lord above that bitch could talk!" he said. "And Jane — I never liked her. Your father said she was a good bookkeeper and clerk and that we needed someone, but . . . I never trusted her! I was almost too late, but someone is watching out for us. Ah, well, Danni, lass, I'm sorry I failed you at the house. I should've known not to eat that dreadful woman's terrible sandwiches — but I'm mighty thankful I got here in time!"

Danni laughed a little hysterically and threw herself into his arms.

A week later she sat at a table with Natasha, Billie and Father Ryan in the Midnight Royale café off Magazine Street.

It had been a wonderful night. The three of them and Quinn had met Jenny and Brad for dinner, and now they were listening to their group.

Quinn was sitting in on guitar. He wasn't Brad's caliber, but he was pretty good, Danni thought proudly, and when he left the stage, she greeted him with the wildest applause possible. It was fascinating to see someone go from handling the threat of death and the not-quite-believable to smiling as he casually enjoyed a night on the guitar.

"Not bad," she told him.

"Not bad at all!" Billie said.

"Wonderful," Natasha assured him.

"Let's not get carried away," Quinn said. He smiled, though, slipping an arm around Danni. "It's great to be out, tonight."

Danni touched his chin. "Living," she agreed.

Billie cleared his throat and complained to Natasha. "They always seem to forget

I'm around!"

"Not at all, Billie!" Danni insisted.

Natasha drummed her fingers on the table. "Not that I want to ruin the music of the night, so to speak, but I'm still confused. Hank Simon was a good man and Gladys Simon was a good woman. Somehow their daughter turned into a monster. She didn't kill her parents, did she?"

"If I understand this right," Father Ryan said, "no. But urban legends abound, so there've been all kinds of stories floating around about the bust of Pietro Miro. To start with, it surfaces because Shumaker, who was willing to believe in the occult if it would get him what he wanted, does some research and knows the bust is in New Orleans. Our crazy convict still in lockup, Vic Brown, hears that the call has gone out and there's big money being offered for the bust. But he thinks that Hank Simon — who knows the story, too, or at least part of it, thanks to his daughter and Bertie — is the one who wants to buy the statue. He sells it to Hank. Before that, though, the spirit, soul, *evil* of the bust has invaded Vic, and he shoots three gang members and winds up in jail. Hank Simon is a good guy. The bust was trying to get him to kill and the pressure was so great he killed himself.

The bust's already in the house and Bertie, of course, calls the little princess she'd tended to all her life — Cecelia. Before Cecelia can tie up her business and get home to take possession, her mother hangs herself. So, enter Leroy, who steals the bust because he's heard Shumaker is after it. But he wants more money. He hides the bust in the cemetery while he tries to negotiate with Shumaker. Then Shumaker kills him in a fit of rage and sends his thugs to the cemetery — and you know the rest of the story. That's the best I can figure it, at any rate. Thankfully, Danni, you read the right part of the book in time to know the bust had to be totally destroyed."

"I will read it from cover to cover, inside and out," Danni vowed.

"And stick with your artwork. Obviously, it can be a *warning*," Quinn said.

"I have no control over it. I painted the second picture in my sleep."

"Maybe it's a talent that will grow," Billie mused.

"Well, now I'm sorry I brought all this up," Natasha said. "But I do understand it better." She paused. "It *is* fantastic to be out tonight. Agreed, Father Ryan? You might be scaring a few of these people into good behavior with that collar of yours, but . . ."

"Serving God doesn't mean I have to miss out on good music and good friends," Father Ryan told them. "Good music by your friends, Danni — and you, too, Quinn. And good company. To evil put down, and the rise of the new Cafferty and Quinn," he said, lifting his cup.

"Peace, and no more evil objects!" Quinn chimed in.

"But there will always be something else," Father Ryan said gravely. "That's the way it is, a constant battle. At this table, we all know that."

"That's why we seize the moments," Natasha reminded him.

Smiling, Father Ryan nodded.

"Changing the subject, I'm in need of a new clerk," Danni said.

"Hmm. A new clerk certainly needs to be carefully hired," Natasha said thoughtfully. "I have my Jez, and everyone needs someone like him."

"I may have the right man for the job," Father Ryan said.

"Oh?" Danni asked.

"Well, he has a bit further to go. Quinn brought him to me. Cleaned up and detoxed, he's a wonderful fellow. Smart, courteous . . . Bo Ray Tomkins."

"Bo Ray!" Danni said with surprise. She looked at Quinn.

"Some of us just need a second chance," he said with a shrug. "We'll think on it, Father Ryan. You may have something there."

Jenny came rushing over to the table. "Quinn, the guys want you to sit in again. Eighties rock. You up for it?"

"Sure," Quinn said.

He went back to play. The night lasted a bit longer, and then Quinn pointed out that Wolf was still at the shop.

He leaned in and whispered to her, "We don't know when these moments come. I'm all for living . . . and seizing the moments. And I think this is one. . . ."

His whisper was suggestive. She smiled, feeling the thrill that seemed to sweep through her every time she saw his face.

She stood quickly. "We're going to call it a night," she told the rest of them.

"Excellent idea. You need to get a room," Billie said.

Danni grinned. "Yes, and I have one!"

They bade the others good-night and returned to the shop, strolling slowly.

"How is this going to work?" Danni wondered. "Our relationship, I mean."

Quinn was silent for a minute.

"It won't, will it?" she asked him.

He was thoughtful. "Well, we have tonight. We owe ourselves tonight. As to the future . . ."

"We should back away a bit, shouldn't we?" she asked quietly. "Things between us are very . . . intense. But we have responsibilities."

"I don't have the answers, Danni."

"I do. We back away for a while. We see what the future brings."

"I can't imagine not being with you," he said.

"But you're right," she told him firmly. "We have to see what the future brings."

Wolf, standing guard, greeted them and they petted him and gave him a few treats.

New treats. Treats Danni had gotten at the pet shop on Royal.

And then . . .

Whatever the future, they were taking the night. Seizing every moment.

ABOUT THE AUTHOR

New York Times bestselling author **Heather Graham** has written more than one hundred fifty novels and novellas, has been published in nearly twenty-five languages, and has over seventy-five million copies in print. An avid scuba diver, ballroom dancer, and mother of five, she still enjoys her south Florida home, but loves to travel as well. Reading, however, is the pastime she still loves best, and is a member of many writing groups. For more information, check out her Web site, theoriginalheathergraham .com.